PRAISE FOR DELPHINE ROSS

For *The Dance of Desire*:

"Ross will steal your heart with this utterly delightful, romantic friends-to-lovers retelling of Beauty and the Beast."
—HEATHER WEBB, *USA Today* bestselling author of *Queens of London*

For *The Poetics of Passion*:

"A beguiling Victorian romance filled with secret identities, hidden passion, and family loyalty...for fans of Evie Dunmore, Mimi Matthews, and Emily Sullivan."
—*Historical Novel Review*

"Charming and sexy...Ross's debut historical romance is definitely a novel that will enchant readers!"
— ELIZA KNIGHT, *USA Today* bestselling author of *The Rebel Wears Plaid*

"Chock full of compelling characters, charm, and heartfelt emotion."
— HARPER ST. GEORGE, author of *The Duchess Takes a Husband*

"Delphine Ross conjures...the era with a master hand. A fascinating read!"
—MIMI MATTHEWS, *USA Today* bestselling author of *The Belle of Belgrave Square*

The Dance of Desire

The Dance of Desire

A MUSES OF SCANDAL NOVEL

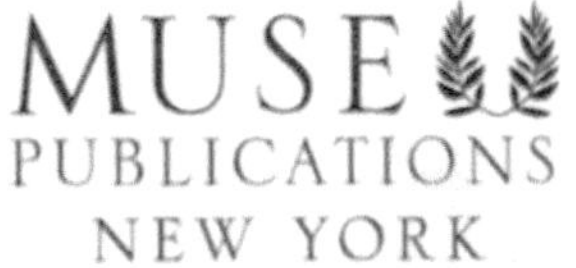

DELPHINE ROSS

MUSE PUBLICATIONS
NEW YORK

Books *that make you think.*

Books *that make you feel.*

Books *that inspire.*

Library of Congress Control Number: 2024903768

Trade softcover: ISBN 979-8-9853512-8-6

E-book: ISBN 979-8-9853512-7-9

Cover and interior design: Kris Waldherr

First print and ebook publication March 2024.

No AI was used to write this book.

For Karen,
who loves all things French and and all things feline.
Here's to the D & S!

PROLOGUE
AUGUST 1859

ON THE SULTRIEST day London had seen all year, Virgil Sydenham, Viscount of Sunderland, was locked in an artist's closet.

This hadn't been Virgil's intention. He'd only gone inside the closet to steal a moment of solitude before rejoining his father and mother, who'd been arguing again. Hiding had become a habit since Virgil's tenth birthday some months earlier: go someplace quiet where no one could find him, preferably with a thick wood door. Breathe deeply until he felt able to confront the world anew, before anyone noticed his absence.

Never before had the door locked behind him.

Prior to this occurrence, Virgil and his parents had been visiting the artist who owned the closet, a certain Neil Bartham. Virgil's father, the Earl of Sunderland, had engaged Bartham to paint Virgil and his mother as a surprise for her birthday. Bartham immediately dazzled Virgil with his looks, charm, and talent—all elements Virgil believed he lacked. (Even at the age of ten, Virgil held few illusions about himself.) As for Bartham, he was a tall man of perhaps five and thirty years. He wore a cobalt blue jacket that had little similarity to the Savile Row tailoring Virgil's father favored. Bartham bore thick chestnut hair, a broad smile, and an easy, engaging manner. (Also unlike Virgil's father.) Bartham possessed a large family—Virgil overheard several children playing in the lush garden outside the studio, which was in a wing of the artist's home —and a fair-haired wife, who doted on the artist as though he was the sun and she the moon. Clearly, Neil Bartham was someone fortune favored.

However, his mother had not at *all* been pleased when the earl's birthday gift was unfurled. Her mouth pursed, her eyes widened. Virgil sussed there was something uncouth about Neil Bartham for all his pleasantness. Something disreputable.

"You do know his wife is an adulteress?" his mother hissed once Bartham stepped away to request refreshments for them. "The newspapers call her the Muse of Scandal. She was married to some art critic when she ran off with Bartham—"

"Her first marriage was annulled years ago, Eliza," his father interrupted in a tight voice. "Consider Bartham's talent, darling. He'll paint a masterpiece worthy of you."

"Talent is no substitute for moral rectitude, Richard." She stamped her silk-clad foot. "I do wish you'd warned me before we ambulated here on such a hot day…"

Once his mother's voice began to rise, Virgil slipped from the studio toward the hallway. Toward the artist's closet, which turned out to be the first door on the left.

No one noticed.

The closet was filled with several tall canvases and a folded easel. Enough room for a boy to hide. But once the door locked behind Virgil, he understood the worst: he was trapped. Yet he didn't panic despite the smoldering heat and the pervasive stench of turpentine. Instead, he felt an odd gratitude. A locked closet was an excuse for him to escape the arguing. The strife. The sense of being perpetually underwhelming to his parents.

I suppose I should yell for help, he thought. He didn't.

A moment passed. Another.

Outside the closet, Virgil heard a scuttle of voices. Not his parents, thankfully—perhaps they thought he'd gone to play with the artists' children. Speaking of which, Virgil heard a young boy lisp in a high-pitched tone, "One, two, three, four…"

A game of Hide and Seek. Well, hopefully no one would find Virgil until he was ready.

But then the closet door opened and shut—and he was no longer alone.

A slender body slammed against him in the dark. A girl, judging by the flounces of her diaphanous skirts, which made his skin itch. Some sort of fluffed up netting.

"Musa, is that you?" the girl hissed under her breath. "I called the closet!"

"Not Musa," Virgil answered, trying not to stammer. He'd never been so close to a girl before. Not like this. She smelled of floral soap and newly mowed grass.

The girl pulled away though her skirts still brushed his legs; the closet wasn't meant for two. "So sorry! Zeus, you must think me rude. I didn't know the closet was occupied."

"It is rather."

The girl let out an odd laugh. Embarrassed, that's what she was —this was an emotion Virgil knew too well. Perhaps to compensate, she released a soft torrent of words. "You must be the boy posing for Papa. He mentioned you and your family were scheduled for today. A large oil painting. Told us to behave—" another odd laugh "—well, not like *this*, mind. That's why we were playing in the garden, but it got so hot. It is rather crowded in here, isn't it? Anyway, I'll leave—"

"You can't leave," Virgil managed to interject. "Door's locked."

"I forgot about that." The girl let out a sigh, skirts rustling. "Yes, the lock is fussy. I suppose Papa hasn't repaired it yet. No reason to panic—someone will find us soon." More brightly, "Hopefully only after I win the game."

Some distance outside the closet, Virgil heard the young boy shriek, "Ready or not, here I come!"

"Shush!" the girl whispered.

Virgil whispered in turn, "Who are you?"

After several moments of silence, she murmured, "I'm Allegra Jane Bartham. But everyone calls me Angela."

"Do you look like an angel?" Virgil couldn't resist asking. He'd hadn't even caught a glimpse of Angela when she dashed into the closet. She'd been so swift.

In the distance, a shriek of laughter. Someone's hiding place must have been discovered.

"I wouldn't know."

Her bashful tone offered all the confirmation Virgil needed.

Several yards outside the closet door, slow footsteps drew near. Angela grabbed Virgil's wrist.

"They're coming!" she mouthed against his ear.

"Who is?"

"My sisters and brother."

Virgil felt an unexpected pang. He had a brother once—well, he couldn't think of him now. "Aren't they hiding too?"

"I suspect they've all been found. But I want to see how long it takes them to find me. Shush!"

A moment later, the footsteps turned away; Angela released his hand after letting out a long breath.

"That was close! I suspect it was Musa," she whispered. "She knows I'm here, but won't betray me."

"Musa's your sister?"

He sensed Angela's vigorous nod in the dark. "She's the eldest. Bossy."

Virgil knew all about that. His brother had been seven years older. He'd been the dominant one, but not in a bad way. Virgil had admired Robert so much; all of life's gifts seemed centered in him.

But again, Virgil didn't want to think of this. Not now. Not during this unexpected encounter with this peculiar yet enticing angel girl.

"What of your other siblings?" he asked.

"They're twins."

"Identical?"

"No, though they resemble Papa. Their names are Lyra and

Theo. They're only four. Babies really." A pause. "Anyway, who are you?"

Virgil held back a stutter, as he often did when anxious. "It doesn't matter."

And here was the sorry truth. He, Virgil Sydenham, Viscount of Sunderland, didn't matter to the world save for the title he'd inherit when his father passed to his eternal reward (though Virgil prayed this wouldn't be for many, *many* years). He never wanted to become earl—that honor was meant for Robert, not him. Virgil would have been content in a humble country estate filled with fragrant flowers and gentle animals, far from anyone who might find him lacking.

"Surely you have a name," Angela prodded.

"Virgil Sydenham," he finally answered. "Viscount of Sunderland."

"Oh."

Angela exhaled the syllable. Virgil cringed, imagining her thoughts. *You're an aristocrat. Above my station.* What if she fawned over him to gain social advantage? Such insincerity was all too common among the *ton* and beyond.

Before Angela could say another word, the closet door burst opened. Virgil's mother at her most distressed.

"There you are, Virgil!" she cried. "I had no idea where you'd gone—I was worried something happened!" Her eyes narrowed as she took in Angela. "Who are *you*."

His mother's words were a demand, not a question.

"Angela. Well, Miss Allegra Jane Bartham, ma'am. I'm the artist's daughter."

Virgil cringed as he recalled his mother's earlier tirade. *"You do know Bartham's wife is an adulteress? The newspapers call her the Muse of Scandal."* He prayed Angela hadn't overheard.

"'You are to address me as *my lady*," his mother corrected. "I'm the Countess of Sunderland, not your governess."

Out of the corner of his eye, Virgil made out Angela's graceful curtsey. "Forgive me, my lady."

"And why are you and my son in a closet, Miss Allegra Bartham? You led him astray?"

"No, my lady."

To Virgil's surprise, Angela didn't appear cowed by his mother's displeasure. He supposed she was used to judgment, given the gossip about her parents. Still, he recognized his mother's temper rising like the heat outside in the garden.

Perhaps Angela sensed this too, for she quickly added, "Don't be angry with the viscount, my lady. The closet locked behind us. An accident, that's all."

His mother's mouth pursed. "Enough. Both of you, come."

"Yes, my lady."

Angela offered a hand to help Virgil out—he'd been wedged in a corner of the closet against the easel—and at last he saw her in the full light of day.

Angela Bartham had long pale hair, like her mother. A lithe figure. About his age, maybe a little younger. Blue eyes. She wore what appeared to be an enormous lavender tutu and ballet slippers. A costume glittering with sparkles. Was she a dancer then? Or just dressed like one?

She took him in similarly, her soft pink lips curving.

"I had no idea what you looked like in the dark," she said.

With this, Virgil's stomach dropped. He knew he was plump. Ruddy-cheeked. Rude red hair. Freckled. In other words, everything Angela Bartham wasn't. For she was exquisite. Yes, that was the only way to describe her; he imagined his father using the word in the same way he would for a work of art.

Virgil waited for Angela's smile to slip into dismay over his awkwardness. But, to his amazement, her expression appeared decidedly sympathetic. He knew she somehow understood all his sorrows and disappointments…and, even more miraculously, she cared.

And in that moment, Virgil's heart expanded in a manner that felt decidedly new.

Still smiling, Angela set her forefinger against her chin. "I know this is forward, but you don't look like a Virgil to me."

"His proper address is *my lord*, Miss Allegra Bartham," his mother called out over her shoulder. "Virgil is a fine name."

"That's true, my lady," she conceded. To Virgil: "But I'd rather call you Sunny, if I may. Your hair is like the sun before it sets. Warm. Kind. Like you."

Virgil swore he heard his heart knock against his ribs.

"Sunny then," he agreed. "Thank you, Miss Allegra."

"Angela," she corrected. "Because we're friends now, aren't we?" A last curtsey in his mother's direction. "Well, I should let you go pose for my father. I've already taken much of your time."

And then she skipped away to join her siblings, taking Sunny's heart with her.

As the years passed and they grew into adulthood, Angela proved to be a worthy guardian of his heart. She and Sunny became the best of friends; his heart grew in devotion despite his mother's disapproval. As children, they'd spend spring mornings walking about the rose gardens of Green Park, winter afternoons reading novels aloud in her sitting room. His heart expanded further when he escorted her to the ballet, where he watched her rapturous face drink in *Giselle*, her favorite. After he learned to play the piano, he became her only audience when she danced alone in Neil's studio and, on several memorable occasions, under the full moon on summer evenings, when he thought his heart would burst from bliss.

Alas, some things cannot last. Thirteen years after their first meeting in a closet, Angela would break Sunny's heart.

He would not take it well.

CHAPTER 1
THIRTEEN YEARS LATER

BARTHAM DAUGHTER TO WED TRADESMAN

The Times, 27 December 1872. Lady Minerva Hadley of Grosvenor Square is pleased to announce the imminent marriage of her great-niece Miss Angela Bartham to Mr. John Carles of Surrey, a noted sherry importer. The nuptials will take place on the morning of December 30th at Holy Trinity Brompton.

Miss Bartham, a noted beauty, is the middle daughter of artist Neil Bartham, whose elopement decades earlier with the former Mrs. Clio Sutton née Hadley—aka 'the Muse of Scandal'—drew much censor. In 1866, Mr. Bartham disappeared whilst traveling to Jerusalem to paint religious subjects. His unexplained absence left his family on the edge of financial and social ruin. Fortunately, the artist was recently located alive in Egypt.

Many will recall that Lady Hadley sponsored Miss Bartham's brilliant introduction to society earlier this year. Miss Bartham's grace and silver-blonde hair drew much attention despite her notorious parents.

ON THE LOVELIEST winter morning in the sweetest church one could imagine in all of London, Angela Bartham possessed only one question before her wedding.

"You're certain Sunny's here?"

The person Angela addressed was her elder sister, Musa, her matron of honor—Musa, who'd unexpectedly married that spring to an up-and-coming artist named Sebastian Atkinson. Their union had gained much attention thanks to a popular children's book they'd collaborated on.

"Completely certain," Musa answered, glancing up from the train of Angela's gown, which she'd been arranging. Sewn of a delicate silk brocade, the train was easily wrinkled, something Angela hadn't taken into consideration when she conferred with the modiste.

Musa added, "That solves one mystery, though there's still no word about where he'd been all this time."

Six months earlier Sunny had asked for Angela's hand in marriage, a proposal Angela promptly refused for reasons only Musa understood. Afterward, he'd disappeared from London to heaven knew where. Rumors flew high and low. Some said Sunny purchased a commission in the military, which seemed ridiculous— after all, Sunny was an earl, not a second son without prospects. Others said he'd simply gone off on a Grand Tour to soothe his broken heart. Even his mother was uninformed as to his location. She'd taken the surprising task of approaching Angela to see if she knew where her son had gone.

Now Sunny was back in London without notice…and a guest at her wedding.

How? Why? Angela fretted, her usual cheerfulness muted. She knew she should be relieved. Perhaps Sunny's presence meant he'd forgiven her, though she doubted it. They'd been the best of friends until his proposal. He'd since refused to speak to her.

She wondered who could have invited him. Certainly not her mother, Clio, who'd been disappointed when Angela refused

Sunny's hand. Nor her great-aunt Minerva, who was relieved when Angela promptly agreed to marry a sherry merchant named John Carles soon after Sunny's proposal. (Not the same as an earl, but definitely a step up for the Barthams.) Carles even had a home in Surrey. Angela had always wanted to live in the countryside surrounded by animals and flowers. More importantly, he adored Angela…or so she told herself.

As for Angela's feelings for Carles, those were more complicated.

You're very fond of him, she told herself. *That's enough for a happy marriage.* John Carles ticked all the boxes off her list of Gentleman Worth Marrying. He was well-off, kind, and handsome enough. Her great-aunt Minerva assured Angela he was a wonderful match, with a good reputation and honorable family name. Anyway, Angela didn't believe in true love, the sort of passion that brought flutters to your stomach and heady kisses. Not anymore.

She'd experienced such a love once. It nearly destroyed her.

She'd learned her lesson. Now Angela was determined to be happy no matter what—she'd take her joy where she could find it. She understood there were more important considerations when it came to choosing a husband. There was respectability, the possibility of children, financial stability, even futures for her sixteen-year-old siblings, Theo and Lyra, who yearned to become musicians.

Anyway, passionate affairs of the heart rarely lasted…save for a few lucky couples.

Angela stole a glance at her mother and her sister, Musa, who were adjusting each other's floral garlands.

Mama and Papa are the exception. So are Musa and Seb.

Everyone who encountered the couples could tell they were meant for each other. Musa and Seb spent their days finishing each other's sentences as though they were of one mind and heart. As for Clio, such was her devotion to their father that she hadn't been the same since his departure for Jerusalem. Now that Neil Bartham been found in Egypt, she was scheduled to leave in three days to help bring him home; he'd been seriously injured there.

Angela told herself she didn't envy her mother's and sister's marriages. At the age of three and twenty, she already understood life was filled with inequities. All things considered, she really was fortunate. Carles would be a good husband. She was delighted to become his wife. Really.

As for Sunny…that was an entirely different matter.

"I'm surprised Sunny's here," Angela forced out. His presence in the church was an uncomfortable reminder of the romantic love she'd given up on. Soulmate love. The kind of love that doomed lovers in ballets.

For Sunny *did* believe in such a love…but Angela couldn't love him that way. She cared enough not to wed him without reciprocating his affections. Unlike Carles.

On that front, Angela tried to suppress the guilt roiling her stomach.

"I invited his mother," Clio admitted sheepishly. "I should have told you, but I never expected she'd attend, and with Sunny, no less. I thought she'd still be in mourning for the previous earl."

Angela couldn't think how to respond. On one hand, her heart leapt to see her old friend had returned for her wedding—perhaps he'd gotten over her refusal. On the other hand, it was all so awkward.

"Well, this is a surprise," Musa said dryly, adjusting her spectacles. "Sunny looks so different. I hadn't recognized him until I heard his mother bleating in her usual way."

Angela was saved from her uneasy ruminations by the arrival of her great-aunt Minerva, who was overdressed for a wedding. She appeared to have decked herself in every diamond she owned.

"Posh, the Earl of Sunderland is old news," she clucked to Angela. "Look at this article, miss! I'd hoped someone would write about your wedding."

Aunt Minerva held out a newspaper folded to the society

section. BARTHAM DAUGHTER TO WED TRADESMAN, the headline declared. The article lasted for all of three brief paragraphs, flattering to Angela but touching on her spotted family history. Angela supposed it couldn't be avoided.

"There's three journalists here," Aunt Minerva added. "They came right up to me, the rascals! I hoped this article would be enough to satisfy them. Well, one must accept such hardships when one is a famed beauty such as yourself, miss."

"I suppose," Angela said.

"I'll see you inside the church! Soon your family will be received at the most elite addresses in London—and it's all because of my sponsorship." Another cluck of pleasure. "Oh, no need to thank me, Angela. Not yet. There's time for that later."

Once her aunt bustled out, Angela peeked out the rectory doors, taking care to remain hidden.

The church was full on the Barthams' side, but scant on Carles'; he claimed it was too far for his family to come from Surrey. He'd considered applying for a special license, so they could be wed near them, but settled for a common license to avoid declaring banns for their wedding. ("That's for plebeians who can't afford privacy," he said.) Still, a common license required them to be wed in the parish church closest to Angela's home.

Carles awaited her at the head of the aisle with the vicar. As for everyone else in the church, Angela made out the dowager countess—well, she remained the Countess of Sunderland until Sunny chose a bride. She appeared as always, with her receding chin and haughty demeanor, only more annoyed, if such a thing was possible. She was seated near a man Angela didn't recognize.

Then she did.

Angela's stomach dropped as though she were about to tumble down a hill. She must have let out a gasp, for Musa said, "I should have warned you."

Lyra, Angela's youngest sister, added, "Wherever Sunny went—"

"He came back quite…" Angela's words faded away.

"Altered," Clio finished.

Angela stole another glance at the man who'd replaced her old friend. It couldn't be. But there he was.

Virgil Sydenham, the former Viscount, now Earl of Sunderland. Sunny, her dearest companion from childhood. If not for his bright auburn hair, she wouldn't have recognized him.

Angela's heart panged. Given the scandals surrounding her parents, his friendship had been especially precious—he saw Angela as who she was, not as people gossiped. Sunny was kind, good, and compassionate. For a moment, she recalled picnicking with him in Green Park as children. The two of them laughing as they chased rabbits at his country estate in Berkshire. Reading books together. His piano and her dancing to his playing. Days of innocence that could never be regained or revisited.

Sunny was seated directly on the aisle—Angela would have no choice but to pass him directly on her way to the altar. His hair had grown markedly longer since they'd last met. The length subdued his unruly curls into something sleeker, vaguely scandalous even. His hair nearly reached his shoulders, like one of Papa's bohemian friends.

His clothes were different too. Though Sunny always dressed in accordance with his station in well-tailored clothes from the finest Saville Row tailors, today he was completely dressed in a black morning suit save for a dark red necktie. He looked leaner. Powerful.

But it was more than this that made him appeared so changed. There were new creases across his brow, a hard set to his jaw. His brown eyes colder. The sweetness she'd loved about him was gone, along with the gentle, wondering way he approached the world that made him appear stumbling and awkward at times. Angela had known differently.

To Angela's shock, her old friend looked angry. Defiant. A bit dangerous. Not at all like himself.

Even more surprising was the fashionable young lady seated

beside him. Her chestnut-hued hair was arranged in tight ringlets to her shoulders beneath her be-plumed bonnet. She appeared several years older than Angela. No one could deny the lady was beautiful in a showy way. She reminded Angela of a peacock, all display and dazzle. The lady stared down at her navy-blue lace mitts, her lips pursed with ennui.

As for the Countess of Sunderland, every so often she threw an alarmed glance in Sunny's direction and fluttered her purple fan.

"I can't believe it," Angela whispered.

Lyra replied, "You can believe it. I even spoke to him when he arrived, to make sure I wasn't imagining things."

"What did he say?"

Lyra shrugged. "Just hello and fine morning, did I think it was going to snow, that sort of thing. But he spoke French to the lady. I understood enough."

"Aren't you going to tell me what he said to her?" Angela asked, her mouth dry.

Lyra's voice dropped to a breath. "That he'd buy her a new gown once this was over."

Angela pulled back from the door. If Sunny was courting the lady, it was decidedly forward to take her shopping. This proved that either they were engaged or she was his mistress. Worst of all, she was French—or so Aunt Minerva would say.

"It seems he's been on the continent after all," Musa said. "Like the rumors claimed."

As though sensing Angela's presence, Sunny's head pivoted toward the door. Angela scuttled away. The church doors slammed so hard that the sound reverberated.

"He saw me!" Angela cried.

"And what if he did?" Musa soothed, taking Angela's hand. "You're trembling. Has this really upset you so?"

"I'm only trembling because I'm so happy," Angela claimed. "That's all."

"Happy people don't look as though they're about to faint."

Musa whispered, "If you've doubts, you needn't marry Carles. I hope you know this."

"I want to marry him," Angela replied.

That, at least, was the truth. Wasn't it?

Clio swept Angela into an embrace just as the church bells struck ten. "Come, beautiful. It's time."

"Indeed it is," Seb added; he'd come in from the church to escort Angela down the aisle. He offered Angela his arm. "Are you ready?"

"As ready as I'll ever be," Angela answered, grateful for her brother-in-law's steady warmth. She forced a smile. All was well, really. "I'm going to be married!"

It was enough she was fond of Carles. Love of a sort would come in time. Anyway, love made you vulnerable; marriage made security—and security would hopefully lead to love. And if love didn't come, Angela would survive. There'd be children to adore, a home to create. There were worse things than a loveless marriage…though right now she felt queasy enough to vomit.

I swear I will be happy no matter what. There is beauty, there is goodness in this world. I'll make it so.

"The music's starting!" Lyra squealed, clapping in anticipation.

Inside the church, the organ swelled with the majestic chords of the wedding march from *Lohengrin*. Angela gathered her bouquet, a generous spray of exquisite pink roses with soft yellow stamens. Clio settled Angela's veil over her eyes, transforming the vestry into a blur of white. Seb led her toward the door, with Lyra and Musa following as her bridal attendants.

Before they entered the church, Angela stole a last look through her veil at her family, all whom she adored beyond measure. Clio was wiping away tears of pride. Musa and Lyra looked beautiful dressed in pink gowns, Seb regal in his best suit, and Theo grown up beyond measure. Once her mother brought Papa back from Egypt, the Barthams would all be together again. Even better, her family would gain security and respectability thanks to Angela's marriage. That would have to be enough.

Suddenly Angela realized she was marrying for love after all.
For the love of her family.
And with this, joy filled her heart.
I will be happy no matter what.

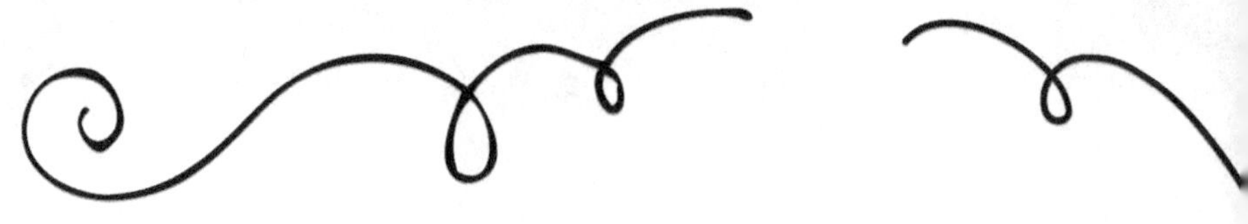

CHAPTER 2

ONCE THE ORGAN began to play the wedding march, Sunny, or more properly Virgil Sydenham, Earl of Sunderland, decided the worst day of his life wasn't the day he'd lost his brother Robert, as awful as it was. Nor was it the day his father died, which happened to be the same day that Angela Bartham refused his proposal. No, it was today, but not for the reason one would expect.

His head was splitting like the devil's anvil was smashing into it.

Sunny rarely drank, not anymore. One would have thought he'd learned his lesson after his previous experiences. Last night he hadn't been able to resist, knowing Angela's wedding was this morning.

Damn it. I shouldn't have attended. But he'd forced himself to come. Forced himself in order to prove to himself, his mother, and the world that he cared nothing for Angela Bartham. Not anymore. That he was doing better than ever and even had a beautiful woman by his side.

As for that beautiful woman, her name was Hélène Charlotte de Castel-d'Albret, an appropriately grand name befitting her aristocratic lineage. Hélène, seated between Sunny and his mother, sniffed dismissively. She whispered to him in French, "She's beautiful, but rather ordinary."

He replied in a low tone, "What of it?"

He'd brought Hélène to prove he wasn't at a loss for feminine companionship. Wasn't someone to pity. Hélène's arrival had horrified his mother, even after he assured her Hélène was the daughter of a former French noble from the Second Empire. Sunny didn't dare tell her the extent of their relationship.

"And she's wearing white," Hélène added. "*Trés bourgeois, non?*"

He nodded wearily. Yes, wearing white as a bride was very middle class. White had always been his least favorite color…especially on Angela.

To his horror, she looked lovelier than ever. Glowing, as she approached her future husband, that tradesman. Joy-filled. This was one of the qualities he'd always loved about her—no matter what, Angela found good in the world. This extended to the people surrounding her. He'd been a desperately awkward, lonely child; she'd seen the good in him.

But not enough to wed him.

"We shouldn't have attended, Sunderland," the countess muttered to her son. "If this is your idea of revenge, you've wasted my morning."

The Countess of Sunderland had long despised the Barthams for reasons too copious to enumerate. Which was surprising, considering that Sunny's father, rest his soul, had esteemed the art of Neil Bartham and ignored the family's reputation. Then there was the matter of Neil and Clio's four children, three girls and one boy, of which Angela was the middle daughter.

As well as the kindest, most beautiful and grace-filled woman in England. Angela was sunshine and kittens and bright smiles. Mozart on a summer night and roses in a summer garden. Or so he'd once believed.

"I wish this was over," his mother whined beneath the swelling organ music. "I feel degraded."

"Je suis d'accord," Hélène agreed, tapping her fan against her thigh.

"That's exactly why we're here," he muttered, grumpier than usual. "To prove we're above them."

All too soon Angela drew close, her brother-in-law Sebastian clasping her arm. She progressed down the aisle as though she were floating in a sea of silk, revealing her years of ballet dancing. Her face was soft beneath her long ivory veil, her eyes trained on the huge bouquet of luscious pink roses clutched in her arms. Her lips curved in a gentle smile.

His head gave another pound.

To his dismay, Angela didn't meet his gaze as she passed Sunny on the aisle; he could have been dressed as a chimney sweep for all it mattered. Her lacy skirts brushed his hand, which he'd rested against the pew to steady himself. He flinched at the unexpected contact. Yet he didn't remove his hand.

Worse, his fingers flexed to caress her skirts.

The pale cream silk was crisp against her petticoats, the lace trim soft. Just like that day long ago, when they'd been trapped together in that closet as children.

This is as close as you'll ever get to holding her.

He unwillingly recalled the future he'd envisioned when he proposed to Angela six months earlier, before she'd broken his heart. He'd imagined summers in his ancestral home in Berkshire, countess of all she surveyed as they walked along the lush woods and gardens. Winters in London in his townhouse in North Kensington, where they'd attend ballets and she'd visit her family. Private soirées where he'd play Mozart, and she'd dance for their friends.

Most of all, he imagined clasping Angela in his arms in their nuptial bed, her pale gold hair falling across the bed linens as they made love. Warm sunlight gilding her shoulders, birds chirping outside their window. Dandelion clocks and rose petals and teacakes dusted with sugar.

Suddenly Sunny wanted to bolt for the door. Run. Though that would undermine the point of his attending the wedding: to prove Angela had made a mistake in refusing his proposal. He glanced at Hélène. Thank goodness she was there, though what sort of revenge could it be if it went unacknowledged?

At last, Angela arrived at the altar, where Carles awaited. He really did look like a weasel, Sunny decided. Too tall. Thin. Lanky brown hair draped across his forehead. Darting eyes.

The vicar cleared his throat in preparation for the ceremony. Angela raised her eyes from her roses. Sunny made out a subtle flush cross her face as she gazed up toward her future husband; Carles was much taller than Angela. He took her hand in his, returning her warm gaze. He beamed—that was the only word for it.

Sunny resisted the urge to gag.

"Dearly beloved, we are gathered here to witness the union of Allegra and John…"

The vicar's drone circled Sunny's ears like a mosquito. How many times had he witnessed the service of marriage? As a boy, he'd found it enthralling, the hope that one would meet your true love and live happily ever after like a fairy tale. Today, the ceremony irked him more than he'd ever expected to be possible.

He jiggled his foot against the pew. His eyes smarted from lack of sleep.

Revenge only hurts the bearer.

This was a saying Sunny's father trotted out regularly after the death of Sunny's brother. Sunny hadn't wanted to believe him, for he had plenty of fodder for revenge. When another boy at Eton shoved him into a pile of horse manure. When his mother criticized his waistcoat straining at the buttons. When someone at his club ridiculed the stammer that emerged when he was stressed. Most of all, when Angela refused his suit to choose Carles.

But now he knew his father was right. When this was over, Angela would live happily ever after. He'd take to his bed until his headache subsided—Hélène could shop on her own. As for his mother, who appeared to be dozing, he'd follow her lead.

"Wake me when it's over," he whispered to Hélène as he shut his eyes.

She offered a warm chuckle. "*Exactement.*"

He didn't look up when the church doors creaked open. A late arrival.

The vicar continued despite the interruption. "Do you, John Francis, take Allegra Jane as your lawful wedded wife?"

"I do," Carles finished. To Angela: "Your turn, darling."

Despite everything, Sunny's heart thudded in anticipation. He forced himself to look at Angela. To his surprise, Angela looked pale beneath her veil, queasy even. Her gentle smile had become a rigid seam.

The vicar began, "Allegra Jane, do you take—"

A baby's cry interrupted the vicar. Angela's mouth grew tighter. Carles' gaze darted toward the door.

How loud the baby was! Angela's heart gave a thud, especially after the vicar's words came to a halt. Her cheerfulness drooped like an unstarched collar as she glanced over her shoulder.

Through the haze of her white veil, Angela made out a lady, someone she hadn't met before, enter the church. The lady wore respectable navy blue broadcloth, her dress fuller than the current fashion. She stood in front of the church doors, cradling a swaddled infant. A little girl about three years clutched her skirts. The lady was pretty in a delicate way, like Angela, though her hair was dark, not blonde, beneath her straw bonnet.

It must be someone from Carles's side—that was good. Angela had been distressed by how few showed for their nuptials from his family, though Carles had prepared her. Still, Angela wished the lady hadn't interrupted the ceremony. For a moment, when those church doors creaked open, she imagined someone interrupting their wedding, like Bertha Mason's brother in *Jane Eyre*. She and Sunny had read the book together long ago.

Her heart gave another thud at the thought of Sunny's presence. She'd never seen him so fashionably dressed. The French lady by his side really was stunningly beautiful.

It's good he's here. It proves he bears you no ill will.

The vicar cleared his throat and began anew.

"Allegra Jane, do you take John Francis as your lawful wedded husband?"

This was it. The moment that would tie them together forever. No turning back.

A deep breath. "I-I..."

I do. Two syllables. That's all. It should be easy. But Angela couldn't seem to get the words out. That lady's arrival had rattled her.

As for the lady herself, she let out a cough. But it wasn't the sort of cough one would make if ill. It was more the sort to gain attention if one was too polite to make a scene.

Angela's skin prickled as whispers rose in the church.

"Answer the vicar, darling," Carles said, his smile tight.

"Who's the woman?" Angela whispered, her stomach clenching anew.

"No one important," Carles said. To the vicar: "We've a train to catch."

They were to honeymoon in Wales, which wasn't Angela's choice. Wales felt so far away with her mother leaving for Egypt— what if something arose with the twins? Anyway, their train wasn't until much later that afternoon. First there was the ceremony to complete, the registry to sign. Then the wedding breakfast, which her great-aunt would host in her townhouse in Mayfair. All markers of church and state—markers that would finally return Angela and the Barthams to social respectability.

The vicar's brow creased. "Is there something we should discuss in private, Mr. Carles?"

Though his tone was low, the implication was clear.

No scandal, Angela prayed, all of her cheerfulness gone. *Please, no scandal.*

Another murmur ran through the church. Angela couldn't resist peeking over her shoulder. The dowager countess's brow arched. Sunny sat upright as though his spine had turned to steel.

Something bad is going to happen. They know it. Everyone knows it.

"All is well," Carles snapped. "Continue."

"If you please," the dark-haired lady called out in a broad West Country accent; her baby wailed anew. "We should speak in private, John—"

"You're not to call me by my christian name," Carles scolded.

The lady ambulated down the aisle with her children in their direction. As she drew near, Angela smelled something damp and rank seep from her cloak. Travel. Horses. Mud.

"Mr. Carles then. Regardless, we should speak." She shrugged in Angela's direction. "Sorry, love."

"Sorry for what?" Angela asked, suspecting the answer she was about to receive would make her *very* unhappy. "Who are you?"

The young lady answered, "Perhaps you should ask John—I mean, Mr. Carles—that question."

Angela's gaze darted between Carles, this rather shabby looking lady, her children, and the vicar.

"I'd rather hear it from you, madame," Angela replied.

"He's the father of my children. My husband."

Angela would have told herself she'd misheard had not a collective gasp rise in the church.

"Your husband?" Angela said weakly. Perspiration beaded on her forehead beneath her veil.

A nod. "My name is Mary Elizabeth Carles. Mrs. John Carles, yes. We wed in Surrey four years ago as of last May. I've papers, certificates, whatever proof you require. I'd suspected Mr. Carles had a pretty piece on the side, but had no proof until I read this."

She brandished a clipping of a newspaper article from her reticule—the same article Aunt Minerva had been so proud of moments earlier.

This can't be happening to me.

"Papa!" the little girl cried, her arms straining for Carles. "I missed you!"

"Liar!" Carles grabbed Angela's hands; his palms were unpleasantly moist. "Angela, say you believe me! That woman is not my wife." Carles's voice dropped to a whisper. "She's Catholic. We all know papist ceremonies don't count."

A long moment passed, a moment in which Angela sensed her family's future melt like snow in summer. Musa and Seb's books avoided by anyone respectable. Lyra left without prospects for marriage or as a musician, Theo laughed out of school. Worst of all, her mother wouldn't leave to help her father return home from Egypt because she'd be too busy fretting about Angela.

"That's not exactly a denial," Angela said at last.

Another lady stood up. Well, staggered really—she'd been seated in the back on Carles's side of the aisle apart from everyone else. Angela noticed her earlier; she'd appeared so out of place in her magenta evening gown, like she'd come directly from a ball. However, the bump rounding her stomach was impossible to ignore despite the generous flounces on her skirt.

"He's my husband too!" the pregnant lady called out in a heavy Cockney accent. "We wed in Gretna Green two years ago. I wasn't going to say anything unless I had to—" she nodded at the first wife "—but then I realized I'd been a coward." To Angela, "You're better off without him, duckling."

A hiss swept around the church. Angela's face burned, her knees trembled beneath that lovely silk and lace gown she'd been so proud of that morning. Her head buzzed with light. She wasn't going to faint, was she?

Instead, her mother fainted; Seb caught her before she hit the stone floor of the church. Musa dashed to Clio, waving smelling salts over her face. Angela couldn't bear to look anywhere else, knowing what she'd witness. Lyra's mouth would be agape, her great-aunt flailing, Theo slinking in the pew as though to disappear.

And then Angela knew. She wouldn't be getting married that day, or any day for that matter. Once word got out, she'd be the laughingstock of all of London. Worse, England. It didn't matter she was a famed beauty, or how noble her intents had been in agreeing to wed Carles and his supposedly good family name. All that mattered was that Angela Bartham, daughter of Clio Bartham, the Muse of Scandal, had been abandoned at the altar after nearly wedding a bigamist.

She'd join her mother in infamy…and so would the rest of her family.

A sharp cackle broke the horrified silence of the church. The Countess of Sunderland—Angela would know her laugh anywhere.

She muttered, "It figures a Bartham daughter would choose such a husband."

With this, what felt like all hell broke loose. The middle class woman thrust the baby into Carles's arms—"Take your child, sir!"—and the little girl coiled her arms around his knees like an attacking octopus. Tiny as she was, the child's weight threw Carles off. He crumpled to the red-carpeted aisle, nearly hitting his head against the altar.

Next, the pregnant woman kicked Carles in his thigh. Angela sensed she'd intended to aim for parts further north.

"Bastard!" she hissed. "I suspected as much about you, but didn't want to believe it!"

Then Aunt Minerva fainted next to Clio, Lyra's eyes bugged out, and Musa caught their aunt while her ever-active brain clicked away in search of How To Fix This.

But no one could fix this; this Angela knew without a doubt.

It's all true, Angela thought in an oddly detached manner. Now it all made sense: Carles's anxious manner after she'd accepted his proposal, his refusal to show her his estate in Surrey. Even the common license so they wouldn't have to post banns, and how few showed from his side for the wedding.

This is the worst day of my life.

With this, Angela's emotions returned in full force. A rush of embarrassment—how could she have misjudged Carles so?—along with a bright blade of fury.

He ruined her life. Well, now she'd ruin his.

"I'll kill you," she hissed.

She stared around for a weapon. Something. Anything. Meanwhile Seb strode forth, his fists raised—he had a temper when provoked—but that wouldn't provide enough satisfaction for Angela's liking. The prayer books were too small to wreck any damage save for a bruise or two. The brass candlesticks too far away. Her eyes finally settled on the generous bouquet of pink roses in her arms.

Roses had thorns. Thorns were sharp. They would do just fine.

Just as Angela was about to smash her roses into Carles's face, another burst of laughter from the Countess of Sunderland. She cackled like a seal drunk on gin.

"Shut up, Mother," Sunny snapped.

"Oh come, it's hilarious, Sunderland!"

In lieu of an answer, he majestically rose from the pew, looking more self-possessed than Angela had ever witnessed. Was he going to leave? That would be a kindness. How humiliating this all was!

No, instead he approached Angela.

Sunderland, no," his mother called out, any amusement banished from her tone. "Don't!"

Don't what? Angela thought.

Sunny dropped to his knees before Angela.

"Angela Bartham," he said, "I'd like to offer for your hand in marriage."

And then it truly was the worst day of her life.

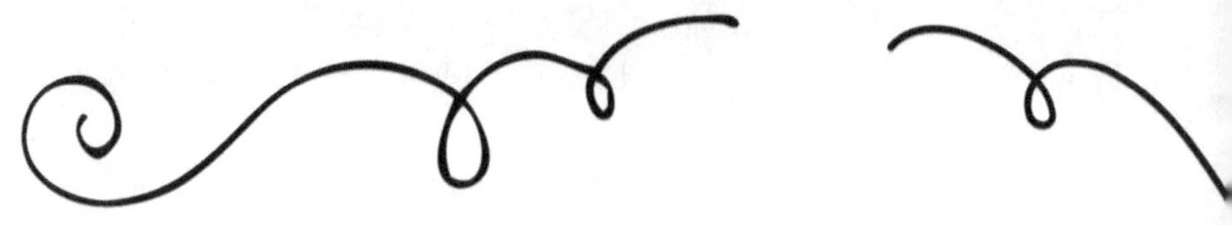

CHAPTER 3

As soon as Sunny made his declaration, Hélène stood up in a huff and slapped his cheek so hard that his teeth rattled. But what was done was done.

"You can't marry her!" John Carles flung out his arms, nearly smashing his eldest daughter's head, who continued clutching his thigh as though it were a raft on the Thames. "I gave Angela a dowry," he yelled at Sunny. "She accepted it *very* willingly. That's an implied contract between us, one she's broken. Ask any solicitor."

"He's correct, Sunderland!" Sunny's mother shouted from her pew, where she was fanning herself furiously as though to keep from swooning. "She's not yours to wed. Give her to the bigamist like a good boy. Now step away from the Bartham chit or I shall faint!"

"I'll marry whom I like," Sunny growled, forgetting his pounding head, his jaw where he'd been slapped. "As for you, Carles, though you haven't much of a leg to stand on—" he pointed to the child still coiled around Carle's thigh "—I'll repay your so-called dowry."

"That's right! He's the one who broke the law, not me," Angela shouted, smashing her bouquet of pink roses into Carles' chest with great vigor. "As for your dowry, you can shove—"

"Thief! Doxy!" Carles' insults drowned out Angela's words, which were assuredly more vulgar than anything she'd ever spouted in her life. "Cheap bit of fluff!"

That was enough.

Sunny raised his gold-tipped walking stick and leisurely approached Carles. The taller man cowered—he may have had some inches on Sunny, but he appeared delicate beside the earl's stockier form.

"I'm sorry, I didn't hear you, Carles," Sunny said, cocking his head. He thumped his walking stick against the palm of his left hand. Once. Twice. "Could you please repeat yourself?"

"I said she was a c-cheap—"

Sunny clasped his palm over Carles' mouth and raised his walking stick above his head. Everything in the church gasped, even the dowager countess. One of Carles' wives screamed.

"You didn't say that about Miss Bartham, did you?" Sunny challenged.

Carles' pale eyes blinked. Fear, that's what he felt. But he didn't breathe a sound.

"I thought not." Sunny let his lips spread into a rather cruel smile, one hadn't known himself capable of until recently. "You have no idea what I might do, Carles. You're welcome to find out, if you care."

The vicar nervously interjected, "This is a house of God, my lord. Let us not taint it with anger."

"I'd say it's Mr. Carles who's tainted your house of God," Sunny replied in a soft voice that afforded no argument. He removed his palm from Carles' mouth. "Now go. Shoo!"

"We'll help!" young Theo called out, rushing toward the altar. "Sebastian, shall we?"

And so they would have had not Carles dashed out of the church so quickly that his eldest daughter had no choice but to release her father's leg. Later, Sunny would question whether

Carles' departure had been spurred by fear, or the desire to avoid his wives and children.

Sunny addressed the vicar. "Send for a special license for Miss Bartham and myself—I'll pay whatever it takes. I'm sure your church could use a donation, yes? We'll wed immediately." Then, to Angela, "Shall we?"

For a moment, he half-expected Angela to turn away. To refuse his suit. But she only offered a tight nod.

And then Sunny's mother did indeed faint.

Outside the church, news of Angela and Sunny's unexpected nuptials must have spread, for the three sleepy reporters in the church had multiplied into a ravenous pack of chattering journalists. They confronted the newlyweds as soon as they stepped foot outside the church after the ceremony. The reporters churned with questions, daring to sweep the couple away.

"My lady, did you suspect the earl would propose this morning?" a grey-bearded bear of a man shouted at Angela. A second, who appeared younger and more desperate, interrupted, "Had you any suspicion about Mr. Carles' bigamy?" A third, "This is the most romantic story of the year—our readers will devour it! My lord, how fortunate you were present to rescue her from such a nefarious man. True love prevails!"

Angela remained too stunned to respond outside of an occasional syllable; her cheeks drained of color until they matched her bridal veil. But Sunny took immense satisfaction in her shock…and in his mother's.

Once the dowager countess recovered from her faint, she'd rushed out the church no doubt to find a solicitor to void the union. Hélène followed in a huff after throwing a second slap in his direction. Not that it mattered. Sunny had never felt better. Nothing like upsetting others' expectations to soothe a hangover.

Powerful, that's what he felt. Dominant. A lion instead of a lamb.

"My bride confided her suspicions to me some weeks ago," Sunny lied smoothly. "However, she felt compelled to honor her promise to Carles. I knew it was a matter of time before the truth would emerge."

As he spoke, he recalled all that occurred after they'd thrown Carles out. How the church fell into a peculiar hush more suitable for a funeral than a wedding. How somehow the special license for the wedding arrived more quickly than he'd imagined possible. How shaken Angela appeared as she repeated the vows. Hopeless, that's what she felt, for she understood how ruinous Carles' bigamy was for her reputation and her family. Distraught, for she probably loved Carles.

Yet Sunny hadn't turned back from marrying Angela despite his attachment to Hélène. He couldn't, though he wasn't exactly sure what had spurred him to make Angela his wife beyond his mother's cruel laughter. It certainly wasn't because he loved her. Not any longer.

Revenge. That's what it was, though it wasn't the revenge he'd envisioned.

Instead of Angela regretting not choosing him as her husband, he'd imagined Angela in debt to him. Angela knowing he was the one who'd saved her family from ruin—he hadn't been able to resist.

And that was the crux of it.

Revenge, he thought anew. Revenge against Angela. Revenge against his mother, against anyone who'd ever ridiculed or compared him to his brother, considering Sunny of no import save for his title. This need felt stronger than love, greater than desire. He hadn't been able to turn away from it. Well, he supposed there were worse reasons to wed, though he hadn't considered the aftermath.

And now here they were, tied together in unholy matrimony.

Angela Bartham, his wife. His countess.

His enemy.

He threw a look at Angela, who stood by his side before the bank of reporters, who'd grown raucous with their hungry gazes and demands. She was shivering with cold. With everything going on, she'd left the church without her cloak.

The questions rang out, more than Sunny could discern amid the rush of male voices.

"It was fortunate you were there to rescue Miss Bartham—I mean the countess—my lord," one reporter shouted. "Care you speak of your unexpected nuptials?"

Sunny said, "Love is a powerful force."

Hopefully that was cryptic enough to throw them off.

"And what of you, my lady? Do you love the earl? I understand you were childhood sweethearts," another reporter barked. Angela blanched again.

Before Angela could respond, a lanky boy of not more than a dozen years pushed his way to the front of the crowd. "Special Edition! *Times*, fresh off the press! Read it!"

The front page screamed: BARTHAM BEAUTY NEARLY WEDS BIGAMIST! Sunny could well imagine the rest of the article. He ordered the newsboy away after buying his pile of papers for more money than the urchin had probably ever seen in his life.

"This no longer matters," he declared, dumping the newspapers into a pile of snow. "Now, if you'll excuse us, we've a breakfast to attend."

A black-painted carriage bearing his seal arrived—his coachman must have brought it around in anticipation. Sunny swept Angela into the carriage, squeezing their way through the crowd.

She flinched at his touch but didn't pull away.

Once they were alone in the carriage on their way to Mayfair, Angela spoke for the first time since she'd accepted the signet ring that stood in for a wedding band.

"You didn't give me a choice."

"A choice?" Sunny felt his forehead wrinkle.

"To marry you or not." A breath. "But I suppose I hadn't one. It was either marry you or let my family be ruined."

It was true. And now here they were, seated across from each other in the carriage. He could feel her warmth through her gown despite the chill. Smell the perfume from those roses she'd carried…or was it the scent of her hair? She'd arranged it in plaits, all coiled about her lovely head like a madonna from a Renaissance painting, with white silk ribbons and silk flowers.

Despite everything, she still affected him, damn it.

"I suppose I should thank you. Be grateful and all that. My mother would never have left for Egypt unless I was settled. But why did you do this, Sunny? You despise me—I can see it in your eyes."

"Sunderland," he corrected, disconcerted by her presence. "My lord. Formality is better in such a situation."

"A marriage of convenience, you mean." She shook her head, eyes hooded with sorrow. "Once we were friends. The dearest of friends…"

He replied in a bitter tone, "You want the truth, Angela? I need a wife. You'll do."

"Rubbish! You could have any woman in London. You're the Earl of Sunderland, for heaven's sake! Tell me the *actual* truth why you married me."

"Despite everything, I care for your mother. Your family."

"But not me," she said, the words choked.

"Not anymore," he replied, wanting to believe it. The pulse of his heart claimed otherwise.

The carriage bumped as it crossed the Green Park toward Mayfair. Outside, the sky grew heavier with clouds. Colder. Angela swiped at her eyes. Was she weeping?

It doesn't matter what she feels.

Angela asked after a long moment, "What sort of marriage will this be, with you not caring for me?"

He stumbled in his old awkward way, "The marriage won't be consummated, if that's what you mean. I've no desire to touch you."

Liar, his body answered…his body that had grown to know over the past six months since he'd last seen her.

Now that he was near her—the closest he'd been since she'd refused his suit—he felt his skin prickle in that old way with the hunger to touch her. To embrace her as more than a friend. To possess her. During his time in France, he'd tried his best to exorcise Angela from his heart and body. Though he hadn't taken a lover, he'd had flirtations. Well, more than such, even if it was only to prove he could survive without Angela.

But now that she was beside him, he couldn't resist recalling all his cherished dreams to hold her in his arms. To know her as intimately as a woman could be known.

He supposed old fantasies died hard.

Angela implored, "What happened to you since your father's death? Where did you go? What did you do? We were all so worried about you."

Her pale blue eyes raked his face. Did she still see him as he'd been before she broke his heart? Or as he was now? Could she discern the effects of the past six months on his soul? Where he'd gone? What he'd done? He could scarcely believe it himself.

He couldn't tell anyone. But he could confess the aftermath of her rejection.

"*You* happened to me," he said. "Your pity."

She frowned. "My pity?"

"I saw it in your face when you refused my proposal. How you felt so sorry for me for loving you as I did. Like I was nothing more than a lap dog you'd grown fond of." He drew a deep breath. "And then that letter."

Angela had sent him a letter the day after she'd refused his proposal. He couldn't bear to think of its wretched contents, let alone speak of it. Yet the letter was ever present in his mind, like a nightmare one couldn't subdue.

The letter consisted of five pages detailing why she would

could never be his wife. She'd phrased everything tactfully enough, he supposed. However, anyone could read between the lines to comprehend what she really meant. Much of her letter lingered in his memory still.

She'd written: *I understand the honor you have offered with your proposal, but it is impossible for me to reciprocate your affection to the degree required for such a union.*

She'd written: *My heart is closed to you. I beg you to understand this is a failure of imagination on my part, not yours.*

She'd written: *I do not consider you the kind of man I could ever choose for a husband.*

She'd written: *I beg you to give up whatever attachment you feel for me. I do not love you.*

She'd written: *I can never love you.*

That letter changed him. Cursed him. It served to prove everything he'd ever feared about himself. That he was essentially undesirable. Unloveable. Unworthy. A joke. Oh, yes, at the end of those five devastating pages she'd written she'd always care for him as a friend—or so she claimed. A sop to his ego. But that wasn't what he wanted of her. Or needed.

She drew a shaky breath. "I only wrote that letter to free you. I-I wanted to…"

Destroy your love for me.

Her words drifted into silence, but Sunny understood too well. She'd succeeded…and more. That letter had engendered something dark inside him. Something that still entrapped his soul.

At the memory, a rush of bitter heat rose—an anger he'd grown too familiar with these past months.

She added in a desperate tone, "I thought I was doing you a kindness."

He laughed. "A kindness? You have an interesting idea what constitutes such."

"Believe me, I immediately regretted sending that letter."

"But you didn't come to me to confess such, did you?"

His words grew low and insistent, as all the hurt simmering

inside him surged forth. His sense of being cursed by that letter. By her.

"If your words weren't hurtful enough, my mother found your letter. She had no right to search my chamber, but she was so damn curious after I returned home distraught. As for her reaction to your letter…well, it only confirmed what I'd known since my brother's death." A pause. "She laughed at me, Angela. For my sentimentality. For caring for you. For being upset you wouldn't marry me."

Just as she laughed at you today.

His mother's reaction to the worst heartbreak of his life only reiterated that he was a constant disappointment. Unable to live up to the promise expected of him as a son, an earl, a man. Unlike his brother Robert, whom even now years later, he missed deep in his bones. Robert, who'd been meant to become earl until he'd snapped his neck while riding a horse.

Strange how he still missed Robert, but not his father who'd passed much more recently. But Robert had never made him feel like a failure.

"I was very wrong, though I'd meant otherwise," Angela said in a low voice. "I'm so desperately sorry! I wrote that letter because I cared about you so very much. I know you don't believe me, but it's true."

"As a friend," he snapped. "Never a lover or a husband. You made that abundantly clear, Angela."

"And yet here we are." She lifted one shoulder, let it fall. "Married. Tied to each other for the rest of our lives." Her voice grew very small. "At the least we can be friends still, can we not?"

His body tensed at her offer.

"Make no mistake, Angela. We're not friends. Not any longer."

She flinched, but didn't protest. Instead, she simply turned away as though he were no longer in the carriage. Every so often, her shoulder shuddered. She was weeping. But he couldn't comfort her, though his old feelings for her rose despite everything. He couldn't forgive her. Couldn't risk the possibility of caring for her.

Revenge only hurts the bearer, he thought again. Now all the sweetness he'd felt turned to ash. It was the worst torment to gain what you most yearned for, but to no longer want it. Worse, to disdain it. Had he not given way to his desire for revenge, he would have married another woman to lead another life. Such as Hélène.

A lifetime is a long time to be trapped with your enemy.

Well, he supposed he and Angela could lead separate existences. She could take the country house in Berkshire, he the townhouse in London. Or he could purchase a residence for her elsewhere. Someplace far away where they wouldn't see each other unless absolutely required. Still, they'd be tied together for the rest of their lives. He wouldn't be able to honor his legacy as earl, provide an heir.

Yet again, Sunny would be perceived as a failure. A disappointment.

What am I to do?

A solution rose in his mind. A desperate solution, but one that could work. One that would allow him to provide continuity to the earldom. One that could leave him free of Angela and her family's reputation unscathed. Despite everything, he still cared about her mother, who'd always treated him kindly.

But he couldn't say it. Not yet.

And then it was too late, for they'd arrived at her great-aunt Minerva's townhouse on Grosvenor Square, where everyone awaited them with awkward smiles and bottles of champagne and beribboned gifts as though Sunny had been intended as Angela's husband all along.

All he could do was bear it like a fool.

CHAPTER 4

THE WEDDING BREAKFAST—NOW lunch because of the fiasco at the church and the wait for the special license—lasted far too long for Angela's comfort, yet was far too short. It was excruciating. Aunt Minerva had themed the breakfast to double as a belated Christmas celebration: plum pudding, decorations of holly and firs, and even a sprig of mistletoe placed for convenient kissing. However, the festive atmosphere made the day into even more of a mockery.

Her wedding day.

Looking back, Angela could scarcely recall the ceremony itself, which concluded without a kiss. The next thing she knew, she'd somehow signed the registry and was outside the church on the cold December day without her wool cloak. Sunny stood beside her, the ground beneath her embroidered slippers as icy as his demeanor. And the reporters! How many there'd been! The questions they'd thrown at them! Sunny refused to meet her eyes. She couldn't meet his. She'd stared down at the signet band that seemed to have come out of nowhere. It was set on her left hand on her ring finger. Her stomach gave an odd flip.

He is my husband now. I am his wife. And he despises me.

As soon as he'd proposed marriage, she'd understood. He wasn't saving her. He was punishing her. And she understood why.

The ride in the carriage to Mayfair confirmed all she'd suspected. The letter. She knew she'd been unkind to write it, but she could think of no other way to free him from his devotion to her. *"Make no mistake, Angela. We're not friends. Not any longer…"* His cold words proved she'd been all too effective.

As for the wedding lunch, Angela half-expected the Dowager Countess to show up half-way through shouting at her. She also cringed in anticipation of the French woman making an appearance, whether she'd confront Sunny. (Where had she gone after she'd slapped Sunny? She'd seemingly disappeared.) Then there was Angela's parting from Clio, understanding she might not see her mother for as long as a year. How painful it had been to bid her mother farewell, knowing how far she'd be traveling to be reunited with her father!

But Angela also knew she had no choice but to marry Sunny. Clio wouldn't have left England otherwise; her father couldn't travel home without her assistance.

All too soon, the wedding breakfast was over and she and Sunny were again alone in his carriage. Alone as husband and wife. The trunk she'd packed for her honeymoon on top…the trunk that had once held her hopes for her future. Her aunt gave her one of her coats, clucking in sympathy over Angela's loss of her cloak at the church.

"Where are we going?" she asked in a low voice. It was already dark, for the sun didn't last past four in late December in London.

"My home." Sunny's tone was dismissive. "For tonight."

Our wedding night.

Once the carriage was underway, she stared out the window into the shadowed streets, willing herself not to think of another wedding night she'd dreamed of, but not with Carles. No, a night with someone no one in her family knew, though Musa had an inkling.

He'd been a dancer, like herself. Angela had loved him madly. Desperately.

Like Giselle for Albrecht.

Like Isolde for Tristan.

Like Juliet for Romeo—

"Annulment," Sunny said, interrupting the frigid silence in the carriage.

His pronouncement rattled Angela from contemplations of wedding nights and doomed love. Her stomach plummeted. Her eyes opened.

"Excuse me?" She hoped she's misheard.

"Annulment," he repeated. "That's how we'll end this farce."

"I know you're angry with me, but not that!"

Annulment. She couldn't even say the word. It felt a curse returned, like something out of a fairy tale. For a Bartham, an annulment would be nearly as bad as marrying a bigamist. Her family would never survive the scandal.

Her mother's first marriage to a famed art critic ended in annulment soon after their honeymoon. Though her mother had never shared the details, whatever happened was too tawdry to be spoken of directly. All Angela knew was her mother had run off with her father soon after their first meeting at a ball in Venice. Since then, Clio Bartham had been whispered about. Laughed at. Snubbed by anyone with a reputation to protect save for Sunny and his father. So had all the Bartham children until recently, when Aunt Minerva sponsored Angela's entry into society to find a husband.

"Hear me out, Angela. The annulment won't be as you fear. I'll do my best—"

"What 'best'?" Angela folded her arms, shivering despite her aunt's coat. "There is no such thing as 'best' when it comes to an annulment."

"Our situation is not your mother's."

"It doesn't matter! I don't care about scandal for myself. I can survive anything, I know that." Hadn't her broken heart proven as much? "But the twins. My sister Musa. My family. The scandal."

"It won't be a scandal if the annulment is uncontested," he countered in a tight voice. "Which is what it will be. And we won't annul the marriage immediately. That would definitely create a scandal."

"How long?" Angela's tone was flat.

"A year. Long enough for people to lose interest in our marriage. Long enough for your mother to be reunited with your father. But not so long that the church will refuse—we'd have to apply for the annulment earlier so it would be completed by then. Much can happen in a year. By then, there will be other scandals to distract the press…especially if we handle our situation correctly."

Angela let out a long breath. Surprise, that's what she felt. He'd thought this through. Considered the ramifications.

Annulment. Now the word felt like an offering. A gift.

Still, she wouldn't give in so easily. She distrusted him, especially after his "we're not friends" declaration.

"And what would handling 'our situation correctly' mean?" she asked in a prim tone.

"We live quietly."

"Apart from each other?" That would make the year so much easier to stomach.

His teeth flashed bright in the shadows of the carriage. "I wish. Any public separation would encourage speculation. Gossip. So we live together for a year. Someplace quiet—I've a few ideas."

"If we live together like a married couple, wouldn't that undermine our case for an annulment?"

"We shan't share a bed. I promised I wouldn't touch you. I meant it."

Because then we won't be able to end this sham of a marriage.

From what Angela knew about annulment, you had to swear under oath you hadn't consummated the union. Worse, the woman's most intimate parts could be examined to prove she was still untouched. Her face burned even considering it.

As though sensing her embarrassment, Sunny said, "You shan't be humiliated by a physician. I'll prevent such."

Because you're a man. An earl. Angela had heard whispers that her mother hadn't had that protection for her annulment.

"You do know I'll be in your debt for the rest of my life."

"Yes, you'll be in my debt," he replied in a low voice. "But you already are, aren't you? And neither of us wants to be wed to each other. I need an heir. I, for one, had other matrimonial intents prior to today."

Again, Angela thought of the French woman fleeing the church. She was a showy beauty, so different from Angela. Perhaps that's what her rejection had pushed Sunny toward.

"No, I don't wish to be married to you," Angela replied.

"Well, there you have it. We're in agreement," Sunny said, turning away to stare out the window. "If it helps, I'll settle you after the annulment, so you need never worry about funds."

By then they were nearly at Sunny's home in North Kensington, which was set in the area known as Little Venice; Angela could tell by the glint of gas lamps reflecting in the Regent Canal. Outside the carriage, the snow began falling in thick clumps of white. It would have appeared magical, except there was nothing magical about the day.

As the carriage slowed, she drew a long shaky breath.

"A year then, my lord."

"A year and not a day more, Angela."

To her astonishment, an unexpected hope rose, tender as a green shoot in spring.

And perhaps by then you'll find a way to forgive me.

However, this she doubted.

The carriage approached a townhouse set facing the Regent Canal, though to call the mansion a townhouse seemed ridiculous. It was a palace, Angela decided, but such was the wealth of the Earl of Sunderland.

Angela glanced at him, this old friend who'd be her husband for a year. To her shock, she noticed a pale pink rose tucked inside his breast pocket of his greatcoat, one she hadn't noticed before.

A rose from her wedding bouquet. It must have fallen while she was wrestling with Carles.

Sunny made out Angela's recognition the same moment she did. He explained, "It's not every day a man marries the woman he once loved."

Again, her eyes stung. Before she could decide how to respond, Sunny announced, "We're here."

The carriage came to a juddering halt. A footman approached, clutching an umbrella against the snow. He opened the carriage door for Angela. She peered out as the wind whipped tendrils of hair from beneath her bonnet, plastering them against her cheeks.

To her astonishment, all the servants were standing in a line before the entry doors despite the weather. Had they received word of their marriage? If so, who'd told them? The French woman? Sunny's mother? Angela half-expected the dowager countess to jump out from behind a tree to throttle her.

"My lady."

As Angela reluctantly accepted the footman's assistance, a shrill female voice shrieked, "Minx! Slattern! You planned this all along, didn't you?"

Angela made out the Dowager Countess's approach from behind the line of servants; her fears hadn't been for naught. The look on Sunny's mother's face suggested something sinister. Unhinged. Her shouts were quickly overtaken by the rise of song. Holiday carolers…or were they? No, it was the clatter of male voices mingling with bells on the wind. Reporters.

"My lady," the first one cried, reaching Angela as she stepped onto the pavement, "did you always love the earl?"

Another: "Is it true you plotted to wed the earl all along?" To Sunny: "My lord, care you to comment on your wife's family? After all, she's the daughter of the Muse of Scandal herself."

"I'd forgotten about that!" another reporter rejoined.

"Let the countess be!" Sunny growled, his voice close to her ear.

Angela whirled. To her surprise, he stood beside her, that walking stick raised to separate her from the reporters by force. "Come!" He grabbed Angela by her forearm, dragging her back inside the carriage.

Once the door was shut, he banged on the roof of the coach with his fist.

"Drive!" he shouted.

The carriage lurched forward, the horses neighing and rearing as though they'd become possessed by demons. For a moment, Angela thought the carriage would tip on its side into the Regent Canal as the reporters surged after them, shouting.

She slid against Sunny. He pulled away from her, brushing off where she'd touched him.

"We'll lose them soon," Sunny muttered, staring over his shoulder. "They're on foot."

To her surprise, he didn't seem distressed. Cool, that's what he was. How he'd changed.

Her heart was still pounding as she glanced outside the carriage. The Regent Canal gave way to shadowy silhouettes of winter trees swaying in the wind. Soon the streets were empty and cloaked with snow; Angela supposed most people were home with their families, warm and cosy and preparing to celebrate the New Year. Not fleeing voracious journalists and irate dowager countesses.

"Thank you," Angela said once the carriage slowed to a regular pace. For what else could be said? She'd never free herself from her obligation. Nor would he ever forgive her.

"I didn't get rid of them for you, Angela. I did it for my title. My position. What I owe my legacy. I owe it to my father and brother to bring honor to my family, not scandal. Continuity." A breath. "The less attention to our marriage, the less people will notice when it's annulled."

"You really can't bear me."

Sunny didn't answer for a long moment. More church bells and snow and wind.

"What I feel," he said at last, "is none of your concern."

He opened the carriage window and shouted up to the coachman. "To Paddington Station. Now."

"Where are we going?"

Sunny replied in a tone that brooked no reply, "Somewhere no one will bother us for a year."

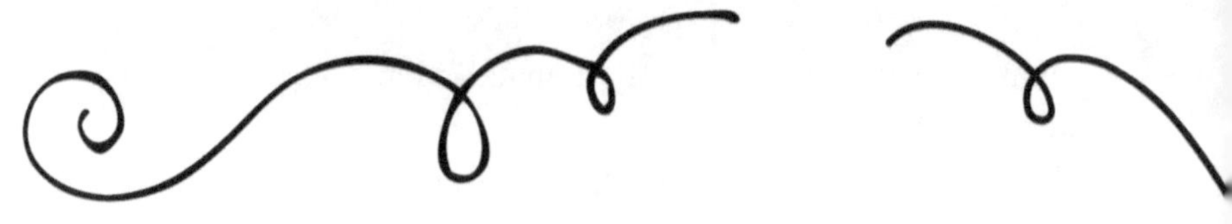

<h1 style="text-align:center">CHAPTER 5</h1>

"Paris?" Angela replied in a distressed tone. "I can't go there."

Sunny hadn't confessed their destination to Angela until they were at Paddington surrounded by travelers all filled with good cheer. Meanwhile, he'd managed to locate what was probably the last open haberdashery in the city, where he bought a change of clothes for himself. On this that was to be their wedding night, which had turned into a farce, they sat waiting for the last train to Dover before New Year's. They were in a private waiting room, where he prayed no one would recognize them.

Again, he thought of his father. His brother. His legacy. On top of that, his jaw hurt like hell where Hélène slapped him.

Angela's voice broke. "I don't want to Paris. *I can't.*"

He supposed she couldn't bear to leave her family behind in England. Well, too bad.

"We've no choice, not if we're to do this right. No journalists will find us of interest there. They'll simply believe we're on an extended honeymoon, Angela."

He had other reasons for returning to Paris—reasons he couldn't share with her. Or anyone else save those directly affected. A matter of honor, especially after the way he'd abandoned Hélène. She'd surely return there.

"There must be other places we could hide, Sunderland. Anywhere else. Please." Her eyes were bright with emotion.

He explained in what he hoped was a reasonable tone, "One of the properties my father left is a small chateau near the Bois de Boulogne. It's rather isolated. No one will follow us. Nor will my mother. She despises the French."

"Regardless, I'd rather not." She folded her arms across her chest.

"You don't have a choice, countess."

He couldn't resist the sarcasm. *Countess.* Well, she wouldn't be one forever. Just a scant three hundred and sixty-five days.

Damn her. Damn me. Damn the situation.

On the train to Dover, neither spoke to each other, but this couldn't last forever.

Once they were underway, Sunny realized he'd made another miscalculation. He hadn't taken into consideration the intimacy of travel, how you had no choice but to interact with your companion. He'd forgotten what it was like to find one's way to a hotel while traveling to a new town. Forgotten the intimacy of breaking bread in an inn where you knew no one. Forgotten what it was like to share quarters…not that he ever had with Hélène.

Fortunately, the hotel in Dover was one where he could get two adjoining rooms so he could avoid seeing Angela in her most intimate moments. He wrote a lie of a name on the registry, praying no reporters had followed their path. He avoided the newspapers… but there they were, all over the breakfast room.

Their marriage hadn't made the front page, thankfully. But the society section sported headlines ranging from FAIRY TALE WEDDING BETWEEN EARL AND COMMONER! to EARL AWAY ON SECRET HONEYMOON. Several included an illustration of Angela standing awkwardly beside Sunny outside the church. Whoever the artist was, they'd captured the two of them more accurately than not.

Angela's mouth twisted into a grimace when she spied the papers. But, to her credit, she didn't complain, though she blanched. She folded her napkin away and left the breakfast room as though it was any other morning. He supposed her life as a Bartham had taught her how to respond to scandal.

And then Sunny saw a journalist, or someone he suspected to be. The man bore all the markers of the profession: ink-splotched fingers, leather shoulder bag.

The journalist stared at Sunny brazenly, his head tilted in calculation. Suddenly, he rose to his feet.

"You're the Earl of Sunderland, are you not?" he called out, nearly knocking over his teacup in his eagerness to approach.

Sunny didn't acknowledge his address. Instead, Sunny bound upstairs toward Angela's room.

"We must leave for the ferry," he whispered from the other side of the door. "Now."

Again, Angela didn't linger. They snuck out of the hotel through the servant's staircase, though the ferry wasn't due for another hour and a half. As soon as they were onboard, they separated, Angela to the deck, he inside.

"Better that way," he said, thinking of the illustrations so like them in the newspaper.

"Agreed," she'd said tersely. "No need for you to be tormented by my presence."

"Or you by mine," he countered. "We'll meet when the ferry docks in Calais."

No matter that they were to be on the ferry for hours and Angela was unescorted. Yet he couldn't stop himself from spying on her at a distance. Watching her on the ferry deck, which was surprisingly calm for a channel crossing.

She'd thought herself alone, he knew. It was so cold no one else ventured outside.

By then, the moon was rising. He watched her stare out toward the sea. Then she curled her hand about the railing of the deck after nervously glancing over her shoulder to make certain she was alone.

As if listening to some music no one else could hear, she danced.

He'd gone to the ballet enough times with her over the years that he recognized the steps of her barre exercises. There she was with her pliés, her arabesques, her grand battements, all on *demi-pointe*. She didn't release the railing, but he knew her balance was such she had no need for a barre, even on a moving ferry.

Her exercises complete, she moved away from the railing, toward the center of the deck, her limbs growing loose in their motions despite the cold.

He couldn't turn from her.

As she danced, her hair loosened from beneath her bonnet. She set her bonnet on the wood decking. He continued watching, disquieted. After she'd sent that letter, was easier to judge her, to despise her. But now, all he remembered was how ardently he adored her.

He adored her like Tristan for Isolde.

Like Lancelot for Guinevere.

Like Romeo for Juliet.

Somehow, the removal of her bonnet freed Angela's dance. She smiled to herself, lost in invisible music. Her soft pink lips tilted upward as though the horrors of the previous day had never occurred. That she'd never been abandoned at the altar by a bigamist, or forced to marry someone who resented her.

Whenever Angela danced, she embodied joy. She was grace incarnate and beauty, an otherworldly force—that's why Carles and all those suitors had been so drawn to her. And Sunny had yearned to possess her as though one could clutch a moonbeam or a dandelion clock.

To his horror, he realized he still yearned for her, God save him. Desired her. There, on a frozen deck of a ferry, on a cold winter night, all he thought of was taking her into his arms. Imagining what it would feel like to press his lips along that graceful neck of hers. To unplait her gold hair until the tresses spilled around the flesh of her shoulders.

Still. After all they'd been through. After that cruel letter.

He slunk away, feeling even more miserable and irritated, if such a thing was possible. When he went back inside the ferry, he'd sought cold water in the men's washroom and splashed his face until it stung.

Revenge only hurts the bearer.

His father had been right. If her letter had cursed him, now he'd cursed himself.

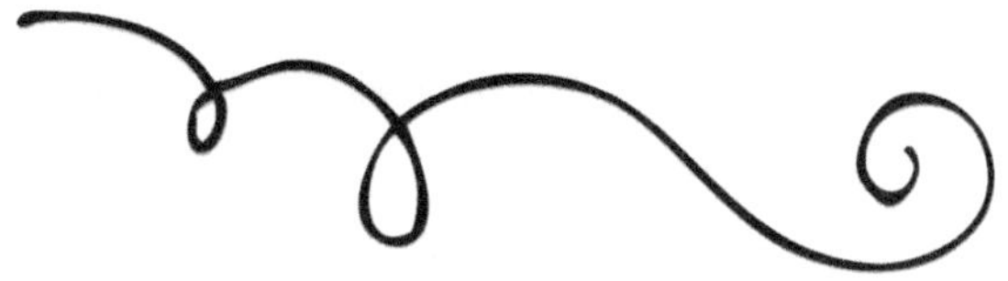

CHAPTER 6

WHEN THEY ARRIVED IN PARIS, it was just past midnight two days after New Year's—a New Year's that was the most miserable Angela had ever known. Save for those moments on the ferry when she'd danced under the moonlight, she'd felt no joy since before her wedding. Sunny remained as aloof as he'd been, but what was done was done. Anyway, she'd destroyed their friendship once she sent that letter—she understood this now. She'd been so very wrong.

I should be grateful, she told herself. A year wasn't that long, not really. She'd be freed and so would he. It would be fine. Really. As for John Carles, what a close call that had been!

But Paris. Why did it have to be Paris?

The dancer she'd loved was from Paris. Despite Sunny's explanation about his father and the chateau and how Paris was the only place they'd be left alone, she felt she was being punished.

She'd never been to Paris before. She could have gone there with her true love but hadn't.

Don't think of this, Angela.

"Are we nearly there?" she asked Sunny, breaking the silence in the carriage he'd engaged at the train station. They'd barely exchanged words since they'd fled London. The few they had were oriented around physical needs: *Here we will sleep. Here we will eat. Here we will wait for our next conveyance to our next destination.*

"Yes," was Sunny's terse reply.

All too soon Angela made out a tangle of trees gilded by moonlight. The Bois de Boulogne, or so Sunny muttered. They'd just passed the Arc de Triomphe, which was taller than she expected from the illustrations she'd seen of it.

The Bois looked wilder than any London park, a new land far from anything she knew. She half-expected to hear a wolf howl at the moon before turning their yellow eyes on their carriage. Angela couldn't resist a shiver, thinking of dark fantasies from ballets she loved. Giselle and the Wilis. The sylphide and her earthly lover.

The carriage came to an abrupt halt before a house silhouetted against the dense night sky. No moon, for the sky was heavy with clouds. Not even a solitary light shone from its windows, which appeared copious of number even in the dark. The house appeared to have two stories save for the turrets marking each corner.

Once she'd disembarked from the carriage, Sunny ordered the coachman to pull down her trunk. He remained inside the carriage.

"Aren't you coming?" she asked once the trunk was set near the chateau's door.

"Not now—I've tasks to take care of. A servant will see to your needs."

He offered her a brass key. Then, without another word of explanation, he knocked on the roof of the carriage and drove on, leaving Angela alone in the night in a new land.

Well, a pox on him. A pox on this marriage, Angela thought. Anger and nerves warred inside her. She should be grateful he was leaving her be. Really. For all his talk of tasks to take care of, he'd probably gone to a hotel to avoid her. (Good!) Or maybe he'd gone to that French woman, if she was his mistress...though how could this be? She was surely still back in London.

Unless she followed us here.

Angela sat on her trunk, resentment rising. Surely Sunny would return, wouldn't he? He'd just wanted to upset her. As for the servant, judging by the lack of light inside the chateau, they'd probably gone to bed.

A moment passed. Two.

Sunny didn't return.

He'll never forgive me. This is his way of punishing me. Well, what did she expect? They weren't friends. She was in his debt. It's not like he'd dumped her in the middle of nowhere…though it felt akin to this.

Especially once a wolf did howl, or something that sounded akin to one.

She shivered. It was so *so* cold—Angela had never been in such a frigid, desolate place. Years ago, she'd imagined Paris as the center of the world, a place of art, beauty, and ballet despite its tumultuous history. Not a place where she felt exiled from all of humanity.

A rush of wind rose, hissing against her ears. She half-expected snow to start falling. Instead, a flash of lightning split the sky. Rain despite the temperature.

That decided it.

Angela turned the key in the door lock, which was stiff as the icy air slicing her lungs.

The cylinders of the lock clicked, but the door hinges were frozen. Her struggle was noisy enough that a grey-furred cat leapt from beneath an overgrown boxwood before disappearing into the shadows.

Angela forced the door open. It creaked like it hadn't been opened in decades. Then, using all of her weight, she forced her trunk over the threshold.

Inside, the chateau was nearly as devoid of light as the night sky. Fortunately, she found a gas lamp and a box of flints on a small table inside the entry hall, as though in anticipation of her arrival.

She lit the lamp with hands stiff from the cold. A rumble of thunder.

"Hello?" she called out, hesitant. "*Bonsoir?*"

No one replied. For all Sunny's talk of servants, the chateau felt empty as could be. The rain began, slanting hard against the window. Or was it hail? Another rumble of thunder. Her heart began to thud. Vulnerable, that's what she felt. Unwelcome. A prisoner.

Don't be ridiculous, she told herself. *It's the hour. In the morning, this will all seem very different.*

Angela raised the lamp, illuminating the chateau. The golden light revealed a twisting marble staircase. It was high of ceiling and decorated on every possible inch. She imagined it resembled something Marie Antoinette would have commissioned before the Revolution. As for the frescoes decorating the ceiling, her father would have taken exception with their gilded brightness.

And then she heard *it.* Or rather a scampering of low-pitched howls and chirps too low to identify.

Another cat scampered across the marble floor. Pale-furred, unlike the one she'd spied outside.

"Here, kitty," she whispered. The cat turned its bright green eyes in her direction before howling anew and darting off to parts unknown. A mouse skittered.

The cat knows there's something off in this house. Something sorrowful.

"Stop being so fanciful," she muttered into the darkness.

Her stomach grumbled. Hungry, that's all she was. It was making her anxious—she would not allow herself to be spooked. It had been hours since she'd eaten. She'd turned down Sunny's offer of food at the train station, eager to get to their destination.

In the morning, she'd seek out food. That's when the servants would reappear, bringing life to the chateau. Life would return. In the morning, she'd decide what to do, especially if Sunny didn't come back.

But first, to find a bed. Sleep would make everything seem less threatening.

Angela squared her shoulders and climbed the stairs.

~

Upstairs, the rooms were surprisingly scant for such a large house. Though it appeared the chateau had been recently inhabited from the state of the housekeeping, many of the rooms contained furniture covered in white sheets, appearing like ghosts.

A library led to what appeared to be a music room, where there was both a spinet and a grand piano; she wondered whether Sunny still played. Next, a salon paneled in mirrors with tall glass windows along one wall. Then, a dressing room with shelves and hooks for clothes. Locked doors leading nowhere. More mice. Emptiness. A water closet adjoining a spacious tiled room with a huge clawfoot bathtub in its center. The bathroom appeared surprisingly modern, with brass taps and baskets of soaps and towels. The chateau was a mix of new and old, it seemed.

And then a solitary bedroom. At last.

The bedroom was smaller than she'd expected. Humbler too, given the grandiosity of the entryway with its gilded frescoes, the mirrored room, even that absurdly large bathroom. The bedroom was also the first room to reveal any sign of life, though it was presently uninhabited.

To her surprise, a cozy fire glowed in the fireplace grate, near where an oversized upholstered chair had been set before a small round card table. On that table: a platter of bread and cheese and fruit beneath a glass bell, a carafe of red wine. There were persimmons, scarlet pomegranate seeds, clementines, sap-green apples. A rustic boule, a slender baguette.

Moving slowly as though the feast might disappear, Angela removed her bonnet and coat. She placed her gas lamp on top of the fireplace mantel.

She ate, tearing at the bread and cheese with her hands like a desperate animal. The wine burned her throat—it was a rougher vintage than expected—but she didn't care. Nothing in her life had ever tasted so delectable to her.

Afterward, head spinning from food and alcohol, she collapsed on the bed, a grand curtained affair that required a small footstool to climb into. The bed was soft, comfortable, and smelled of lavender. It had been aired—a servant expected her arrival, just as Sunny said. But her trunk was still downstairs. And she hadn't a lady's maid—she and Lyra usually helped each other dress. While traveling, Angela had managed with a buttonhook; she didn't dare ask Sunny for assistance.

Somehow she removed her day suit, petticoats, and stays. Once she was in her chemise, she took out her hairpins. At least she had her reticule, which contained a comb. It felt good to untangle her hair, to feel it loose against her shoulders. To no longer have hairpins pressing against her scalp.

She climbed into the bed, feeling very small and very enveloped in feathered pillows and duvets. Suddenly she was shivering in that big soft bed, but not from cold or exhaustion. How alone she felt, so far away from her family. What were they doing? Probably asleep by now.

Still, she imagined Lyra and Theo pounding on the piano together in Musa and Seb's home in Bexley. Then she imagined Musa and Seb collapsed on a settee, their laughter rising as they teased each other in their usual way. Somewhere beyond England, her mother seated on a train traveling toward her father...

As for Angela herself, everything had changed. As for being a countess, she wouldn't be one for long. The important thing was she'd protected her family, even if it meant fleeing home for Paris.

And then her thoughts returned to the dancer she'd loved and the future he'd offered her in Paris—a future she'd refused.

"Don't think of this," she whispered to herself. "It's too late."

Angela curled into herself and tried to sleep. She couldn't. Instead, she recalled his dark curls and warm eyes. His rather Gallic nose and wide mouth. The way he tilted his head when he was searching for a word in English. His infectious laugh.

The euphoria of his embrace.

And then her mind returned to the past. To when she first met him, before her heart had been so irrevocably broken.

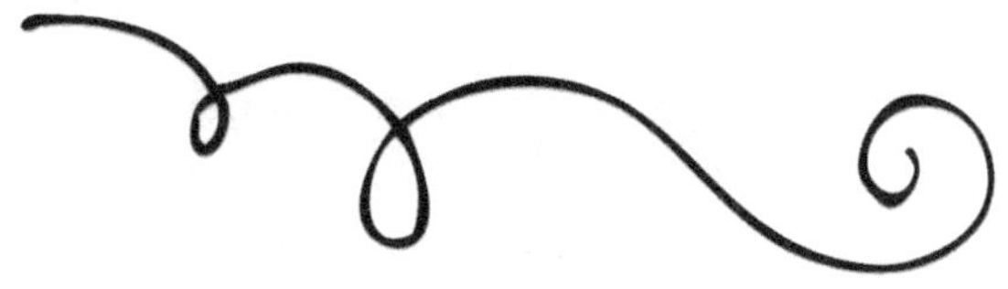

CHAPTER 7

His name had been Philippe. Philippe Claremont.

Whether or not Philippe had been her soulmate, Angela had loved him as much as it was possible to love someone. Even now, five years since she'd last seen him, she still felt this deep in her bones.

Angela had been all of eighteen when she met Philippe at the dance class she'd been secretly taking. Because of her family's troubled reputation, Angela had no interest in courting controversy. Respectability, that was her favorite word. It was aspirational. Aspirational was forward thinking, something she needed to be in the wake of her parents' scandalous marriage. Angela had spent her childhood snubbed by other children, save for her siblings and Sunny. Aspiration offered hope for the future. Respectability.

As a child, she considered her parents desperately romantic. As an adult, she saw they were scorned by society. Snubbed. Trapped…especially her mother, Clio, whom everyone gossiped about.

Therefore, Angela resolved at the tender age of twelve to restore her family's reputation. To do so, she'd use her only possession: her beauty. For as long as she could recall, she'd been told what an extraordinarily pretty girl she was. When she grew into womanhood, her mirror confirmed their praise. But she didn't take pride in her beauty—she wasn't vain. She simply saw her beauty as a commodity that would help her family granting her siblings a future, her mother respectability.

Still, when Angela considered how she *felt* when she danced… well, that was hardly respectable.

Angela had been dancing since she was a small child. She happened onto ballet in the same way that Theo and Lyra happened upon their love of music: it called to her. She taught herself what she could, assisted by Lyra and Theo pounding away ballet scores on the Barthams' out of tune spinet. She consulted books and prints of prima ballerinas of the past. Sunny fed her obsession by taking her to performances at Covent Garden.

Ballet became as seductive as a suitor whispering love poems on a perfumed summer evening. The music. The costumes. The yearning. The doomed love. The beauty. Since she'd vowed to wed for respectability, ballet would be her true love. Romance was for dance, practicality for marriage…unlike her parents, who'd married for passion.

However, one aspect of the craft eluded Angela: dancing *en pointe* in the manner of the great Taglioni. The virtuosic technique was one that enabled a ballerina to appear as though floating mid-air. Yes, Angela could obtain a pair of toe shoes—the newest models could be ordered from Italy, if one had enough money. But Angela knew point dancing wasn't something to be attempted without careful instruction. She could end up seriously injuring herself and destroying her feet.

If I don't learn to dance en pointe, Angela thought, *I won't be able to bear it.*

After a discreet search, the ballet teacher Angela located was a wizened French woman of about sixty years named Madame Claremont. She agreed to allow Angela to take a private point class every Thursday, as long as Angela's family approved. "You must promise to never go on the stage," Madame Claremont told Angela.

"You're not meant for that. You don't know what they say about dancers."

Harlots. Dollymops. Prostitutes. Yes, Angela did know—remember, her favorite word was respectability. Not that she had any plans to go on the stage. She simply wanted to dance *en pointe*.

"I'll chaperone you for your class," Musa acquiesced after Angela begged for help. "We'll find the money, though it's not wise with Papa gone. People will assume the worst." At that time, Neil Bartham was away in the Holy Land for just over a year; people were beginning to whisper he'd abandoned his family.

And so it became established that Angela would sneak into the back door of Madame Claremont's every Thursday afternoon, hoping no one who knew her family would notice her arrival. Just in case, Musa accompanied her.

But one fine spring day Musa was unavailable, so Angela stubbornly went alone…and Philippe was there.

Philippe, whom Angela felt inexplicably drawn to as soon as she spied his tall, dark-haired self.

Philippe, who made her heart leap in a grand jeté before he ever pirouetted in her direction.

Angela hadn't a chance. Later, she'd learn her experience was what the philosophers call a *coup de foudre*—a love at first sight akin to what her parents experienced when they met.

Madame Claremont acknowledged Angela's arrival. "*Ma petite*, are you well? How pale you turned!"

"I-I'm fine," Angela stammered, watching Philippe leap across the studio. He was a little older than she, perhaps just over twenty. She recognized the solo: one of the Albrecht variations from Act Two of *Giselle*. "It's warm today, isn't it?"

Madame helped Angela to a seat. "No more than usual for April. Sit, *ma petite*. I'm sorry, but I need to cancel our lesson for today. I would have sent a note had I known he was going to show. Where is your sister today?"

"Not here," Angela answered, still staring at him. "Who is he?"

"My youngest nephew Philippe. He's a gift, hasn't he?"

Madame Claremont smiled, a rarity for her acerbic but good-natured self. "He just arrived from France—I'm still not sure why he's here. A feud with his parents. *Alors,* he's talented, *n'est-ce pas?*"

N'est-ce pas indeed. Now Angela's heart was really thumping. She watched transfixed until Philippe's solo ended. It was then Madame introduced them in her courtly old-fashioned way.

"*Enchantée,*" Philippe said, brushing his lips against Angela's knuckles.

Madame explained to Philippe in a mix of English and French that Angela was one of her more gifted students. "This is usually Mademoiselle Bartham's lesson time with me—"

"*Et voilà ! Je suis une bête—*"

"A beast," Angela translated, charmed; she knew a few words in French from studying ballet. If he was a beast, he was the most fetching one she'd ever met.

"*Oui,* because I'm stolen your time away from *la danse,* mademoiselle."

Angela replied, "You speak English?"

He shrugged. "Some. Enough." He offered her his hand. "Shall we? I'd like to see what *ma tante* has taught you, Mademoiselle Bartham."

Though Angela was still dressed in her street clothes, she couldn't turn away. She quickly tied on her toe shoes, tucking the ribbons as Madame taught her. By then, her toes were already quite battered from going *en pointe,* but she didn't care. The pain was worth it. *Was love the same way?* she thought absently.

And then Madame's pianist launched into the *pas de deux* from *La Sylphide.* Another favorite. She glissaded into his arms.

He felt strong against her. He was tall enough that even when she was *en pointe,* he still had a good four inches of height over her. She gazed up at him. His eyes were more green than brown, she decided. More like a tree in the rain than chocolate. His brow strong. His nose could be considered a touch too large, but it suited his face. His mouth wide. Soft. Ripe. She found herself wondering what it would be like to kiss it.

"How you stare at me," he murmured, his hands firm yet gentle on her waist as he guided her through the steps. She pirouetted, then went into the fouettés.

However, the truth was he was staring at her. For the first time in her life, Angela felt something akin to a molten warmth rise from within herself. It made her breathless.

This is dangerous, she thought. Though she didn't yet know the particulars of what men and women did together in the privacy of the bedroom, she suspected enough…and that it could lead her into ruin. Wasn't that what happened to her mother when she'd abandoned her first husband for Angela's father?

No matter. She couldn't turn away from Philippe.

"Leap," he prodded. "Now."

And she did—and he readily caught her midair. She felt like she was flying, even after he gently set her down.

When the pianist played the final chord, she didn't move for some moments. Nor did he.

That *pas de deux* was their first of many. Their final one would come six months later, but Angela didn't know that then.

Angela must have dozed off remembering Philippe, for she recalled nothing more, not even her dreams. When she awakened, the room was a soft pink. The rain had stopped. Dawn had arrived, despite everything in her life.

Paris, that's where she was. France. The chateau the Earldom of Sunderland owned near the Bois de Boulogne, with the darting cats. She recalled how empty the house was upon her arrival, Sunny abandoning her in what appeared the middle of a wild wood. The lack of apparent servants. But there'd been a fire to warm her, food to fill her stomach. She'd been provided for.

Then she noticed: the trunk containing her trousseau laid on the floor of her room. Someone had brought it up while she'd slept.

A note written in English laid across it, but not in Sunny's hand:

My lady, I shall be downstairs should you require me. Until then, seek what you want and take what you need.

No signature, but she knew who: the mysterious servant who'd left her dinner. He or she must have brought it up while she slept. They'd also renewed the fire in the grate—the room was pleasurably warm.

She knew she should feel disturbed—had they watched her as she slept?—but of everything that had occurred, this hardly seemed of note.

"I'll feel better after I bathe," she told herself. Then she'd go downstairs, seek breakfast.

A bathroom with a water closet—she'd noticed one down the hall. It had looked surprisingly modern, with hot and cold taps. She hadn't had an opportunity for a bath since before the wedding.

She wrapped her shawl about her shoulders, barely covering the bodice of her chemise, as she padded barefoot down the hall. It was far colder outside the bedroom; her skin rose with gooseflesh. Out of the corner of her eye, she made out a darting shadow near where the stairway curved into the hall. Another cat chasing a mouse? The more time she spent in the chateau, the more deeply its firmaments seemed caught between abandonment and luxury.

The bathroom door opened easily, unlike the chateau's entry the previous evening.

Inside the bathroom, the curtains remained tightly drawn. One solitary candle burned, barely illuminating the room. She made out the murmur of water. Perhaps her unseen servant had already drawn a bath for her, anticipating her desire. The scent of sweet-smelling soap rose in the steamy air. It felt deliciously sultry. Luxurious.

Once Angela's eyes adjusted to the darkness, she saw she wasn't alone.

She made out a stocky form in the clawfoot bathtub, his muscled back turned from her while he bathed. He appeared powerful, dashing. The color of his hair was impossible to discern in the shadows. His thick hair was long for a man, though it fell to just above his shoulders.

Sunny. He'd returned while she slept.

And now she'd happened upon him. While bathing.

Angela nearly slammed the door in her haste to escape, but she feared drawing his attention. She backed away silently, slowly, as though retreating from a lion who'd escaped his cage.

Still, she must have made some sort of sound, for Sunny twisted in her direction, splashing water onto the tiled floor as he rose from the tub. He raised his arms in protection, water sluicing off him.

"Who goes there? Show yourself!"

And then the whole of him was exposed to her eyes.

Completely unclothed. Naked. Like a statue in the museum.

His body gleamed in the dusk, flesh wet from the bath. Though his most intimate parts remained hidden in shadow, she'd never seen him so exposed in all their years, not even when they'd swam together as children in the pond on his country estate.

She had no idea Sunny had chest hair, which covered his torso in a fine layer save for the sides of his belly, where his pale flesh reappeared. The fur tapered into a triangle toward the dip of his hips. She'd never known that, for all his bulk, he was solidly muscled across his chest and along his arms.

"I'm sorry," Angela began to say, but the words froze in her mouth.

And then she recalled she was half-dressed herself. No doubt he could make out the curves of her body beneath her chemise, which left her feeling as naked as the day she first drew breath.

Flushing, she tightened her shawl and folded her arms across her breasts.

Yet, to her shame, part of her *wanted* to let the shawl drop. To be exposed as he was, though a thin lawn chemise was not the same as emerging unclad from a bath. To entice him in some unkind revenge, proving she still held some power over him, despite his claims to the contrary.

Sunny broke the impasse with an angry shout.

"Get the hell out! Go!"

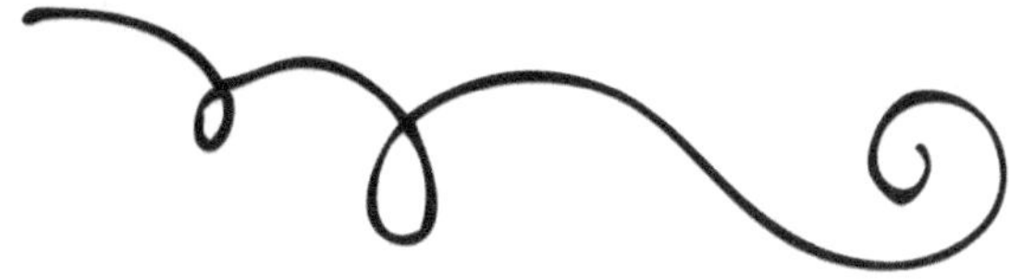

CHAPTER 8

THE BATHROOM DOOR slammed in Angela's face, just missing her nose. She barely noticed.

Sunny. In the bath.

She'd no idea he'd appear that way, not that she'd ever considered it. He'd been her friend, not someone to be desired. It was disconcerting…as well as her reaction to viewing him.

"My lady."

A brittle male voice behind her. French-accented English. Refined.

Now it was Angela's turn to be startled. She whirled.

Behind her stood an elegant gentleman of perhaps sixty years, his hair peppered with silver and dressed in the servant's livery of an earlier age. He clutched a lit candelabra, for the hall was still dim with dawn. Long face, sharp-nosed, clean-shaven.

The servant dropped his eyes from her half-clad form. Discreet, that's what he was.

"I'm glad you didn't walk into this." He indicated the candelabra with a jerk of his chin. "It's my fault. I apologize for startling you, my lady. You are the Countess of Sunderland, I presume."

"I am," Angela admitted, feeling like a fraud. "You're the—"

"Manservant. Butler. Whatever his lordship requires," he interjected. "You may call me Dubois, my lady."

"*Du bois*. Of the woods," Angela said, tightening her shawl within an inch of its life. "How appropriate. Here we are by the Bois de Boulogne."

"Fate has a sense of humor," he said smoothly. "I attend his lordship when he's in residence. But I'm also here to serve you, my lady."

He gestured with the candelabra toward the stairway.

"*Le petit dejeuner* is in the dining room." A delicate pause. "It can wait if you care to dress."

To Angela's relief, Dubois didn't depart after he'd brought her freshly baked croissants, hard-boiled eggs, and milky coffee with cubes of sugar. She was as ravenous for answers as she was for food after a night of solitude. Fearful the servant might disappear, she'd dressed in a rush in a green wool polonaise, which she'd brought in her trousseau in anticipation of the honeymoon in Wales. She'd prided the outfit for its slim silhouette, which was more fashionable these days. How long ago these considerations seemed, from another life.

Dubois was tactful enough not to refer to her presence during Sunny's bath. Perhaps he thought they had a real marriage and were on a real honeymoon. Not this farce of a charade. Well, Angela would say nothing to dissuade him.

Angela looked about the dining room, which she hadn't seen during her explorations the previous night. The dining room was more intimate than expected, given the florid decoration covering the entryway. Clean white walls with a few framed botanical prints. Its windows overlooked the Bois de Boulogne, which appeared as wild as she'd suspected upon their arrival. It unfurled like a fairy tale kingdom as the mists of dawn gave way to day. The rain must have turned to snow overnight, for white dappled the park like frosting on a wedding cake.

The dining room table was smaller than Angela would expect for an earl's residence: an oval hewn of gleaming mahogany barely large enough to fit six. The table displayed a variety of newspapers—she presumed Dubois had brought them. Some were in English, others in French. Angela knew a little French from studying ballet, but not enough for fluency. She anxiously paged through the newspapers, searching for any mention of her marriage.

Dubois swept the newspapers off the table. "No need for those, madame. The earl would prefer not to see them."

Angela had no desire to see them either, but hadn't been able to resist.

"Thank you for leaving the food last night in my chamber," Angela said. "The fire was appreciated too."

"I don't reside in the chateau," Dubois explained as he offered more coffee. "Therefore, I wasn't here when you arrived last night. *Je vous demande pardon*, my lady—I'm sure it was disconcerting to find yourself alone." A careful pause. "His lordship arrived this morning. He had matters to attend to last night—I'm sure he regretted leaving you alone."

Angela nearly laughed in disbelief. *The only thing he regrets is marrying me.* But she said nothing, only waved away Dubois's apology.

"It matters not. I felt very fortunate to have a meal waiting for me, after such a long journey."

"I do this every night in case his lordship arrives without notice," Dubois said, clearing croissant crumbs with the edge of a silver knife against the tabletop. "It's a tradition since his lordship's father, whom I also served."

"The previous Earl of Sunderland, you mean." Angela leaned in eagerly. Aside from curiosity, she was hungry for someone to talk to her. She'd felt so alone these past days. "He was very kind to my father. I was sad the earl died so unexpectedly last year."

"*Oui*, the previous earl," Dubois confirmed. "He's responsible for the chateau in its current form." His voice dropped. "One might say this chateau was born from tragedy. The previous earl acquired and renovated it after his eldest son died."

"As a place to mourn?" Angela knew Sunny's brother Robert had died at the tender age of seventeen, leaving Sunny heir to the title. In all their years of friendship, Sunny rarely spoke of his brother or the riding accident that led to his death.

Dubois nodded. "After the loss, the previous earl required a place to—"

"You've said enough," Sunny interrupted brusquely. He'd arrived while the two were in conversation. Despite his bath, his eyes were dark with exhaustion. If he'd been out all night, he'd probably not slept. "You may go."

A bow and a muttered "*Oui,* my lord," and Dubois departed.

Now alone in the dining room with Sunny, Angela felt her skin prickle with something she couldn't name. It wasn't nerves. Nor was it embarrassment over viewing him in the bath.

Anticipation. How strange.

She felt as though she was in a battle. Was it to prove her worth? Or win his approval?

He settled beside her at the small table. Took the last croissant and poured coffee from the silver urn. He refused to meet her eyes. Perhaps he felt as disquieted as she did. Still, she noticed how more, well, *masculine* he seemed now that she'd glimpsed him nude. She had no idea. Nor had he shaven; she supposed she'd startled him enough that he'd skipped that grooming ritual.

"I apologize for interrupting your bath," she ventured.

Though Sunny kept his tone even, his face grew red. "Do you always burst in while people are bathing?"

"Not intentionally."

"Don't get too comfortable here, Angela. A year will seem very long if you do. Or get too familiar—"

"With servants," she finished.

"Servant," he corrected, breaking off a piece of his croissant with a studiously unaffected air. "Singular. Dubois will be the only one we interact with during our year here. Better that way. Less opportunity for gossip. There are others servants, but they will only come as needed and will remain apart from us. Think of them as hands helping behind the scenes."

"I see. I assume you've paid them well to keep our secrets."

Sunny said matter-of-factly, "They have a vested interest. As do I."

Again, Angela's skin prickled. There was something more he was going to say. Despite their estrangement, she still knew him better than anyone else in the world…or so she'd believed. What was it? It took all her control, but she remained silent.

"I must insist," he said at last, "we establish rules for our marriage. Rule number one: don't go into rooms that aren't meant for you."

"The bathroom wasn't locked. An honest mistake. Again, I apologize."

He flushed, avoiding her eyes. Humiliation, that's what he felt, she realized. Well, she'd felt vulnerable too in her chemise. But she didn't feel shame.

He said, "There are other rooms forbidden to you besides bathrooms while people are inhabiting them."

"Locked, you mean. Like Bluebeard's castle."

The analogy slipped out before Angela could think twice. The chateau brought to mind a book of fairy tales they'd once read together, nothing else. But Sunny, to her astonishment, slammed down the silver coffee urn on the table.

"Everyone is afforded secrets, Angela, including me. But no, I don't have anything that interesting in my past. This brings me to rule number two: you're not to leave the chateau save for short walks. No visits to public places such as shops or theaters, no interactions with anyone outside this chateau."

Angela understood why—to avoid discovery—but this still rankled her. "So I'm essentially a prisoner then?"

"More of an esteemed guest," Sunny said, sidestepping her

question. "Finally, rule number three: you may have noticed there's only one bedroom since the chateau isn't fully habitable at this time."

This was getting to be ridiculous. "What kind of chateau has only one bedroom?"

"This kind. And it has only one bed."

Angela's voice rose in frustration. "Then I'll find somewhere else to sleep. On a sofa. A floor. I don't care—you take the bed."

"That's unnecessary. Until I can arrange for other sleeping arrangements, we'll share it. Don't look so alarmed! I promised I wouldn't touch you. I meant it."

Angela set her arms akimbo. "That will be a challenge if we're sharing a bed."

"I've a solution. I'm nocturnal by nature."

"Since when? You usually get up at dawn."

"Since now. I'll sleep during the day. You'll occupy the bed at night. Even better: we'll avoid encountering each other that way, yes? No need to speak to each other."

Without waiting for her reply, he swept out of the dining room, grabbing the remains of his croissant. It was only after he slammed the door behind him that Angela recalled Dubois's whispered confession.

"One might say this chateau was born from tragedy. The previous earl acquired and renovated it after his eldest son died."

And then she realized. His father had arranged for the chateau to have only one bedroom, so no guests could stay. So he could grieve in solitude.

Anger is good, Sunny told himself as he stormed from the dining room upstairs to the bedroom. *Anger is better than desire or shame.* Better he should hate Angela than yearn for her...and for a moment when he'd witnessed her in the bathroom, all he'd wanted was her.

When she'd appeared amid the steam as he'd bathed, he thought he'd conjured her out of heartbreak and resentment. He'd been exhausted enough. He knew he'd been unkind to abandon Angela as he did when they arrived at the chateau, but he couldn't bear her any longer.

He spent the night alone, waiting for the dawn to arrive, so he could go home without encountering her in his bed. Unsurprisingly, Hélène hadn't yet returned to her home on the left bank. He'd left a written apology, begging to speak when she showed, before turning to other preoccupations. Tasks. Once the sky lightened, he turned west toward the chateau, too exhausted to remain out any longer. He'd find a way to avoid Angela. He had to, for a year was a long time. Lord knew there were enough corners of the chateau suitable for hiding, even if there were scant beds.

She'd awaken, leave the bedroom. Then he'd lock the door and finally sleep. Alone. In that sole bed.

He'd miscalculated on Angela waking so early.

For a moment, when he'd seen her in shadows of the bathroom, he didn't trust his senses. Wearing only her chemise with her silvery-blond hair down, she was glorious. A naiad who appeared not of this world. Worse, *his* world, the one he'd yearned to bring her into if she'd married him when he'd first proposed.

And she'd seen him in his most vulnerable moment in the bath. What had she thought? Had she pitied him? He knew he appeared ridiculous. Plain. Worse, ugly. An animal even, with hair covering so much of his form. Hadn't he been told such over the years?

Sunderland the slug. Virgil the victim. Fat Sunderland—he'd heard all the nicknames, the cruelties. Sunderland the unwanted, though few said this to his face now that he was an earl. They knew better.

No matter. He knew what they thought.

A knock on the bedroom door brought Sunny's ruminations to a halt. Dubois…though Dubois was more than a servant to him by now.

It had been Dubois who had witnessed Sunny at his worst

earlier that year. After Angela refused his proposal, Sunny fled to Paris to ruminate over his wounds in private. Dubois had intervened several times to protect his new charge, especially when Sunny's behavior spiraled into alcohol and debauchery. *"I do this for your father's sake,"* Dubois always said. *"And yours."*

Once Sunny met Hélène, everything changed. She'd given him a purpose…though it wasn't one he'd expected.

"If I may, my lord," the older man said without preamble in his French-accented English.

"I know what you're going to say," Sunny replied once he'd locked the door behind them. "Out with it."

They switched into French in case Angela should overhear.

"You insisted you were only attending the wedding to prove you no longer cared for Mademoiselle Bartham. That's why you'd brought Mademoiselle de Castel-d'Albret with you, *n'est-ce pas?*"

If it had been any other servant but Dubois, Sunny would have snapped at him for his insolence.

Sunny hid his face in his hands. "I lost control of the situation."

A long sigh. "That's an understatement."

Sunny looked up from his hands. "Did Mademoiselle de Castel-d'Albret write you? She's not in Paris. Well, not yet."

"Write? She sent a wire here. She's furious and understandably so."

"I-I couldn't help myself," Sunny replied, stammering in his old way. "I'll make it up to her." He'd somehow keep his promise to Hélène, as tricky as it was. That is, if she ever acknowledged him again. "But now that you've met Angela…"

He gestured weakly into the air, feeling more ineffectual than he had since Eton, when he'd been regularly bullied.

Dubois sank into the armchair and leaned forward. The gesture might have been seen as familiar save for their history.

"If I may speak freely, your bride is a beauty. Charming. I can see why you're so besotted with her. Does she love you then, my lord?"

"No." If there was anyone Angela loved, it was Carles, the bastard. "The next thing I knew, I'd asked her to marry me. I can't explain what happened exactly."

Actually, he did know. He'd never admit the truth, not even to Dubois who knew his darkest secrets.

"I'll fix it. We'll only be married for a year," Sunny added. "She agreed to an annulment—we'll do it discreetly to avoid gossip. Mademoiselle de Castel-d'Albret will hopefully understand."

"A year! That seems an invitation to trouble. Will Mademoiselle de Castel-d'Albret be so patient?"

"I have no idea," Sunny answered, too weary to think further. "I'll send flowers after I get some sleep."

With this, Dubois left and Sunny staggered into the bed, which remained unmade since Angela's occupation of it. Despite the coffee he'd taken with breakfast, he was fatigued beyond measure. He didn't care the sheets had touched Angela's skin—they were clean enough. He'd be able to sleep even if the sheets were from a brothel.

It mattered not: he tossed and turned beneath the duvet, imagining the bed bearing the imprint of Angela's soft body, the pillows holding the floral fragrance of her hair. Then he recalled how she materialized from darkness while he'd bathed, the way her curves pressed against the translucent lawn of her chemise, revealing her secrets to him.

When he finally slept, his dreams were of his wife pirouetting by a turbulent sea beneath the moon.

Twelve hours later, Angela took his place in the bed. Unlike Sunny, she changed the linens in her fastidious way. Life as a Bartham had accustomed her to all manner of housework; they'd only possessed one maid of all work.

Despite the clean sheets, Angela still sensed her husband's

presence. The scent of his shaving soap, the clean tang of perspiration from the exercise he must have taken. His anger. His hurt.

When she finally slept, her dreams were of a fierce lion nudging her palm.

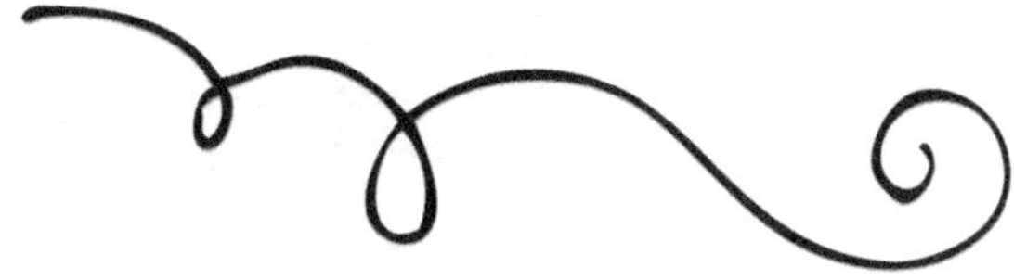

CHAPTER 9

Dearest Musa,

Forgive my delay in writing you. I'm sure my abrupt depar-ture from London worried you—I hadn't known our destination until we were on our way. I hope this letter will put your mind at rest. All is well!

We remain on our honeymoon and shall be for some months, perhaps through the end of the year. As for our location, Sunder-land thought it prudent we keep our location secret for obvious reasons. However, you may write me care of his family home in Paris, whose address I've written below. (I implore you not to share it with anyone for obvious reasons.) Sunderland's home is a chateau built by his father on the edge of the Bois de Boulogne, which is far wilder of appearance than our London parks. Though the chateau is only partly habitable, it serves our needs well.

We live a quiet existence without visitors save for a stray cat or two—I've tried to tame them as companions, but they're ever so fast. Nor have we partaken of Parisian life. Alas, much of the city remains in transition, given the turmoil of recent years. In the meantime, the chateau has a library with plentiful books in English, though I've been working on my French too.

On an unrelated note, has Mama written with any news of

Papa? I expect it's much too soon—Egypt is so far away—but I think of them every day and hope she isn't fretting about me. If you write her, pray convey my love and assure her of my well being.

I hope you, Seb, and the twins are well. I miss you all dreadfully. Write me soon as you can!

With much affection from
your devoted sister
Angela

BY THE START OF FEBRUARY, Angela still hadn't received a reply from Musa though she'd sent a letter several days after they'd arrived in Paris. Such was Angela's impatience that she nearly wrote her sister again. She resisted, for what was there to say? She'd already avoided confessing the truth: she was essentially a prisoner in a forlorn chateau with a man who abhorred the sight of her. The truth rankled Angela, but what was she to do?

Angela supposed her elder sister was busy with the twins and her new publishing house. Musa and Seb had a new children's book coming out that spring entitled *Tales of Clever Animals and Witty Birds.* As for Sunny, he and Angela continued their uncomfortable arrangement of sharing the bed. He refused to speak to her, using Dubois as his intermediary.

On top of that, he'd allowed his beard to grow in, granting him a rather wild appearance. She'd no idea his beard would be a dark copper, contrasting against his bright auburn hair. It hid the freckles on his cheeks and made his chin appear stronger, his mouth ripe. His lack of grooming seemed intended to dissuade Angela from approaching him.

Not that she would have dared, though her sorrow over losing her friend had shifted into a resentful irritation. She hadn't known Sunny possessed such a temper.

That letter. I should never have written it.

To add to the frustration, Dubois claimed a new mattress would arrive any day, but was delayed. Angela had no idea what would happen once she and Sunny shared the same schedule. Would they simply continue avoiding each other as they had been? Or would they be expected to share meals like they weren't enemies?

Anyway, Dubois and his invisible army of servants took care of her needs well enough…though that didn't explain the neglected corners of the chateau. The locked doors. The sense of being trapped like a princess in a tower.

Angela missed her family desperately. Missed interaction with someone who didn't resent her existence. She spent hours listlessly reading in the library or wandering from room to room like an unwanted ghost. She considered using the mirrored salon on the second floor for dance—it was certainly large enough—but anticipated Sunny's anger. At least the mice had become better at hiding; she'd barely seen them of late.

The mirrored salon felt forbidden. To start with, it was covered in cobwebs and dust, all markers of abandonment. The few pieces of furniture were covered in white sheets. But other rooms bore similar neglect save for the library, which was the only welcoming corner of the chateau. Sunny's father had been a voracious reader and in multiple languages too.

Even so, how alone Angela felt.

All this changed on the second day of February. That was the morning that Angela received an unexpected visitor at the chateau: her brother-in-law Seb's best friend Luke Ward. A journalist, or had been when Angela last heard.

Ward arrived about an hour after Sunny had taken possession of the bed, just as Angela finished with breakfast. The journalist once worked at the same printer Seb had before his art gained notice; the men had grown up closest of friends in Kent. Angela barely knew Ward but she remembered him well. He'd once stolen letters from Seb for a newspaper story that nearly ruined Musa's reputation. But then again, it was thanks to Ward's professional connections that Angela's father had been located alive in Cairo.

As for his appearance, Ward was dressed as outlandishly as

always, perhaps more so. From the few times she'd met him, Angela recalled he always wore a mustard-yellow bowler. Today, he'd tucked a small purple iris in its ribbon band. When he tipped his hat, Angela saw that his longish, fawn-colored hair was thinning. He was clean-shaven save for an elaborately groomed moustache.

A dandy, that's what he was, an aesthete. Ward reminded her of several artists who'd fawned over her father before he'd left England to paint in Jerusalem.

Angela was uncertain whether to be concerned by Ward's arrival or not. Musa always described him as little more than a charming but sly opportunist. There was also the matter of Sunny's second rule: *You're not to leave the chateau save for short walks…no interactions with anyone outside this chateau.*

"I'm sure you're startled to see me, my lady," Ward said by way of introduction. "After all, we've only met, what, three or four times? Before you toss me out, let me assure I'm no longer writing about current events—yes, your sister informed me of your unexpected nuptials."

Angela was about to turn him away, but found herself too alarmed.

"What did my sister say?"

"No need to worry!" Ward's voice dropped. "I swear I won't write about you and the earl and your fairy tale wedding and all that. Won't report on your honeymoon. Anyway, my usual readers would have no interest." In a normal volume, he added, "I now write about art and culture for periodicals, my lady. Reviews, interviews, essays. I'm employed by an English language weekly in Paris, have been for some months—"

"My sister sent you to check on me?" Angela interrupted, raising a hand to get in a word. He spoke so quickly.

"She did." He smiled, looking rather rakish. "She warned my arrival might alarm you. Here." He thrust into Angela's hand a letter bearing Musa's handwriting. "Proof I'm not lying, my lady. So, without further ado, may I come in?" He rocked on his heels. "It's frightfully cold out here."

Well, this was unexpected…and unexpectedly welcome. The truth was Angela was desperate for company. Save for an occasional feral cat, she saw no one outside Sunny and Dubois, unless she counted the people glimpsed while walking alone in the Bois de Boulogne.

"Hurry," Angela said, looking over her shoulder to confirm she wasn't being watched. She suspected Dubois, whose loyalty laid with Sunny, wouldn't approve of Ward showing up in such a manner. At least as a married woman she didn't require a chaperone, or so she hoped. "Inside, Mr Ward. And please be quiet, if you will."

Ward arched a brow in inquiry.

"The earl is sleeping," Angela evaded, uncomfortable referring to Sunny as her husband. "He's a nocturnal sort."

Ward laughed brightly. "As am I, if I'm to be honest. I'm usually up all night because of my employment. However, I decided a morning call seemed more appropriate than calling at midnight."

Angela smiled despite herself. Well, if Dubois showed, she'd find a way to smooth things over.

"If you'll follow me," Angela invited. The library would do. So many of the chateau's rooms remained unused or closed away. With such few servants, it was to be expected. It really was astonishing that she hadn't happened upon any of them but Dubois. Such was Sunny's determination for no one to meet her, she supposed.

To her surprise, the library was locked for once. She briefly fantasized about picking the lock, a covert skill she'd acquired after getting trapped in that closet with Sunny years ago. Well, she'd use the dining room instead.

Once they settled at the round table before the fire, Angela sliced open Musa's letter with a butter knife. Her sister's note confirmed Ward's account.

Dearest Angela,

I know you asked me not to share your address, so forgive me for sending Luke Ward your way. I was so distressed by your letter that I required confirmation you were well. I would have never expected Sunny to whisk you away to France as he did! But then again, he is so very changed, isn't he?

But, if I am to be honest, it's good you're not in London. I fear the newspaper stories are just as wild as we feared— it's wise you'll be away for so long. I've refused to speak to them about your union with Sunny. The same for Aunt Minerva, who feels awful about what happened with Carles. Hopefully, by the end of the year, the press will find some-thing of greater import to write about. In the meantime, Seb and I will do all we can to dissuade interest in your marriage.

In other news, no letter yet from Mama. I promise to let you know as soon as I've news about Papa. She'd warned it might be some time before she could write, but it still concerns me.

"I must thank you for all you did to find my father, Mr. Ward," Angela said she'd folded away the letter, which confirmed her fears about the scandal. She breathed deeply. How would she ever extri-cate herself from Sunny without affecting her family?

"I was pleased to be of assistance. I owed your sister and Sebas-tian a favor after…" His brow crinkled beneath his receding hair-line. "Well, I'm sure you heard I stole letters she sent Seb for a newspaper story. Not my finest hour."

Musa had been devastated, Angela recalled. "But then you located my father—"

"And justice was restored in the universe," he said in his quick way. "Musa said as much."

"Is that what you call my sister? By her christian name?"

"Yes. Just as I call your brother-in-law Sebastian."

"Then you may address me as Angela."

Yes, it was overly familiar of her. But it was more comfortable than being called 'my lady.' For all her ambitions for her family,

Angela never desired a title. It felt akin to wearing a ballgown to church.

"Ward will do for me, Angela. Or Luke, if you prefer. After all, Sebastian is practically a brother to me."

"Luke," she repeated. He was the first person she'd addressed by their christian name since leaving her family after the wedding breakfast. For some reason, chatting with him reminded her of her brother Theo, though Theo was much younger and usually overshadowed by Lyra's gregariousness.

Family, that's why. Luke Ward was the nearest to such she'd encounter since she left England.

"Since we're on a first name basis, let me share this with you, Angela."

He pulled from his satchel a newspaper; Angela sucked in a breath at the sight of them. She'd enjoyed not encountering newspapers in the time she'd been in Paris. Outside of the morning of her arrival, Dubois had been careful to keep signs of the outside world at bay. She'd only learned of the death of Napoleon III in January two weeks after the event. Not that it mattered, given how removed she was from everything.

As for Sunny, she had no idea what he knew or read. They alternated their time awake in the chateau like the moon and the sun. Some days, the only sign of his presence was his dressing robe in the bedroom and his cologne lingering on the pillow. It reminded Angela that not only had she gained an enemy, she'd lost a friend.

"I promise it won't bite," Luke said.

Angela reluctantly picked up the newspaper, which was folded to the society section. A London *Times* from two days earlier.

THE EARL OF SUNDERLAND ABROAD WITH BRIDE

Virgil, Earl of Sunderland will be away from Parliament whilst on honeymoon with the Countess of Sunderland, whom he unexpectedly wed last month. Their destination remains unknown.

So strange, Angela thought. It was perhaps the shortest article she'd ever read. No mention of her by name. But why?

Her wariness must have shown, for Ward explained in a tone barely above a whisper, "Your sister suspects you may wish to part from your husband at some point. The less you're named in relation to the marriage, the better."

Angela was incredulous. "Even with all the scandal?"

"Time passes." A world-weary shrug. "It may seem impossible now, but eventually no one will remember who the Earl of Sunderland ever wed. His wife will be some forgotten lady who slipped out of his life, never to be heard from again."

"My sister asked you to write this?"

Luke grinned like a Cheshire cat. "She did."

Angela's foreboding lifted. Somehow Musa knew. Somehow Musa was trying to protect her.

"How on earth did you get it published?"

"Let's just say someone owed me a favor…and I owe Musa many, *many* favors." Those stolen letters again. "Once your sister asked for help, I was happy to help. Consider this a small counteroffensive in the war against scandal."

Angela would have hugged Luke if she knew him better. She settled for offering what she hoped was a beatific smile.

"I'm grateful," she said. "Truly."

Luke's tone grew serious. "You have to think of the press as a beast requiring regular feeding. Fortunately, I had what they hungered for in that moment."

He rose abruptly from the upholstered chair, smoothing his trousers, which were a fashionable green plaid.

"If we may, what I now require to feed me is a walk—I've warmed up enough. May I invite you to join me?"

"I shouldn't." Angela remembered Sunny's second rule not to interact with anyone outside the chateau, especially in public places. She'd already broken part of the rule in allowing Ward's visit.

"Ah, but I promise to protect your reputation with the greatest care. We won't go far. We'll avoid humanity, that cursed species. As for journalists, they're another breed here—I'm still learning who's who. But if I was a betting man, I'd venture there's enough local game in Paris to distract them from you."

Angela stood, unable to resist. "I'll get my coat."

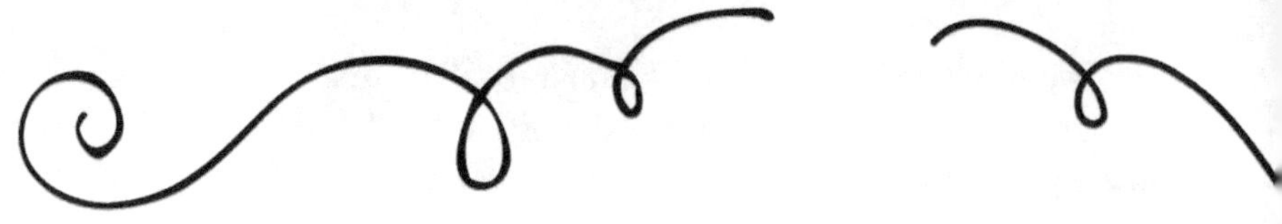

CHAPTER 10

ONCE THEY PASSED the gravel drive surrounding the chateau, Luke confided, "I sense there isn't much comfort in your home, though it's quite grand. I also had the sense of being spied on, if I may be so blunt." He rubbed his hands and blew on them before shoving them into his greatcoat pockets. "Anyway, it's warmer now than it had been."

He was correct. The sun had come out, making everything around the chateau appear bright and sharp. Angela smiled at the sparrows darting from tree to tree, the low hum of life that seemed to rise from the earth despite the purgatory of winter. January had turned especially snowy after their arrival. As for the feral cats that lived outside the chateau, they darted away immediately; Angela had given up trying to gain their friendship. She hadn't seen one inside the chateau since her arrival the first night.

"How long have you been in Paris?" Angela asked. "I recall Seb mentioning you'd been positioned here for employment."

"Just a few months. Soon after his wedding to your sister. I met someone who lives here, which was an enticement. Speaking of which, I recall you dancing a very pretty solo at your sister's wedding reception. Didn't you study ballet once?"

Angela's mood shifted. She'd stopped taking ballet classes once she'd become engaged to John. Dance seemed frivolous, potentially scandalous. Exactly what she shouldn't do as a Bartham seeking respectability, though she hadn't been able to resist dancing under the moonlight on the ferry to France.

Dance was what she returned to when most troubled of mind…which made the temptation of the mirrored salon so difficult to resist despite her lack of toe shoes and appropriate clothing.

"Not anymore," she answered. "The life of a ballerina isn't one I desire. I mean, I still dance for myself—oh, that sounds wrong! I meant to say it pleases me to dance, but I have no aspirations beyond that."

"Meaning to go on the stage," Luke said thoughtfully. "Fame. Fortune. To exchange art for money to please the public."

"That sounds so vulgar stated that way," Angela replied. "But yes."

"Art doesn't require material aspirations to be worthy of endeavor," Luke said. "I write about artists all the time. No one goes into the arts to become wealthy. They go into the arts because they want to make something beautiful. Inspiring. Like Seb, for example. Your father. If you expect more than that, you're naive."

Naive. Was that what she'd been? Her devotion to ballet wasn't because she wanted fame or wealth. It was because to because she'd wanted to *live* through dance. To experience the stories she so loved. The passion. The romance. The drama. The eternal love.

Anyone respectable knew ballerinas were one step away from courtesans, especially in the *corps de ballet*. Angela had no delusions about her talent: she was no Maria Taglioni or Fanny Elssler, who transcended the grit of the stage to attain greatness. Nor did she have the resources to study for the endless hours required to perfect her craft.

Still, in those moments while she danced, Angela felt as though she was touching something greater than herself.

"You're right," she agreed. "That's what my teacher used to tell me about art and commerce. They're an unhappy marriage of convenience." Well, Angela knew all about this. "She only agreed to teach me because I promised not to go on the stage." A short laugh. "She was protecting me before I knew to protect myself."

"Understandable," Luke said. By then they'd walked around the perimeter of the chateau in a direction Angela had never explored before. The gravel walk led to a private rough and tumble footpath marked by stones and tree roots. She'd been too cautious to attempt it alone. With company, she gave way to her curiosity.

She felt free. Happy. Almost like the girl she'd been when she'd danced under the moon.

And then she knew: she'd reclaim the mirrored salon for herself. Begin to dance again for herself. She'd use her year wisely, instead of mourn. She felt her heart perk up, her optimism return.

"Look!"

Luke pointed toward the sky, which was bluer than it had been in weeks.

Before and beyond, Angela could make out the Bois de Boulogne. There were fields surrounded by paths and roads, several lakes, and more trees than could be discerned. She'd only been able to see a small fraction from inside the chateau.

Angela let out a long sigh. "It truly is lovely here. I haven't appreciated it. Thank you for escorting me."

"As a newlywed, I'm sure you had other considerations for your attention," Luke replied. "If it's any consolation, I've been informed Carles was run out of town after your wedding—no one had any idea about his secret marriages. His younger brother took over his sherry importing business and made fiscal amends to his wives and children."

"I hadn't known he had a brother," Angela replied, her stomach dropping as though she missed a step on a staircase. So much she hadn't known about Carles. Yet she'd agreed to wed him, to trust him with her life, her reputation…unlike Sunny, whom she'd known since she was a child.

"I should return," Angela said, suddenly uneasy.

"I've disquieted you by speaking of disquieting subjects, haven't I? Forgive me, Angela."

Angela assured, "No, I'm grateful for your help. In time, interest in my personal affairs will go away, I'm sure."

Still, Luke was right: she was disquieted. She'd felt so giddy after reading that article. Meanwhile, Carles and his scandals had continued on in her absence.

You'll find a way to be happy again. You always do. Wasn't that how she'd survived heartbreak?

The mirrored salon. I'll dance.

"In any case, I think the article will help—hopefully it'll gain some attention. I'll write your sister and inform her of your well-being." Luke offered his arm. "Let me accompany you back. The path is lovely but treacherous."

"Was that meant as a commentary on my situation?"

"Well, you are a Bartham," he said gently. "Barthams aren't exactly known for living quietly."

Before they turned away, he took a last look, circling in all directions. "This is so beautiful. For all my time in Paris, I've yet to visit the Bois de Boulogne. Hadn't the time." A laugh. "Well, I found other attractions. The garden about your home looks so over-grown and lush. That greenhouse especially. Are those flowers blooming inside? And in winter too! It must be a refuge on sunny days."

"What greenhouse?" As far as Angela knew the chateau didn't possess one. She squinted. Could that be a glimmer of glass?

He shrugged. "Perhaps I'm mistaken. I'd assumed it was yours."

And so they returned, this time in silence to avoid stumbling. When Angela glanced up, she noticed the bedroom curtains shift.

Sunny—he'd been watching Angela from the window.

Upstairs in the chateau, Sunny paced back and forth in the bedroom even after he'd forced himself to close the curtains.

Despite his claims, he struggled sleeping during the day. When Angela's caller arrived, Sunny had been in the library after returning from sending flowers to Hélène yet again. (She still refused to see him.) Once Sunny heard the bell pull, he staggered from the library, taking care to remain hidden from Angela. After he realized the visitor was someone Angela knew—he could tell by the way she led the gentleman into the dining room without hesitation—Sunny gave up on sleep.

Who was he? Had he courted her once? Including himself, Angela had attracted four suitors before she'd settled on that ass Carles—proof of her poor judgement.

Confront her! Rule number two, you coward!

However, this would involve deigning to speak to her, which would be a capitulation. He'd snubbed all of her previous efforts and apologies.

By the time Sunny decided to go after them, Angela and her companion had departed the chateau for parts unknown. Sunny darted upstairs into the bedroom like a disobedient child. He again attempted to sleep, but then a new preoccupation rose: the greenhouse. Had she noticed it?

As for Angela's companion, Sunny told himself he didn't feel jealous. It was simply in his interest to know whether she was consorting with someone who might undermine their privacy. The less people knew of their marriage, the less notice their annulment would attract.

Liar.

After some minutes, Sunny pulled the bedroom curtains open. There she was, chatting with the gentleman on the pathway outside the chateau. They must have returned from their stroll. The gentleman was wearing a mustard-yellow bowler. He was probably some sort of artist, no doubt a friend of her family. They appeared in animated conversation. Was she laughing? She was.

She once laughed like that with me.

Against his will, he remembered the times they'd chased squirrels and climbed trees in Kensington Gardens, though that changed once she started wearing long skirts. The summer day their rowboat had tipped into the Serpentine because they were daring each other to catch a fish with their bare hands.

"She's not your friend anymore," he muttered. "Ignore her."

He couldn't speak to her. That would only afford Angela the opportunity to argue. Instead, he settled for writing a note.

My lady,

It has come to my attention that you took a walk with a gentleman caller this morning. In case it's slipped your mind, here's a reminder of Rule #2: No leaving here save for short walks, no interactions with anyone outside this chateau.

Persist in such unwise behavior and I'll begin to believe you wish to remain married to me.

With gravest concern,
Sunderland

He pinned the note to the bed pillow, feeling rather satisfied with himself. He hadn't lost his temper. Hadn't broken his rule of not speaking to her. He'd taken control of the situation, as he should. After all, he'd done her a favor by marrying her, revenge be damned.

The next morning, a note in answer awaited him in Angela's neat handwriting. It was also pinned to the pillow.

My lord,

Let me assure that remaining married to you is the last thing I desire. However, one must recognize that a year is a long time to go without conversing with a friend, now that you no longer fulfill that role in my life.

I apologize for breaking Rule #2. In the future, I promise to limit any gentlemen callers to unlocked rooms inside this chateau. To make this easier to abide in the coming months, I will be using the mirrored salon for my own needs. (I presume this doesn't fall under Rule #2. Or was it Rule #1 that concerned forbidden rooms?) One must have space to dance if one is to be compliant.

Respectfully yours etc,
Angela, Countess of Sunderland

In reply, Sunny wrote one word in large block letters on a full sheet of paper. He knew it would infuriate her, but that was too damn bad.

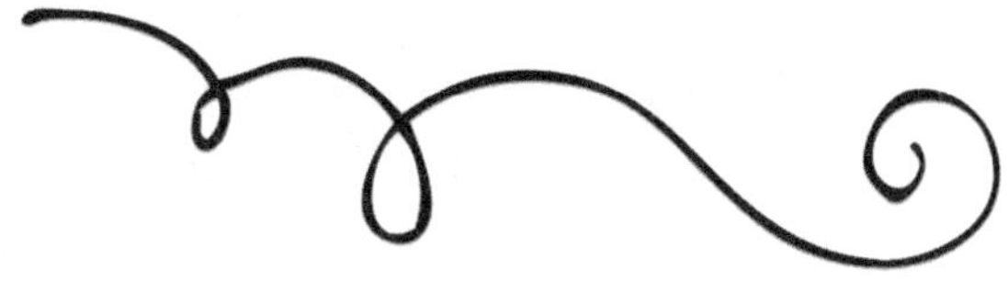

CHAPTER 11

ANGELA DIDN'T TAKE his refusal without a fight. To Sunny's annoyance, she confronted him in the dining room about an hour after he'd awakened.

"Why did you say no?" she demanded.

Sunny looked up from his dinner, which was really breakfast in his topsy-turvy day. A full meal of roast duck and potatoes with greens, which Dubois had left for him as a matter of habit. The food wasn't necessary. Sunny had dinner plans for the evening with Hélène—after many written apologies and flower bouquets, she'd finally agreed to meet with him. Still, he poked at the food, restless in his uneasiness.

To avoid overwhelming Dubois, Angela usually took her dinner at the same time but in the bedroom, which was when she probably discovered Sunny's last note. She appeared more distressed than enraged, he decided.

"I didn't *say* no, Angela. I left you a note stating such," he said, glancing at the clock. He should leave, but couldn't find the will to do so. "I told you I don't wish to speak to you."

"We're speaking now."

"Notes are sufficient, countess. The briefer the better."

He knew it was petty, but all he could think of was her gentleman caller. How she'd laughed with him like she once had with Sunny. Now that she was so close—the closest they'd been in some weeks—all he sensed was how differently she treated him. Her posture was tight. Unwelcoming. Protective. Like that of a stranger.

"This requires more than a note." Angela slid into the chair across from his. "Please, Sunderland, let me use the mirrored salon for my own needs. A year is a long time, especially if I'm not to venture beyond the chateau grounds. It's such a small thing."

"If it's a small thing, it can be ignored." The duck had grown cold. Unappealing…just as he imagined he looked. Strange how he hadn't thought of his appearance since the wedding, when he'd yearned to impress Angela. He hadn't bothered to shave to go out, though he should have for Hélène's sake. At this rate, his beard would soon overtake his face.

"Would it help if I apologize for breaking your rules?"

"You already apologized in your note." His tone was short.

She leaned in toward him. "If this is about my caller, he's only a family friend. Not a risk—my sister sent him to check on me. We only walked around the perimeters of the grounds, that's all."

He'd figured as much, but now that she'd confirmed such, he especially burned to ask for further details. He couldn't bear to. It would reveal he still cared about her. That she could make him jealous. Vulnerable.

"You can also apologize by leaving me alone, Angela."

To his chagrin, she poured herself a glass of wine, which Dubois had left on the table. Her hands were trembling. Courage, that's what she was drinking for.

After a long moment, she asked, "No Dubois tonight? I wager he'd agree with me about the salon."

"He has a cold. Or allergy. Or something." Allergies or no, the truth was Sunny ordered Dubois to leave once dinner was served, to avoid inflicting his rotten mood on the servant.

Still, he didn't leave to meet Hélène though he was uncertain if it was his reluctance to see her or his jealousy over Angela's caller. He sensed there was something else Angela wanted to say. Something he wouldn't want to hear.

Behind him, he heard a log on the fire crackle and break.

"You and your talk of forbidden rooms," she said nervously. "There's a greenhouse behind the chateau. It's yours, isn't it?"

He felt his face go rigid; he'd thought the greenhouse better hidden. "It's not part of this estate."

"Oh. I thought it might have something to do with your brother. This chateau…it's all about him. I can tell. The only one bedroom, how closed off everything is."

Why did she have to bring up Robert? It only reminded Sunny of all he'd lost. The title he'd gained.

He pretended not to hear her. He turned away, setting a silver cover over his meal like it was the most fascinating act he'd ever undertaken.

She pressed, "Is your brother why so much of this house is forbidden to me? Because your father acquired it after Robert's death?"

He took a sip of water. Once he swallowed, he said, "You're a persistent one tonight." He affected a lighter tone than he felt.

"I wish you would tell me more, so I can understand. All the years we've been friends. All the years I knew of your loss. Your sorrow." She gestured about the dining room. "I truly had no idea about this chateau."

"Make no mistake, Angela. We're not friends. Not anymore."

"I-I know. You've told me this multiple times." To his surprise, she sounded sorrowful. "Is this chateau where you went after I…"

Her words drifted into silence, but he understood.

After I refused your proposal.

"That's a long story, one I'd rather not share."

And a story I shan't tell anyone. Especially you.

Uneasy, he chucked Angela under her chin. "Cheer up, countess. I won't hold your curiosity against you. Now what about you?"

"What about me?" He watched the slender column of her neck as she swallowed a gulp of wine. She was uneasy too.

Good. Only fair.

He said in a low voice, "You asked me questions that weren't your business. Now it's my turn."

"This wasn't meant as an exchange, Sunderland."

"Now it is, Angela. First question: who was the gentleman who visited you today? Besides being a family friend, that is."

She let out a soft laugh, more confident. "Don't tell me you're jealous."

"That's an answer, I suppose." It took all his self control not to press further. "Second question: did you know Carles was already married when you accepted his proposal?"

She shoved her glass of wine back. "Heavens, no! What do you take me for?"

"Well, that's a relief to hear." A pause. "Still, I envy him. You loved him enough to wed him willingly."

"Can we not speak of Carles?"

"Too heartbroken?"

"The state of my heart is not your concern."

She took a nervous gulp of wine, her cheeks flaring. Guilt, that's what she felt. He'd seen her like this before, the time she'd lied to her mother about having a headache in order to stay home and read books with him. *"It's more pleasant, with just the two of us,"* she'd told him once they were alone.

Suddenly he knew. "You weren't in love with him, were you?"

She blinked as though she'd been pinched. "It no longer matters."

"It matters to me. You were willing to marry Carles without love. But not me."

He knew he was being awful, but he couldn't seem to stop himself. Next thing he knew, he'd be harping again about that letter she'd sent. But he felt possessed by a force he couldn't name. No longer himself. Wild.

Angela, to her credit, kept her voice even. "Would you want me to marry you under such circumstances? You deserved a wife who loved you as more than a friend. You deserved far better."

"Such as that charming letter you sent me?"

There, he'd done it. Lost control.

Angela lost control too. She stood from the table so quickly that her wine glass nearly tipped over.

"Damn it, will you ever stop harping on that stupid letter? I told you how much I regret sending it! It was ill conceived, poorly written, unkind—I know that now. I wish I'd never—"

"Last question, Angela, then I'll leave you be. If you didn't love Carles, why did you agree to marry him? Was it for position? Money?"

"Don't be vulgar!"

"Or for a family? You've always been fond of children."

His voice broke despite himself, thinking of the family he'd once yearned to have with her. A daughter. A son. To his surprise, he yearned to caress her cheek, imagining how velvet-soft her skin would be. Even now, even after everything he'd learned about her.

She answered after a long moment, "Perhaps I believed I loved him."

Unlike you.

The implication was clear, but the flare of her cheeks told Sunny she was lying again. She'd known all along she wasn't in love with Carles but accepted his proposal anyway.

Because you're unworthy, Sunderland. A disappointment. Everyone says as much.

"Well, that's a relief to know, Angela. That will make it all the easier."

She offered a delicate frown. "How?"

"To forget I ever loved you once this year is up."

She flinched. He understood his words were cruel as well as untrue—he'd never ever forget loving her even if he lived a century. But, in that moment, he again felt possessed…especially when she bit the soft of her lip.

And then he did the most ridiculous thing he could possibly do in reaction to his lie, as wrong as he knew it was. He grabbed Angela by her shoulders and slanted his mouth against hers, closing the distance between them in a single step.

He awaited her protest, for her to slap him even. To his surprise, she didn't struggle. Instead, she leaned into his kiss, her body soft against his, after the briefest moment. He involuntarily stroked her cheek, her hair. He felt her intake of breath, her shudder.

This is what it's like to kiss her. To hold her. He'd wondered for so long, fantasized about it, desired it so deeply. And now that the kiss had happened, there was scarce satisfaction in it. For the kiss had been stolen from her, not given freely.

Still, he was pleased that he pulled away first from their kiss, not she. Then he remembered himself, felt regret.

He expected outrage. To his surprise, her eyes were dilated, face flushed. Her mouth appeared ripe and swollen. Welcoming.

I did that to her, he thought, shocked. *Despite everything, she desired me.*

That would have to be his consolation. His revenge.

"For someone who no longer loves me, you act otherwise," she said, touching her mouth.

"Desire isn't the same as love. I think you know this too. You see, I realized something after your confession about Carles. It's a simple truth, but so important."

She raised her chin, defiant. "Tell me."

His voice was as soft as his words were sharp. "Angela Bartham, you're incapable of love for anyone save your family."

As soon as he spoke, he flooded with remorse, and her eyes pooled with hurt. *I'm sorry,* he wanted to say. *I didn't mean it.*

It was too late. Before he could apologize, she pulled off the signet ring he'd given her in lieu of a wedding band and set it on the table.

"Incapable of love..." She shook her head. "You know nothing about me. Nothing at all."

She turned and left the dining room.

"Where the hell are you going?" Sunny demanded, following her into the entry hall, where she grabbed her coat.

"Anywhere you're not!"

CHAPTER 12

Before Sunny could stop her, Angela rushed from the chateau out into the dark night, mustering as much dignity as she could in the face of insult. She'd never tell him about Philippe. Ever. He didn't deserve the truth. Sunny deserved nothing from her. Not after that conversation. That kiss.

Outside, that's where she needed to be—she didn't care how cold it was, how bitter the wind. Outside, past the mangy grey cat who lived under the stairwell, beyond the curling trees whose limbs appeared alive in the wind.

Outside, where she wasn't trapped in a dining room with a beast of a man she'd once considered a dear friend—a man who'd just kissed her in a manner that made her forget her beloved Philippe, to her shame.

Once she was outside, she'd walk for as long as she could bear the cold February night. Until she outraced her anger. Her sorrow.

And then she realized: she'd broken Sunny's second rule again. Well, damn him.

Angela walked on, uncertain of her direction. The night was thick with fog, the air moist in that peculiar way that suggested spring could be around the corner or a snowstorm. She'd forgotten her bonnet too. Her hair felt wild against her face; with no one to see her in the chateau, she'd only twisted it into a simple knot at the base of her neck.

Where am I?

She stopped, turning in all directions. Where had she run to? All she'd sensed were her legs swishing beneath her skirts as she'd rushed out into the night, away from Sunny and his accusations. She'd yearned to get as far away as she could as quickly as she could.

"Mademoiselle, *attention!*" a gruff worker dressed in overalls and a thick coat. He was carrying a ladder.

"I'm so sorry," she stammered. "*Je suis désolée.*"

Angela stepped to the side of the pavement. She squinted, trying to make out the silhouette of the Arc de Triomphe. Had she gone in that direction? At least then she'd have some idea where she was.

Wherever she was, she stood in the middle of a pavement facing a wide boulevard. The boulevard shimmered with gas lamps, though they illuminated little in such foggy weather. All around her, people rushed. They appeared shadowy silhouettes as they passed. Her ears made out the clatter of horse hooves, carriages. Her nose inhaled the scent of rotting cabbage, horse manure. A woman dressed in a tattered cape glared as she strode by, offering a string of French that sounded more irritated than not.

Just move, Angela told herself. *Find some place to sit.* Then she'd untangle where she found herself—she couldn't have gone that far. Perhaps she'd even find someone who spoke English to help.

Within the fog, she made out the shimmer of bright lights across the boulevard. A café. It looked invitingly welcoming. Warm. Her fingers strained inside the pocket of her coat. No coins.

She'd stay only long enough to figure what to do, where she was. She could even ask for directions in her rudimentary French. After all, how far could she have gone? Hopefully, no one would question her right to be in the café. In time, she'd have to return to the chateau—what choice did she have?—but surely by then Sunny would have disappeared to wherever he went most evenings.

To her dismay, her eyes stung. The old Sunny, the one who'd been her friend, would have followed her, made sure she was safe…but the old Sunny wouldn't have said such unkind things.

"Nothing to be done," Angela whispered. Well, she'd do her best to make a good impression.

She smoothed her hair and approached the café.

The sign on the café was brashly painted in bright scarlet letters surrounded by gold. La Fleur Interdite, it said—The Forbidden Flower. Whether French or English, La Fleur Interdite was bright with gaslight and welcoming in its warmth; Angela's cheeks and fingers thawed once she crossed its threshold.

La Fleur Interdite was also incredibly loud and crowded. Too crowded. Smoky, though Angela was uncertain if it was from tobacco or something else.

She looked around, hoping no one would pay her mind. A group of men dressed in an odd melange of clothing hung together in a mass as they bent over a table, shouting out encouragement. Gambling. Dice or cards? Either way, it was rougher than anywhere Angela had ever come across in her life, even with Philippe. During their courtship, he liked to visit small cafés run by French émigrés, where he could get the food he missed from home.

Several gaudily dressed ladies hung on the men's shoulders, their loud laughter rising like a taunt. Their brightly colored silk gowns looked ill-fitting, too shiny. Garish. So did their necklaces of beads and the kohl lining their eyes. Toward the back of the café, a trio featuring an accordion and two violins played an aggressively lively tune. A mazurka, Angela recognized.

Upon her arrival, four men, one of whom wore a top hat and opera cloak with what appeared to be a sable collar, turned slowly from the long quartz bar that ran along one side of the café. Their eyes raked along her body, eyebrows raised; Angela's skin prickled as though they'd come across her wearing only a chemise. Then they grunted and turned back to their glasses, which were filled with a cloudy green substance.

Well, all except for one, the gentleman with the top hat.

He raised a ruddy glass of wine in Angela's direction. He appeared well into his third decade, with an air of hauteur that seemed out of place in the café. He was perhaps the handsomest man she'd ever seen, though not in a way Angela appreciated.

He winked.

Angela's stomach tensed. *I should not be here.*

The café plunged into silence, leaving Angela feeling even more exposed. Or did it just seem that way because the trio finished their mazurka?

"*Excusez-moi,*" Angela began weakly, her cheeks flushing. "*Je suis—*"

How to say "lost" in French? Was it *perdue? Oublié?* She couldn't recall. No matter: the trio immediately began another piece, this one a waltz, drowning out Angela's voice as she fumbled for words. Her hands clenched inside her pockets. Her eyes burned from the smoke-filled room.

A woman dressed in a severe black gown punctuated by neat lace cuffs and a matching collar approached. The café's proprietress, Angela assumed.

"Mademoiselle?" Her tone was inviting as she addressed Angela. "*Puis-je vous aider?*"

How can I help you?

Angela forced a smile, uneasy. "*Parlez-vous anglais, s'il vous plait?*"

The proprietress took Angela's hand and began caressing it. "*Oui,* I speak English, mademoiselle."

Angela shoved her hand back in her pocket. "Oh good! I'm lost—"

"Not necessarily, mademoiselle." She pulled Angela to the side of the café toward the door; her grasp was startlingly firm on

Angela's wrist. "If you wish to be here, you're most welcome." In a lower voice, "You'll need to pay me a commission, of course. After you pay the fee for the room, of course."

Now Angela understood. She resisted the urge to run.

"I-I don't wish to be here, madame," Angela countered, growing more flustered by the second. "I'm not what you think—I'll leave soon as you tell me where I am. Please."

"Perhaps a glass of wine first?" The top-hatted gentleman slid alongside the proprietress to address Angela; his English was astonishingly good. "You're new here, little one. From London perhaps?"

"It doesn't matter, monsieur."

He laughed, showing bright sharp teeth. He turned to address the proprietress in rapid French. After some back and forth, he addressed Angela anew. "Dance with me?"

"No, thank you." Even had she wanted to, there was no room to waltz in this overcrowded, smoky café.

"He's really asking you to go with him upstairs," a barmaid interrupted before the proprietress shushed her. "For a private—"

Angela's embarrassment gave way to anger. "I'm not what you take me to be! I'm simply lost."

"That's what they all say," the gentleman replied. "You look familiar, little one. English, blonde, pretty. In trouble. If I were a betting man, I'd say you're a member of the aristocracy, *oui*? I've been waiting here for something to write about."

Angela's mind recalibrated in a panic. *A journalist. He'd recognized her.* He'd probably seen those illustrations in English newspapers.

She said in her haughtiest tone, "You're very much mistaken, monsieur."

"I can smell a good scandal." He pulled out an array of bank notes. "*Combien?* How much for the truth? Don't be shy! I can afford whatever you ask for an exclusive interview." A rather lupine grin. "On the other hand, if you're not whom I believe, I'll pay for that too…once we're upstairs, little one."

Before she could think otherwise, Angela's hand flashed against his cheek. The slap rang out louder than the waltzing trio. The violins screeched to a halt, the accordion let out a rude belch. And then, as one, everyone in that sordid café turned in her direction. The gamblers, the prostitutes, and what felt like the whole of Paris.

Angela felt like a lamb surrounded by wolves.

"I'm so sorry," she muttered, backing away toward the door. "*Pardonnez-moi.* I'm leaving. Really."

Before she could race outside, the top-hatted gentleman clutched her arm.

"Enough. Come with me."

"Ow! Let me go!"

The proprietress intervened. "Let her go, Willie. She's no one important, dressed like that."

She spoke in English, perhaps to reassure Angela. Or was something else going on? While Angela puzzled this, a man dressed in a brown hooded cloak slid inside the café. He clutched a walking stick tipped with gold.

Her attention was pulled by a shout from the table where she'd witnessed gambling. A pair of dice fell onto the floor. Some had cheated, or so Angela surmised from the scattering of French she understood.

The table tipped over and a chair thrown, much to Angela's gratitude, for everyone turned their attention from her.

La Fleur Interdite erupted into a melee of fists and shouts. The musical trio rushed to protect their musical instruments as though they were children. A woman screamed from the back of the café, where a second man, this one dressed in a military uniform that had seen better days, smashed a wine bottle in half. He flourished it above his head as he staggered toward the front of the café, where Angela stood with the proprietress and the others.

Angela turned for the door. But then something—no, someone—grabbed her by the waist. The top-hatted man.

"Hello, little one." His breath was hot on her ear. "Come with me."

Angela raised her knee directly into his groin. He doubled over, but recovered. His arms tightened.

"Leave her alone!" a deep male voice shouted in French.

The cry came from behind Angela. She watched as the gentleman cloaked in brown rushed forth, his face shadowed beneath his hood. He wedged his walking stick between her and the top-hatted gentleman, freeing Angela just as the fighting reached a climax of shouts and crashing furniture. Angela half-expected a fire to break out.

Her cloaked rescuer handled his walking stick with the skill of a rapier, granting Angela the opportunity to break for the door. How dashing he was, so daring! Somehow she squeezed out onto the pavement, just as the police arrived in a loud clash of shouts and whistle-blowing.

She looked over her shoulder at the café. Her rescuer had disappeared.

What to do? Where to go?

A hansom cab halted in front of Angela just as she was about to cross the street. The carriage matched the slatternly quality of the neighborhood. Its door opened, revealing the beaded hem of an evening gown.

"Get in!" a female voice ordered in accented English.

"No, thank you," Angela replied.

A bemused chuckle from the shadows of the carriage. "You'd rather remain here?"

"It's not that…" Angela said just as the front window of La Fleur Interdite shattered. (Again, where had her cloaked rescuer gone?) "I'm fine, madame."

A gloved hand reached out from the shadows of the carriage.

"Come. Don't be proud."

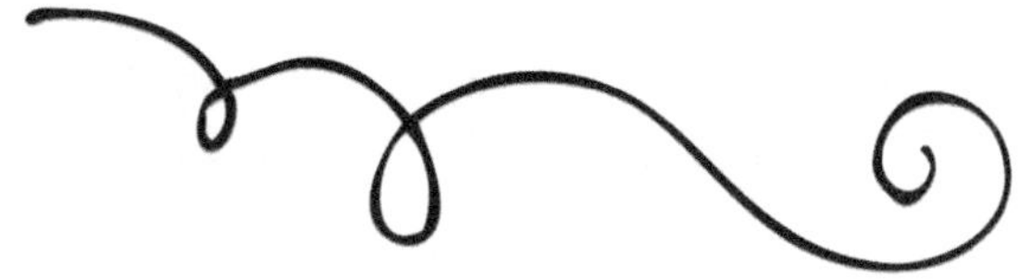

CHAPTER 13

"I PROMISE I'm not kidnapping you," the woman said as the carriage lurched forward into the night. Her tone remained that disconcerting mix of amusement and aggression.

"I presume not," Angela said primly. Still, it was deeply troubling that the interior of the carriage remained as shadowy as it appeared from the boulevard. She strained to make out the face of her rescuer. So far all she'd heard was her voice, seen the hem of her dress, her gloved hands. She'd also smelled her perfume. Floral with a hint of spice, perhaps musk.

The carriage turned a sharp corner. At last, a slant of light fell on Angela's rescuer, illuminating the elaborately draped skirts of her gown. It was a rich green satin that didn't appear cheap, unlike the prostitutes she'd encountered in the café. However, the gown appeared to have seen better days; Angela noticed a neatly mended seam here, a worn hem there.

Angela suddenly realized the woman had addressed her in English, not French.

"How did you know I was English?" The evening had turned so peculiar. Worse, dangerous if not for her cloaked rescuer. La Fleur Interdite was indeed well-named.

Another bemused chuckle from the shadows. "Between your

hair and your clothes, you don't dress like a Parisian. Plus you appear far too innocent to be lingering about La Fleur Interdite."

Angela's neck prickled with new anxiety.

"However, there's another reason I stopped my carriage," the woman added. "You're the new Countess of Sunderland."

Merde.

Now Angela's panic really rose. She recalled the top-hatted journalist in the café. Could the woman be another member of the press? In all the years of Bartham scandals, she'd never encountered a female journalist.

Don't feed the beast.

"Thank you for rescuing me." Angela reached for the door though the horses were gaining in speed. "You can stop the carriage."

The woman set her hand on Angela's. "I wouldn't dream of abandoning you here, my lady."

"It's not abandonment if I ask."

"Again, I promise I'm not kidnapping you. Where would you like me to bring you?"

"But I'd be taking you out of your way."

Another dry chuckle from the shadows. "I've no place to be. My dining companion never showed. Where to?"

Angela gave way, for what was she to do? "Toward the Bois de Boulogne, just north of it. I don't have the address, but I'll recognize it."

"I know exactly where." The woman opened her window to call up to the driver. When she finished, she told Angela, "We're near there. I told the driver to take the long route."

"Whatever for?"

"Because I want to converse with you."

"Is that so?" If she was a reporter, best to meet the beast where they lived, Angela decided. Not that she had a choice. "How did you know who I was?"

"Ah, but first I have a question. How did you end up at La

Fleur Interdite? That's no place for you, if you care to avoid scandal."

"I'd rather not say."

"You needn't play coy. We've met before, my lady."

"Have we? Forgive my poor memory, madame."

"Mademoiselle," the woman corrected.

"You're a journalist, aren't you?" Angela asked as the carriage hit a bump.

The woman arched a brow, bemused. "*Mon dieu,* no."

"Then who are you?" Angela knew her question was rude, but she didn't care. It wasn't every evening one was nearly molested, survived a fight in a café filled with gamblers, and was rescued by a dashing, cloaked man.

"I'm not surprised you don't recall me, my lady. You had other preoccupations during your wedding."

The woman bent toward Angela, where the light lay. Finally, Angela made out her face in full.

The French mistress, or so Angela had presumed at the wedding. Unlike when she'd seen her with Sunny, the woman appeared more refined in her beauty—Angela had judged her unkindly. No, the woman was striking. Her chestnut-hued hair was ornately curled, her grey eyes luminous above her aquiline nose. Still, she still reminded Angela of a peacock. Proud. Disdainful.

Angela let out a long breath. "Now I recall. Forgive me for not recognizing you."

The woman settled beside Angela, rearranging her skirts. "I should be flattered I made an impression considering the chaos that day." Her face turned rigid. "I did not expect Sunderland to marry you."

And then Angela knew. "You and Sunderland were courting."

"With the intent to wed," the woman replied in a cool tone. "No longer, thanks to you. Not only that, he stood me up for dinner tonight." She shook her head, mouth tight with anger.

That's where Sunny planned to go tonight.

Their argument had interfered. A rise of regret, of remorse rose amid Angela's uneasiness. Angela knew too well what it felt like to lose the man you loved. To settle for a future other than the one you'd dreamt.

Angela couldn't think how to reply beyond a muttered, "I'm so sorry."

An even more disquieting thought rose.

"You followed me to La Fleur Interdite to confront me after Sunderland didn't show."

The woman's bemusement gave way to a full-throated laugh, which showed off her lovely white teeth. "That would take cunning beyond my capacities. I was on my way to confront Sunderland— and there you were, standing like a little lost lamb. You still haven't told me why you were at La Fleur Interdite."

"I went for a walk. I got lost."

Angela recalled the top-hatted man's breath against her ear, then her rescuer, who came out of nowhere to protect her. In retrospect, there was something oddly familiar about the gentleman's walking stick. She supposed walking sticks were all the same though.

The woman replied, "Those men at La Fleur Interdite would have ruined your life far more than marrying a bigamist, my lady. Gossip columnists. Journalists. Oh and absinthe drinkers, opium smokers, and gamblers." A pause. "Was there a man there wearing an opera cloak with a sable collar? Top hat? Handsome in a dissipated way?"

"Yes."

The woman's tone turned bitter. "He's the worst."

"I'm grateful to you for rescuing me," Angela said, remembering her manners. "Improbable, you must admit."

"Timing is everything, as the saying goes. And here we are." The woman offered Angela her gloved hand. "Shall we begin again? I know who you are, but you don't know me. Hélène Charlotte de Castel-d'Albret."

That's quite the name, Angela thought as she accepted her hand. "Mademoiselle…or have you a title?"

"Not since the end of the Second Empire. You may as well call me Hélène—Sunderland calls you Angela, *oui*? It'll make things less complicated between us. Woman to woman."

"I'm so sorry," Angela said anew. "I truly had no idea about Sunderland's intentions toward you."

"No matter." Hélène offered a rather Gallic shrug, which made her lovely curls crinkle about her shoulders. How cynical she appeared! Her gestures made her appear older than her years—she was in her late twenties at most. But perhaps this was all a show. As Angela knew too well, everyone had their own way of dealing with heartbreak.

Sunny courting another woman—Angela had never considered this. How self-centered she'd been. She glanced at Hélène, the woman who might have become Sunny's wife. She was surprised by a stab of jealousy. Against her will, she recalled how he'd kissed her. How she'd responded.

Had Sunny kissed her like that too?

Angela was no fool. She understood his kiss that night was nothing more than a way for him to establish dominance. To humiliate her. And yet, to her shame, she hadn't once thought of Philippe in that moment.

Perhaps she's where Sunny goes while you sleep.

Angela asked in a careful tone, "Have you and Sunderland seen each other in Paris before tonight?"

Hélène shook her head emphatically. "He sent flowers and notes though."

"How often did he send them?" Angela had to know.

Hélène arched an eyebrow. "My, aren't you full of questions!"

"You had questions for me," Angela countered. "Only fair."

"Well, instead of a question, here's a fact. Don't pity me, Angela. I knew Sunderland was in love with you when he began courting me."

"I assure you he doesn't loves me." Angela's throat grew tight. "He only married me because he cares about my family. Well, among other reasons."

"It no longer matters, does it?" Hélène met Angela's gaze boldly. "I'm the woman he refuses to meet for dinner. You're the woman he made his wife."

Not for long, Angela yearned to say. *Only another nine months. Sooner, if possible.* Anyway, the state of their marriage was for Sunny to confess, not Angela.

Instead, she settled for an anemic "Sometimes things aren't as they appear."

～

Several moments later, Hélène's carriage left Angela on the gravel drive outside the chateau. "Do you wish to speak to Sunderland?" Angela asked.

Hélène shook her head. "I've changed my mind. I'm too angry —it's to his benefit I don't."

"I suppose we won't see each other again."

"I think not, Angela. Still, I'm glad to have encountered you. I was curious about the woman Sunderland married. Now that we've met, I shan't think of you again."

Angela was too taken aback to respond. However, Hélène wasn't finished.

"Before I leave, one last piece of advice. Don't seek out places where you're unwelcome. Next time, someone may not rescue you."

"Next time I'll rescue myself," Angela retorted.

Once Hélène was gone, Angela lingered for a moment outside in the chill air, distressed by all she'd learned that evening. If all Hélène claimed was true, Sunny jilted her to protect Angela's family from ruin, undermining Hélène's future. Even more troubling: he'd yearned for revenge more than he cared for Hélène.

In her heart of hearts, Angela wished she could flee France, to abandon her marriage so Sunny could reunite with Hélène. To make things right. But Angela knew that wouldn't do even it was possible. Best to lay low, to avoid scandal. To follow the plan they'd agreed on—hadn't her experience at La Fleur Interdite proven such? Anyway, Hélène's anger precluded any hope of reunion, or so it seemed.

Nothing to be done.

Angela squared her shoulders. As she approached the chateau, a cat yowled, probably from the garden. The chateau was illuminated as though for a soirée.

Sunny was still there, she knew it. He'd insulted her, watched her stomp off in the night, then had the audacity to wait for her return. He probably intended to hurl more insults in her direction.

Her stomach ached. She'd hoped he'd be gone by now…though if he wasn't with Hélène, where did he go while she slept?

Angela girded herself as she opened the door. As she feared, Sunny awaited in the reception area. But the tableau greeting her eyes was nothing she expected.

He was bent over a litter of kittens.

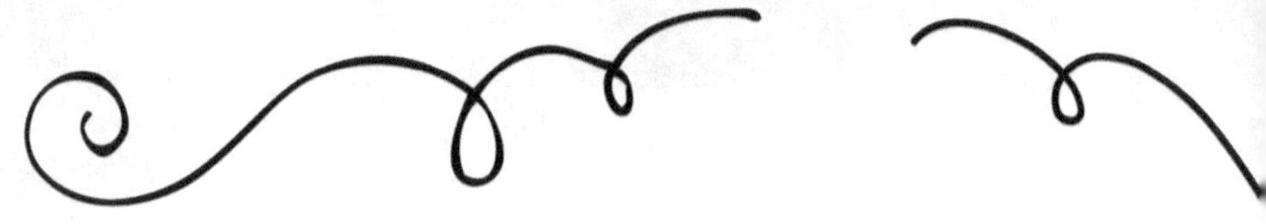

CHAPTER 14

"Angela," Sunny said, forcing a degree of normalcy into his voice he didn't feel.

Of course, he swelled with relief when Angela opened the door. Of course, he'd followed her after their argument, though he was careful to remain out of sight as she rushed into the foggy night. Of course, he'd intervened at La Fleur Interdite when she was attacked. But he'd never ever confess the truth. He prayed she hadn't glimpsed his face beneath his hood or recognized his gold-tipped walking stick.

When she entered the café, he'd imagined the most awful fates befalling Angela, especially after he saw the gentleman wearing the opera cloak approach her. Sunny knew of him too well.

Edmond de Williem was notorious for his society column in a popular scandal sheet that made many a Parisian with secrets quiver with anxiety…especially Hélène. Known more commonly to the masses as Willie, the journalist's column was too powerful by half, for he wrote with a pen dipped in venom and an eye for personal enrichment. It took all of Sunny's self control not to sweep in and confront him—this would serve no one. Then, when Sunny lost Angela amid the melee, he'd never felt so distraught, especially after she disappeared to god knew where for nearly an hour.

Anyway, there was no time now for explanations or apologies, not with a passel of kittens mewing on the floor. He hoped she couldn't notice the scratches on his face, which he'd gained at La Fleur Interdite while fighting on her behalf. Most of all, he hoped she didn't hate him after he forced that kiss on her.

He wouldn't blame her.

And still he still took pleasure in recalling her response, that she hadn't pulled away first. How ripe her mouth had felt, soft and warm beneath his. He'd imagined kissing her in such a manner for so many years, but not under such circumstances.

"If you're giving me kittens to make up for being so awful," she began, "don't bother."

"I would never," he said, his throat unexpectedly tight. Vulnerable, that's what he felt. And then he realized why.

Across the room, his brown cloak was in full view along with his walking stick, both set across a chair. Damn it, he'd forgotten to put them away after the distraction of the kittens. There was no way for him to hide either without drawing attention to them. The walking stick's gold tip especially seemed to gleam in the candlelight.

"So now you're speaking to me?" she said.

"For the moment, yes."

He felt childish. Anxious. His signet ring felt strange on his hand. He'd grown used to her wearing it. But it was more than this—he glanced anew at the cloak and walking stick.

Still, she didn't flee from the room. Didn't run out the door. Nor did she seem to notice his cloak and walking stick. Instead, she knelt on the floor beside him, avoiding his gaze.

She picked up a kitten. Two. The others crawled into her lap.

A corner of her mouth lifted. And then he recalled everything he ever believed about her before she broke his heart. That Angela Bartham was made of rainbows, kittens, and sugar. Ballet slippers and sonatas and moonlight. No woman could live up to such adulation. Letter or no, he'd been unfair to her. Unforgiving. Merciless.

How wrong he'd been.

Angela's tone was studiously disaffected. "Where did the kittens come from?"

"Dubois found them in the kitchen pantry. He promptly had a sneezing fit and fled."

"Poor Dubois! I suppose we're down to the invisible servants then."

"For the time being." He had no idea she thought of them that way. He'd just been glad they'd been so discreet.

Angela at last met his gaze. Her lovely blue eyes appeared weighed by exhaustion. "The grey cat in the garden?"

Sunny shrugged. "If she's their mother, she appears to have abandoned them. I'll look for her in the morning. See if I can encourage a family reunion."

Angela tutted. "Poor kittens. No parents. No family."

There were five kittens in total. Not newborn, but not grown. Probably just over two months old. They mewed softly, their mouths opening and shutting like guppies, he thought.

"We should get them milk," he said. "Let's take them into the kitchen." That would gain him the opportunity to hide his cloak and walking stick.

She appeared surprised by his concern for them. He supposed he'd proven himself otherwise of late.

She rubbed her nose against the tiniest one, which was a tortoiseshell, and cooed. "So tiny. So sweet."

So vulnerable, Sunny thought again…but this time he knew he was thinking of Angela, not himself.

I treated her like I was a monster. A beast.

He knew what had gotten into him. Jealousy. Desire. Pain. And he'd lashed out at her and she'd fled. He'd followed her to make sure she was safe, but he didn't stop her when she'd gone into La Fleur Interdite. He hadn't, for he feared her seeing him and knowing he cared.

He'd never have been able to forgive himself had anything had happened to her. He'd never be able to tell her that. No, his pride precluded it.

But she'd returned safe. Alive. While she was gone, he felt as though he'd been cursed by a spell. And now the spell had broken, leaving him surrounded by hungry kittens and filled with remorse.

He felt like himself again. However, in recovering himself, he realized the cruel mess he'd made.

And so he would have to suffer through the mess. His revenge.

~

She took off her coat and gathered the kittens into her arms as though they were a bouquet of flowers. She flowed in her graceful way into the kitchen, where a fire still burned. Once she turned her back, he quickly threw the cloak and walking stick beneath the chair, where it would appear less obvious. Sunny had no choice but to follow, unable to let her out of his sight. Fearful she'd disappear again.

She fetched milk and poured some in a saucer.

"Now that we're speaking, you haven't been honest with me," she accused. She set the kittens on the long wooden table that had seen better days. The kittens immediately clustered around the saucer of milk, their mews silenced for the moment.

His heart stuttered. She'd recognized him despite the cloak.

"What makes you think I haven't been honest?" he sidestepped.

Angela appeared as if she was about to say one thing, but reconsidered.

"I met Hélène."

This he did not expect. Then he remembered: amid the fighting with Angela, he'd missed his dinner with her. He'd been so distracted…or perhaps he'd wanted to be distracted, if he was to be honest. Hélène must be furious. How wrongly he'd treated her.

"When? How?"

"She rescued me in her carriage."

That's where Angela had disappeared to—Hélène must have been on her way to the chateau to confront him. He expected she'd turned around after encountering Angela. (Again, his fault.)

He affected innocence. "You needed to be rescued?"

"I wandered somewhere I shouldn't have. A café where I was unwelcome." Reluctantly: "Someone may have recognized me."

Usually Willie didn't write about scandals from across the Channel. Even if he knew who she was, Sunny suspected Willie's interest in Angela was because of her beauty.

Still, she'd been in danger because of his temper. To make amends, he wanted to drop to his knees before her like a knight of old. To beg forgiveness for all he'd done. To tell her, *Yes, I know you can love. Just not me.*

He couldn't. And now here they were.

"It's unlikely," he reassured. "You wouldn't have wandered into that café if I hadn't lost my temper." He forced himself to say the words that were so difficult for him. "Angela, I'm so sorry. I was very wrong to say what I did."

"Is that an apology I hear?" she mocked.

"It is. I was such an ass tonight."

"Yes, you are an ass," Angela agreed. "While you're at it, you can also apologize to Hélène. You were to have dinner with her tonight—"

"I was preoccupied with you. You stomped off."

"Because I broke your stupid rule about not leaving the chateau grounds?"

"No. Because I feared something might happen to you. Because I knew I said something unforgivable." His voice was very small.

"That's no excuse. You should have sent Hélène a note."

He flailed his arms. "How? Remember, no servants. Only kittens."

"And you were courting her when you married me! Talk about being scandalous. Cruel." Her voice broke. "I now know I owe you a greater debt than I realized, Hélène too. I hadn't known you were courting."

Hélène told her about their relationship. Well, only what he deserved.

"It's not what you think, Angela. My situation with Hélène is…complicated."

"Generally it's fairly clear what a courtship with the intent to wed is, except in our situation."

"And what exactly is our situation? Marriage of convenience? Farce involving gentleman callers? A way station until Carles untangles himself from his mess?" He couldn't resist the question, as unkind as it was.

Angela set her head in her hands. He'd upset her again.

Shit, now I've done it.

"Angela, I'm sorry. Should I apologize again? Go find more kittens? I know I've been at my worst tonight."

"Yes, you have been. But no, it's not you, though I appreciate the apology." A hint of a smile. "That makes three apologies from you tonight. Apologies suit you."

"A fourth apology then. I apologize for kissing you." He didn't regret it though, wrong as he'd been.

"It's not that either."

"Is it Hélène? I intend to make it up to her. More. She deserves better. Or the mirrored salon?" After all, that had started their argument in the first place.

She finally met his gaze, her eyes weighed with emotion. "You're right. I-I didn't love Carles." Her tone grew earnest. "It's so complicated…but you should know my reasons for refusing your proposal, why I accepted Carles instead…and why it had nothing to do with you."

Now it was Sunny's turn to sit down.

I've a blow. A pain. But he resolved to bear it. No more cruelty. No more jealousy.

While they were speaking, one by one the candles in the kitchen had dosed—he hadn't thought to bring in an oil lamp. They were plunged into darkness when the last candle in the kitchen blew out, snuffed by wind sweeping down the chimney, leaving them in darkness save for the fireplace, which still glowed. It would have been terribly romantic…except it wasn't. For a February night, the wind was particularly noisy in that gothic manner he'd grown to love, being so close to the Bois de Boulogne.

The wind grew louder. Wilder. But he didn't mind.

"So uncomplicate things for me, Angela," he said at last, his voice rough. "Pretend I'm your friend, like I once was. Confide in me like you might have before we married."

"I can't," was all she said.

He yearned to press for an explanation. He didn't—he'd done enough damage for one night. He should just be thankful she hadn't recognized him or his cloak. Anyway, the mantel clock chimed midnight from the hall, breaking the impasse. By then, the kittens had slipped into a milk-induced nap. They piled together inside a wicker basket lined with a tea towel. One of them mewed, fostering a tenderness in Sunny he thought he'd lost in the past year.

Without another word, Angela gathered the basket of kittens. She turned to go upstairs to the bedroom where she'd sleep alone, but stopped.

Sunny's heart thumped. Was she going to say something more?

"My shawl. I left it on the table."

"I'll get it," he offered, just as she stumbled against him.

Into his arms.

She only remained in his embrace for the briefest moment before she pulled away with a murmured apology. But it was enough time for him to inhale the curve of her neck, her hair. To recall what it was like to kiss her.

He could smell the lavender soap she used to wash her hair. The cool scent of air from the outside world, where she'd run after he'd been so cruel. She reminded him of rain and sunshine, flowers and grass. The world he'd turned his back on when she'd broken his heart.

And then she was gone, along with the basket of kittens.

～

He'd followed me tonight, Angela thought as she laid in bed. *It was him in the cloak—I could swear it.*

That was one reason she'd been so tempted to confess about Philippe. Somehow, once she realized he'd rescued her at La Fleur Interdite, she felt she owed him an explanation why she'd refused his proposal to accept Carles instead. To confess her secret about Philippe.

For all of Sunny's gruffness, he'd protected her. She'd noticed the cloak and walking stick in the entryway, which led her to recalling how he'd threatened Carles on her wedding day. But why the disguise? The subterfuge? He'd acted as her friend, not her enemy. Yet he refused to admit such.

Angela remained awake for far later than she wished, even after she settled the kittens at the foot of her bed. They mewed softly in protest before settling back into sleep. Outside, the wind still rushed, the trees knocking against the walls of the chateau.

She supposed her insomnia was due to the drama of the evening. There was much to mull between the revelation Sunny had been courting someone, the violence she found at La Fleur Interdite, the knowledge he'd broken another woman's heart to rescue her from scandal. The kiss he'd given her, which she still couldn't set from her mind. The traitor she'd been to Philippe's memory.

But it was more than this.

He still cares about me. This felt a miracle greater than any she'd expected.

And then she knew: she still cared too.

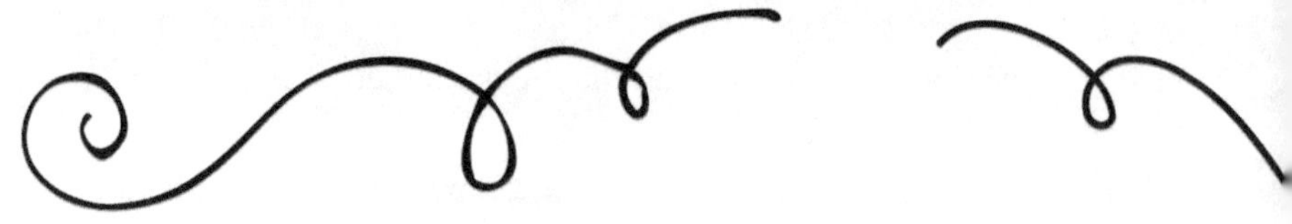

CHAPTER 15

In the morning, Angela didn't delay. She began clearing out the mirrored salon after breakfast. She yanked dust clothes off furniture. She managed to find cleaning implements and a bucket, which she filled with soapy water. She even sang as she swept cobwebs from corners, with the kittens scrambling at her feet.

That was the thing about Angela. Despite the melee at La Fleur Interdite, despite Sunny's unkindness, she was resilient.

So cheerful, he thought. *It's sickening.*

As for Sunny, he was miserable. He hadn't gone to Hélène after Angela went upstairs with the kittens. Nor had he sent a note to apologize. Instead, he'd sat for hours in the library, seized by an impulse. He could propose they burn her awful letter, start anew. Plus, if he was honest, he hoped she might slip and reveal what was bothering her—she'd seemed so close to a confession last night. If she hadn't loved Carles, had there been someone else?

He'd lost his nerve.

The clock struck a bright ten in the morning. So damn early. Glowering from the hallway, Sunny stifled a yawn as he watched her clean. He should go to bed—it was his turn between the sheets —but found he couldn't look away from her. Lord knew he was exhausted enough to sleep for a week after the turmoil of the previous evening. How had she recovered so quickly?

"My lord, if you will," Dubois interrupted in a low tone. "If I may have a word in private."

"What is it now?" Sunny grumbled. Dubois had returned despite his allergies to the kittens. The poor man's eyes were swollen red, his nose dripping. His loyalty was impressive.

"I can hear you there!" Angela called from inside the mirrored salon, affecting her sweetest voice. "Are you spying on me, Sunderland? Perhaps you've a secret to share?"

"Heavens, no!"

Again, he wondered if she'd seen the cloak, known it was him. Hadn't he used the walking stick on Carles at the wedding too? His methods were too consistent.

"Sunderland, you need to become more discreet with your moods. Otherwise, how shall we survive the rest of the year here?"

"That's your problem, countess, not mine."

She tsked. "And to think you were full of apologies last night, my lord."

"I did mean them." Sunny countered. "I also gave you kittens."

"And I accepted your apologies, though I must admit preferring kittens over them. Yet you're the one who sounds moody, not me. La la la!"

She offered a little pirouette around the mop. Sunny resisted the urge to grab the mop from her, especially when the kittens batted at it. One jumped onto Angela's skirt as though it were a sail. A tuxedoed one. She picked the kitten up and kissed its little nose before settling it on a sofa. Dubois raised an aristocratic eyebrow.

Sunny grumbled, "I never agreed you could use the mirrored salon." He knew he was being ridiculous, but he felt as though he was losing control of the chateau's secrets.

"Maybe not, but you apologized with kittens! That's nearly the same as a yes," she sang out. "Anyway, aren't you supposed to be sleeping? That bed will be mine soon enough."

How could he sleep when she was singing? And he was fretting over her cheerfulness?

"No need for you to be here. Your bed awaits," Angela called. "Or shall I offer another dance for you? Perhaps one about a gentleman caller? Are you still ruminating on that?"

Damn it, he'd sworn not to bring up the gentleman caller again. Here she was tempting him.

He folded his arms before his chest. "Remember, annulment, not scandal."

"What's all this about?" Dubois asked, concerned.

Angela ignored his question. "I have no interest in scandal, Sunderland. Rest assured, I'm counting the days until we can go our separate ways. But until then—" she gestured around the mirrored salon "—this will fill my time nicely. Unless you prefer to entertain me yourself?"

"I'd rather visit with the kittens," Sunny growled.

Angela brightened. "I'll introduce you if you like."

"No kitten visits," Dubois interrupted, sniffling. "Can't they go outside?"

"No!" Angela protested. "They're mine."

Dubois tried again. "If you please, my lord—"

Now it was Sunny's turn to ignore Dubois. "You named the kittens?"

Angela smiled. "Of course! I'll bring them with me when I return to England. Let's see, the calico is Clover, then there's Dandelion, Ivy, Marigold—well, Mari for short, that's the smaller tuxedo—and Hyssop."

As she recited their names, Sunny felt his chest puff up. He had pleased her after all.

"What gender are they?" he asked just as the calico began climbing his trouser leg. He hadn't considered the ramifications of *that*.

"I'm sure they're all girls—I checked." Angela continued, "Oh, I should warn you I have callers coming. Perhaps later today, tomorrow. Worry not, no gentlemen. A lady, I think. Maybe two. Before you fret, they have no idea who I am. Surely that doesn't break your second rule, Sunderland?"

Sunny disengaged the calico from his leg. Such sharp little claws. It distracted him from a tap on his shoulder. Dubois again.

"My lord," he said in a low tone. "I must insist you come with me."

~

"What is this about callers?" Sunny asked once they were alone in the library. "She says two? Or are there more?"

"I tried to explain to you earlier but—" Dubois gave way to a large sneeze "—they're coming to fit her for shoes and clothes. I've done all I can to contain the risk. I told them she's Mademoiselle Dubois, my daughter."

"You couldn't get us another bed," Sunny grumbled, "but you can get her shoes."

"One can always share a bed, but not shoes. Such are the priorities of Parisians." Dubois shrugged in his precise way. "If it makes the situation any easier, I've been assured the new bed will arrive in a week."

"Not soon enough."

In the two months they'd continued sharing the bed, Sunny had grown to know Angela's scent, to find strands of her silver-blonde hair on his pillow…which led to other, more intimate considerations he wished had been banished when she'd broken his heart. To his dismay, he regularly woke up painfully aroused.

He told himself it meant nothing. It was like the cats rutting outside in the garden. Biological. Not emotional. And now he that he'd kissed her—well, that didn't equate into things. Not at all.

"I don't care about the money, mind. But why does she need new clothing? It's not as though she's going to be exploring Paris."

"The clothing is for dancing, my lord."

"You mean toe shoes? Tutus?"

"I presume so, my lord. Plus spring is coming. She only has winter clothing, she says. Surely you don't want your wife—"

"She's not really my wife."

"If you say so."

Upstairs, he heard the clatter from the mirrored room. It sounded like Angela was moving furniture.

Sunny frowned. "She's not planning to dance in public, do you think? She couldn't be that unwise." As improbable as the logistics were for such an endeavor, who the hell knew with Angela?

Dubois let out an awkward laugh. "I can't imagine so. However, I found out about her gentleman caller. He's a family friend. I made discreet inquiries."

Sunny knew as much but yearned for details. "Tell me about him."

Dubois explained that Angela's friend was none other than one Luke Ward, a reporter from London—well, he had been until he turned to reviewing art in Paris. Sunny recalled Ward was a close friend of Musa's husband, Seb, who came from a more bohemian milieu than Sunny was accustomed.

Journalist bad. Family friend good. Did they cancel each other out?

Dubois reassured, "I believe Ward has no romantic interest in the countess, if it matters. I found this in her possession in her coat pocket. I believe he brought it yesterday."

Dubois offered a folded sheet of newspaper.

"Snooping, Dubois?" Sunny felt secretly pleased. Such loyalty.

"I think you'll approve, my lord."

Sunny grabbed the newspaper. The London *Times* article was barely a paragraph long. The headline said THE EARL OF SUNDERLAND ABROAD WITH BRIDE. The article had no mention of Angela at all. It was as though they'd never married.

Once Sunny finished reading, a wave of sadness struck him. How ridiculous. He should be happy. Relieved.

"This is good. Very good," he forced out. "And my bride is unnamed—she could be anyone really."

As soon as he said this, a disconcerting thought rose.

That's why Angela's so cheerful this morning. She sees an escape from our marriage. How could he blame her?

Sunny asked, "How was this done?"

"Monsieur Ward wrote it, I presume," Dubois replied. "However, even if Monsieur Ward is a friend of her family, he's still a journalist. *Le quatrième état.* He's helped you now, but will he in the future? If you wish to avoid difficulties, keep an eye on him. Think of your legacy as the Earl of Sunderland."

Legacy. That's all Sunny ever thought of these days. Along with revenge and secrets involving cloaks and walking sticks. And forbidden kisses.

"In the meantime, if I may be so bold, I advise you to let the countess have what she wants. The toe shoes, the tutus. She'll be happy, you'll be left alone. You made a concession with the mirrored salon—"

"I didn't make a concession. She took it."

"Still, that should satisfy her for some time. She won't go nosing in places you'd prefer her not to."

The greenhouse—Sunny didn't need to say it. It had shocked him when she'd mentioned it. The thought of her inside it made him feel so incredibly vulnerable.

As though anticipating his employer's concerns, Dubois said, "Perhaps we need a higher fence around the greenhouse?"

"Is that possible, considering you can't even get a bed here? Anyway, that'll only draw attention to it."

Dubois' reply was overtaken by a sneeze of the most violent variety. Another sneeze. A third.

"Never mind." Sunny patted the older man on his shoulder. "Go rest. We'll speak later."

Once Dubois departed, Sunny turned to correspondence regarding his estate, all the things required of him as an earl in exile. It helped fill the empty days, now that he was trapped here with Angela. Dubois had found a way for him to take care of his responsibilities without revealing his location. Especially necessary when it came to his mother, who was no doubt distressed Sunny had left England again without notifying her. So far, she hadn't found him.

Or so he'd thought until that moment. His stomach churned, for in a new pile of letters, he made out a too familiar hand.

Sunny tore open the letter from his mother. It must have arrived earlier, when he was distracted with Angela and the kittens in the mirrored salon.

Sunderland, she'd written:

After much trouble and many inquiries, I finally figured where you are: Papa's chateau. (May he and your brother rest in everlasting peace!) This is despite that dreadful Musa Atkinson, who was no help at all. I was forced to pay her a call to find out where you ran off with Angela Bartham. (I refuse to call her your wife— you know too well what I think.) Mrs. Atkinson was most reluctant to tell me anything of substance though I pressed her repeatedly.

Still, I have my ways. But why did you have to go to France?

Rest assure I shan't share your location with the press, though they still clamber for information. You cannot imagine how it tries my nerves! I've a headache most days that nothing can soothe—but enough about me.

Let me assure I have done all I can to preserve your legacy to our family from being tainted by your association with Angela Bartham. I've informed the press I was not at liberty to reveal your bride's identity, but I could assure it was not a Bartham. (Yes, I know the newspapers reported otherwise, but I informed them posthaste this was a grand joke on your part. Still, it has been most trying to keep them all at bay.) My denial of your marriage will make it all the easier when you finally remove your Great Mistake from our family tree...which brings me to the reason for this missive.

Last week, I spoke yet again to our family solicitor. After much back and forth, we've come up with a plan to rescue you from Angela Bartham. It's quite simple: first, we secretly annul the marriage. (We'll pay the Barthams whatever it takes.) Then I'll find someone else for you to marry, assuming you haven't consummated your union. (If you have, no one need know, most of all me. Discretion is so important in these sordid situations.)

A replacement bride! It's rather brilliant, I think. With this in mind, I have several debutantes in mind, all of whom can be trusted to remain silent in exchange for a title and a generous allowance. More importantly, they'd make a far more suitable wife than that Bartham adventuress.

I urge the greatest haste on this. The sooner we set the wheels into motion, the sooner you can return home from France. No one will ever guess the truth.

From your most concerned mother,
Eliza, Dowager Countess of Sunderland

Sunny paced back and forth in the library. For once, his mother was right: if he returned to England with another bride, no one would believe Angela had ever married him.

It bothered Sunny to be on the same side as the dowager countess, however inadvertently. However, there was no way he'd let his mother choose his bride. Plus, if he was to be honest, he still resented how little his mother mourned his father.

Hélène. She's the answer. They'd discussed marriage in the first place, before all had gone to hell in that Kensington church on a December morning. It wasn't love between them. Nor was it lust—how could it be? It was understanding, which was often as precious and hard to find.

No doubt she was still furious at him, but how could he blame her? He'd have to find some way to make it up to her. Beg her, if necessary. She had needs. He could fulfill them.

But first, to the greenhouse.

To be safe, he locked the door to the library, though Angela was upstairs in the mirrored salon. He grabbed his walking stick, just in case.

He approached the second bookshelf on the wall without windows.

The latched lock to the secret passage and greenhouse was hidden behind a thick copy of Hugo's *Les Misérables* on the third shelf from the bottom. However, it was a Greek translation, of all things. His father had chosen such out of caution, thinking no one would ever choose to read it.

When his father purchased the chateau after Robert's death, the former earl had been concerned about uprisings in Paris; hence, he found the secret passage deeply appealing. The chateau's original owner had built the passage, which led beyond the greenhouse onto the Bois de Boulogne, allowing escape if necessary. Sunny had heard of a similar hidden passage at Versailles, which had saved lives during the Revolution. Such structures were akin to priest holes tucked inside English manor houses, used by Catholic clergy during the reign of Elizabeth I.

The irony of escaping into what was essentially a glass house did not go unnoticed by Sunny. Sunny, however, used the greenhouse for another purpose, one he didn't share with anyone save Dubois. The consideration of others discovering his secret abode brought up dark memories of old humiliations and vulnerabilities. Well, no longer. He'd changed…and it was due to Hélène as much as Angela.

The bookshelf easily slid open once Sunny turned the latch. Today, the passage smelled particularly moist and green. Spring was in the air, he sensed it. Whatever season or time of day, the passage was always dark, for it was walled in mahogany, though on bright days one could make out a faint glow emanating from the greenhouse. No matter: Sunny could find his way even with his eyes closed.

Once inside the secret passage, Sunny slid the bookshelf neatly back into place. He hurried. With luck, Hélène wouldn't turn him away.

CHAPTER 16

IN ALL OF Sunny's fantasies about his reunion with Hélène, he never expected her to set a knife against his throat. Nor did he expect her to pin him against the doorway of her rather shabby flat on the Left Bank near the Champ de Mars.

Her greeting was equally welcoming.

"You don't deserve to be in my presence," she said in rapid French. "You didn't show last night."

Sunny shouldn't have been surprised. He couldn't blame Hélène for being peeved at him after all he'd done. (Perhaps *peeved* was an understatement.) He'd hoped the out-of-season irises from the greenhouse would smooth things over…along with groveling for forgiveness.

"Look, darling!" He shoved the flowers in her direction. "Your favorites!"

The irises were a rich purple so deep they were nearly black. Gorgeous and dramatic. Like Hélène herself.

She didn't remove the knife. "I anticipated you'd show up once you heard I met your bride—and outside La Fleur Interdite, of all places. What a scene! Did you see Willie's article in *La Tête-à-Tête* today? They're closed now, thanks to her. Here, read it."

Hélène waved the article in front of Sunny's face with her free hand.

SCANDAL AND DESTRUCTION AMID CLOAKED CHAOS!

Last night at La Fleur Interdite, a gentleman wearing a brown cloak invaded the popular café and attempted to bludgeon your faithful correspondent whilst we were in intimate conversation with a mysterious blonde beauty. Though we escaped with nary a bruise, La Fleur Interdite did not fare as well. It is expected to be closed for a week until repairs are made and fixtures replaced.

The reason for the attack remains undetermined. However, one anonymous source questions whether the blonde beauty might have some connection to a certain scandalous English lady who made a certain advantageous marriage shortly before the New Year. If so, one must question her judgement for loitering in cafés during the dark hours…though we would not be averse to meeting her again in private.

Sunny didn't have to see *La Tête-à-Tête* to know what happened last night at La Fleur Interdite. Still, he was surprised to see it in print.

"It's hard to read with a knife at my throat. He didn't identify Angela?"

Hélène let the article flutter to the carpet. "Not by name. But insinuated, yes."

Shit. All the more reason to make amends to Hélène.

"Let me go, darling. I'm not here about Angela. I've come to apologize for not showing last night. Really."

It seemed all he did these days was apologize.

"Why is this apology any different from your previous ones? Just because you swanned in here with irises this time doesn't make things different. Anyway, you look little better than an animal.

What have you done to yourself?" She flicked her knife against his chin. "You know I prefer you clean shaven. "

Sunny forced what he hoped was a winning smile. "No need for violence."

"It's not violence unless I use my knife."

At last she released him; Sunny nearly fell to the floor. Once he recovered, he said, "Let's not use the knife then. It's not my favorite weapon."

"Favorite weapon. . . " She laughed, leading him inside her rather shabby sitting room. "You are witty! I miss the old days. Remember?"

How could he forget? In the time he'd known her, Hélène had proven herself a worthy ally in love and adversity, one consideration in offering for her hand. For all of her drama, she had a good heart. A soft side she rarely showed. She was just unpredictable. Tempestuous. It was appealing, if one didn't mind feeling emotionally seasick at times.

More importantly, she'd saved him when he was at his lowest. If he was to be honest, he owed her his life, and he'd repaid her with abandonment and humiliation. Such was Angela's hold on him.

"Well, what is your favorite weapon then?" she teased.

Sunny pulled the rapier hidden within his walking stick. He nodded in her direction and raised it.

"Shall we? For the sake of old days?"

A slow smile spread across Hélène's face; she couldn't resist a challenge. She glanced down at her gown, which was of a deep crimson brocade. It had clearly seen better days, like her sitting room.

She offered a moue. "You're in trousers, Sunderland. Unfair advantage."

"You wouldn't let a silly thing like skirts get in your way, will you? Anyway, I can buy you a new gown."

That's what he'd said to her the morning of Angela's wedding, he recalled too late. But Hélène didn't take offence. Instead, she slashed her knife across her skirts just above her knees.

The satin fell to the floor, revealing neatly shaped legs clad in bright violet stockings and satin garters.

"Now it's a fair fight," she said, stepping out of the fabric circle. She set down her knife and drew a rapier hidden beneath the chaise longue. "Ready?"

"Ready. *En garde!*"

Fencing was the only sport he'd excelled at while at school, but fencing with Hélène had refined his skills to a new level. They were well matched, something Sunny always appreciated about Hélène. She was no simpering English miss seeking to land an earl for the sake of social climbing. He'd fenced often enough with her to know what to expect. She was only two inches shorter, but had long arms and a quick brain. Sunny, however, had the advantage of strength and persistence.

She taunted, "I promise not to slice up your pretty face, *chéri*, though you deserve it."

"Pretty face? I think you must be referring to yourself, darling. Gentle now!"

"I'll show you gentle!" She thrust a parry in his direction.

As they fenced, it always shocked Sunny how *normal* Hélène made him feel, as though he wasn't the Virgil mocked at Eton and Oxford, or the Sunderland disdained in London save by those who sought him out for social advantage. (Well, if *normal* was comprised of sword fights and insults.) With Hélène, you always knew what she thought. She hated you or she accepted you. She was going to stab you or love you…except he knew she didn't love him that way. But he felt similarly about her.

It was refreshing. Freeing. Something he thought he could take a lifetime—unless she stabbed him first.

All marriages of convenience should be so uncomplicated, he decided.

"You're slowing down," she accused.

"I'm wearing you down. A difference."

"Boring," she scoffed.

Back and forth they went, their rapiers clashing, their words tossing, using all the available corners of the room. There were few belongings to get in the way; Sunny knew Hélène had been forced to sell many of them. Nor would any servants interrupt. She'd let her last maid go some months ago. As they fenced, he also knew how her brain worked: she'd aim to surprise him, but he'd overtake her through sheer resilience. They were a good partnership. In Hélène's world, Sunny was dashing, desperate, and brave…and so was she.

"Tell me when you're ready to surrender," he said, raising his rapier.

"I'll never surrender." She lifted her rather sharp chin. "Will you?"

And then she delivered the *coup de grâce*, just when he'd been distracted by a bell ringing. Someone at the door, probably a bill collector.

"You win," he said, sidling away from the rapier pointed at his heart.

"Of course I win…unless you let me win." She scowled. "You didn't, did you?"

"Never! I wouldn't insult you."

"Good."

Out of breath, she collapsed onto the chaise, one of the few places to sit in the nearly empty room.

"Come then. Talk to me. Apologize. That's why you're here, *n'est-ce pas?*" She patted the seat next to her. "Yes, I'm still furious with you. But I must admit I'm glad to see you despite everything. You amuse me. It's a shame you're not a woman, Sunderland."

"Can't help that." He settled beside her, inhaling her exotic perfume. It was a bit much. "How is Julie?"

Hélène's face darkened. "Not well." She brushed a sudden tear away with the back of a hand. "It didn't have to be this way." She threw a pointed look in his direction.

"I know, I know." Sunny panged with guilt. All things considered, she'd been very generous to even allow him to speak to her, let alone fence.

"I'm back now," he said gently. "I've a proposition for you."

She rose from the chaise. "I don't want to hear it. You let me down. Julie too." She pointed to the door. "It was amusing fencing with you. You can see yourself out—"

"Just listen. My marriage is not what you think."

"I know what I think," Hélène snapped. "You still love her."

"Not anymore. A childhood infatuation."

"Don't lie! It's me you're talking to. Every time you speak of her—"

"I know, I know. It makes you angry."

"But I *like* being angry," Hélène replied in a cool tone. "You deserve my anger, you bastard. Now my situation is even more dire."

"I'm truly sorry, Hélène. I can fix it."

Hélène waved her hands. "Too late. You're married now."

"The marriage isn't real."

"You forget I was in the church when you exchanged vows."

"It's a marriage of convenience."

Hélène laughed in disbelief. "So your marriage of convenience undermined the possibility of our marriage of convenience?"

This was getting to be ridiculous. "She's agreed to an annulment."

"Let me guess: then I'm to marry you as your second choice? How insulting."

"Second time's the charm?"

Hélène slapped him. "This isn't funny."

"Nor is it to me." He rubbed his cheek. "Ow, did you have to do that?"

How could he explain his marital situation without making it seem even more of a farce than it was? When he'd come to Hélène, he'd aimed to suggest exactly what his mother had written: that they wed as soon as the annulment was finalized. He'd return to England with Hélène as his countess, presenting her to the press as a *fait accompli*. True love and all that. So what if she was tempestuous and a mite unpredictable?

Hélène would make a fine countess for all her ways. He cared for her. Respected her. Appreciated her beauty. She was also willing to give him an heir despite their lack of sexual compatibility. She wasn't his soulmate, but she was his equal. That would have to be enough since Angela could never be his true wife.

Anyway, Hélène had her own reasons for wanting their marriage. Without marriage, there wasn't much he could do to help her save offer funds, which were a sop on a gaping wound. Save for the occasional gown, she usually turned down his offerings with a terse "I'm not your mistress."

If all went as planned, no one would be any wiser he'd ever wed Angela. Even better, he could arrange for the annulment as soon as possible, rather than wait the full year out. Despite his mother's dislike of the French, he suspected she'd prefer a French woman with a noble past to a scandalous Bartham.

Hélène considered her knife anew. "Even if you hadn't insulted me, you're of no interest. You're married."

"Annulment, remember? Anyway, I wouldn't have been your interest even I didn't have a wife."

He'd known all along that Hélène had no desire for men…but she did have an interest in protecting her lover, who was being blackmailed by Willie. Hélène had done all she could to protect Julie, but there was only so much two unwed women with limited resources could do. As a result, they were being systematically ruined. Hence, the shabby flat, the out-of-season gowns. The desperation.

One reason they'd discussed Sunny marrying Hélène was to stop the blackmail. Surely Willie wouldn't dare once Hélène was attached to British nobility.

It wouldn't have mattered as much except Hélène's lover had a daughter due to be launched in society—a daughter Julie had secretly given birth to after being seduced by a much-older rake. The baby had been raised by another aristocratic family. Céline had grown into a lovely young woman who believed Julie a family friend, not her mother.

Julie loved her daughter desperately. Protectively. Céline's future would be promising as long as no one found out about her scandalous parentage. How could Sunny not be sympathetic? In Julie and Céline, he thought of Clio and her daughters: women aligned against a world ruled by careless men.

"What's all this chatter?" a sweet voice asked from the hall.

An exquisitely beautiful woman entered the sitting room. She was about half a decade older than Hélène and delicately thin, with thick ebony hair and tawny-brown skin. Julie du Moreau, Hélène's beloved.

If Hélène was like a flamboyant peacock, Julie reminded Sunny of an anxious dove flittering from branch to branch. Systematic blackmail would do that to a woman.

Julie offered Sunny an annoyed glare. "You've returned. Back to break more promises?" To Hélène: "Why is he here, *mon amore?* I thought you'd exiled him."

Though her words were bold, Julie's eyes darted around the room, as though imagining invisible threats in corners.

Hélène greeted her lover with a warm embrace. "I'd thought so too. He wants me to take him back. What do you think?"

Julie answered, "Tell me, how can he take back what he never truly had?"

"Exactly, *mon amour.*" Hélène waved in dismissal. "Go, Sunderland. Surely you can find some other girl to marry. You're an earl, after all."

Sunny swallowed back his irritation. If it wasn't for Hélène, he didn't want to think where he'd be. Anyway, how could he trust another woman, let alone woo her under such circumstances?

Sunny said, "I'm choosing you, Hélène Charlotte de Castel-d'Albret, as my wife. My countess. And I think you understand why."

"Because you feel guilt," Hélène replied in a bored tone. "That's all."

"Not only guilt. Affection. Desperation."

"Now he's honest!" Julie interjected. "Do go on, Sunderland."

"Glad this is amusing you," Sunny said, understanding he needed Julie's approval as much as Hélène's. "What would it take for you to marry me, Hélène? Tell me. I'll give you whatever you want. My protection. Title. Wealth."

"Anything?" Hélène asked, arching a brow.

"Anything," Sunny agreed.

At last, Hélène nodded. "Very well then. Revenge."

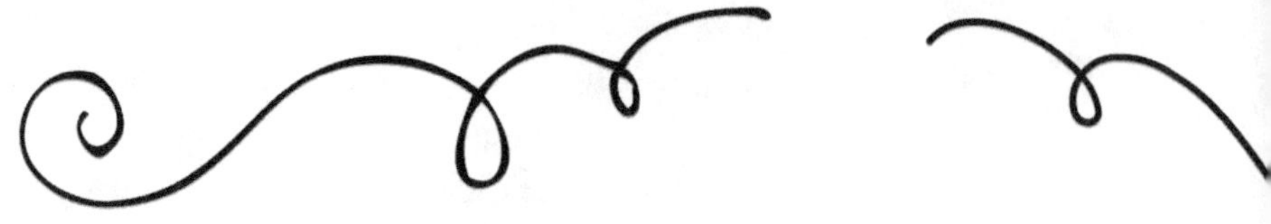

CHAPTER 17

A SCANT HOUR LATER, Sunny made his way home to the chateau. He didn't enter from the greenhouse passage this time—anyway, no need with the irises deployed on Hélène's behalf. The chateau looked so different in the daylight than it did at night. It appeared bright, not gothic. Welcoming, not foreboding. But that was because everything felt different. Nostalgia, that's what he felt. Nostalgia for the life he'd led before he'd gone to visit Hélène.

Same day, different life. Different bride.

I can't believe I agreed to Hélène's terms. But if that's what it takes...

The terms were one Sunny never imagined. He was to best Willie in a duel. *"It's not murder if it's a duel, Sunderland,"* Hélène said as though she was describing a jaunt in the park. *"All you need to do is challenge him over some insult. An affair of honor. You'd easily win. You'd also win the appreciation of half of Paris. They'd wish they had your nerve."*

"I'm not going to kill anyone," he'd answered.

Hélène shrugged. *"We'll have to see what happens, won't we?"*

When he'd gone begging for Hélène to consider his suit anew, he had no idea she would suggest such an undertaking. Even in his darkest moments, Sunny never considered using his rapier for bodily harm. Fencing was exercise, a way to calm his mind. To feel less dominated by the world.

And so Sunny's bargain with Hélène was settled with a handshake and his signet ring, which now rested on her hand instead of Angela's. As for when the duel would occur, that was up to Hélène.

"*When?*" he asked after she'd agreed to marry him.

"*When it's time,*" she answered.

There were several considerations. First, La Fleur Interdite needed to be reopened. Then Sunny had to insinuate himself into Willie's circle to lay the trap for the gossipmonger's fall. It would be too obvious if Hélène challenged him to a duel, too inviting of scandal. Though there'd been instances of women dueling in Paris, Hélène couldn't risk such. Not with Julie's situation as it was.

Months earlier, when Sunny had first discussed marriage with Hélène, it was with the understanding his title would protect Hélène and Julie. But in recent weeks, the situation had turned even more perilous for Julie and her daughter, Céline. Céline had become engaged to wed someone she loved. Someone who'd give her a good life. Sunny had seen Willie's behavior toward Angela. He'd wanted to throttle him. How would Willie torment Julie if he learned of Céline's future?

As Sunny approached the chateau, he glanced down at his walking stick, thinking of the rapier hidden inside. It was sharp, balanced, the finest francs could buy—he'd made sure of that. When he'd been at his absolute lowest, Hélène encouraged him to fence again to build his spirits. Now that same rapier would free Hélène and her lover from blackmail, if all went as planned.

If Sunny didn't end up killed himself.

I won't kill him, only scare him. That will have to be enough for Hélène.

Upon his return to the chateau, the kittens scampered to greet Sunny. Already they'd grown used to him, it seemed. Dubois was nowhere in sight—he probably fled to avoid the kittens—but

Angela's laughter rang down from the mirrored room. He supposed she was in the midst of being fitted for toe shoes and sundries. No matter what she'd find joy, even when trapped in a chateau with him.

He really had loved her so much. It hadn't been enough. No, *he* was never enough.

You'll feel better once you get some sleep. You'll figure a way out of this mess.

He went upstairs to the bedroom, where someone had made the bed during his absence. Angela, no doubt, for she'd left a fresh note on the pillow. It was written in pencil along the top of a piano score.

Sunderland,

Even if one is to dance alone, one still requires music. I hereby request the removal of the spinet from the music room to the mirrored salon. I'm sure you can comply with this simple request, given how generous you've been thus far.

Extremely respectfully yours etc,
Angela, Countess of Sunderland

PS: The kittens send their regards.

Sunny immediately recognized the score. Mozart, of all composers. His favorite movement from his favorite piano sonata, the adagio in E-Flat Major. She was needling him. Tempting him, damn it. He'd pushed music aside in recent years, especially after his father's death.

Against his will, he recalled the pleasure of playing the Mozart adagio years ago, when he was home from Oxford. Angela dancing to it…and now he was contemplating a duel to free her from their marriage. How things had changed.

He placed the sheet music neatly on top of the dresser before he settled into the bed with a grunt. Sleep would make everything better. His mood especially. Tomorrow he'd write his mother to move forward on the annulment. Tomorrow he'd tell Angela his plan to marry Hélène, though never about the duel. Nor would he tell Dubois—the duel would remain Sunny's secret.

Tomorrow would mark the beginning of the end of their marriage.

As for today, he left her a new note.

Countess,

Mozart is fine for some, but not for me. If I agree to your request for the spinet, in exchange I must insist you honor Rule #2 without deviation, especially regarding a certain café you recently frequented. A certain newspaper has taken note of your recent misadventure there—I've enclosed the article for your perusal.

Sorry to be the bearer of unpleasant news, but I'm sure you will agree discretion is required during these trying times. I trust the kittens will provide you with adequate company.

Yours etc,
Sunderland

In reply, Angela wrote only this:

Of course I will comply. Yes, the kittens are adequate company. In fact, they're delightful—thank you again.

Tomorrow became a week, two weeks, then a month. March arrived, bringing the end of winter. Sunny was relieved no further articles were published by Willie about Angela or about La Fleur Interdict. Nor did Luke Ward return for a visit—Sunny's last note must have set the fear of discovery into Angela. No matter: he still couldn't seem to tell her about Hélène and their plan to wed. Not that his path crossed with Angela's, though it could have if Sunny tried. He knew this was a situation that should be discussed in person, not in a note. *"By the way, I've found myself another bride so we can annul our marriage soonish. Problem solved, yes?"* wasn't going to work.

Anyway, he hadn't written Angela since her last note. He told himself he was too busy. Too distracted, for he spent his spare time practicing his fencing in the mirrored salon once Angela took over the bed. It would help to have a sparring partner, but he didn't dare return to Hélène lest she change her mind about their bargain.

In the meantime, he'd heard back from his mother, who'd been effusive in reassurances that the paperwork for the annulment would be taken care of immediately. *"I swear all will go well, Sunderland—I am so delighted!!!"* the dowager countess wrote in an exuberant hand. Sunny supposed annulments were two a penny these days, if one possessed noble blood. His mother had also enclosed a clipping of an article for which she'd agreed to be interviewed. Sunny scanned it, his mouth pursed. DOWAGER COUNTESS WELCOMES NEW BRIDE, the headline announced, accompanied by a flattering illustration of his mother clutching her favorite Pomeranian.

"My son is a most private person when it comes to his private life, as is his very private bride," she told some society rag. (Sunny resisted the urge to roll his eyes—how many times could a person use the word "private" in one sentence?) *"The Earl's announcement of Miss Angela Bartham as his bride was a jest on his part. The Earl and his new countess requested discretion until their return home. One must agree that a honeymoon is a sacred time. As his mother, I swore to honor my son's wishes."*

She must have paid well for the article's publication, Sunny decided. How else could the press not have located the wedding registry they signed? The special license? His mother had always been a mistress of manipulation.

"You must inform the countess of the change in plans, my lord,"

Dubois said one afternoon, soon after Sunny had awakened from his shift in the bed. "It would make your situation easier here if she were to know your misadventure will end soon. Consider her needs. She'll want to plan for her future."

"I know, I know. But I haven't seen her."

Angela was still avoiding him. Or was Sunny avoiding her? It was hard to tell. He supposed apologies and kittens only went so far…though he didn't sense the resentment he once had from her. In the scant hours when both were awake in the chateau, he often heard Angela in the mirrored salon, especially once he conceded to have the spinet moved. For all their ethereal grace, toe shoes were incredibly noisy. As for her piano playing, she wasn't very good. He suspected the music inspired her dancing more than anything else.

"I know what to do!" Dubois exclaimed, nudging Clover—that was the calico—off the bed with a sneeze. "I'll arrange a dinner for the two of you tomorrow night. You'll be forced to have a civil conversation for once. You can tell her about the annulment then."

Sunny grimaced at his coffee. "She won't consent to take a meal with me."

"Now that she's dancing, she's in a better mood."

Sunny set down the coffee and rose from the bed. Stretched. "Not possible. Remember, she sleeps when I'm awake. I sleep when she's awake. Sun and the moon. Never to meet."

This wasn't exactly true, but close enough.

"Not anymore." Dubois looked rather pleased with himself. "The new bed is due to arrive tomorrow morning."

Sunny scoffed, "I don't believe you."

"It's true, my lord."

"Really? After so long?"

"Really. Use that as an excuse to dine with her. If it helps, I'll issue the invitation." Dubois strode toward the door. "Here, I'll do it now."

"No!" Sunny pulled him back into the bedroom. "I'm telling you, she won't want to see me."

"You're probably right." Dubois cocked his head, frowning at Sunny. "Not if you're looking like this."

"Like what?"

Dubois shoved Sunny in front of the standing mirror. "For one, you could shave. You haven't bothered since you arrived here."

Sunny refused to look at himself. He knew what he'd see. Nothing to be done about it. He'd accepted he'd never be viewed as handsome among the *ton*.

"Whatever for? Better to hide my face."

"After you shave, you could use a hair trim."

"I prefer my hair long. It's the style, isn't it?"

"If one combs it, my lord." Dubois tutted. "And your clothes!"

Now Sunny was getting irritated. "I've plenty of stylish clothes. Mademoiselle de Castel-d'Albret chose them for me. She's excellent taste."

"It doesn't matter how *à la mode* your clothes are if you don't wear them, my lord. Most days I see you in the same trousers and waistcoat. Shirtsleeves, like a laborer." His voice lowered. "Or that old cloak when you go out."

"You're full of opinions today, Dubois. What other advice do you care to share? If I didn't know better, I'd think you were trying to get me to court her."

Dubois's laugh sounded a trifle uncomfortable to Sunny's ears. "Just to ease the situation with the countess. You haven't done well on your own—"

"Dubois!"

"I'm being honest. And on that front, perhaps consider offering a smile when you greet her tomorrow night."

This was going too far. "But I gave her kittens!"

"If I may be honest, even I tire of your grumpy routine. Your father, rest his soul, would be appalled—"

"My father would be appalled by me no matter what."

"That's not what I meant, my lord. Every time you speak to the countess, she's either provoking you because you're so difficult or she's running away in tears." Dubois let out a long sigh. "I understand the situation is uncomfortable. Unorthodox."

"It won't be unorthodox for much longer," Sunny retorted, his temper rising. He turned from the mirror. "Go then. Issue the invitation. Tomorrow night. Seven o'clock. I promise to be at my best." He nodded toward the dressing table. "I'll even groom myself for the occasion."

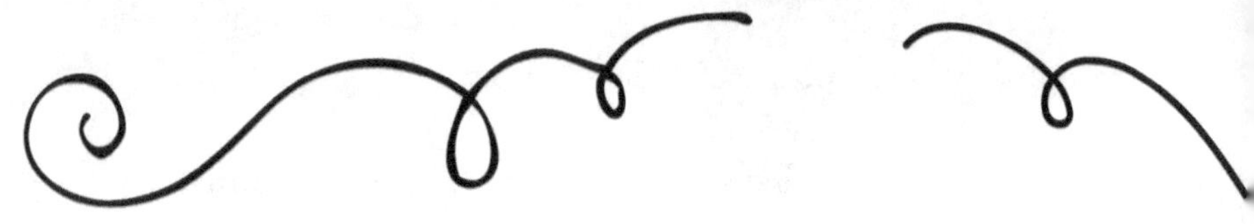

CHAPTER 18

Angela was surprised when Dubois issued Sunny's invitation to dinner. She accepted despite her sour mood. She'd received a letter from Musa that morning stating there was still no news from their mother regarding their father. Angela wished she could reach out to Luke Ward. Perhaps he could help—hadn't he located Papa in Cairo in the first place?—but this remained unwise.

Calm down, Angela, she told herself in an attempt to stir up her optimism. *You knew it might be a while before you'd hear anything. You need to be patient.*

But she'd been patient. No, more than patient. She still had months ahead of her in Paris. Months before she could leave her marriage without repercussions; months before she could see her family. Luckily, no further articles had been published about her misadventure at La Fleur Interdite, but Angela didn't trust the matter to be closed. From personal experience, she knew how quickly a scandal could grow from whispers.

Sunny must have sensed her heightened mood, for he behaved in a civil fashion when she appeared in the dining room at the stroke of seven. He'd even dressed in a stylish black jacket she recalled from their wedding. Beneath it, he wore a silk embroidered waistcoat that appeared so deep a red it was nearly sepia, a similarly hued necktie.

To her surprise, he'd also shaved, revealing his face for the first time in weeks; she'd grown used to seeing him obscured behind a thicket of a beard. Despite his dark clothing, he was clutching a kitten who was engaged in shedding fur all over him. Marigold, or Mari, as she called her, the other tuxedo cat. Angela watched Mari crawled up his arm, licking his bare cheek.

For a moment, Angela's heart lurched as she recalled her friend of so many years. His kindness. His gentleness. It was still there—he hadn't lost it.

He still cares for you, she reminded herself…though this was easy to forget. After all, they'd barely spoken since the night when he'd rescued her at La Fleur Interdite.

Sunny rose from the table as soon as she entered the dining room, collecting Mari in the crook of his arm. He recoiled in a manner most would not notice, but Angela did. Perhaps it was the way she was dressed, for she'd taken out her favorite gown from her trousseau, a cobalt blue silk velvet that set off her pale blonde hair. Though it required stays, the gown was cut in the aesthetic manner. Simple, elegant. The neckline was low enough to hint at the curve of her breasts, but not so much to feel vulnerable. Tasteful, the modeste had said. Suitable for evening or an afternoon event.

At the time she'd been fitted for the gown, she'd envisioned romantic evenings of sweet words and soft kisses; she'd been hopeful then about marrying Carles. As for Sunny, his dinner invitation had made her so uneasy that she'd decided she needed armor in the form of a favorite gown.

It appeared to have worked, for he flushed before offering a bow, carefully depositing Mari onto the oriental rug. The kitten scampered beneath the dining table, no doubt in search of her siblings.

"Madame Countess."

She curtseyed in return. "Monsieur Earl."

It's good I dressed as I did, she decided. There was a formality about the dinner she hadn't anticipated. The dining room was set as though for a royal feast with plates decorated in gold and fine crystal goblets. Napkins folded like swans and silverware gleaming from a recent polish.

Her anxiety flared.

"Is someone joining us?" she asked in a careful tone.

"No," Sunny replied. "I simply thought we could have a discussion that didn't involve notes on pillows."

Unable to resist, Angela said in a sly tone, "But we do that so well."

A hint of a smile finally crossed his lips. "Speaking of pillows, you'll be pleased to learn a second bed has finally been procured."

She clapped slowly. "Bravo. Where?"

"Downstairs. The morning room. It's a quiet room. Small. I think you'll find it to your liking."

"The one next to the library?" The room had been locked when she'd last checked.

"No. Other end of the hall. Nice view of trees, sunlight."

"I hadn't heard the bed being delivered." She raised a brow. "When did this miracle occur?"

"This morning. You were in the mirrored salon with the doors shut. We didn't want to disturb you."

"So we won't share a bed again."

To her surprise, she felt a surge of emotion. How embarrassing. She'd grown used to his scent on the linens. The sense of his presence.

"No, we won't." His voice sounded weighted with disappointment. Or was she imagining such? "I'm sorry it took so long for the bed to arrive, Angela. I wish it could have occurred sooner. It's just the way things are in Paris these days, or so I've been informed."

"I'm sure."

Their rather stilted conversation was thankfully interrupted by Dubois's arrival.

"My lady, my lord." He filled their glasses with champagne, bustling all the while. He indicated a variety of platters, all crowned with ornate silver covers. "I've set your meal along the sideboard. I'll allow you to serve yourselves *à la russe. Bon appétit.*"

Dubois bowed and departed, leaving her alone again with Sunny. His eyes met hers. Brown and soft and warm. She sensed there was something he was going to say. Was he finally going to confess about the cloak, the rescue at La Fleur Interdite? Or something else?

He's not going to try to kiss you, Angela. Not after last time.

She felt her face heat at the memory. Shame, that's what she told herself. Or was it something else?

And then, to her horror, she wondered what it would be like if she were to initiate a kiss of him. Like he was another man, not the Sunny she'd grown up with…a man she yearned to know in the carnal sense. How would it differ from kissing Philippe?

Impossible. Improbable. Disloyal.

"I'm being rude," he said. "I'm staring at you."

"It's my gown. I'm overdressed, aren't I?"

"No, not that at all." He finally looked away, biting his bottom lip.

"What's all this about?" She gestured toward the dining table, her confusion rising. "A feast? Champagne?"

He flushed anew. "Because I've good news for you. For us."

Sunny offered her a seat, remembering his manners. He'd found himself tongue-tied with nerves once Angela showed for dinner.

She was even more exquisite than he recalled.

That blue velvet gown was the loveliest garment he'd ever seen her wear. It was the color of a sky at twilight, just before night overtakes the day. It was cut in such a way to set off the slope of her shoulders, the gentle curves of her breasts, without revealing more than a hint of the trim figure beneath. The gown was modest yet seductive. In a strange way, its simplicity made it all the more alluring: no lace, no beads, to detract from her beauty. It reminded him of the simple gowns her mother wore, which were more artistic than fashionable. Nor did Angela wear any jewelry save for a pair of simple pearl drop earrings. She'd dressed her hair in loose curls, which she'd gathered at her nape in a display of cultivated naturalism that left the nape of her neck bared.

Despite himself, he wondered what it might feel like to press his lips against the length of her neck. How warm her skin might be. How soft…

But it was more than this, Sunny decided. Angela herself glowed with vivid life. Perhaps it was the freedom she felt, having the mirrored salon all to herself to dance. Or perhaps it was hardly seeing her the past month while he avoided her. All of his wonder at her presence in the world reignited, his sense of her being a miracle, an otherworldly force for beauty and joy.

Whatever it was, all of Sunny's old stumbling ways returned. He nearly knocked over a glass, fumbled with the silverware. Next thing he knew, he'd take to stuttering again.

Dubois had advised him to offer a toast first. A way to smooth out her suspicions…and she *was* suspicious, he could tell. Her hands clenched by her sides, a wariness in her eyes. She didn't even pick up Mari or Clover when they tumbled near the hem of her gown.

Well, he'd earned her distrust. Not even a cluster of kittens and apologies would take that away.

He pulled out a chair for her, reminding himself of his manners. Once she was settled, he raised his coupe, which Dubois had filled with champagne. He didn't care much for wine—not any longer—but had been assured it was an excellent vintage.

"What are we drinking to?" she asked, still wary.

"To endings and beginnings." That sounded innocuous enough, didn't it?

She set down her coupe. "You're making me nervous. I sense you have something to announce."

He felt his throat tighten. "The end of our marriage."

"The annulment?" she asked, the words practically a whisper.

Disbelief. Shock. That's what she felt. He understood.

"Underway." He'd already received assurance that documents had been filed with the appropriate ecclesial authorities in England and expedited. "With luck, our case will be resolved by July."

"I'll have to testify?"

"No, just sign papers. As it turns out, our marriage will be annulled over a technicality."

She frowned. "I don't understand."

"We set the wrong name on the marriage license. Angela Bartham, not Allegra Jane Bartham—a small but important distinction that allows us to claim we were never wed. Blame it on the excitement of the moment."

Angela's eyes widened. "You can annul a marriage for that?"

"Apparently so. There's three reasons a marriage can be annulled: fraud, incompetence, or impotence. These don't include non-consummation unless the man is impotent—" an embarrassed grimace "—something I most ardently prefer not to prove."

"Signing the wrong name is considered fraud?"

"It can be."

"Are we even married then?"

He let out a long sigh. "Oh, we're married. It's grounds for annulment, not invalidation."

A moment passed. Outside the dining room, he heard a kitten run down the hall.

She leaned forward. "There's something else, isn't there? I can tell."

This was the part that he found so difficult to speak of. He drained the rest of his champagne. For some reason, once he'd made his little announcement about the annulment, he turned deeply melancholy. He should have expected such. After all, he'd yearned for Angela to be his wife for much of his life. Despite the unfortunate way their union had occurred, there was still sorrow in the loss of a dream.

He met Angela's eyes across the table. Forced himself to speak.

"I won't be returning to England without a wife. It's necessary, given the interest in our nuptials." A pause. "Mademoiselle de Castel-d'Albret has consented to marry me as soon as the annulment is finalized. She'll be introduced to society as the Countess of Sunderland. Not you."

~

He'd made amends to Hélène, Angela thought. *Found a way to regain her affections.* She knew she shouldn't be shocked. For all of Hélène's anger, Angela understood too well that the line between anger and attraction could be exceedingly mutable. Perhaps he did love Hélène after all. That was good, wasn't it? He'd be another woman's husband. No longer hers.

Relief, that's what I feel, she told herself. *Happiness.* By marrying Hélène, Sunny would detract attention from her. No one would ever believe she'd ever been his wife. Angela's reputation would be preserved and he'd have a countess he could be proud of, a family in time. Not a wife who didn't love him as he deserved.

While Angela was thinking all this, Sunny refilled their coupes with champagne.

"Shall we have another toast? Your turn, countess."

She felt lightheaded. Was it champagne or emotion?

"To old friends and new futures," she finally said. She could think of nothing else.

Sunny repeated her toast in a low voice. She drank her champagne, her hands suddenly cold. Nerves. In a moment, she'd either weep or laugh.

"I suppose I should congratulate you," she said. "I'm happy for you both. Truly."

A bashful smile. "It was difficult to convince Hélène, but all worked out in the end."

A new question rose. "Will we see each other after your marriage?"

What she really wanted to ask was *Will things be as they were between us?* But she knew this was impossible.

He let out a soft laugh. "I'm surprised you'd want to. I haven't been at my best."

"Nor have I," Angela admitted. "But you did save my family from scandal. Despite everything that's happened, I'm deeply grateful for that."

"Rest assured I'll honor the promise I made when we married. You'll be settled as you desire." Sunny set down his coupe, ran a finger around its rim. "But no, it's probably best we don't see each other again, I expect. Not intentionally."

Her eyes stung. "Then this really is the end."

"The beginning of the end," he corrected. "You've much to ponder regarding your future, Angela. When you're ready…"

"I'll inform you," she finished.

She took another gulp of champagne. She knew she should take pleasure in her life unfolding before her, revel in the possibilities. The freedom.

How strange all this is.

"I suspect this is a shock, Angela. Perhaps it'll help to eat?"

"Yes, of course."

He reached for the platter nearest him from the sideboard. After he removed its silver cover, the delectable scent of warm butter rose forth. Chicken *de volaille*, her favorite. Angela's mouth watered—Sunny must have informed Dubois. Another platter revealed rice slivered with almonds and currents, a third, spring-green asparagus glistening with hollandaise the color of sunshine.

They ate without conversation, this dinner marking the beginning of the end of their marriage. To fill the silence, Angela considered confiding in Sunny about her parents, her worries, as she once might have. She also considered confessing an idea she'd been mulling for her future: a dance school for children. Sunny had sworn to settle her after their marriage was annulled. She'd be able to devote her life to ballet without going on the stage, even gain financial independence in time.

The idea came to her one night while she'd laid awake with the kittens, who'd grown stronger and sassier. Kittens weren't children, but she enjoyed their playfulness. It reminded her of her desire for children, one reason she'd accepted Carles' proposal. Hopefully, no one would think anything scandalous of her sharing dance with children. She'd even read that the great Maria Taglioni had taken to teaching dance and comportment in London to the nobility.

But enough had been said that evening, she decided. Enough that needed to be digested beyond a fancy meal.

After the chicken *de volaille*, they moved onto a cheese plate, then finished with fresh fruit. Like the night of her arrival at the chateau, there were pomegranates, apples, persimmons, clementines.

While they ate, Angela snuck glances at this man who had been her childhood friend, then her husband, and would soon be gone from her life. She recalled the only other meal they'd shared at the chateau, the breakfast after their arrival. There'd been croissants and eggs and coffee accompanied by recriminations and rules. This meal was so different, for it bore a sense of death akin to the first yellowing of leaves on an October tree. Soon the tree would be bare and winter would arrive.

But after that, the spring will come, Angela reminded herself. *It always does.*

The clock struck the hour. To signify the end of their meal, he stood from the table. So did she. She half-expected him to flee—she knew him well enough to sense his discomfort in her presence. Everything had changed: he'd soon be another woman's husband.

She'll love him as he needs. I should be happy for him. And yet part of her wanted to linger. She found herself yearning for more time with him.

Impulsively, she took his hand though she couldn't explain why.

"I assume you can locate your way to your new bedroom," he said, holding onto her hand a moment too long.

"I can, thank you." Her hand tingled where they'd touched.

He reminded, "The morning room."

She nodded and fled after a muttered farewell.

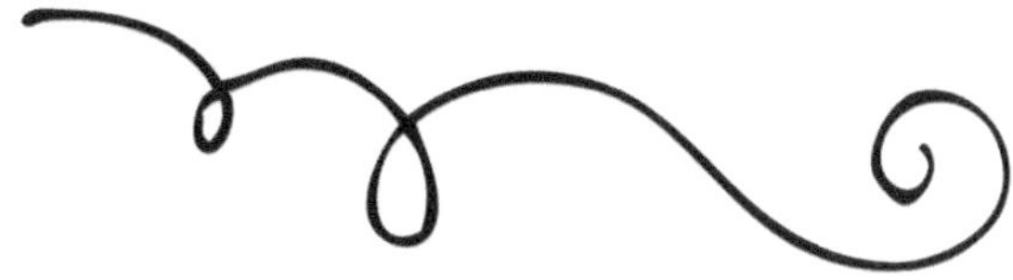

CHAPTER 19

Sunny was unable to sleep that night, though the cause went beyond being accustomed to his usual upside-down hours. Usually he'd have gone into the library to take care of paperwork, or out into the night. He found he couldn't bear to leave the chateau, not after that dinner with Angela.

Now that the end of their marriage was at hand, he felt weighed by the knowledge they'd never share another bed, even at opposite hours of the day. He'd never inhale her fragrance on the sheets again. Never find one of her notes pinned on his pillow.

He recalled one of the last she'd left, which she'd scrawled on the score for the Mozart adagio. He'd kept it. He lit a candle to reread it, imagining the warmth of her hand against the page.

Sunderland, she'd written. *Even if one is to dance alone, one still requires music.*

For some reason, this phrase opened something in him, like a key to a forgotten room. All of his emotions rushed forth: the loss of Robert, his father, even Angela after she'd refused his proposal and sent that letter. Sunny inhaled deeply, pressing his fingers against his eyelids until he regained control.

Fortunately, he was distracted by the kittens; they'd shown in his bedroom, no doubt expecting Angela. He tried to nudge them away, but they were persistent. And so he pulled on his trousers beneath his nightshirt, left his bed.

The kittens followed him into the mirrored salon, where the spinet awaited. He shut the door.

Downstairs in the morning room, Angela also found herself unable to sleep, though it wasn't because of the new bed or her new bedroom. Both had been made as comfortable as could be.

She'd arrived in the morning room to find it transformed into the most welcoming sanctuary she'd ever encountered. While the new bed was smaller than the one she'd shared upstairs with Sunny, it was piled with linens and pillows in soft hues that reminded her of the promise of spring. Someone had brought down her trunk—Dubois, she assumed—from the bedroom upstairs. It was placed in a corner of the room next to a delicate dressing table painted a lovely cream color. On top of a tall dresser, she found a water jug and bowl, towels scented with honeysuckle and lavender, and her hairbrush.

Yet something was missing in the room. Something that went beyond the absence of Sunny's belongings, the rather dark masculine furniture, the thick Persian carpets, the heavy velvet bed curtains.

No kittens, she realized. They hadn't followed her into the new room.

Usually the five of them slept on the bed with her, though they'd begun crowding her now that they'd grown larger. Their absence felt emblematic of the evening, how loss felt such a key presence. She recalled Sunny's face when he announced his planned nuptials to Hélène. He hadn't looked happy…or was it Angela's presence that displeased him?

Soon this interlude in their lives would be over. It would be for the best. A memory to forget.

But do I want to forget?

She tried to push her worries away, to simply be grateful. For one, it was easier to unfasten the blue dress than it had been to don. For another, the new bed was even more comfortable than the one upstairs.

Once in bed, she lay there for what felt like hours, sensing the turn of the earth in the night. The tick of a clock from the hall.

And then Angela heard something unexpected.

Music. From upstairs. The spinet. Someone was playing it. Softly to be sure, but it was the Mozart sonata she'd written that note on. The adagio in E-Flat Major.

Sunny. He was still awake, like her.

She'd chosen the score without thinking, just wanting to nudge him into remembering happier times in their friendship. Now she wondered how wise that had been.

Years ago, when she was sixteen, she'd created a simple dance to the Mozart sonata, for which Sunny had accompanied her on a summer evening. It had been a special moment they'd shared. Two friends creating art and beauty.

"So lovely, Angela," he praised in his awkward but kind way. *"I think this is your best dance yet…"*

"It's in the past," she whispered. Sunny would soon be gone from her life, but she'd survive—she always did. She had her family, a future, even kittens. She hadn't believed she could survive the loss of Philippe, but she had.

I cannot bear this. But I must.

Angela continued listening to the sonata. His piano playing wasn't as schooled as it once had been. Now there was a hesitancy about it, the occasional wrong note, an unevenness of tempo. But his playing had gained a bittersweet quality she found more appealing than precision, like that of an unrequited love come to naught.

The yearning. It called to her.

Unable to resist, Angela tiptoed upstairs as quietly as she could muster.

The door to the mirrored salon was closed, but that didn't deter her. Squinting through the keyhole, she made out Sunny seated before the spinet with only a candle to illuminate the music. Several kittens lay on the bench beside him—that's where they'd disappeared.

She silently opened the door. She'd dance, for this was how she banished sorrow from her life.

~

Silent or not, Sunny knew when Angela entered the mirrored salon without looking. He didn't turn from the spinet, for he'd just reached a section involving a complicated run of sixteenth notes— he was determined to make it to the end of the adagio. Still, he sensed Angela's arrival even before Clover jumped off the bench and ambled in her direction.

From the corner of his eye, he watched Angela dance while he played. Her feet were bare beneath her simple cotton nightgown, her hair loose. A glissade led to a jeté, then a piqué into a piqué turn, all performed with abandon as her hair whipped around. He'd never seen her dance in such a manner before, but he understood. In the shadows of the salon, she felt hidden. Safe.

Suddenly, he hit a sour note. The music jangled to a stop.

Angela stumbled from a pirouette though she didn't fall. She stood in the middle of the salon, her chest rising and falling beneath her nightgown. Her hair was tangled about her shoulders, down past her waist. He hadn't realized how long it had become.

"Angela…" He rose from the bench. "I woke you. I'm sorry."

"I couldn't sleep. I-I went looking for Clover." Recognizing her name, the calico rubbed against Angela's ankles and mewed. "You couldn't sleep either?"

"That. Among other things."

He took a careful step in her direction.

Angela picked up Clover, who began to purr loudly. "I must admit I'm shocked we won't see each other after the annulment."

Her eyes glistened with emotion. He understood.

"I know. But for the best. No scandal. No insinuations."

"I'm glad you patched things with Hélène."

"I am too. But it's still sad. All of this."

"I-I know. And we won't see each other again."

Now she was openly weeping. He supposed her dance opened her emotions, just as the music had his. In response, he opened his arms. She set the cat on the piano bench and stepped into his embrace. Friends, that's all.

"I'm so, so sorry again about that awful letter," she murmured against his ear. "You do know that?"

"I never want to think of that letter again." His voice vibrated against her. Against her body, which felt so soft yet so strong. "I'm sorry too, Angela."

"For what?"

"For this."

His mouth met hers—he didn't think twice of it. She could have deflected his kiss by shifting her head ever so slightly to the side so his lips would find her cheek instead. It would become a kiss of friendship, not one of desire. She didn't.

Perhaps she realized this time his kiss wasn't to punish her, like that night when they'd argued and she'd run off. No, this time his kiss was a farewell. That he knew they couldn't be together and had finally accepted it, now that he'd agreed to take Hélène as his wife.

As with all farewells, he didn't want to be the first to turn away.

Don't turn away, Angela thought. Her life had been filled with too many partings, between Carles and Philippe and even her father and mother. But she wasn't thinking of those now. No, not at all.

Sunny's kiss differed from their previous one, Angela decided. There was a tenderness to it, a searching quality. His lips were soft. Seeking. Worshipful, but she didn't mind. She felt a soft moan swell from her throat, one she couldn't contain even had she wanted.

Hunger, that's what she felt. Arousal. Curiosity.

And so she let herself relax into Sunny's embrace.

His arms tightened about her. He was stronger than she'd expected. Muscled. Protective. Hadn't he proved such on their wedding day, when he'd confronted Carles, and later, when he'd rescued her at La Fleur Interdite?

She let her lips part ever so slightly, instinctually. He traced them with the tip of his tongue. She opened her mouth, letting him take possession. It all felt natural. Inevitable. Most of all, surprising.

I hadn't known it would be like this.

A warmth pooled from the center of her stomach, an arousal she hadn't felt in so long. She hadn't thought she could ever feel that way again, not since Philippe.

You don't love him like that. It's only you being sentimental.

Perhaps Sunny sensed her confusion, for he pulled away, breathing heavily. He caressed her cheek.

"I know that was wrong, Angela. I'm sorry. It won't happen again."

"No, no," she reassured. She took his hand in hers as though he was still her friend, though her desire was more than what she'd expect for such.

The mirrored salon had but one small settee, barely enough for one person to recline upon, let alone two. After another muffled kiss, he pulled away, his eyes meeting hers. Yet he remained silent. So did she.

"*I should leave,*" she wanted to say. "*You belong to another woman. Not me.*"

But then it was his turn to take her hand. He led her down the hall. Into the bedroom they'd once shared, though never at the same time. He shut the door, locking the cats outside the room.

In silence, she pulled him beside her on the bed, which seemed smaller now that it bore both their bodies. Also in silence, he shut the bed curtains, sealing them in darkness from the world beyond.

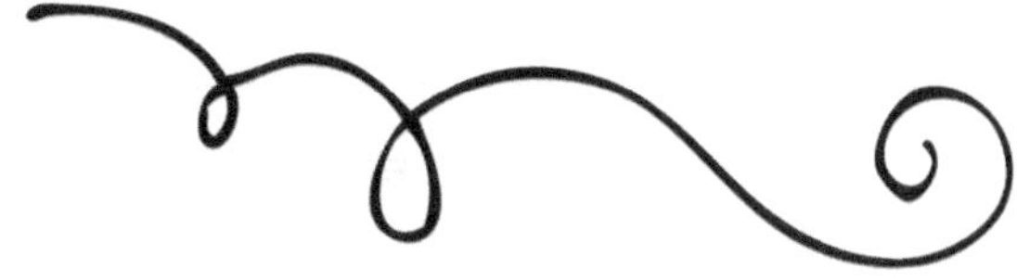

CHAPTER 20

THIS IS WRONG, Sunny told himself as they lay together in the dark within those bed curtains. *Very wrong. She's only doing this out of pity. Not love.* Plus there was the complicated matter of Hélène and the promises they'd made, though it was understood their marriage wouldn't be one of physical fidelity. But he couldn't turn Angela away. Not now. Not ever.

For he still loved her. Deeply. Irrevocably.

He always would—he'd been a fool to believe his angry attempt at revenge could end that. *Revenge only hurts the bearer*, he remembered. Well, the only thing hurting him now was his erection, which was raging. He'd never felt so aroused in his life.

If his attempt at revenge at brought him to this point in time, so be it. It was only what he deserved.

"We can't consummate this," he said, drawing upon all of his self control. Even if it wouldn't invalidate their annulment, it would still be wrong. A risk. His trousers felt tight around his cock, his skin too sensitive. (Thank god he was wearing them.) He hadn't much experience with lovemaking save for a few fumbling encounters, but he knew enough to understand where a bed and a willing partner led…though part of him yearned to take her and make her his wife in deed, damn the consequences. She'd never forgive him.

"No," she agreed, her voice soft. "I should leave."

She didn't make a move. Nor did he.

He forced himself to say, "You can leave anytime, Angela. You've a bed downstairs now."

He felt stupid as soon as he'd said that, for it was growing increasingly clear they weren't sequestered in his bed for the sake of slumber.

"You could leave too," she countered in a sly tone.

"But it's my bed now."

"Maybe I like your bed more than my bed."

This was getting to be ridiculous. Not that he really minded. The longer they lay there, the more he knew that if she made any move to leave his bed…well, he wouldn't be proud of his behavior. He'd beg her to stay if necessary. Somehow, lying there in the dark, the only sound being her soft breath, it made everything he'd ever fantasized about her seem possible.

As though testing the temperature of water, he reached for her in the dark. His hand fell on her shoulder—he could feel the soft cotton of her nightgown, the subtle texture of the weave. The small pearl buttons along the front, which were done up to her neck.

He ran his thumb gently along the curve of her clavicle. The hollow of her throat, where her pulse vibrated. How warm she felt, so soft. He heard her take a steep inhalation of breath. But she didn't pull away, to his relief.

"I'll stop anytime you tell me," he murmured, turning onto his side toward her. "Promise."

He waited to see if she'd respond. Another breath from her. A sigh, which he took as assent. Her hand fell against his thigh, where his trousers were taut against his muscles. Her touch was caressing, gentle…though she avoided his most intimate parts before sliding her palms beneath his nightshirt.

No consummation, he reminded himself.

Somehow he managed to shimmy beneath the bed linens, setting the sheet over their bodies. She didn't refuse. For whatever reason, this seemed to grant permission for him to continue touching her. Plus there was the matter of her hand on his chest, which she'd moved up his ribs.

At last, her palm came to a stop against his heart. Whether or not she could feel it pounding, he took courage in her exploration.

He unbuttoned the neck of her nightgown, releasing each pearl button gently. Slowly. He felt the fabric slip from her shoulders. The warmth of her skin beneath his hands. He yearned to cup her breasts, but didn't dare lest she pull away. But when his hand brushed against her heart, it was pounding just as his was.

She was affected too.

"Come here," he murmured. "Closer."

She did, to his amazement.

This time when they kissed, her mouth was as greedy as his. Her tongue laced with his, readily meeting him in this silent place of darkness where desire and uncertainty met. Fearful of losing control, he broke away to brush his lips against the curve of her neck, her shoulders. He twined his fingers into the soft silk of her unbound hair, breathing deeply to calm his arousal…though his thoughts continued onward.

He imagined sucking her nipple into his mouth, how it might pebble against his tongue. He imagined her moans and sighs as he caressed the delta of soft fur cresting her secrets. Her body arching against his, her thighs parting in welcome. How it would feel to possess her in full, after so many years of loving her…but he did none of this.

Instead, he rested his head against her shoulder and closed his eyes. He inhaled the floral fragrance of her hair, the subtle musk of her flesh, and tried his damnest to be content. To be grateful for this encounter, as unexpected and peculiar as it was.

And then, after what felt like an eternity, he slept the soundest he had since she first broke his heart.

∿

In the morning, Sunny was the first to awaken. It took him a moment to realize where he was—part of him wondered if the previous evening had been some strange dream. Nothing more had happened between them to his simultaneous relief and disappointment; they'd slept as chastely as children, he in his clothing and she in her nightgown.

He pulled himself up against the bed, careful not to wake Angela. He was aroused, but he silently willed the erection away, for he couldn't bear to leave her. Not yet.

He inched the bed curtains open, letting the light spill on Angela as she slept. He'd dreamt of this moment for so long, so many years. Angela beside him, her hair spilling over the pillows. The murmur of bird song beyond. The sweet sound of her breathing. Her eyes shifting beneath her lids as she dreamt. As friends, he'd seen her nap at picnics and doze off during boring lectures. But he'd never seen her sleeping in a bed. Not like this.

Angela asleep wasn't as he imagined. For one, she snored. Though her snore was soft, it resembled a low moan that bore nothing erotic in it; if he hadn't been so exhausted, she probably would have kept him awake. She'd also kicked the bed covers off her feet, revealing that her toes were calloused and crooked from toe shoes, the heels of her feet reddened. As for her hair, much of it had tangled like a nest over her face.

She was still the most beautiful creature he'd ever encountered.

He watched her shift onto her back, her mouth open. Drooling, that's what she was doing. However, his attention was drawn to her nightgown, which remained unbuttoned at the neck. It served as proof of all that had occurred between them the previous evening. He hadn't imagined their encounter. That she'd allowed him to kiss her. Undress her.

Though her breasts remained covered, the unbuttoned nightgown revealed a scattering of freckles across the center of her ribcage. He'd no idea she possessed them. He resisted the urge to trace the freckles as though they were a constellation of stars.

"I know you're watching me," she said, eyes still shut. "I can feel it."

At the sound of her voice, he felt his cock stiffen anew, damn it. He shifted away, setting his feet on the floor. "Nothing happened last night," he said, drawing a deep breath. "Not really."

Much as I wish otherwise.

"I know, Sunny. You're a gentleman—thank you for that." She settled onto her side, pushing her hair back from her eyes. She sat up. Met his gaze. "But what did happen was very wrong. Unfair to Hélène. Unfair to you."

"I-I know." He looked away from her. His arousal fled. Nothing like the mention of another woman to kill desire. "It won't happen again."

"I would be a liar not to admit last night was very enjoyable," she said in a low voice. Ashamed, that's what she was, an emotion Sunny recognized too well. And yet that wasn't all he sensed.

"What is it?" he pressed. "Just tell me already, Angela."

After a long moment, she said in a very small voice: "You should know the truth about why I refused your proposal. Why I couldn't love you the way you deserve."

Much as it had last night, his heart began to pound. This time, it wasn't because of lust.

"There's someone else." He'd been right, damn it.

She gave a tight nod.

"Who? When?" He couldn't resist asking, much as he despised himself for it.

"It no longer matters. I met him while you were away at school. Five years ago. He's gone."

"He abandoned you then." A rush of protectiveness rose, overtaking his jealousy. "I can't imagine anyone doing that to you, Angela."

"No, no. He didn't abandon me. Not at all."

She turned away just as a single tear made its way down her cheek.

"You see, I abandoned him."

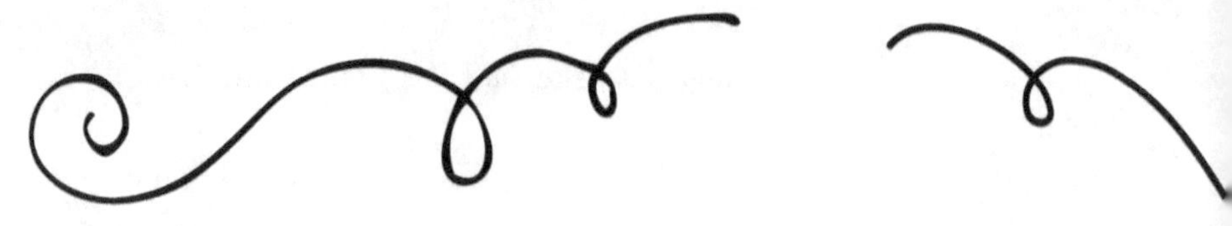

CHAPTER 21

ANGELA HADN'T INTENDED to tell him about Philippe's fate—a fate she'd never confided in anyone. Somehow, once they'd been so intimate, she decided she owed him an explanation.

And so she spoke, telling him little about Philippe save he was a dancer, like herself, but was French, unlike herself. That she'd met him while Sunny was away at school.

She didn't confess of his kisses that burned her soul, the times they snuck away to his small room upstairs from his aunt's ballet studio. He and Angela were Giselle and Albrecht. Tristan and Isolde. Though they didn't consummate their relationship, it wasn't from lack of desire. Still, they'd done nearly everything else a man and a woman could do to pledge their love using their bodies; they were dancers, after all.

But there was one thing they couldn't do: marry.

Though rich in ambition, Philippe was poor as a church mouse. If not for his aunt, he'd be homeless. He'd run away from Paris after falling out with his parents over their demand for him to give up dance to join his father's business.

Angela walked around with her head dizzy with desire. Musa made fun of her absent-mindedness. As for Sunny, he never noticed; he was finishing up at Eton before heading to Oxford. Not that she would have confided in him—she already suspected his tender feelings for her. Even had she felt similarly, Angela knew Sunny's parents would never condone a match with a scandalous Bartham daughter.

"*One day we will wed*," Philippe swore to her. "*One day we'll be together always.*"

And then one day, that day was to come.

Philippe received a letter from a former teacher in Paris. An audition, one that could lead to a place in the *corps de ballet* of a small Russian ballet company; they were in Paris for the winter. "*I've recommended you for the position*," Philippe's teacher wrote. "*You must return immediately.*"

Even now, Angela could recall the scene as though it had occurred days ago, not years. Philippe packing his scant belongings to return to Paris for the audition. His excitement. "*You could come with me*," he said. "*You and I, we'll dance together on stage. Take a leap of faith, mon amour.*"

She hadn't told her mother, who was in the throes of her own heartbreak after her father's departure for Jerusalem. But she had tried to tell Musa, who was overwhelmed with running the household. Anyway, Musa hadn't taken her seriously.

"And so I agreed to elope," she said. "We were to meet at Paddington. He'd use the last of his funds to book our tickets to Paris. And then…"

Angela covered her face with her hands. Sunny, to his credit, didn't press. Still, she forced herself to continue telling her tale.

For she'd abandoned Philippe on a cold winter night, never to see him again.

"My abandonment wasn't from a lack of love," she explained. "It was from a lack of courage. For when all was said and done, I couldn't do that to my family. I imagined the scandal. The ruin, especially if I went on the stage. The look on my siblings' faces once they realized I'd stolen their futures from them, especially Musa, who was doing everything she could to support us with Papa gone."

But what happened after she abandoned Philippe was far worse.

"About a year later, I went to see his aunt," Angela continued in a low voice. "By then, I'd stopped taking class with her, for I was too ashamed—I had no idea what Philippe had confided about his intentions toward me. But I was so desperate for information—I missed him so much! And yes, I still loved him. By then I realized my mistake in abandoning him in such a manner. At the least, I should have written him of my change of heart, apologized."

That was when she learned Philippe had taken ill and passed away while traveling with the ballet company in Russia. *"Cholera,"* his aunt confided. *"His parents are heartbroken."*

"I wish you'd told me about Philippe," Sunny said once she'd finished her confession. "Wish you'd trusted me."

How different things might have been. Yes, he still would have loved Angela desperately, still yearned to marry her. But he would have understood. Would have been gentler with his courtship. More patient. He would have realized she was woven of shadows as well as light, that her cheerfulness was borne of desperation, not optimism.

Instead, after she refused Sunny's proposal, he'd come to Paris himself, taking shelter in the chateau. During his sojourn, he'd done things he could never confess…unlike Angela, who'd been so brave and frank with him.

"And now you know the truth of how cruel I was," Angela said. "I abandoned Philippe. I could have at least told him in person, sent a letter, anything. How could I do that to someone I loved? That I nearly married? And now he's gone forever. I can't help but think that if I'd been with him, things might have been different, that he could have survived."

"Or you might have also died," Sunny countered, the fear gripping him like a frigid night.

"It matters not—he's gone!" She began to weep in earnest, her body shaking with emotion. "Since then, I've tried to be strong. To find the good in things. To be grateful. Cheerful. But sometimes… it's so *so* hard."

To comfort her, Sunny simply pulled her into his arms. This time there was nothing erotic in the gesture, only the desire to comfort a friend.

Stay close to me, he thought. *Don't leave.*

He felt his heart thump. Again. The pain of it was just as acute. Yet somehow it felt bearable.

Compassion. That's what I've been lacking.

"Now you know why I couldn't marry you," she sobbed against his chest. "I knew you loved me, Sunny—you were always deserving of having that love returned. But…but…"

"You didn't have love to give."

He understood now. How sad he felt, though there was also a measure of peace.

She blew her nose. "Anyway, it's for the best, with Hélène. I'm truly happy for you both. I really am!"

"I suppose," was all he said. "I suppose."

A cautious knock on the bedroom door interrupted their conversation. Angela pulled the covers over her body, closed the bed curtains. Shame, that's what she felt. Even if nothing had really happened beyond a few kisses and caresses, Sunny could tell it wasn't something she took pride in, especially now that she'd revealed her darkest secret.

"My lord?" A sneeze from outside from the hall. "Are you awake?"

It was Dubois. No doubt he was curious how last night's dinner went.

"Yes," Sunny called out. "Just a moment. I'll be out…"To

Angela, whispered: "You can remain here, if you like. Go back to sleep."

He left the room after donning a jacket over his nightshirt. He threw a last glance at Angela reclining in his bed, yearning to commit the sight to memory.

Outside in the hall, Dubois was eager for conversation, just as Sunny expected. But Sunny found he couldn't bear to speak of the previous evening. Instead, he requested breakfast be brought to him in the library.

Once alone, he unlocked a drawer in his deck.

He took out that letter she'd sent him way back when, the one explaining why she couldn't marry him. Though he'd memorized much of its five pages, he forced himself to read it anew, now taking into consideration everything Angela had confessed that morning.

Toward the end of the letter's devastating conclusion, she'd written:

I can never love you.

Now he understood. The letter had never been about him. It had been about Philippe and her broken heart. Her loyalty to his memory. Her guilt over his death. How unfair—no, unkind—Sunny had been.

After a long moment, he fed Angela's letter into the fire. Once nothing remained of each page but ashes, he removed a fresh sheet of paper from his desk and a pencil.

Sunny wrote only two words on the page, for that was all he needed.

Upstairs in Sunny's bed, Angela didn't sleep, but she did linger, especially once the kittens wandered in. They distracted her from remembering all that had just occurred. She still couldn't believe she'd told Sunny about Philippe. She could tell from Sunny's expression that he felt as though her confession had punched him in the gut. She felt awful, but what was done was done.

Still, he'd reacted with compassion. Kindness. Like the Sunny who'd been her dear friend for so many years. Not the beast she'd married.

And then her thoughts returned to how it had felt to dance in the mirrored salon while he played the Mozart. The way he'd kissed her afterward and led her into his bedroom. His gentleness as he unbuttoned her nightgown. How his heart sped while she stroked his chest…and hers had too.

Only that one night, she reminded himself. What was the point anyway? She was still in love with Philippe, or at least his memory. He was going to marry Hélène. The situation was impossible.

After some moments, Angela reluctantly left the bed. However, when she arrived at her room downstairs, she discovered a note pinned to her pillow.

"Friends again?" Sunny had written.

She clutched the note to her chest, her cheeks lifting into a painfully wide grin. He'd forgiven her; she'd forgiven him. But more than this had occurred. She'd told him about Philippe—Sunny had responded with kindness, freeing her in a strange way.

She immediately began writing a response to his note. What to say? And then she knew: this time, she'd answer him in person, not with a note.

Angela rushed from her room down the hallway toward the library, the kittens trailing at her heels. She'd probably find Sunny there, immersed in paperwork as he often was—she thought she'd heard him speaking to Dubois earlier.

The door to the library was closed.

She recalled the first rule of the chateau: *Don't go into rooms that aren't meant for you.* Well, did the rules matter anymore, after all that had happened?

She knocked once, then twice. When no answer came, she tested the doorknob.

Unlocked.

Inside, the library was empty. Angela turned to confirm Sunny wasn't hidden in an overstuffed chair—perhaps she'd imagined hearing him.

Hyssop, the most acrobatic of the kittens, scrambled toward the furthest bookshelf. She climbed to the third shelf and clawed at what appeared to be an expensive leather binding. A Greek edition of *Les Misérables*—the title was in both English and the Greek alphabet.

"Down, Hyssop! No!"

Angela grabbed Hyssop before the kitten could inflict further damage. She returned upstairs, where she settled for leaving a reply on his pillow.

And so she did, answering his two words with two of her own:

Friends always.

No matter what happened, this she'd hold in her heart forever. But Sunny's note wasn't the only happy correspondence Angela would receive that day. Soon after lunch, Dubois announced a telegram had arrived at the chateau from her sister Musa.

Success, it read. *Mother with Father in Alexandria.*

CHAPTER 22

"You're certain he'll be here tonight?" Sunny whispered to Hélène in French.

"He comes by most nights, *chéri*," Hélène replied, gesturing around the floor of La Fleur Interdite. "He'll show any minute—I know it."

It was a rainy March night, about a week after Sunny's dinner with Angela. He and Hélène were sequestered on the far side of the cafe, where the shadows lay deepest, their heads bowed toward each other over a small ironwork table. It was so late that the music trio had already packed up their instruments and a barmaid was wiping down the quartz counter of the bar.

The two were waiting for Edmond de Williem to show, better known as Willie to the masses who avidly followed his gossipy columns. Sunny hated calling him by the familiar nickname. It reminded him too much of Angela's favorite ballet, *Giselle*. The second act involved Wilis, supernatural women cursed to destroy men who'd ruined their lives. Ironic that it was Willie who was after Hélène and her beloved Julie, not the other way around.

As for Angela, they'd spent the days since the dinner pretending they never slept together. She seemed exceptionally happy since she received the telegram from Musa about her parents. Most importantly for Sunny, they were friends again.

He wished Angela wouldn't be in Paris for the duel—what if someone discovered her presence at the chateau? He'd do his best to minimize any press attention. Though with Willie, who knew what might happen?

"I should kill him myself," Hélène muttered darkly, staring into her nearly empty glass of red wine, Sunny's signet ring on her hand. "I could stab him like Marat in the bath. Or shoot him."

She hadn't heard from Willie in some weeks, but was convinced she'd seen him loitering near her flat on the Left Bank. This occurred on the same day Julie's daughter announced her betrothal.

"I would not recommend that," Sunny said, the hair on his nape rising at the prospect of Hélène with a pistol. "I promised I'd help you. And I will."

She scowled. "You're a gentleman. You've a code of honor and all that. You'll drag your heels until it's too late."

"We agreed nothing would happen tonight. Tonight is for research, that's all. To decide on a plan."

What that plan would be, Sunny had no idea, especially since there were no options that wouldn't involve violence and the potential for scandal. The contemplation of confronting Willie made Sunny feel nearly as flustered as he'd been at school, though he'd been the bullied then, not the bully.

The front door opened abruptly, letting in a sheet of rain. Two men pushed their way inside, their faces shadowed beneath their top hats. The taller of the two shook out a black umbrella. They appeared too well dressed for La Fleur Interdite, compared to other journalists they'd seen loitering earlier that evening. Sunny had even thought he recognized Luke Ward from his trademark yellow bowler; he hadn't stayed long enough for Sunny to be certain.

"That's Willie," Hélène whispered. "He's wearing the opera cloak."

Sunny grunted, wishing the light was better.

Though their encounter had been quick and nasty, Willie appeared exactly as Sunny recalled from that night when he'd rescued Angela. The journalist was handsome enough, with his dark hair and immaculate grooming. His eyes were heavy-lidded, like he spent more time in the shadows than the light. His mouth was thin, nose slightly crooked. The asymmetrical quality of his face made Willie appear more handsome than not, suggesting a secret history of dominance and intrigue. Sunny suspected he was skilled at wooing information out of people as needed.

Once Willie and his companion settled at the bar, Hélène lowered the veil of her black bonnet over her face and hunched her shoulders. A widow, that's what she appeared. This did not raise Sunny's spirits.

"*Messieurs*," the barmaid greeted brusquely. "We're closing soon."

"We won't be long." Willie insisted with an ingratiating smile, "If you please."

The barmaid nodded reluctantly.

Willie ordered claret for the two of them. The gentleman seated beside him seemed on edge. Anxious. Well, if he was with Willie, he probably had cause to be.

Once they were served, the two men turned to each other. Willie radiated confidence, the other not so much. More mumbled conversation, too low to comprehend. And then something happened that set Sunny's teeth on edge.

An orange cat jumped on the quartz bar, probably kept on the premises for mousing. The proprietress greeted the cat's arrival with a small saucer of milk.

"Come here, kitty," Willie invited.

The cat obliged by raising its head before turning back to the saucer, the feline version of a dismissive shrug.

Willie asked his companion, "You like cats?"

"Well enough," he answered in a nervous voice. "They're useful."

"I despise them."

Without warning, Willie swatted at the orange cat. The feline was quicker than the journalist; it leapt over Willie's shoulder, drawing blood from his clean-shaven cheek in the process.

Serves you right, Sunny thought.

Willie set a handkerchief against the scratch. He swore softly.

His companion muttered, "You asked for it."

"Perhaps."

By then the orange cat found its way to Sunny and Hélène's table. The cat coiled around Sunny's ankles beneath the table, meowing with a determination that suggested it smelled the *coq au vin* they'd picked at an hour earlier.

The feline leapt onto Hélène's lap.

Sunny felt Hélène tense beneath the table. The cat took no notice, only settled in for the duration. Hélène began to pet the cat in a manner that appeared more agitating than soothing, though the feline didn't seem to care.

The barmaid threw a nervous smile in their direction. "My cat likes you."

"I suppose," Sunny said, uncertain what to do. He turned his attention back to his glass of wine, feeling more vulnerable than he had in months.

You can defend yourself now. You're not as you had been.

Willie picked up a fork abandoned on the bar. He rose from his seat at the bar and slowly approached their table, still holding the utensil.

Was he seeking the cat…or had he recognized Hélène?

Sunny's hand tightened about the handle of his walking stick, his heart pounding. Why had he not been so intimidated that night when he'd rescued Angela?

Because it was for Angela. Because you didn't know who he was then.

"Here we go," Hélène whispered, swallowing hard. She squared her shoulders and offered a tight smile. But then the unexpected happened.

Willie's companion tapped his shoulder and handed him an envelope.

"Let the cat have its revenge," he said. "The rain's stopping. I'm leaving."

"I'll go with you," Willie replied. "I insist."

"You needn't. Really."

But Willie did as he wished, leaving Hélène and Sunny with the cat. Then the two men left La Fleur Interdite as suddenly as they'd arrived.

The barmaid let Sunny and Hélène remain for another quarter-hour and even offered another round of wine. Sunny, however, found he had no thirst. He sensed the barmaid feared Willie's return.

Outside on the pavement, the rain had slowed to a drizzle. Willie and his companion were nowhere to be seen.

Hélène let out a long breath. "I should have confronted him. Or rather *you* should have, if you truly want me to marry you. I'm serious."

"I know you are, darling."

"Don't humor me, Sunderland! Are you going to duel him or not?"

"I will. But not yet. Soon."

I won't kill him, he thought anew. *I can't.*

And then he thought of Angela back at the chateau. No doubt she was asleep in her bed, surrounded by kittens. He suddenly wished he'd spent the evening with her, not Hélène. He'd have to find some way to keep the duel secret from her. But how?

There's no good solution.

Once Sunny arrived back at the chateau, he staggered into the salon they used as a sitting room, determined to forget his disquiet in a brandy. To his surprise, Angela awaited him there, clutching Clover on her lap.

"I thought you'd be asleep by now," he greeted. "It's so late."

He wondered if she could sense Willie's presence about him, Hélène's perfume. His anxiety.

"I couldn't wait until morning," she explained, her eyes bright. "My mother's written. She and Papa are on their way to Rome—they'll be there by mid-April."

"That's wonderful news!"

"Isn't it, though?" Angela rose from the settee and twirled with Clover in her arms. "She says that if all goes as planned, they'll remain in Rome through the summer." A pause. "So I had a thought. What if I were to join them in Rome after their arrival?"

"Rome?" he repeated weakly. "But…but…"

Once you go, we'll never see each other again.

He sank into an upholstered chair, feeling as though the air had left his lungs.

Clover jumped from Angela's arms, perhaps alarmed by her exuberance. "I can tell you think this is a bad idea."

"I didn't say that, countess. But the annulment won't be finalized yet."

"I know you said July, but if I'm with my parents in Rome, no one will believe we were ever married. I promise I'll sign whatever papers you send. I won't get in the way of you and Hélène. I swear!"

She really wants to leave. How could he blame her? Even if they were now friends, she was still essentially a prisoner in the chateau. Save for her misadventure at La Fleur Interdite, she'd barely left the grounds save for strolls in the Bois de Boulogne.

"Mid-April is only a month from now."

She nodded. "Yes, it's soon."

A month. He could put off the duel with Willie until after she left—he'd been uncomfortable with the prospect of her being at the chateau while it took place.

A month. But then he'd have to move onto the next phase of his life. Without her.

He must have revealed his reluctance, for Angela's tone turned pleading.

"Hear me out, Sunny. I'd be ever so discreet traveling to Rome. I promise! No scandals! Of course, I suppose you'd still have to remain here. Or perhaps not. The important thing is you'd have your freedom back—I know you've been trapped here as much as I've been." A pause. "Well? What do you think?"

He thought, *I can't bear for you to go.*

But what Sunny said was very different.

"It's a good solution. A clever one." A forced smile. "Well done, Angela."

He gave in so easily, Angela thought as she made her way back to her bedroom. For all her excitement over seeing her parents, she felt an unexpected sense of loss once he agreed to her request. *He's relieved I'm leaving.* But how could she blame him? Even if they were now friends, their situation was complicated…especially since the evening when they'd shared a bed and she'd confessed of Philippe.

In the week since this occurred, she and Sunny pretended nothing had occurred. Still, Angela found herself thinking about their encounter when she least expected. While they were conversing, she'd lose her train of thought as she recalled his soft mouth as they kissed. Folding her nightgown brought back memories of him unbuttoning it. In the mirrored salon, her body would rise with heat as she recalled that Mozart adagio he'd played. Looking back, it had been a dance of desire they'd shared, for it had led them to his bed.

Then Angela recalled another dance she'd created, but one performed without music. She'd choreographed it soon after she parted from Philippe. Instead of a dance of desire, it had been a dance of loss, for she suspected she'd never see Philippe again. She'd been right.

I cannot bear this, she thought. *Yet I must.*

Though it was late, Angela found herself upstairs in the mirrored salon, too agitated to sleep. She tied on her toe shoes, trying to recall that dance she'd created for Philippe. It had been lyrical and slow, reflecting her emotions. It wasn't her showiest piece in terms of technique, but it had been heartfelt. She never intended it to be performed again.

Until now.

Once Angela stretched her limbs, she rose into an arabesque.

While she danced, she closed her eyes and tried to imagine Philippe accompanying her in a *pas de deux*. In her fantasy, he remained as tall as she remembered, his hair just as dark. His eyes were still more green than brown, his brow strong, his mouth still wide.

And yet for all of her efforts, it was Sunny Angela imagined, not Philippe. Sunny with his rude auburn hair and freckles. Sunny with his soft, comfortable body that was strong and broad and welcoming. Sunny, who'd entered her heart as a friend and surprised her as a lover.

Suddenly, Angela found herself unable to continue. She sat on the floor, her chest tight. In a month's time, Sunny would join Philippe as her past. In a month's time, they'd part.

I'll feel better once I'm in Rome, she told herself. *I'll find joy again.*

But, in the meantime, she'd mourn.

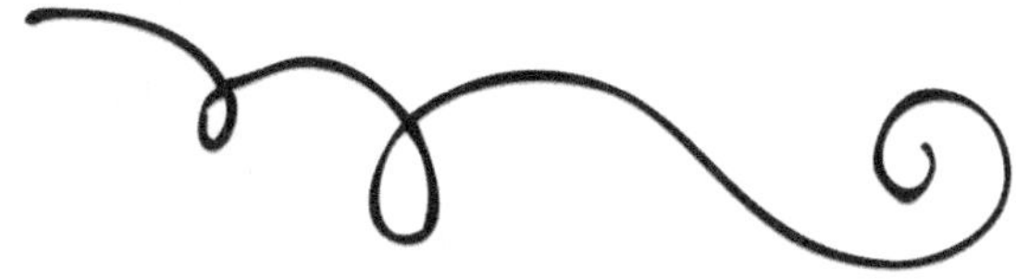

CHAPTER 23

Darling Angela,

It pleased us so much to hear of your intention to join Papa and me in Rome! Your presence will help his recovery. Though his health has improved, he's still weak from his ordeal, which is why we've decided to remain here for a few months before continuing onto London.

Below is the address of the flat we've let near the Spanish Steps, which has ample room for all of us. We should be there from April 12th on—if you depart Paris on that date, we should be nicely settled by the time you arrive in Rome. I must admit, though, to some confusion. You wrote Sunderland won't be accompanying you. Is this correct?

With much love
from your mother

PS: Papa sends his love too. He cannot wait to see you, sweetheart.

ONCE ANGELA RECEIVED a reply from her mother, she began counting down the time to her departure. As the weeks passed, she and Sunny settled into a rhythm at the chateau…a rhythm that had become deeply pleasurable to Angela.

Too pleasurable, damn it.

They spent their mornings with the kittens in the library. They read aloud to each other in English and French; as a result, Angela's French had improved quite a bit. He encouraged her to spend afternoons dancing in the mirrored salon without interruption. Sometimes he'd accompany her on the piano, like he did long ago. They even took meals together.

And then the weeks became six days, then five. Angela's travel was booked to Rome. The kittens would remain at the chateau until Angela returned to London. She considered bringing Clover to Rome with her, but decided it would be unkind to separate the calico from her sisters.

Four days before Angela's departure, Luke Ward showed up one afternoon at the chateau to wish her well. She was astonished to learn Sunny had invited him.

"Your husband explained you were leaving to visit your parents in Rome," Luke explained. "I come bearing a parting gift." He offered her a newspaper in his usual way. "Read it, Angela. Go on, don't be afraid!"

BARTHAM DAUGHTER IN ITALY

The Greater London Gazette, 7th April 1873. *After much inquiry, Lady Minerva Hadley of Grosvenor Square confirmed her great-niece Angela Bartham departed London in January for Italy, where she is taking the air in the Alps. The noted beauty was reputed to be wed to Virgil, Earl of Sunderland, an account vehemently denied by Eliza, Dowager Countess of Sunderland and Miss Bartham's family. Whether Miss Bartham's lovely face will be seen this season in the drawing rooms of London appears unlikely.*

"Taking the air in the Alps?" Angela laughed as she folded the newspaper, pushing away any melancholy she felt. "I haven't even left Paris yet. Really?"

"Really," Luke Ward confirmed. "Anything to protect your reputation, my lady. I had a devil of a time getting your great-aunt to agree to the article, but she gave in after your husband wrote her —ah, and here he is!"

"Ward," Sunny greeted, emerging from the dining room. "Excellent job with the article. Thank you."

"I'm pleased to be of assistance, my lord," Luke said, offering a quick bow. "As for the other part of your request, all is arranged as you asked—"

"What request?" Angela interrupted.

Sunny offered a mysterious smile. "You'll find out soon enough." He glanced at his pocket watch. "I estimate they should arrive any moment, if Mr. Ward has come through as I trust."

Outside the chateau, Angela heard the rattle of livery, the rumble of horse hooves. She ran to the window. An elegant brougham pulled into the gravel driveway, drawn by two matching grey horses.

"They've arrived," Sunny said. To Angela, "Perhaps you'd like to spend the day exploring Paris, countess?"

And then she knew: this was Sunny's farewell gift to her.

As bittersweet as Sunny's gift was, the carriage ride was completely delightful. Angela stared out the carriage windows with ecstatic pleasure at the world beyond. How lovely everything was, with the sun so bright, the flowers so lush! She'd arrived in Paris in deepest winter; she'd be leaving in the heart of spring.

"It's kind of you to accompany me, Luke," Angela said once they were well on their way along the Champs-Élysées. They'd just passed the entrance to the Bois de Boulogne and the Arc de Triomphe.

"Your husband wanted you to see Paris before you left for

Rome," Luke explained. "He enlisted me because he feared it was too risky for him to take you about, even with a carriage."

Angela supposed there was wisdom in this. Still, she felt a pang that Sunny couldn't accompany them.

"As long as we're careful, there should be little danger of scandal—" he winked "—especially since you're off taking the air in the Alps."

"Sunderland was behind the article too?"

"Yes, but I'll take some credit. I must admit I miss writing about more than art. However, the bonnet was all his doing. Who knew a man could have such good taste?" Luke tipped his customary mustard-yellow bowler. "Save for myself, of course."

Part of Sunny's surprise had included a new spring bonnet for Angela to wear during her travels. It was the loveliest one she'd ever owned, with grosgrain ribbons the color of the sky and pale silk roses along its jaunty brim. Hats were so different in Paris, smaller than in London. Most importantly, the bonnet had a veil to hide Angela from prying eyes.

"If I may be blunt, Angela," Ward continued, "he seemed shamefaced about keeping you so isolated from the world when he called on me."

"Sunderland visited you?"

Angela's amazement grew. She'd confided to Sunny about Luke Ward and his relationship to her family, but not where he lived.

"He did, Angela, but it was the strangest thing. He appeared at my door one night, just as I was dragging myself home from a soirée. If I didn't know better, I'd think he was trying to disguise himself. He wore a brown cloak—"

"With a hood," Angela finished, holding back a broad grin. This confirmed her supposition that Sunny rescued her that night from La Fleur Interdite.

"Yes." A soft chuckle. "He reminded me of a monk from medieval times. I half-expected him to chant in Latin. Though to be honest, I think I've seen him before, though I'm not sure where, perhaps at a café or such. His red hair is very noticeable. Anyway, he said he wished he'd thought of my escorting you about earlier during your time here."

"No matter," Angela replied, enjoying the play of sun on her cheeks. She tried not to think of the loss the outing signified, only the freedom it promised. She sighed, "How lovely this all is!"

Luke grinned. "There's far more for you to see. I think you'll be pleased by what's been planned for today."

Along the Champs-Élysées, the carriage made their way deeper into what Luke explained was the right bank of the Seine. "The Bois de Boulogne is just outside the boundary of the city. You can't claim you've properly been in Paris until now, Angela."

"Where are we now?" Angela asked. She resisted the urge to hang her head out the carriage window to drink in all the details. How grand it all was! Despite the troubles Paris had borne in recent years, the city appeared dipped in gold and ivory. She made out formal gardens on each side of the boulevard. Down the avenue, a tall obelisk pointed toward the cerulean sky.

"We're nearly to the Place de la Concorde—that's where the obelisk is. I won't bore you with history you already know, but Louis XVI did not come to a happy end here." Luke gestured across his neck with a wince. "Back then, this was called the Place de la Revolution."

"How peaceful it looks," Angela observed.

"Such is the crawl of history, Angela. Turmoil becomes peace. Enemies become friends."

Angela mulled how true this was. "Where are we headed?"

Luke pulled out several folded sheets of paper from his jacket pocket. "Your husband was very particular about where I should take you. He's actually written an itinerary with eight—no, nine —destinations."

Angela's heart swelled. "That sounds like Sunderland."

For her fourteenth birthday, he'd created a scavenger hunt filled with clues that took them all around London, from St. Paul's to Hyde Park. This was the Sunny she knew and adored as her friend for years. The Sunny she'd regained in the past month…and that she'd lose after she left for Rome.

I won't think of this today. For today, I'll be happy.

"What's next?" she asked, pushing away sorrow like sour milk. There was too much to enjoy. The Place de la Concorde was unlike anything Angela had experienced in London, as though all of Paris was using the square as their drawing room on a beautiful spring day. Children giggled as they floated paper boats in the fountain while their parents looked on indulgently. Pigeons clustered and flew in response to shifts in the wind, while white-haired dowagers clutched lapdogs.

"Let's see," Luke replied. "Your husband says that when we arrive in the Jardin des Tuileries—we're nearly there—he wants us to continue toward the Louvre to enjoy a view of the royal palace. We won't stay long. After this, we're to travel along the Seine toward the Île de la Cité to view Notre Dame, then the Pont Neuf."

"I'll veil myself," Angela said.

The hours passed quickly. Sunny had chosen each destination thoughtfully, with an eye toward protecting Angela's privacy as well as what would offer interest. She and Luke remained inside the carriage save for brief stops to stretch their legs where few people congregated.

Luke read out Sunny's notes, which were droll yet thoughtful; Angela had the sense he was there beside them. Indeed, if she closed her eyes, she imagined she could smell his cologne, which she'd grown used to while they shared the same bed. His warm scent of bergamot and musk…

"When you arrive at the Isle de la Cite," Sunny wrote, *"give a salute to the gargoyles at Notre Dame and mourn the fate of poor Quasimodo. Remember when we read his story together, Angela?"* At Angela's first sight of the Seine from the Pont Neuf, he offered the following observation: *"Breath in the history—this is the oldest bridge in Paris—but one would be wise to avoid the stench of*

summer. *Still, isn't the water lovely with the sun glistening in late afternoon?"* He even arranged for a late lunch at a well-regarded café, where a private dining room had been reserved for them. *"Order the blinis with caviar, Angela,"* he wrote. *"You'll adore them with crème fraîche."*

Each of Sunny's notes brought a wistful smile to Angela's lips, a melancholic sensation. They made her wonder what their life might have been like had she returned his affection…especially when she made out a couple's indiscreet display inside a passing carriage. They appeared lost to the world, their eyes closed in ecstatic delight while they embraced.

And then Angela recalled how it had felt to lie in Sunny's arms a month earlier. The tenderness as he rested his head against hers while they slept. How surprisingly pleasurable the encounter had been. It differed from what she'd experienced with Philippe, but in a way she could now appreciate.

Welcoming rather than dangerous. Gentle rather than frantic. Accepting rather than desperate.

"Too late," she murmured to herself.

"What's too late?" Luke asked; he'd been in the midst of reciting another of Sunny's observations. This one was about the building of the Palais Garnier, which would house the Paris Opera and its ballet in the coming year. By then, the sun was growing low in the sky.

"I said it's late now," she said, her face hot.

Her thoughts had turned so unruly…and then she wondered: Was Sunny courting her? Was that what this day was all about?

Impossible, she decided. He knew she was leaving for Rome, that was all. He was going to marry Hélène. No, the outing today was a kindness he wanted to show her. A farewell, that's all.

To think I'll soon never see him again.

"Sweet Jesus, you're not crying, are you?" Luke asked. "I can't handle tears, Angela—you'll make me break out in hives. Did I do something I shouldn't?"

She forced a laugh as she dabbed her handkerchief against her eyes. "No, not at all. It's just the day. The beauty of Paris. You've been very kind."

Luke said thoughtfully, "Too much stimulation after too much time in solitude."

"Perhaps."

And then she heard a scrap of music from beyond the carriage, the sweetness of violins and cellos. Mozart…and she knew which piece. The adagio from the piano sonata, but arranged for string instruments.

"A last stop before we return," Luke announced. "That is, if you're not too tired, Angela."

"Not at all."

Luke helped her down from the carriage. This neighborhood was far less grand than those they'd visited that day; it wore the results of the recent struggles in Paris with far less grace. It reminded Angela of the night she ran away from Sunny and found herself near La Fleur Interdite: the clattering footsteps, the scent of cabbage. But in this moment, the quartier was transformed into something transcendent.

They stood on the pavement and listened.

The Mozart sounded like a prayer as it rose from a grey stone hall that appeared ancient; perhaps it had been some type of temple in another century. The moment felt sacred, exquisite. The setting sun filtered the sky into so many colors that Angela couldn't name them all. She'd never beheld such a beautiful sight.

Angela was grateful for the veil over her bonnet, which hid her emotions—or so she hoped. In every note of the music, she sensed Sunny's yearning. His devotion…and he'd arranged this beautiful, perfect day for her. Only her.

How he knows me. How he loves me. She recalled their past in all its messiness and beauties. Now Hélène would be his wife, the mother to his children. Not her.

Did Sunny love Hélène? She'd never thought to ask. Not that it mattered. Not anymore.

And then she knew. Whatever she'd felt for Philippe was a

chimera. A flash. Nothing like her connection to Sunny. She and Philippe had shared passion, but not understanding. Obsession, not devotion. It had been young love, exciting and bright. Not the slow love of friends nurtured into blossoming.

Too late, she thought again. *Far too late.*

"*Merde*, you *are* crying," Luke said. "Forgive my crude language." He awkwardly patted her shoulder as he pulled her back inside the carriage. "There, there. Ugh, I'm no good at this, am I? Come, I'll escort you home."

"I've made a mistake," she said. "An awful mistake."

Before Luke could respond, shouts rang out nearby. Across the boulevard, Angela made out a café with bright paint on new windows. She squinted from behind her veil. *La Fleur Interdite*, she read.

It can't be, she thought. But it was.

A couple was arguing outside the café, a man nearing five and thirty and a younger woman. Their figures were shadowed beneath the twilight sky. Their voices were so loud that they drew a circle of bystanders. The woman suddenly threw a punch at the man, missing his nose. She settled for spitting at him.

"*Je te verrai en enfer,*" he shouted, "*après t'y avoir envoyé d'abord.*"

I'll see you in hell, after I send you there first. Angela's French had improved enough that she understood.

Luke pulled Angela away from the carriage window as the dark-haired man strode toward their direction. As he passed, Angela recognized his fur-collared opera cloak and top hat with a shock. Edmond de Williem, the journalist who'd propositioned her that evening before Sunny had intervened. Willie.

However, Angela had no time to mull this significance of his presence. Her attention was drawn by the woman chasing Willie. She was regal and beautiful and brunette...and Sunny's future wife.

CHAPTER 24

"I saw them," Angela told Sunny as soon as Luke brought her back to the chateau. "Willie and Hélène. They were arguing on the street outside La Fleur Interdite."

"What of it?" Sunny replied, avoiding her gaze. He'd seemed uneasy at her arrival; she'd found him in the library pacing before the fire. Anxious, that's what he was. But this only proved something Angela suspected.

"There's something going on," she said. "Something involving you and Hélène—I can tell. Something beyond your engagement."

An uneasy laugh. "I'm not married to Hélène yet. How would I know?"

To Angela's dismay, he turned as though to dismiss her. After that gorgeous day too; if Angela didn't know better, she'd think something occurred while she was on her outing with Luke.

"I wish you'd tell me the truth before I leave here," she burst out. "There's so much I want to know. La Fleur Interdite, Willie, Hélène—"

"It's not your business." Sunny's tone was resolute as a closed door.

"I believe it is. You rescued me at La Fleur Interdite, when I ended up there with Willie. It was you in the cloak, with the walking stick, wasn't it?"

"You grant me greater powers than I possess, Angela."

"I thought we were friends." Her voice broke to her embarrassment.

"Yes, we're friends, but we're not intimate, Angela. We can't be. Not anymore."

The silence hung between them.

He bit his lip. "This is so difficult, isn't it?"

"I-I know. Soon we'll be strangers, won't we?"

"Never strangers," he assured, taking her hand. "Always friends. Just apart."

Angela turned away, her eyes prickling. *I won't cry. I can't cry. Gratitude, that's what I feel.* She wanted to tell him about her wonderful day. Thank him. If she did, she feared she'd fall apart.

"Forget what I said about La Fleur Interdite, Sunny. Aren't we going to have dinner together?" If they only had four more days together, she'd aim for harmony.

"I'm not hungry, countess." A strained smile that Angela didn't believe. "You go on without me."

Sunny's heart lurched as he forced that smile for Angela, as he watched her turn away. He'd had been listening for her return from Paris, waiting for her reaction to all he'd planned—how could he not? He'd planned the day so carefully, wanting to make up for all those months she'd been trapped with him. Wanting to make her happy so she'd think kindly of him after she left…and, if he was to be honest, wanting to woo her, though it was far too late for that.

As the afternoon passed, he'd checked his pocket watch, imagining where she might be at that moment. Imagining her reaction. Wishing he was there beside her, not Luke Ward. Thinking how it pleasurable it would be to hear her tell him everything she saw that day, her response to his notes.

Too late.

Once Sunny received Hélène's letter, his plans for the evening immediately changed. He hadn't expected her to confront Willie in such a manner at La Fleur Interdite, but she'd grown impatient. He'd begged her to wait until after Angela's departure for Rome, but Willie had issued a new threat that morning. As for Sunny, it had been two months since he'd made his bargain with Hélène—he'd put her off too many times. Was it his cowardice? Or avoidance?

And now, everything had changed. There was no way he was going to admit to Angela he'd rescued her at La Fleur Interdite—her accusation caught him off guard. Best she know as little as possible. Come what may, she'd remain protected. She'd probably learn about the duel, but at least she'd be leaving Paris soon.

Dawn, it would happen. The duel. Hélène had challenged Willie.

Sunny knew he should try to sleep, but how could he? He'd never dueled before, though he knew what to expect. As Hélène's second for the duel, he'd already exchanged letters with Willie, setting the terms for the encounter. Usually only seconds would communicate, but Willie insisted the duel take place without delay —he hadn't located a second yet, or so he claimed.

Rapiers. The Bois de Boulogne at a glade commonly used for such furtive encounters. Sunny would stand in Hélène's place. If Sunny won, Willie agreed to never bother Hélène and her lover again.

They'd fence to the first blood, not to the death—Hélène would have to accept this. However, Sunny knew not to trust Willie. He thought of that orange cat, how Willie swiped at it.

I shan't kill anyone, no matter what happens.

Sunny locked the library door behind him after he shooed the kittens out. They insisted on following him everywhere when Angela wasn't near. He'd grown fond of the kittens, but even more fond of Angela's devotion to them. If nothing else, he'd given her something to remember him by after they parted. The kittens would be her friend as he'd been.

As for himself, he'd do the best he could with his life with Hélène. Without Angela.

What if you don't survive tomorrow?

Time to think. Time to write out his thoughts in case the duel went awry. If he was killed, Angela would be left his widow, his mother forced to reckon with his marriage. As for Hélène, he'd find some way to provide for her and Julie.

He took out paper and began writing a letter for Dubois to find in the greenhouse. Outside the hall, he heard the clock strike eight.

He lied to me, Angela thought as she laid in bed. *I know it.* By then the clock was well past midnight—she'd lost track of the hours. Tonight the kittens had followed Sunny save for Clover. She remained with Angela in her lovely room. Clover had grown into an affectionate cat, with an insistent meow louder than her sisters. She wished she could bring the calico with her to Rome, as impractical as it was.

Angela glanced out the window through the crack in the curtains. The sky was still dark. Stars dotted the sky like a gathering of lights. It was really was lovely, not at all as though they were in a city; she recalled Luke's explanation that the Bois de Boulogne wasn't truly part of Paris. How desolate the chateau seemed when she'd first arrived, the sense of being in a wood possessed by wolves and other wildness. Now everything felt transformed, like a spell had been lifted.

Despite herself, Angela couldn't stop thinking of how it had felt to listen to the Mozart that day on the pavement. The sense of possibility and loss accompanying it. The sudden realization that things could have been very different with Sunny had she not been so mournful over Philippe.

She'd been so obsessed with Philippe that she truly never

considered the possibility of loving anyone else. She believed love had to be like Tristan and Isolde or Albrecht and Giselle—fated, tragic, all-encompassing. Now she understood love could be as gentle as a Mozart adagio or a litter of kittens.

Too late.

Angela turned from the window, feeling as though the constellations were mocking her. Fate written in the stars. Possibilities lost. Futures to come. In all of them, she'd be without Sunny—he'd have Hélène as his countess.

I cannot bear this. Yet I must.

Well, if she couldn't sleep, she'd take a bath. The warm water could soothe her so she could sleep. In a scant five days, she'd be on her way to Rome. She'd be fine. She always was.

Will you really?

Angela ignored the question as she wrapped the kimono she used as a robe over her nightgown. She padded upstairs, her bare feet quiet on the marble steps. Sunny's door to his bedroom was shut. No doubt he was asleep, unlike her; she recalled the shock of happening upon him in the bath that first morning after their arrival.

As for the bathroom, the door was ajar, but it wasn't unoccupied. Angela heard running water, the splash of a washcloth against flesh. Someone chatting in a low voice.

She peered through the crack in the door.

Sunny. He was bathing, the room nearly as dark as it had been that first day. His body was turned from her, immersed in suds. All she could see was the back of his head, his arms draped along the rim of the tub.

To her surprise, four cats sat on the floor surrounding the clawfoot tub. He'd been speaking to them as though they were friends. "I thought cats didn't like water," he said, "but suit yourself."

Ivy, the tiniest of the kittens, had her back leg extended as she groomed herself in a matter-of-fact manner, while Mari had stretched out her entire body, setting her paws on the edge of the tub near Sunny's hand. She rubbed her jaw against Sunny's hand, marking him with her scent as cats do.

Sunny had purposefully left the door ajar so the cats could leave the bathroom should they want. This was so adorable that Angela struggled not to laugh.

She must have made some sort of sound, for Sunny's head turned in her direction. Toward where the door was ajar. In response, Mari trotted toward Angela, pushing the door open with a nudge.

Angela bent down to pet Mari. The cat mewed softly.

"Angela?" Sunny asked, meeting Angela's gaze.

Three syllables, but so much more. An acknowledgement. An invitation.

He said nothing more. Unlike the last time when she interrupted him in the bath, he didn't yell or tell her to go. He remained still. Calm, as though he was waiting for Angela's reaction, like an animal spotting the hunter. Watching her to see she'd do next.

As for what that would be, Angela's pulse tripped in a manner that had little to do with fear.

His soft brown eyes met hers. There was something vaguely defiant yet sorrowful in their depths. As though he was inviting her to join him in the bath. Daring her.

Her fingers wrapped around the edge of the door.

Before Angela could decide what to do, he stood from the tub and wrapped a white towel around his hips, hiding his most intimate parts.

He stretched his arms in her direction.

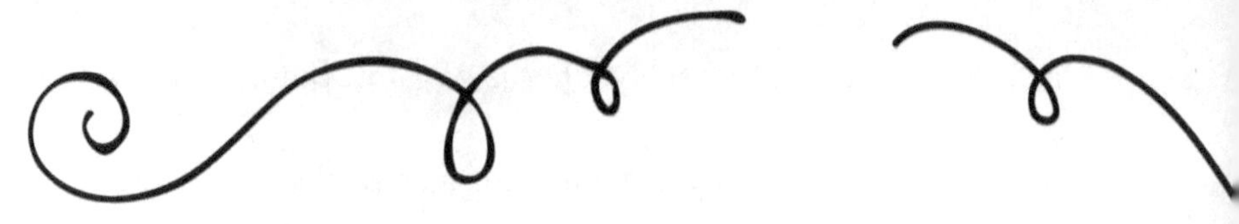

CHAPTER 25

Without another word, Angela stepped into Sunny's embrace, not caring that her kimono would be soaked. Her feet grew wet from the water that had already spilled on the floor. And then Sunny's mouth slanted against hers, so soft and eager, and he was pulling her towards him. Against him. Toward the water, which splashed over the side of the tub.

In response, the three remaining kittens fled the bathroom. This was Sunny's cue to firmly shut the bathroom door once they broke away from their kiss.

This is so wrong, Angela thought. *But I can't turn away.*

He offered his hand. Again, an invitation. A goodbye.

A moment passed. Another.

Only this one night. That's all we have.

Before Angela stepped into the tub, she let her kimono fall from her shoulders to the tiled floor of the bathroom.

He reached for her, helping her down into the water. The warm water turned her nightgown translucent, and her nipples hardened into nubs, but she was beyond modesty. Once she settled in the tub, he caressed the fabric barrier of her nightgown, gentle yet hungry. She arched her back in the bath, then let out a long sigh that became a moan. Her head rest against the edge of the tub. Her eyes shut.

She was floating in water. In darkness. She felt adored. Worshipped. A warmth blossomed within her, a sense of spring returning. A yearning. As he shifted to make more room for her, she felt the hardness of his erection beneath the towel, which he'd tucked beneath him.

She didn't pull away.

More water splashed onto the floor—there'd be a flood by the time they were done. Still, as good as his attentions felt, the fabric between them frustrated her. She wanted his flesh against hers, wet and sluicing and warm. She couldn't bring herself to remove her nightgown, as awkward as all those layers of clothing were in the bath. Somehow, if she didn't undress, they weren't betraying Hélène.

She recalled what he'd said that night the first time they'd kissed, before she'd run off on him. *"Desire isn't the same as love."*

This isn't love. This is desire, she told herself. And yet she couldn't stop thinking of how she felt that afternoon. Her regret.

Too late.

Sunny rose from the bath, his sturdy torso painted in shadows. He turned away, letting the towel drop, revealing surprisingly taut buttocks before he wrapped his robe about himself.

He reached for her.

The next thing Angela knew, he'd gathered her in his arms, holding her against his chest. Water trailed from their bodies as he carried her down the hall, into his bedroom. How strong he felt! How muscled! How had she never realized this? All those years, he'd hidden himself beneath slumped shoulders and bashful manners. She should have seen him for who he was, not how he presented—how obtuse she'd been.

Once they'd reached his bed, he opened the curtains and set her down on the edge of the mattress, soaked nightgown and all. Though she'd begun to shiver, she kissed him, his mouth soft and welcoming against hers.

He broke away to shut the door to the bedchamber, cloaking them in darkness.

The water had swollen the buttonholes of her nightgown, making them difficult to unfasten. She felt as though she couldn't breathe as she tugged each one open, fumbling in the dark. She must not have been fast enough, for Sunny took over, pulling the garment from her shoulders. Down to her waist. Onto the floor, where it landed in a sodden whisper.

She lay back on the bed, feeling no shame, only desire…and something more she couldn't bear to name, knowing that they'd soon be parted as husband and wife. She didn't dare speak, fearing they'd come to their senses. Didn't dare do anything that would take him from her.

She felt his weight settle next to her. As he reached for her, her skin prickled anew with gooseflesh, but not from the cold.

As they kissed, she couldn't think. Nor did she want to. But she forced herself to remember where she was, what they appeared to about to do, especially as she felt his erection straining beneath his robe against her thigh. It would be so easy for her to nudge his hips against hers, but it would be so wrong. Besides betraying Hélène completely, it would tie them in marriage. Even if their annulment was to be based on a technicality, she'd know the truth—this dishonesty would hound her for the rest of her life.

"No consummation," she murmured, breaking away from their kiss.

"No consummation," he agreed.

They slid beneath the covers as one, shifting away from the side of the bed where the linens were damp. She reached to light the lamp to better see him—if they were to have only this one night, she'd take what she could from it. Her memories would have to hold her through the rest of her life, after their marriage was over and done.

He grabbed her hands, pulling her back to him. Against him. She gasped, taken aback by his aggression. Yet she liked it and became bolder in turn. She caressed his chest where his robe parted. He was covered in soft fur, his comfortable body welcoming yet tight with purpose.

Before she could change her mind, she arched toward him in invitation. She felt his mouth on her breast, then her nipple. As he sucked, she gasped, yearning spreading to her limbs. Beyond.

She felt herself grow wet. Desire, that's all she was made of. It felt like a warmth, a fire, as it coursed through her limbs, threatening to devour her. This man who'd been her friend for so many years, who'd married her for revenge, was now all she wanted. All she needed.

She pulled him up toward her, needing his mouth against hers. The weight of his body.

His breath mingled with hers as he caressed the soft fur cresting the delta where her thighs met. She opened for him while he stroked her gently. Surely. She spread wider, feeling darkness expand to light inside her. Stars, that's what she was made of. A universe. But this wasn't enough satisfaction.

As they kissed, she reached for his arousal, threading her hand through the opening of his robe. She felt him gasp against her mouth, but he didn't pull away. He felt so hard, so smooth, in her hand. For a moment, she imagined what he'd feel like inside her, how it would be to join with him as husband and wife.

She pushed the thought away, especially once she heard his sharp sigh in the dark in response to her touch. She curled her hand about his thickness and caressed him.

He moved against her palm, growing in urgency. She let out a long sigh as he stroked her slickness with his fingers. And then she felt something grow inside her beyond the stars. Within the darkness of the bed, she heard herself cry out as though from very far away yet very near.

Soon after, his voice joined hers in a sharp cry. He pulled away from her as he shuddered in release. A long sigh.

And then all was quiet save for the sound of their breathing.

～

Afterward, Sunny couldn't say anything to Angela. Didn't dare. She remained silent also, though she kissed his cheek. That acknowledgement of what they'd just shared would have to be enough. He understood what had happened: she'd been moved by the day he'd offered her. Wanted to thank him. Wanted to say good-bye. Felt desire, not love. He was glad they'd remained in darkness, so she wouldn't see him so exposed in body and emotion.

He also feared if they spoke, he'd be tempted to tell her the truth: that at six in the morning, he'd be on the Bois de Boulogne with a rapier in his hand. No matter what Hélène promised, he'd be risking his life.

Still, he forced himself to offer Angela the words that would grant her the truth, should the worst happen.

"Hélène doesn't love me. Nor do I love her, not romantically." His face burned. "I shan't get into the details, but our agreement to wed was akin to a business arrangement, if you will. The important thing is you'll be freed from our marriage. No scandal will fall on you or your family."

"And you'll have a countess." Angela's forehead furrowed in the shadows. "A marriage of convenience to replace our marriage of convenience."

He recalled how Hélène had said the very same thing. He found little humor in it.

He confessed, "She's in love with someone who can't marry her."

Angela replied in a tone barely above a whisper, "Like me with Philippe."

"Something like that." It wasn't his place to confide about Julie. "Hélène is my friend. A dear one."

Angela's words cracked with emotion. "You've always had a gift for friendship."

He laughed softly, but there was little mirth in the sound. "Not that it helped win your love…though now I understand why."

Angela grew very still. But she didn't leave the bed. Sunny took whatever courage he could draw from this and continued.

As he spoke, his words were stumbling and hesitant, like the old Sunny he'd been before his father's death, before she'd refused his offer of marriage and sent him that letter. The Sunny who couldn't imagine a future without Angela by his side.

"I-I will be honest, Angela. Hélène and I agreed to wed," he said, "because I want to protect her. She's being blackmailed by Edmond de Williem, the same journalist who threatened you at La Fleur Interdite."

"*That's* why they were fighting outside La Fleur Interdite."

"Yes. But there's another reason we agreed to wed: I owe her a debt of honor."

"How so?"

Sunny drew a deep breath. "She saved my life."

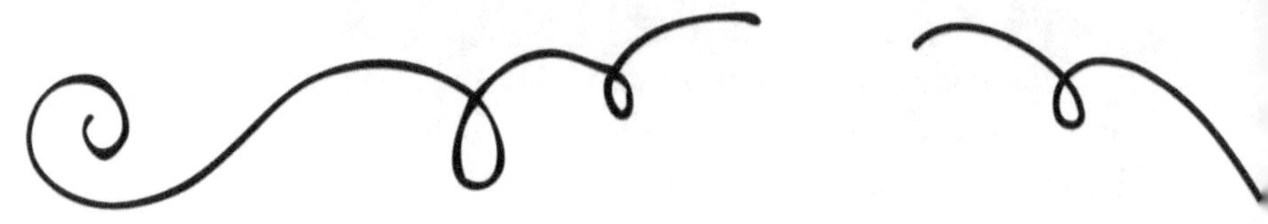

CHAPTER 26

Before he could reconsider, Sunny launched into the truth he'd told no one, not even Dubois. The tale of the curse he felt had plagued him for much of his life, ever since his brother Robert's death.

"I was never intended to be earl," Sunny began. "For as long as I can recall, I've been a disappointment to my parents. Unlike Robert, I was shy, awkward, plain and slow. An object of scorn, not pride. This didn't matter since I was the second son. But Robert's death changed everything. I only hoped that my father would live a long, healthy life…and that you would become my wife in time."

For it was only with Angela and her family that Sunny felt accepted. Valued. Blessed. So when his father unexpectedly died of a coronary, leaving Sunny the Earl of Sunderland at the green age of twenty-four, Angela's refusal left him distraught.

"Despite this, once I inherited the earldom," he continued, "I found myself flooded by debutantes wanting to become the Countess of Sunderland. None who were you, Angela. None who cared or could see my sorrow. It was relentless. All I could think was how do you heal from all this grief? The loss? My father, Robert. My mother's disappointment in me." A meaningful pause. "Most of all, you."

"And so you left England," Angela prompted in a raspy voice.

He nodded. "I had to do something—anything—but feel myself the object of your pity."

"I'm so sorry, Sunny. Again, I wish I'd never written that letter."

He held up a hand to silence her. "I burned that letter weeks ago. Anyway, I'm not telling you this, Angela, because I want an apology. I'm telling you because I want you to understand about Hélène and what I owe her.

"First, I traveled about Europe. I'll spare you the details, but I did not behave well—I drank, gambled, spent more money than I should on amusements I didn't give a damn about. I did not honor my responsibilities as earl—my legacy, if you will. It was as though I wanted to show how unworthy I was, to prove my mother and others correct.

"Eventually I found myself in Paris, partly because of this chateau and partly because I knew my mother wouldn't follow me here—you know how she hates the French. By then I'd truly lost any hope of ever being freed from this sense of being cursed, as ridiculous as it may sound.

"And then late one night, I wandered into the Bois de Boulogne. I knew it was unsafe after dark. Though I'd scarce admit it, I yearned for someone to put me out of my misery. On top of that, I was drunk out of my mind."

He could tell his confession shocked Angela; her eyes grew wide and mouth tight. He forced himself to continue speaking.

He explained how he'd somehow climbed to the top of a waterfall, one that lay in the Bois de Boulogne. Once there, he imagined himself simply falling. Lost in mid-air. He stared at his feet, an awful impulse taking possession of him.

"A simple misstep," he said. "Nothing I would be truly responsible for. An accident. Fate. Bear in mind, I hold no pride in this, Angela. I'm only stating what happened best as I can remember.

"A moment later, I made out a shadowy figure seated on the knoll beside the bottom of the waterfall. A woman—by then the sky had lightened into that greenish-blue preceding dawn. For some reason, I fixated on the woman. Not because I desired her, mind. She was so different from you, with her dark hair and sharp features. It was because I could see she was weeping."

"This was Hélène," Angela said.

"Yes. I made out she was sketching the waterfall, of all things, in the dark while sobbing in a public park. I thought, 'Here's someone as unhappy as I am and as desperate.' I can't explain it, but I suddenly feared for her safety. I yearned to protect her. And this was what forced me to turn away from the waterfall."

What happened next was too fast for Sunny to remember properly. He slowly made his way down from the waterfall. It was a tricky progress: it had been far easier to climb up than descend, for the stones were wet and the grass slick. After this, a crushing pain in his skull and all went dark.

"The next thing I recall, I woke up in a strange bed with a throbbing head. The dark-haired woman sat beside me in a chair. Yes, Hélène, as you surmised." He chuckled softly. "She was peeved, for she had a hell of a time transporting me to her flat. I had quite the gash on my head—you can still make out the scar here, though it's faint. She'd stitched my wound herself, not wanting to leave me alone while I was unconscious."

The rest of Sunny's story came in fits and starts, for it made him emotional. It reminded him too well of of all he owed Hélène, how much they'd shared. The fencing, the secrets, the mutual support after he confided about Angela and she of Julie.

Once Sunny was coherent, Hélène explained he'd slipped on the rocks. However, she'd noticed him before then, perched above the waterfall. She intuited his dark impulse.

"She scolded me—and rightfully so. *'How dare you risk your life climbing up there!'* she said. *'You appear well off, healthy, and young. Think of how many who don't have what you do!'*

"And I realized she was right: even if I didn't want to be an earl, I was in a position where I could help others, even if I was miserable myself. After that, Hélène and I were inseparable...at least for a time." A long pause. "She gave me a reason to think of someone besides myself."

~

Sunny said nothing more after this, but he suspected Angela understood enough. Hélène and Willie, blackmail, journalists, scandal, heartbreak—it was all of a piece. From the pallor on Angela's face, he suspected she felt as he did after she'd confessed about Philippe.

What she did next surprised him.

Angela cried in words more passionate than he'd ever heard from her, "Hélène was right: how dare you risk your life in such a manner! There's so much good in this world, so much beauty—to consider throwing it away because of me or anyone else makes me deeply furious. There are kittens, ballet, dance, music. Family, friends. Goodness, kindness, gratitude. And yes, love. All these things grant life purpose, Sunderland. Like today with that beautiful carriage ride you gave me. The Mozart, the Seine." Her cheeks grew wet with tears. "In my worst moments, when my heart was at its most bereft, I still knew life offered joys I'd yet to experience."

"You don't understand, Angela. Try as I might, I couldn't find any meaning when I climbed that waterfall. Nothing. Everything was so damn black," Sunny countered. "Loving you gave my life meaning. I'm not like you, I'm not beautiful or charming. I don't bring pleasure to the world—"

"That's not true," Angela protested.

"It is. I see it in my parents' eyes. In the eyes of others. The only place I never saw it was in you and your family…and now Hélène."

"And so you'll marry Hélène to protect her, just as you married me to protect me."

Angela's voice was odd, Sunny thought.

"Yes," he replied. "It solves many problems, wouldn't you say?"

He told himself he and Hélène would make a fine couple.

They'd find their own form of happiness, as unconventional as it would be. It would be a relief not to have his heart feel so battered and vulnerable all the time.

"But she loves someone else. And you don't love her." She flailed her hands in surrender. "Around and around we go, and no one is married to whom they love."

He stroked her lovely blonde hair, which was unbound along her shoulders. "I think it's clear who I love, Angela. You. Still. I always have, from the moment I encountered you inside that closet years ago when we were children. You're a force of light in the shadows of life, a brilliant daffodil that makes the world seem worthwhile when I'm at my most sullen. Even now. But I understand you can't love me that way and why," he continued, his throat tight. "Thank you for telling me about Philippe—it's a relief to learn the truth."

Angela burst out, "I wish I had known you before him."

"You did, darling. We've known each other since we were ten."

"I-I know. But not like this." A breath. "What are we to do?"

"There's nothing to be done. If all goes as planned, no one will ever learn of our marriage."

Though I never want to forget it.

He twined his fingers with hers. She didn't resist. Perhaps it was the aftermath of his confession, her emotions, but they lay together in silence in his bed, still clutching hands. Every so often he rubbed his thumb against her palm, as though to reassure her that all was well, that they were still friends no matter what.

Soon he sensed her body relax in slumber, just as the clock in the hall chimed two of the morning. As for Sunny, he remained awake for longer than he wished, awaiting the sounds of the world awakening to a new day.

Four hours to go.

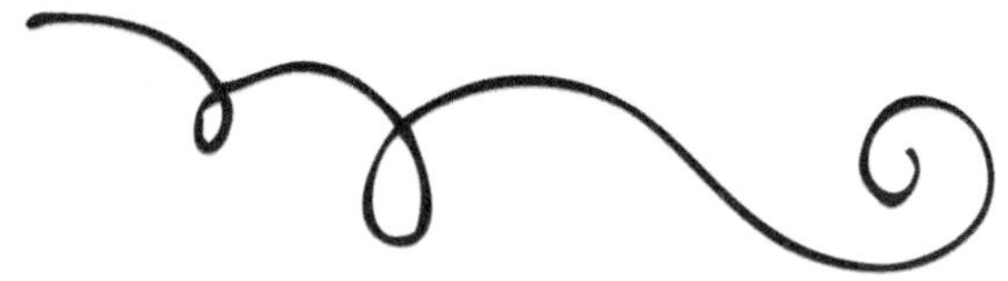

CHAPTER 27

THREE HOURS LATER, Angela awoke with a start, uncertain where she was. She was naked beneath the sheets. Then it all came back to her: the evening with Sunny, the bath, the lovemaking in the dark. How he'd carried her into his bed and they'd been intimate but not fully. His confession, which had shocked her. She felt shaken, thinking of how close he'd come to losing his life, what might have happened had Hélène not been there.

We didn't consummate the marriage. Though she told herself this was good—the last thing she needed was to find herself pregnant in Rome—part of her was bereft.

Especially once she noticed Sunny was already gone from the bed.

Especially now that she knew he didn't love Hélène, not like that.

Especially now that she knew Hélène was in love with someone who wasn't him.

Especially now that Angela knew he still loved her.

Desire, not love, she reminded herself weakly. Yet what they'd shared—the kisses, the confessions—felt suspiciously akin to the latter state.

The clock struck five. The sky was still dark. She raised herself against the pillows, disquieted, and not just because she was alone in his room.

She missed him. Missed what it was like to be with him as something more than his friend. As his lover, damn it. As for now, Sunny was probably avoiding her. It was about Hélène, the past they shared, the protection he owed her. He felt vulnerable after confessing he loved her. Angela understood. Soon she'd be gone from the chateau; he'd remain behind.

Well, she'd leave his bed, go to her room. When she emerged for breakfast, they could pretend the previous evening had never occurred. Go back to as they were as friends. Bid a civilized farewell in several days when she left for Rome. Really, it was for the best, considering Hélène would soon be his wife…though when Angela recalled his confession of love the previous night, her lips widened into a smile so broad that she felt as though the sun had returned after a rainstorm.

Joy. It was like Mozart ringing forth from an ancient hall at twilight, the glimmer of light on the Seine from the Pont Neuf. A hidden meal in a chateau with kittens, an adagio in a mirrored salon. A lover's embrace in a warm bath.

I will be happy, she swore. *These memories will remain mine.*

Outside the bedroom, a scratch at the door. No doubt the kittens. They were probably unhappy to be left alone for the night. Usually they slept with either her or Sunny.

"I'm coming," she murmured.

Angela located her nightgown, which was still damp on the floor beside the bed; she flushed, remembering how it became that way. As for donning something else, Sunny's robe was gone, her kimono probably soaked in the bathroom.

She wrapped a blanket around herself and hurried downstairs to her bedroom. Once there, she dressed quickly for the day in a simple aesthetic-style gown the color of forest moss—no use going back to sleep, she decided, even if she could have. Four kittens trotted at her heels, mewing louder than usual for their breakfast. Ivy, Hyssop, Mari, and Dandelion. But where was Clover?

Down the hall, Angela heard a thin cry from the library. Clover's distinctive meow. She'd somehow gotten caught inside it.

This time, the library door was locked. She knocked.

"Sunny?"

No answer came save for Clover's sharp meow, which had grown louder; the other kittens clawed at the door with distress. Angela considered her options. It was too early for Dubois, if he had the key to the door. As for any of the invisible servants, the only time Angela had ever glimpsed one was in the afternoon and rarely at that.

Angela pulled a pin from her hair, silently thanking Theo for teaching her how to pick locks. A moment later, the library door unlocked with a snap.

The library was empty as could be. Angela turned, suspicion rising. She sensed Sunny's presence, the hint of his warmth.

The kittens followed her into the room, gamboling in their usual way, but they didn't scatter. No, they went straight to the shelf where Hyssop had clawed the Greek edition of Hugo's *Les Misérables*. The book dangled off the shelf. Whoever last read it was in too much of a rush to replace it…and that last person must have been Sunny. She couldn't imagine the officious Dubois lingering over a novel when there were duties to attend.

Sunny had rushed from the library, leaving the book ajar—it had to be that. Yet why had he locked the library door?

There's something off.

Angela turned, seeking any clue. Hyssop jumped up to the shelf, knocking the book down, just as a glint of sunlight illuminated the shelf behind it.

Except it wasn't a shelf. It was an iron latch to a door hidden within the bookcase. But to where?

He's inside there. Why else would the book be amiss, the library locked?

The latch readily turned at her touch. The bookcase slid open to the side, revealing a narrow passage paved in dark wood.

Before Angela could reconsider, she entered the passage, but only after she slid the bookcase back into place to stop the kittens from following.

Enveloped in total darkness, she felt her way along the passage, her feet cautious on the cold flagstone floor. She trailed one hand along the wall, feeling like Perseus in the labyrinth.

As she shuffled forward, her heart began to pound, her flesh prickle. It didn't help that the temperature in the passage was cooler than it had been in the library, similar to that in a cave. Once her eyes adjusted to the dark, Angela walked with one arm before her, fearful of falling, her ears straining for any sound of life.

Just keep walking.

Some feet later, she inhaled a subtle scent of roses, a rush of breeze. The wood wall gave way to cool metal against Angela's hand, then glass. Suddenly the passage opened up: she was inside a tall glass dome bisected by graceful iron swirls.

The greenhouse. Sunny claimed it wasn't on the grounds of the chateau. He'd lied.

Above her, Angela made out a rush of stars, the silhouette of trees. It remained too dark to see much beyond this, for dawn had yet to arrive.

Within the greenhouse, she heard the flare of a match.

"Sunny?" she called out.

"*Non*, my lady." Dubois's thin face emerged from the darkness. "*C'est moi.*"

On a glade in the Bois de Boulogne, Sunny paced as he awaited Willie's arrival. He hadn't been able to sleep at all. Finally, he'd given up just before five, leaving Angela sleeping alone in his bed. It was for the best; he didn't want to have to lie to her about where he was going.

"Six now. No doubt Willie will be fashionably late," Hélène said, annoyance in her tone as she glanced at the pendant watch pinned to her bodice. "He always is, the bastard. He wants us on edge."

"That's a shame. I'd rather get this over with." Sunny drew the rapier from his walking stick. Best to be prepared. "He never wrote who his second is, but he's responsible for the doctor in case one of us gets injured."

"He'll need it."

"I wish I possessed your certainty, darling."

The endearment felt forced, but Sunny was too nervous to resist. Hélène had dressed in black bombazine, which further undermined his confidence. If he didn't know better, he'd believe she was preparing for loss, not victory.

"I know I forced you into this. I know you wanted to wait until after Angela left. But I've good reason to believe in you," Hélène said. She impulsively kissed Sunny's cheek. "Julie is so grateful. You've always been lucky for me, *chéri*."

Sunny forced out, "And you for me."

"Five past six," Hélène announced.

"Where's Julie?"

"At home. I didn't want her anywhere near here."

Sunny indicated the dueling grounds with his rapier. "She knows?"

Hélène gave a little shrug. "Perhaps."

Sunny let out a breath, wondering if Angela had any suspicion. It had been hard to ignore her questions last night. After all, she'd spied Willie with Hélène, when Hélène was performing her little show to provoke Willie. If things went awry, Angela would find out the truth soon enough.

"Ten past six," Sunny said, checking his pocket watch. "I propose we wait to quarter after. If he doesn't show, he'll forfeit—"

"Wait, I see someone," Hélène said, raising her hand. "Over there."

She pointed into the fog, which was burning off as the sun rose.

An open carriage emerged from the grey miasma. As it approached, Sunny made out Willie dressed in a jewel-red sack coat more suitable for a salon than a duel. He stood in the carriage, waving as though addressing an adoring public. Of course Willie would arrive in such a manner, Sunny thought, irritated. (Well, better to be irritated than anxious.) Beside Willie, a white-haired gentleman clutched a large leather bag on his lap. The physician. Seated across from Willie and the physician, Sunny made out a third man in the carriage, his face hidden in shadows.

"I see you found a second after all," Sunny called out. "You're late."

Willie leisurely stepped from the carriage as though he'd all the time in the world. The physician remained seated, but the second rose to his feet. He wore a mustard-yellow bowler.

Sunny squinted in disbelief. Luke Ward—it had to be.

Before Sunny could react, Ward stumbled out of the carriage after Willie. Drunk, that's what he was. Or so he appeared.

"Sorry, Sunderland," he hiccuped. "Didn't have a clue it was you Willie was nattering about. He'd mentioned a feud with a lady. Thought it was for a newspaper story, not this." Ward turned around the glade, his smile hitching. "Where are we anyway?"

Willie rolled his eyes. Sunny supposed few people were willing to risk their lives and reputation for him. Unlike Sunny for Hélène.

As for Hélène, she stepped forth, pointing toward Sunny with a bow of her own. "My second, monsieur. Lord Sunderland has agreed to stand in my place."

Sunny's heart began to pound. He shrugged off his jacket, his waistcoat, and rolled up his shirt sleeves. To his embarrassment, his hands were trembling. This wasn't anything fencing at Oxford or with Hélène prepared him for.

"Lord Sunderland?" Willie asked, his brow raised. "The Earl of Sunderland *Sunderland*? The one who married—"

"You're mistaken," Sunny interrupted coolly.

～

"Where are they?" Angela asked as she and Dubois stumbled across the Bois de Boulogne in the half-light of dawn. She never did get to see the details of the greenhouse, for it remained too dark and they were in too much of a hurry. Once Dubois shared the letter Sunny left behind, Angela understood there was no time to waste—she'd no idea Sunny even knew how to fence. Yet she wasn't surprised. She recalled how adept he'd been with his walking stick when he'd defended her. As for Willie, it seemed Angela wasn't the only woman he'd intimidated with his pen.

The greenhouse had led to another passage, which Dubois said was used during the Revolution for escape. He explained the door exiting it was tucked beneath a tumble of rocks overlooking a duck pond, conveniently depositing them onto the Bois de Boulogne.

"But I don't know where the duel is to be held," Dubois said. "Sunderland didn't write in his letter. There's a section of the park that's popular with duelists. I thought it here, near the vale of cedars." He swore softly. "His father would be so distressed. His brother dead, now the current earl—"

"Don't say that!" This was no time for emotion. "It's quarter past six."

"I think I see something."

"Where?" Angela circled.

Dubois pointed across the field, where the rising sun illuminated an open carriage settled in a glade of oak trees. "That must be where they are, my lady. *Vite!*"

Willie removed his sack coat and unbuttoned his shirtsleeves. "I suppose we're doing this then."

Luke stumbled onto the dueling ground between Willie and Sunny. "Am I to represent you, Willie? Or are you going to do it?" He scratched his chin, circling. "I don't know how to fence. I thought this was for a newspaper story."

"Get to the side, you ass," Willie snapped. To Sunny, "At the count of three."

"I'm to count?" Ward asked, pushing his hat back from his forehead.

"That's what a second does," Sunny confirmed, puzzled by this development. If he didn't know better, he'd suspect Ward was plotting something. But what?

"Very well then," Ward replied. "I'm ready when you are."

"To the first blood," Willie said, throwing an annoyed look at Ward. "Like gentlemen."

"But you're not a gentleman," Sunny countered. "Isn't that why we're fighting?"

"Save it for the duel, Sunderland." Willie raised his rapier. "Ready?"

Once Hélène and Ward were safely to the side of the dueling ground, Sunny nodded in Ward's direction.

"One!" Ward shouted.

Time seemed to slow, the air thicken. As though from far away, Sunny watched himself raise his rapier, a sturdy red-haired man in his shirtsleeves, his forearms bared in the cool April air. Then he stared down at the toes of his boots, which were surrounded by soft, mossy grass. The verdant earth. The flowers growing brighter as the dawn gave way to day. Sunny recognized sweet violets and lilies of the valley, which were among his favorites. A subtle scent rose from the earth, sweet and inviting. He breathed it in…

"Two!"

Now Sunny's mind returned to the life he'd once yearned to live, what he'd imagined it could be before he'd had his heart broken. Before he'd married Angela in a Kensington church on a winter morning and they'd fled to Paris. He saw the flowers growing on his ancestral estate in Berkshire that he so loved. The lambs, the cows. Angela in his arms in their nuptial bed, birds chirping outside their window and all that. Kittens and puppies. Roses and lilies…and he found he couldn't move, though it wasn't fear paralyzing him. Not now.

"Three!"

And then Sunny *did* move. A step toward Willie, rapier at the ready. Willie circled him, his head tilted in concentration as though judging Sunny's worth. The journalist was taller than Sunny recalled, faster too; he recalled everyone who'd ever bullied him and his blood began to rise. From the corner of his eye, Sunny saw Hélène cover her mouth with her hands. For all her steely demeanor, she was scared. Well, she should be. Sunny was scared too, though there was no time for this.

At last, their rapiers met. A clang of metal, the sense of lightning striking—the sensation vibrated along his arm to his shoulder, down his spine. Perhaps it was the knowledge of what was at stake, but this felt nothing like fencing with Hélène.

Back and forth they went, but not for long. Someone shouted, "*Arret!*"

The two men pulled apart. Sunny made out Dubois, who appeared singularly unsettled—where had he come from? He must have found the letter left in the greenhouse, explaining what to do in the event of his injury or death; Sunny hadn't banked on him locating it until later that morning.

But that wasn't all. Sunny recognized a woman following his manservant.

Angela.

She wore a moss-green gown, her expression weighed by an emotion he couldn't name…or perhaps couldn't bear to. His heart seized as he remembered how she'd come willingly to him in the bath, her response after he'd confessed his darkest history. The knowledge that she'd soon be leaving his life forever.

As Angela rushed toward the dueling grounds, the sky above her seemed to brighten with the hues of dawn—the pinks, the purples, the blues—as though life was returning after a long, hard winter. Sunny felt his heart expand, his arms ache to hold her. Even now.

She ran toward him. "Don't do this! I beg you!"

To protect her, Sunny shoved Angela off the dueling grounds;

he had no idea whether or not Willie recognized her from that night at La Fleur Interdite. Willie used the distraction to lunge anew at Sunny, vigorous in his attack. Sunny parried, holding him back, though barely. In frustration, Willie sliced at Sunny's stomach, catching the edge of his shirt with his rapier tip.

No blood was drawn.

A scream shouted, one that sounded frighteningly close. Before Sunny could react, Angela leapt into the dueling grounds, separating him and Willie. The grandest jeté among all grand jetés—she appeared to be flying.

The last thing Sunny saw before he fell against the earth was Willie's rapier slashing at Angela's skirts in mid-air.

And then he heard the blast of a pistol.

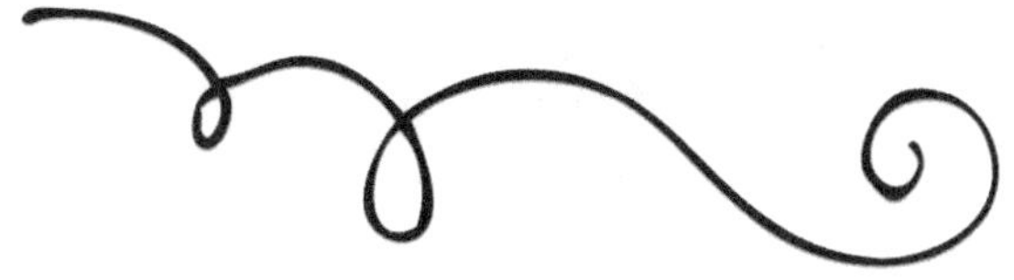

CHAPTER 28

Dubois. He'd fired the pistol—he'd shown it to Angela when she discovered him in the greenhouse. *"I'll bring it just in case, my lady,"* he'd said, tucking it into his waistband. The pistol was an ancient pepperbox revolver, one she suspected hadn't been used in years; Sunny's father kept it in the chateau for protection after the lessons of too many uprisings in Paris.

She'd never expected Dubois to use it. At least he'd the good sense to fire it into the air, rather than at anyone. Thankfully, Sunny remained unwounded.

I love him, she suddenly realized. It seemed a miracle as surprising as a hidden door in a library, a greenhouse in the night, or Mozart on a spring afternoon.

I love him, she thought again. *If anything happens to him, I won't be able to bear it.*

And then Angela knew what she had to do.

Love requires a leap of faith, she told herself.

A deep plié for velocity. Then she leapt with all of her strength. All of her love.

By the time the air cleared of gunpowder, Angela's grand jeté cleared Willie's rapier. She landed on the earth beside Sunny, who remained flat on his back where he'd fallen.

He clutched Angela against him.

"Stay low," he murmured. "Wait."

Dubois fired again into the air. The blast was loud enough to send Luke and Hélène running into the glade, hands clasped over their ears. More importantly, it startled Willie enough that he backed away from Sunny and Angela, stumbling over tree roots.

"Enough," Willie shouted once he regained his balance. "On your feet, Sunderland. Unless you care to forfeit."

Angela squirmed from Sunny's arms. She sat up and folded her arms across her chest—she'd do anything to protect him. Whether or not Willie recognized her, she didn't care. All these years she'd been concerned about her reputation, respectability, protecting her family, stability. None of this mattered anymore.

"I won't move, gentlemen! You'll have to duel over me."

And it appeared Willie would—he raised his rapier, settled his stance. Faster than she imagined possible, Sunny scrambled to his feet.

He set the tip of his rapier at Willie's throat. "Touch her and you die."

But before Willie could back off, Angela heard another gunshot blast, followed by a second. This time it wasn't Dubois clutching the gun.

It was Hélène.

~

"Hurry!" Sunny urged the carriage driver. "Can't you go any faster?"

So much blood, Angela thought. The blood was sticky like molasses, so dark a red it was nearly the brown of chocolate. The substance covered her hands, her skirts. She'd never seen someone shot by a pistol before, let alone someone close enough to bleed on her.

It had taken Angela a moment to comprehend exactly what had happened: not wanting to leave anything to chance, Hélène had shot Willie. The first bullet had gone wide, but the second hit him in his thigh. She'd had brought her own pistol, one far more efficient and accurate than Dubois's, which was too old and slow to do any actual harm.

Inside Willie's carriage, Willie slumped on the seat across from them, blood seeping from the bandage wrapped about his leg, the physician he'd brought attending him. As for Hélène, Sunny held her in his arms, Angela squeezed beside him; Hélène appeared to be in shock. They'd left Luke and Dubois behind on the dueling grounds, for there was no room in the carriage.

"I had no idea," Angela whispered to Sunny. "None of this, even after reading your letter. You, dueling with rapiers. This—" she gestured at Hélène, whose face had drained of color "—even with Willie's blackmail. It makes no sense."

Sunny replied, "Oh, it makes plenty of sense. There's a lot of things you don't know, countess."

"Less talk, if you please," the physician scolded. "Are we nearly to your residence, my lord?"

"Yes." To the driver: "Turn right here."

"Why did you do that?" Willie moaned. "Why, *why?*"

"Because it's time for you to be the scandal," Hélène shouted. "Not me."

"You're not in your right mind! You tried to murder me—I'll swear such."

"You can swear whatever you like, Willie. I'll tell them you and Sunderland were dueling over my affections—I shot you to protect Sunderland's life." Hélène offered a satisfied smile. "You have to admit it'll sell newspapers."

Luke Ward awaited at the chateau, somehow arriving ahead of their carriage—how he'd managed this, Sunny had no idea. But Ward wasn't alone: Julie was waiting outside the chateau. As soon as the carriage came to a halt, Julie ran sobbing to Hélène and embraced her as though she'd never let her go. "*Mon amour*, I was so worried! You're alive!" Angela's eyes widened at their display of affection.

She understands, Sunny thought. He hadn't written of Julie in his letter of explanation—that was for Hélène to reveal, not him. But this consideration fled his mind, for there was too much to do. He led Julie and Hélène to the salon, where Hélène reassured her lover as to her safety. He settled Willie upstairs in his bedroom, where the physician dressed his wound.

Once all this was done, Ward insisted on taking Sunny aside to the dining room.

"I owe you an explanation, my lord," he began after Sunny shut the doors. "The duel, my being Willie's second—"

"You're not drunk," Sunny cut off.

"No, my lord."

"Part of your subterfuge?"

"Yes." He offered Sunny a thick pile of letters, all addressed to Willie. "I think these will explain much."

Sunny's eyebrows rose as he examined the letters, many bearing the signatures of names he recognized. "Stolen? How ungentlemanly of you, Ward."

Luke offered a sheepish grin. "I think we can agree I'm hardly a gentleman. I'm sure we can also agree it would be for the common good to share these documents with certain authorities, and say, to publish them."

"And you'll arrange for such, naturally."

Another grin. "Naturally."

Sunny noticed a brandy decanter on the sideboard. He reconsidered after recalling it was barely half-past seven in the morning. "And here I thought you only wrote about art."

"I write about other subjects when the opportunity arises. Some are more profitable than others." Ward pointed to a chair at the dining table. "Sit, for I've a long story."

Ward explained that when while he was out with Angela the

previous day, he'd witnessed Willie fighting with a woman outside La Fleur Interdite.

"I'd heard rumors about Willie's blackmail under the guise of journalism—after a lifetime of working for newspapers, it's hard not to perk up when you hear something of interest," Ward said with a soft shrug. "I noticed Willie's argument particularly distressed your wife. Once I realized she recognized the lady accompanying Willie, this led me to put one and one together."

"And get three," Sunny interjected.

"Precisely," Ward replied, pouring himself a glass of brandy. "After I parted from Angela last night, I visited La Fleur Interdite with the intention of learning more. As I suspected, people were chattering about Willie's argument with Mademoiselle de Castel-d'Albret. Thanks to inquiries lubricated by alcohol, I found out about a duel rumored to take place on the Bois de Boulogne at dawn."

"And that's how you became involved," Sunny said.

Ward nodded. "It was shockingly easy. By then Willie had returned to the café looking for a second. So I obliged him, thinking if nothing else, I could get a story from the duel…or intervene if things went south." Ward rubbed his hands together. "What I hadn't anticipated was finding gold in the form of those letters at Willie's flat when we returned there to prepare for the duel. If you look through them, you'll find letters from the best families in Paris and some with more complicated reputations. Willie and blackmail are quite the intimate bedfellows."

So it wasn't only Hélène he'd blackmailed. Though Sunny wasn't surprised, Ward's proof was a victory.

"I'd heard rumors of such," was Sunny's noncommittal reply.

"Not rumors. Fact." Ward beamed like a boy at Christmas. "These letters combined with my being present at the duel as Willie's second—let's just say this will generate far more interest than my writing about an art exhibit." His voice dropped. "Of course, I'll be discreet on your behalf. After all, if it wasn't for you inviting me to escort Angela yesterday—"

"You'd never have discovered the story," Sunny finished.

He tried to hide his relief by pouring himself a small glass of brandy, damn the hour. His hands shook a little, but so be it.

He raised his glass in Ward's direction. "To mutual benefit."

Once she'd washed the blood off her hands, Angela waited outside the dining room for Sunny and Luke to emerge, straining for any hint of their conversation, still stunned. She'd no idea Hélène was sapphic—Sunny had only said Hélène was in love with someone who couldn't marry her. But now Angela understood. As for Luke, Angela had been shocked to find him at the duel, but not as much as expected—like many journalists, he seemed to have a nose for when something was about to occur. The kittens gathered at her feet, begging for breakfast; Dubois led them to the kitchen, sneezing all the while.

Some moments passed before Angela gave up any attempt at patience. She pressed an ear against the door. When Sunny opened it, she promptly tumbled at his feet.

"I was anxious," she explained.

"So I see." Sunny helped her up after giving Luke a nod of farewell. "Come with me."

He led Angela down the hall. Toward the library.

"I noticed you picked the lock," he said in a matter-of-fact tone. "I'd forgotten you possessed this skill. How shortsighted of me."

"How shortsighted indeed," Angela said, resisting the urge to rain butterfly kisses all over the bristles of his face. She supposed he hadn't time to shave that morning with a duel.

"How's the wounded?" he asked.

"In pain but not in danger. He'll leave soon."

"That's what the doctor intimated after he removed the bullet." He grimaced at Angela's moss-green gown, which was still stained in blood and shredded from Willie's rapier. "Seems your skirts got the worst of it."

Angela hadn't even noticed, she'd been so emotional. She burst into tears, the blood stains bringing back all that happened that morning. The duel, how she'd thrown herself between Willie and Sunny. Hélène and Dubois with the pistols. How close she'd come to losing the man she loved most in the world.

She threw her arms around Sunny, clutching him as though she'd never let go.

"I thought…I thought…" she gasped.

You would die.

I would be left alone.

You'd never know I love you.

But Angela said none of this, for she felt too vulnerable. Too raw. Instead, she pulled away, swiping at her cheeks like a child.

"Forgive me," she said. "It's been quite the morning."

Sunny offered a lopsided grin. "Don't I know it." He locked the library door behind them. "Come, I've something to show you. We should hurry before someone needs us."

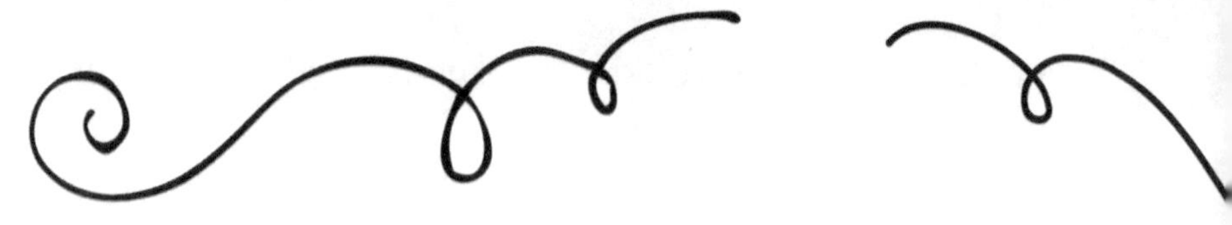

CHAPTER 29

Inside the library, Angela didn't appear surprised when Sunny revealed the secret passage hidden behind the bookshelf. "You've already discovered this, I take it?" he asked.

She couldn't hold back her smile. "The kittens. If you look—"

"Yes, I noticed the claw marks on the book the other day." He offered a wry glance. "Apparently you did too."

He quickly worked the latch and slid the bookshelf door open.

Now that it was later in the morning, the passage wasn't as dense with darkness—Angela made out a faint glow ahead. The greenhouse. She held her tongue until they were well past its entrance. And then she couldn't hold back.

"You lied to me," she accused once they'd made their way inside the glass dome.

But Sunny remained silent...and she understood why.

He wants me to take the greenhouse in first. All of it.

And so she did.

The bright sun illuminated every inch of the greenhouse. While not large, it was perhaps the most beautiful structure Angela had ever seen. Its glass walls were bisected by swirling ironwork that joined and parted in graceful arches. More than this, the greenhouse was filled with more roses than she imagined possible, though there were other flowers, many out of season: irises, tulips, peonies, daffodils.

"I've never smelled anything so exquisite," Angela breathed. "You planted these?"

"My father did the bulk after Robert's death."

"When he acquired the chateau?"

"Yes." To her surprise, Sunny appeared bashful, ashamed even. "The roses are mine. I arranged for them to be planted about five years ago, after the first time my father brought me here. Though we didn't stay, he wanted me to see it. It was then I realized something."

"What?"

He answered in a voice so low that Angela had to strain to understand. "You remember the rose garden in my country estate in Berkshire? The pink ones near the stream?"

"Those were my favorites." That's why she'd chosen similar roses for her bridal bouquet months earlier, Carles be damned. The ones in Sunny's garden had a perfume reminiscent of heaven. That, along with the petals' subtle gradations and soft yellow stamens, made them particularly exquisite.

"I asked my father and learned the botanical name for them: *Rosa Angelus*—Rose Angel." His freckled cheeks flushed. "All I could think…well, you'll think this fanciful, but I wanted to create a garden filled with them, these roses that reminded me of you in beauty and name."

Angela's heart welled with yearning. Sunny continued.

"Soon after, I resolved to plant a garden, Angela, of these roses. A private garden that would be my gift to you after we wed. One that we'd watch bloom together when we visited. For, despite the chateau's history, I do love it here.

"Once I fixed on this plan, I arranged to have cuttings brought from Berkshire, hired someone to cultivate them in my absence…"

He fell into silence. Angela understood why.

"But I didn't accept your proposal," she said. "And you were left with roses reminding you of me."

He nodded. "I'd forgotten about the roses when I fled here after you refused my proposal—well, I wasn't in my right mind, as you know. It was distressing to come across them in bloom, even in the heart of winter. And yet I couldn't destroy them. They were too beautiful. Too precious."

Like you, she sensed Sunny was about to say.

"But I couldn't bear to share them with anyone. Especially you, though Dubois knew of the greenhouse. Hence, the secret."

"I-I understand," Angela replied. She recalled the pink rose in his lapel after they'd wed. It was all of a piece.

Sensing her thoughts, Sunny broke off a small bud from one of the more robust bushes. It was just beginning to bloom.

"Here," he offered. "In memory of our marriage."

And then she realized: he was showing her the greenhouse as part of his farewell. So she'd know the truth before she left for Rome in four days. And now that she understood about Hélène, how could she impede their marriage? Yes, Willie had been vanquished today, but there would be other threats to Hélène and her beloved—threats that Sunny's noble title could offer protection from. He owed this to Hélène for saving his life.

Angela's eyes welled, her throat grew tight. If they only had this short time together, she'd make the most of it.

She didn't trust herself to speak. Instead, she spoke with her body, as dancers do.

She accepted the rose, took a step closer to him. Then another.

She wrapped her arms about him.

I love you, she said with her embrace.

She set her lips against his. He was startled, but didn't pull away.

I love you, she said with her kiss.

He returned her kiss with a deep sigh.

I know you love me. And I love you, he replied as his tongue laced with hers.

Their kiss deepened. The rose dropped from her fingers as they sank to their knees in the greenhouse, the floor soft with moss and soil.

And then she noticed a chaise nearby fabricated in the same ornate ironwork as the greenhouse. Thrown over it was a brown cloak with a deep hood.

And now I've found the cloak you wore to rescue me.

But she didn't question him about it. Not then. Instead, she spread the cloak over the soft earth and lay back on it. She raised her arms, affording Sunny access. He undid the buttons of her bodice faster than she imagined possible. She shrugged out of the gown, relieved to have it far from her, for it smelled of copper and violence, not roses and love. She released the busk of her stays, untied the ribbons of her chemise.

He traced the freckles of her chest before pressing his lips against them.

She let out a long, low moan. *I love you. Only you.*

She faced Sunny, her hand falling over the bulge tenting his trousers. He appeared uneasy as she unbuttoned him.

"I'm not beautiful like you," he whispered, breaking the charged silence.

Despite her teary eyes, her face broke into a broad grin. "It would be strange if you were, wouldn't it?"

Then there was no more room for conversation, for urgency had taken over their intimacies. Need, that's all she felt. Want. Desire…and now she knew her desire included love.

He threw off his jacket, unbuttoned what remained of his clothes—he'd removed his waistcoat for the duel—and lay beside her on the brown cloak. She twined her legs about his hips, eager for whatever might come. Desperate for him.

She nipped at the corner of his mouth, his shoulders, dipping her hand down his chest toward his arousal, which appeared so smooth and stiff. She was about to caress him there, but she still sensed Sunny's reluctance. His shyness. Perhaps she'd misunderstood, for all his declarations of love and rose gardens.

"You don't want me," she murmured, taken over by anxiety.

He drew a deep breath. "I feel so undeserving of you."

"You're not, love."

And then she realized: the same shame that had plagued him all his life, the shame he'd confided to her, had never left. The bullying at Eton, the insults from his mother, the nicknames. For all of Sunny's bravado—his dueling, his anger, his chivalry—he was still that boy she'd met inside a closet hiding from others.

A man who thought himself an ugly beast worthy of ridicule. Unworthy of love.

"I love you. I desire you. Only you," she whispered against his ear. "I'm sorry it took me so long to realize this."

She sensed his smile broaden across his jaw. His body.

He reached for her, granting her permission to continue.

She rolled him back against the cloak, setting kisses along his furred chest, down his soft belly. She licked his nipple, surprised at her boldness before venturing further south. Toward his erection, which seemed to have grown stiffer and larger the closer she drew.

He shuddered and moaned. But he didn't move away.

He set his hands on the slope of her shoulders as she licked and kissed him, being ever so gentle yet demanding. She took him into her mouth. He tasted like salt and musk, desire and need.

Once she sensed he could take no more, she pulled away, meeting his eyes.

His pupils were blasted dark with arousal. Disbelief. Angela felt a strange power she'd never experienced before. The knowledge that she could transform him from a beast into an earl who'd understand his worthiness in the world. His value.

"Now do you understand how much I adore you?"

"God, Angela…"

With a muffled groan, he pulled her toward him, recapturing her mouth beneath his, her body melting against his. And then he caged her in his arms, his erection urgent against her wetness. But he didn't take her. Not yet.

She felt his gentle hands caress the dip of her waist, the swell of her hips before he bent toward her, adoring her. He trailed his lips along her belly, toward the blonde curls cresting her delta. He gently parted her thighs, revealing her swollen vulva, the pearl-like secret tucked within. When his tongue flicked against her, she thought she'd sob with pleasure. She was a constellation of stars. A burst of sunlight.

And then she could take no more. She convulsed against his mouth, her eyes tight as she came undone with a pleasure that startled her.

Oh.

Once she'd settled back into her body, he notched his hips against hers, his cock hard against her softness. She girded herself for what was to come, be it pain or pleasure.

He didn't move. He was leaving it up to her, this deed that would make her his wife in body, if not in deed. Whatever might happen, they'd always share this.

She wrapped her arms about him, pressing down against his arousal.

"Are you sure?" he whispered.

She nodded.

He drew a deep breath, his brow creased. Worry, that's what he felt. And so he didn't take her just yet. He slipped his hand between their hips, caressing her until she climaxed anew.

And then he pushed into her gently. Carefully.

Whatever discomfort she felt passed quickly. He began to move, her hips meeting his in this place where lust and love collided. This was different from what she expected. Deeper. More intimate. More intense and vulnerable, though there was joy in it too, along with their awkwardness and shyness.

And then he cried out and she joined him. She didn't pull away, wanting all of him, come what may.

Afterward, they remained joined together for as long as they could; Sunny couldn't bear to part from her. He pressed his lips against her shoulder, wanting to remain in her embrace for as long as he could. She was so warm, so soft, so beautiful. Around them, the scent of roses hung on the air. Every so often, he noticed a butterfly flutter among the foliage.

She loves me. I love her. And she's leaving soon.

That they'd consummated their relationship wouldn't matter, if Angela still desired an annulment, though he prayed she wouldn't. Whatever scandal might come, they'd weather it together. God knew he didn't care, though Angela might. But there were other considerations. He thought of Hélène and Julie, Willie and his blackmail. The stories that would be published about the duel; he prayed Angela wouldn't be mentioned.

Ward wouldn't do that. He knows better. But what of the others? Had Willie recognized her?

Angela was the first to speak, to Sunny's relief. Who knew what awkwardness he might have spouted with his thoughts in such turmoil?

She accused in a sly tone, "It *was* you rescuing me that night in La Fleur Interdite. I knew it."

Sunny's chest released in laughter. "After everything that's happened between us, this is what you're fixating on?"

"Well, we just made love on the cloak you wore that night." She raised herself on her elbow. She stroked the fur on his chest. "But I have one question for you."

He gazed up at her, her blue eyes sparking amid the sunshine. "I'm afraid what you're about to ask me."

And he was. He felt more vulnerable before this woman he adored than he felt dueling in the Bois de Boulogne.

She jabbed a finger at the cloak. "Why all the subterfuge? The cloak, the sneaking around? The secret passages and such? I understand you might not want me to know you rescued me that night at La Fleur Interdite. But I sense there's been more than an isolated incident requiring you to wear a cloak."

He let out a long breath, relieved. "No secrets?"

"No secrets."

"But you'll have to keep this between us, though Hélène and Dubois know."

"Promise." She plighted her vow in the form of a kiss. "Now tell me! You have to."

Sunny screwed his face, trying to find the words to express without feeling foolish.

"You'll laugh, countess."

"I promise I won't, earl."

"Okay then. The secret passage was already part of the chateau already when my father bought it. A remnant from the French Revolution when aristocrats might need to escape at a moment's notice to safety—there's a similar one in Versailles. As for the cloak, sometimes I go out at night… and help people."

He paused, feeling vulnerable. Why was it that kind deeds always made one seem foolish of the ways of the world rather than wise?

He forced himself to add, "Well, not just anyone. Women in unfortunate straits. If I see someone begging or in need of funds, I'll give them money. Or if they're in a tussle…"

"The walking stick," Angela said quietly. "That's why you're so adept with it."

His face burned with the heat of a thousand suns, or so it felt.

"I know it's ridiculous. Whatever help I give can't really change their lives—the money probably ends up stolen or used by others— but I still try. I should set up some sort of foundation. Perhaps I will in time. I'm still becoming accustomed to being an earl—I've barely been to parliament since I gained my title. Still, I hope whatever I offer helps."

Angela grew very still. "Like you helped me and Hélène."

"I suppose." He sat up, gathering their clothing. "On that note, Luke uncovered some interesting information about Willie. You can expect an article that'll reveal all."

"Including the duel?" Angela tied her chemise.

"Yes," he said, putting on his trousers. "I suspect you won't be named—Ward knows better."

"That's a good thing, since I'm supposed to be in the Alps."

His tone turned lighter; somehow by confessing his secret, his worries didn't feel as oppressive.

"Ah yes, the Alps. We'll have to visit there one day."

"That would be helpful," Angela teased in turn, lifting her hair for help with her stays. "What if someone asks me about my time there?"

"Indeed, countess. And now I'm going to help you again."

"How so, earl?"

He pointed to her gown, which she was in the process of donning despite the blood stains along the skirt. "I want to burn that and take you shopping for something new and spring-like, once everyone leaves here."

As soon as he said this, his anxiety flared. Rome. The annulment. Surely she'd agree it was off. Surely she wouldn't leave.

Perhaps Angela sensed his shift of mood, for her tone turned serious. "What about Hélène? Her lover? Even if Willie is no longer a threat, you still owe her so much."

"Let's not speak of this now, Angela. We'll figure it out."

First, to return to the chateau. Rejoin the world.

Later, Sunny would regret this decision. For when they emerged from the library into the hallway, a wall of journalists awaited—somehow they'd slipped inside despite Dubois's presence. Fortunately, Sunny had the presence of mind to hide Angela in the library before anyone noticed her bright blonde hair.

As a result, there would be no time for farewells, no discussions of what might be next for their marriage. Less than three hours later, Angela would be alone on a train speeding from Paris toward Rome.

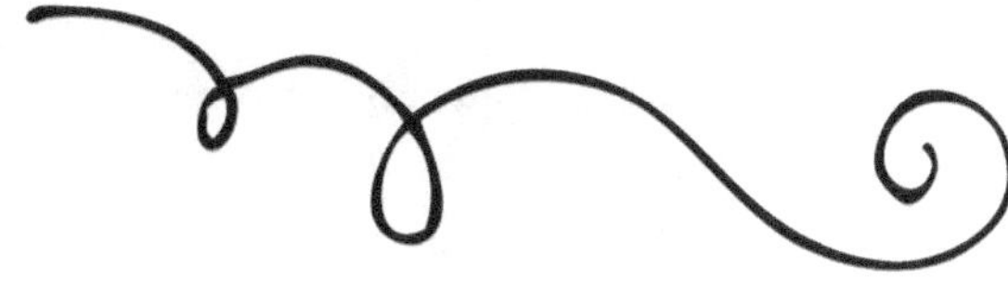

CHAPTER 30

THE TRAIN JOURNEY to Rome felt endless to Angela, for all its abruptness.

Now alone in a private compartment, she wore the veiled bonnet Sunny gave her out of caution—she had no idea when Luke Ward's story would be published, let alone the other journalists who'd caught wind of the duel and its consequences.

While the train sped south, she thought of all that had happened after they'd returned from the greenhouse. Try as she might, all Angela could recall was Sunny's panic once he saw the reporters awaiting them in the chateau. How he'd pushed her back into the library, locking the door so no one would find her. Soon after, Dubois arrived in the library via the secret passage from the Bois de Boulogne with the bonnet and a portmanteau containing clothing and other necessities. *"Je vous demande pardon,"* he said in his formal way. *"It's best we go immediately, my lady—the reporters won't leave. I'll take you to the train station and book your passage…"*

The next day after several train changes and no sleep, Angela's mother thankfully awaited her at the rail station in Rome. She supposed Sunny or Dubois must have wired regarding her arrival.

"Sweetheart!" Clio exclaimed, embracing her daughter. "It's

fortunate we arrived early in Rome. Papa can't wait to see you. No trunk?"

"Just the bag." There'd been no time for anything else. No time for farewells, not even with the kittens.

"We've yet to set up the flat, but no matter. You're here!"

"This doesn't seem real," Angela said, pushing away thoughts of Sunny. "Two days ago I was in Paris. Now I'm in Rome. I feel like I'm dreaming."

"This isn't a dream. Once you see Papa, you'll know it's real."

Over the past seven years, Angela had imagined many times and in many ways what it would be like to encounter her father again. She'd envisioned him arriving on the docks of London, paint box and canvases in tow. Appearing in the hallway of their home in Brompton as though he'd never left. In her darkest moments, she had nightmares of his funeral, his body encased in a coffin cloaked in white lilies.

Now, as Clio led her through the winding streets of Rome, Angela could help but think how lacking in imagination she'd been. She'd never envisioned the ancient city as a setting for their reunion.

Soon mother and daughter arrived at a narrow door set in a narrow building painted in ochre.

"Two flights up, sweetheart."

Angela's heart fluttered with nerves as she climbed the steps. After seven years of separation, her memories of her father were like a faded family photograph and as precious. Neil Bartham was the sort of man who made the world seem brighter and bigger through both his art and his warmth. He was charming and had a robust laugh; Angela always thought she'd inherited her natural optimism from him.

And then there he was, lying on a settee in a humble sitting room spilling with gold sunlight. A man bearing chestnut hair streaked with grey. A man with warm amber eyes, sharp chin, and an intelligent gaze. Her father.

This isn't a dream.

"Papa!" Angela called out, her chest swelling. But she didn't rush to him immediately. No, she'd let herself take him in first—this was a moment she wanted to savor.

Neil Bartham sat up, moving slower than when Angela had last seen him, when he was a vigorous man approaching fifty. He'd lost a leg during his travels, the result of the cart accident that left him incapacitated, penniless, and far from civilization for a longer time than he'd spent painting in Jerusalem. A crutch rested beside him on the settee.

"Aren't you going to greet me, Angela?" he greeted in a more robust voice than she expected. "Or are you going to make me come to you?"

And then somehow Angela was in her father's arms and Clio was embracing them and Angela was weeping and they were all exclaiming how happy they were to be together. For it had all been so very much.

The first hours of their reunion passed in joyful conversation and laughter and somber remembrances. Neil spoke only in general of the travails he'd experienced during the years they'd be separated; those would take more than a single sitting to relate. Angela noticed her father wearied easily. However, he was able to get around with his crutch better than she expected and was drawing again; Angela grinned at the sight of her father's sketchpad.

"I'm simply exhausted," he assured. "We traveled too quickly. I was in such a rush to get home to my family after so long."

"I warned you as much, my love," Clio said, exchanging a soft look with her husband. "You've been through so much."

"I didn't spend time in Rome when I traveled to Jerusalem," Neil interjected. "I'm telling myself it's for the best we linger, though I wish Musa and the twins were here with us too. Once I've improved, perhaps I'll paint some new canvases—I lost everything during my travels save for the ones I shipped home early on."

Neil was particularly invested in hearing about Angela's marriage; he had fond memories of Sunny's father, who'd been such a loyal patron of his art. As for Angela, she was careful not to reveal anything about the annulment.

Still, every so often, she noticed Clio looking at her with an expression suggesting her mother saw more than she said.

~

A full day passed before Angela encountered her mother alone. She'd awakened at dawn after a disturbing dream of Sunny, the duel, and Hélène.

Across the hall, Angela glimpsed her mother seated in the kitchen in her dressing gown, which was a gentle shade of cobalt, her father's favorite color. From the look of things, Clio was brewing some sort of herbal concoction. It smelled awful.

"You're awake already," Mama whispered. "It's not even six."

"A bad dream," Angela whispered in turn. "Making tea for Papa?"

Clio nodded, patting the chair next to her. "I'll give it to him when he wakes. Licorice root, ginger, peppermint along with other ingredients I shan't divulge. It'll strengthen him. He'll complain, but he'll drink it."

"You and your remedies," Angela teased, relaxing into nostalgia. The uneasy threads of her dream faded. All the Barthams had been subjected to Clio's herbal teas and remedies growing up. As disgusting as they were, they did help—or perhaps it was the relief of no longer drinking them.

Clio set the teapot aside to steep. "I'm glad it's just the two of us, sweetheart. How are you and Sunny? I know your marriage was…unexpected. All is well?"

Perhaps it was being alone without her father, but Angela was emboldened. "I wanted to ask you about your marriage. About your annulment."

Clio's blue eyes narrowed. "You mean my first marriage?"

Angela nodded.

"It's not something I care to dwell on, sweetheart."

"Forgive me, I don't mean to upset you, Mama. But I wish you would."

A long moment passed, one in which the fire crackled in the shadows of the kitchen.

"It was a distressing experience," Clio admitted at last, her silvery voice catching.

"I don't mean to pry. But I need to know." Angela tried to keep the desperation from her voice, but was unsuccessful.

"Very well." A deep breath. "My first husband—not my true husband, as I consider your father—did not love me as he should. Looking back, I think he viewed me akin to a piece of art in a museum, not a living woman with needs." Clio glanced down at her hands, which were folded gracefully upon her lap. "The day after our wedding, it was clear we didn't suit. I reassured myself everything would change after our honeymoon. It didn't."

"That's when he took you to Venice, where you fell in love with Papa."

Clio's blue eyes filled with warmth. Joy. "I couldn't look away from your father. Though I know this makes no sense, it felt as though there was a thread connecting us. A *coup de foudre*. But you already know this, sweetheart—your father and I were meant to be, scandal and all." A wry smile. "In the loss of my reputation I felt truly alive, no longer a statue in a museum. Unfortunately, I learned too late that society has a long memory. You and your siblings ending up paying the price, which I regret." Clio's brow knit. "Why all the questions, Angela? Why now?"

"I must confess something. My marriage to Sunny is going to be annulled."

Clio took a sharp intake of air. "Oh, Angela—"

"Not to worry! Our annulment wouldn't be like yours. We've been careful to keep everything under wraps. I know the reasons an annulment can occur: fraud, impotence, or incompetence."

A sharp laugh. "I know all about annulments, Angela. Too well."

Angela plundered on. "We'd claim fraud, which seems the least scandalous. We can argue such because there was a mistake on our marriage license. I didn't use my birth name."

"Allegra Jane Bartham," Clio breathed. "We named you Allegra because it meant 'joyful' in Italian. And so you've been."

"I know, Mama. But now…now…"

Angela blinked back an infusion of tears.

"You're not so joyful," Clio said.

Angela nodded.

"Because of the annulment?"

Angela imagined Sunny's dear face before her, with his freckles and soft lips and mane of auburn hair. "Oh, what a mess I've made!"

"You fell in love with him."

After a long moment, Angela nodded. "I love him more than I thought possible. More than the moon and the stars."

Her mother beamed. "I'd hoped such for years and not because he's an earl. He's a good man. A kind man. He adores you the way you should be adored. He deserves someone like you to love him— he hasn't had a happy life for all his privilege."

Angela's throat grew tight. "I fear it's too late to stop the annulment. It's complicated to explain, but there's another woman involved. I waited too long to return his affections…"

From Clio's silence, Angela sensed her mother somehow understood. Clio reached for her. And so Angela allowed herself to give way to her confused emotions. Her tears felt like a storm held back for too long.

When Angela calmed, her mother asked, "Is Sunny in love with this other woman?"

Angela looked up from her mother's arms. "No. He loves me."

"Has your annulment been finalized?"

"No. But—but—"

How could she explain about Hélène and her lover without betraying their privacy?

"Trust me, it makes sense for him to marry this other woman. He owes her a debt of honor," Angela finally said. "I need to consider our family, the other woman and her reputation, and—"

"Sweetheart, stop!" Clio interrupted. "All I want to know is whether Sunny loves the other woman."

"No," Angela said at last. "He doesn't love her."

"And you love each other?"

"Yes."

In that single word, Angela felt her heart expand as though to reach beyond the seven hills of Rome.

"Then it's not too late. You'll find a way." Clio kissed Angela on her cheek. "Write Sunny a letter—I'll post it for you. In the meantime, would you like some tea?"

Angela didn't wait. She wrote Sunny immediately, using a sheet of paper torn from her father's sketchpad. Unlike that long, hurtful letter she'd sent him way back when, this time her letter was short. For what more was there to say?

I love you, she wrote.

I want to be your wife, she wrote.

I want you to be my husband, she wrote.

I hope it isn't too late for us, she wrote.

Angela sealed the letter and addressed it to the chateau, praying Sunny would still be in residence there. However, she didn't return to the kitchen for breakfast. No, she dressed to go out into the world to post the letter—she wouldn't wait.

"Love requires a leap of faith," she murmured.

This time, her leap of faith felt more metaphorical than physical. But she'd take it.

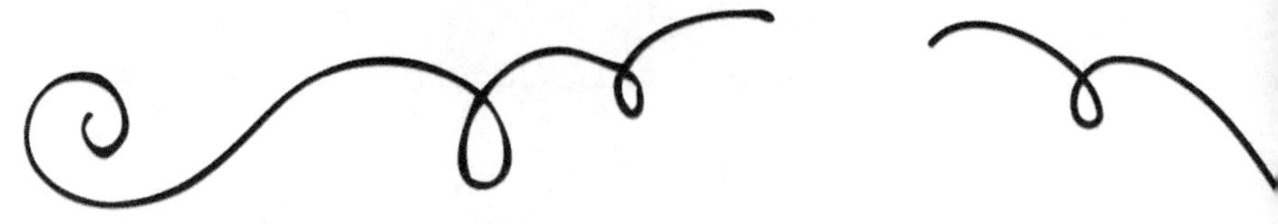

CHAPTER 31

ANGELA'S PARENTS awaited her when she returned from the post office. From their concerned expressions, she realized she'd left without telling them where she was going. "I'm so sorry," she said, removing her bonnet. "I should have left a note."

"It's not that, sweetheart." Clio handed Angela an English language newspaper. "You should see this. I came across it when I went out to buy bread for breakfast."

Angela's stomach plummeted. Those journalists. Well, she knew it would be a matter of time. She only hoped that Luke Ward's article was published before the others.

"What does it say? Am I named in it?"

"No, you're not named," Clio said, a peculiar edge to her voice. "But you should read it."

EARL SAVES WIFE FROM ROGUE WRITER

Yesterday morning Virgil Sydenham, the Earl of Sunderland, was returned to society's attention after dueling the notorious journalist Edmond de Williem in the Bois de Boulogne outside Paris. However, that was the least of what was exposed by the brave earl.

The article continued for some paragraphs, much of it laudatory to Sunny. It also mentioned that *La Tête-à-Tête* had become involved. They'd issued a terse statement that they'd terminated Willie's contract until further notice.

However, the article took an unexpected turn in the second to last paragraph.

～

In Paris, Sunny had only just seen the article that morning. Though he knew press attention was inevitable, he'd avoided all encounters with newspapers until Luke Ward sent a note. *"I think you'll be pleased with my account of the affair,"* Ward wrote. Anyway, Sunny had been too preoccupied with Angela and concerned about Hélène and the possibility of scandal to read newspapers. Angela, he could do nothing about—he prayed she'd write him soon so they could untangle their future. As for Hélène, she remained away from society's eyes in her flat near the Champs de Mars.

Sunny immediately went to her with Ward's article, waiting to read it until they were together.

The article began innocuously enough. "'EARL SAVES WIFE FROM ROGUE WRITER,'" Sunny read aloud to Hélène and Julie. He reminded himself that Ward had been careful not to name his wife in previous articles.

"Ooh, strong opening by Monsieur Ward," Julie said, clapping with glee.

"Go on, *chéri*," Hélène commanded, beaming at him.

Sunny continued with the article. Still no mention of Angela, thankfully. Hélène's shooting of Willie was presented as self-defense rather than anything salacious. Sunny used a dramatic voice as he read, surprised to find himself enjoying himself—he really did seem dashing in the article. Luke's description of the duel made Sunny seem akin to a Dumas hero, with his swashbuckling ways and championship of victimized women. Ward also unearthed further evidence of Willie's malfeasance; it seemed inevitable he'd be arrested in time.

However, the article took an unexpected turn two paragraphs from the end.

Sunny shuffled the newspaper, a frown creasing his face.

"Is that how the article ends?" Hélène asked. She reclined on the chaise in her sitting room, the spring sun falling across her sharp features. He'd rarely seen her so pleased. "It seems so abrupt."

"There's two more paragraphs," Sunny replied in an odd tone.

"What else did Monsieur Ward write then?" Julie prodded.

Sunny looked up from the article. "He announced the name of my wife."

Hélène guffawed. "Best laid plans, *chéri?*"

He set the newspaper in her hands. He couldn't put it off any longer.

"It's not what you think, darling."

"Who on earth is 'the former Hélène Charlotte de Castel-d'Albret'?" Neil Bartham burst out, clutching the newspaper. "According to this article, she's the Countess of Sunderland, not you, Angela. This makes no sense."

Clio made soothing noises to calm her husband. "Did you know about this, Angela? And what is this about a duel? I had no idea Sunny even knew how to fence."

Angela set her jaw. How had the article learned of Hélène and Sunny's intentions? Had one of them told a journalist? Or someone else?

"They're not married. Believe me, I'd know if they were," Angela explained in a rush. "Not yet anyway."

"This Hélène, she's the woman you spoke of," Clio said. "When you told me about the annulment."

"Annulment?" Neil interjected. "Are you married to Sunderland or not, Angela? My head is spinning."

"Yes, we're married, Papa. As for the duel, the article is accurate. Mademoiselle de Castel-d'Albret is the woman who shot Willie during the duel—see, it says so here. Sunny intends to marry her once our annulment is finalized. A replacement bride, if you will." Angela drew a deep breath to stop the quaver in her voice.

"A replacement bride?" Clio interjected. "Angela, pray explain!"

"I warned you it was complicated, Mama. It's a scheme we came up with, so no one would ever know I'd been his wife. Sunny suggested it—he and Hélène were already in discussions to marry before he stepped in at my wedding."

"She was the French woman at the church?" Clio asked.

Angela nodded. "The logic being that if Sunny returned to London with a bride, people would believe he'd married her, not me."

"But don't you love Sunny?" her parents yelled at the same time.

Angela ignored their question.

"Perhaps their marriage was announced prematurely because of the duel. To avoid throwing me to the wolves, so to speak. After all, no one was supposed to know I was in Paris." And then in the brightest voice she could summon while her heart was cracking: "Did you see the article about me in the Alps? Seb's friend Luke Ward wrote that one. All to protect my reputation and our family."

"Mr. Ward also wrote that article about Angela in the Alps, *oui*?" Hélène asked, pacing with agitation. "He's been a very active boy on your behalf, Sunderland. What I don't understand is why Monsieur Ward wrote we were married."

"I told him about your engagement to the earl, *mon amour*," Julie said. "He interviewed me—I didn't know he'd weave it into something more. Did I do something wrong?"

Shit, Sunny thought. Luke probably figured they were going to annul the marriage anyway, thought he'd protect Angela. He prayed Angela hadn't seen the article. What would she think?

Hélène abruptly ordered Julie to leave the room to buy her flowers. Irises, of course. Once she was alone with Sunny, she said, "You need to go to Angela. Immediately."

"I can't. She's in Rome with her parents."

"Sunderland, you do know this is very serious."

"I-I do."

Strange how those two words were akin to a promise. A wedding vow. His voice cracked to his embarrassment.

Hélène cares about me. And I care about her. What a mess this is!

He met her eyes. After a long moment, he said the words he wished he didn't need to.

"Hélène, I won't break my promise to you a second time. We'll wed. The annulment won't take much longer. July, if that."

Hélène waved her hand with impatience. "That's not what I meant, Sunderland. You didn't tell me Angela left Paris."

"It didn't seem pertinent."

"And you let her go?"

"Yes."

Hélène let out a sigh. "You're even more of an idiot than I realized. If I weren't in such a good mood, I'd slap you."

"You're always eager for an excuse to slap me." Sunny forced a weak smile. "That's just our way, darling. It'll make for a lively marriage."

"Marriage…" Hélène finally settled in a chair. "I have a confession to make."

"This should be interesting." His head began to pound. A migraine. He hadn't had one since Oxford. He covered his eyes with his hands, hoping the lack of light would help.

"I hadn't planned to shoot anyone. Just scare Willie if things got out of hand. But once your little ballerina threw herself between you, I realized something."

Sunny looked up from his palms. "What's that?"

"A woman doesn't throw herself between two men with rapiers unless she's madly in love with one of them."

Sunny couldn't think how to respond when Hélène pulled off his signet ring. She offered it to him.

"Take it." Hélène's expression grew unexpectedly tender. "I'm not averse to a marriage of convenience if it benefits me. But our marriage would benefit no one. Especially you."

"But the world thinks you're my wife." He arched an eyebrow. "Congratulations, darling. You're a countess!"

She folded her arms across her chest. "I don't care."

"Of course you care! Julie, her daughter, Willie. Revenge. Wasn't that what this was all about?"

She let out a loud *tsk*. "Julie and Céline will be fine. Willie won't be blackmailing anyone for a long time, not after Monsieur Ward's article."

"What about your future?"

"I'll figure it out." A shrug. "The important thing is I have my revenge. I'm sure Julie would agree."

She again offered the signet ring.

"Sunderland, if you don't take it, I'll throw it out the window."

A moment passed—a moment in which Sunny questioned his emotions. Incredulous, that's what he felt. Most of all, relief. It felt a physical sensation, tingling from his head to his feet. Like spring after winter. Sun after the rain. Kittens in a chateau.

He tucked the signet ring onto his finger, unexpectedly moved. She truly was his friend—he loved her.

He pressed his lips against her cheek. "Thank you, darling."

"You're welcome, *chéri*." She waved him away. "Now go see what's taking Julie so long with my flowers, if you will."

But before Sunny could do so, a disheveled Dubois arrived at the door of Hélène's flat, panting for breath. He gasped out, "I've been looking all over for you, my lord—"

"Sunderland?" a querulous voice interrupted from behind Dubois. In English, "Is that you?"

And then, without waiting for an invitation, Sunny's mother swept past his manservant into the room.

"Good day, madame," she greeted Hélène. "I understand you're my new daughter-in-law. You may address me as my lady or the Dowager Countess. Don't forget!"

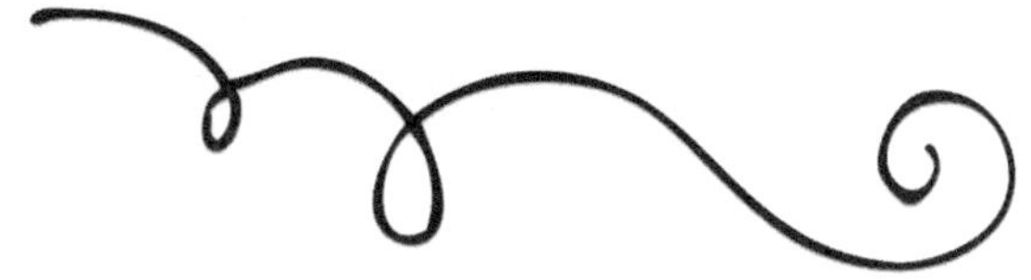

CHAPTER 32

"Well, she's leagues better than that Bartham chit," the Dowager Countess of Sunderland announced a half-hour after she'd burst in on her son with Hélène. "But why oh *why* did you have to marry someone French?"

"We're not married, Mother," Sunny replied, his jaw tight. "Mademoiselle de Castel-d'Albret is my friend."

Mother and son were on their way to the chateau seated inside a soggy hansom cab, one Dubois struggled to find for them. Perhaps representing Sunny's sullen mood, the bright morning had transformed in an instant with a cloudburst. Alas, no hansoms were to be immediately had for hire—they'd become soaked to their skin.

"Don't lie to me, Sunderland! *The Times* states she's your wife."

He felt rather bold. "You shouldn't believe what you read in newspapers. You of all people should know better."

His mother offered a bitter laugh. "Too true. I suppose you'll wed once the annulment goes through?"

Sunny stared out at the passing trees, which were budding green with life. The carriage felt far too small for his liking, too crowded. But then again, even if he was in a giant palace with his mother, it would have felt too small. He suspected Hélène felt similarly in his mother's presence. She'd been taken aback at the Dowager Countess's arrival. The only upside was his mother spoke no French save for *bonjour* and *au revoir*. Therefore, she couldn't understand Hélène's insults, which were delivered with a disarming smile.

"You didn't answer my question, Sunderland."

"I didn't answer because I've nothing to report."

He had no interest in arguing with her. All he thought of was Angela—Angela whom he needed to speak to as soon as he could. Had she seen the article? What would she think?

"I thought we were in accord about the annulment," his mother pouted. "It would mean much to me to be assured the papers have been filed. After all, I traveled all this way here for you. You know how much I hate France."

For some reason, his mother's words returned him to the beast he'd become after his heartbreak. The beast that had enabled him to marry Angela in that Kensington church for the sake of revenge —or so he'd told himself.

"Funny, but I don't recall issuing you an invitation, Mother. Perhaps it's slipped my mind."

His mother smirked. "Gained a sense of humor, have you?"

"Or perhaps I'm simply rude."

After a long moment, she said, "I suppose you want to show your independence, now that you're earl. Fine."

She turned away and ignored him for the rest of the carriage ride.

As soon as they arrived back at the chateau, Sunny showed her to what had been Angela's room. His mother snapped at Dubois to bring her trunk. Perhaps sensing her ill will, the kittens immediately scattered.

She shook her head. "What a shabby environment! So this is where your father spent his time away."

"I love this chateau," Sunny replied, memories of Angela flooding him. Angela dancing in the mirrored salon while he played the piano. Angela reading in the library with him. Angela chasing the kittens up and down the hallway. Most of all, Angela in his arms inside the greenhouse.

He said, "You needn't remain here if you wish. I'm sure Dubois can arrange for a hotel."

The Dowager Countess pursed her lips. "This will be sufficient, thank you."

"I'll see you at dinner. Until then, I've business to attend."

And then he went into the library, locking the door behind him, wishing he had a letter from Angela to reassure himself all was well. Wishing he had some way to write Angela. To let her know he yearned for her with all his heart. That she was his true wife, not Hélène, despite what some stupid newspaper article claimed.

I love you, he thought.

I want you to be my wife, he thought.

I want to be your husband, he thought.

I hope it isn't too late for us, he thought.

In lieu of Angela's presence, he sat on the library floor and played with the kittens, who were nearly full grown.

By dinner, his mother had reconsidered her tactics.

"I'm in a better mood now," she announced. "The rain made me cross. I apologize, Virgil."

Virgil. She'd used his given name, not his title.

"I'm sure," Sunny answered, leaning back in his chair. He moved peas from one side of his plate to the other with his knife, awaiting her next salvo.

"Virgil, I've had a thought," she said abruptly. "Now that you're earl, I understand my importance has changed in your life."

"Indeed," he muttered.

She took a bite from the potatoes au gratin. A sip of white wine.

"I suppose the French woman is fine for your wife. She does seem rather aristocratic. She's beautiful in a vulgar way."

"Mademoiselle de Castel-d'Albret is not vulgar," he ground out. "She's intelligent and witty and loyal. A true friend."

"If you say, Virgil. My main point is I can tell you're fond of her, which is entirely appropriate for a husband and wife." A nervous laugh. "So marry your French mademoiselle! Anyway, everyone believes she's your countess."

That damn *Times* article again. He'd strangle Ward when he next saw him.

"I'm already married," Sunny replied as calmly as he could muster.

He stood from the table, bowed, and left the dining room before his mother could respond.

The Dowager Countess followed him down the hall. "I'm not done speaking to you! Come back, Sunderland!"

He didn't.

Three days passed in this manner, with Sunny avoiding his mother's entreaties. On the fourth morning, Angela's letter arrived from Rome. It was perhaps the shortest missive he'd ever received from her, outside of those notes she'd left pinned to his bed pillow.

Sunny read:

> *I love you.*
> *I want to be your wife.*
> *I want you to be my husband.*
> *I hope it isn't too late for us.*

To his deepest pleasure, she signed her letter:

> *With more love than there are roses in the world,*
> *Angela, Countess of Sunderland*

And then he knew: whatever influence Ward's article might have had no longer mattered. But, to his frustration, she hadn't included an address—he had the sense she'd dashed off the letter quickly in response to that article.

Her letter set Sunny into such a euphoric mood that his mother's jibes didn't bother him as they once might have. He even tolerated her complaints about the kittens with resignation.

On the fifth morning, the Dowager Countess awaited Sunny in the library, seated at his desk. She was staring out the window at the Bois de Boulogne seemingly lost in thought.

This surprised Sunny. He didn't consider his mother a thoughtful person. A plotting person, yes. A gossiping person, absolutely. But a person who ruminated for the sake of such? Not at all.

Her preoccupation meant she didn't notice Sunny's arrival. This allowed him the opportunity to observe his mother as though she were new to him. She appeared older than when he'd last seen her nearly half a year ago at the wedding. More weary. Her tightly coiffed hair had more white than grey, the flesh on her neck more slack. Or perhaps he hadn't noticed before.

Sunny cleared his throat to gain her attention.

"You woke late today," she said, startled.

He'd slept in to avoid her. "I assume you've had breakfast."

"Yes. It was sufficient, thank you, Virgil."

She forced one of those smiles that always seemed so foreign to her nature. But, to his surprise, she met his eyes—a shocking intimacy from her. Her eyes were the same warm brown as his.

She broke from his stare. Disquiet—no, anxiety—flashed across her face. He'd intimidated her.

He didn't feel the triumph he expected.

Outside, he heard a bluejay caw. The clouds shifted.

"If you like, we can take an outing, Mother," he said, gentler now. "The rain's stopped. Sun's out. It feels as though all the world is blooming. Perhaps a stroll through the Bois de Boulogne? We needn't walk far."

To his surprise, she accepted his invitation. "I'd like that very much, Virgil."

~

He didn't take her into the park through the secret passage. Instead, he led her out past the gravel drive, just as Luke had with Angela months earlier, while Sunny jealously spied on them.

Once they'd entered the Bois de Boulogne itself, Sunny and his mother remained in silence for a good quarter-hour save for a murmured "this way, if you please" or "watch the tree branch."

His mother's steps faltered. To his surprise, a tear worked its way down her cheek. Another. She swiped at her cheeks furiously, face ruddy with embarrassment.

Sunny had never seen his mother cry before. Not even when his father or Robert died.

"'Tis the wind," she said, offering a quick grimace.

There was no wind.

"It *is* windy today," he agreed.

To his surprise, he offered her his arm without thinking. She accepted it. She stopped every so often to comment on the flowers, the budding trees, the ducklings in the pond, the waterfall.

"It is rather pretty here, Virgil," she said begrudgingly, her eyes still tearing.

"I sometimes like to come here and just smell the flowers," he admitted.

The Dowager Countess indicated a bench facing the duck pond. It didn't escape Sunny's notice that the bench wasn't far from the one where he'd first encountered Hélène a year earlier. They sat. A robin peeped at their feet, its breast red and plump. Just beyond it, a scattering of sweet violet and alyssum.

He inhaled deeply. How lovely it was! So peaceful despite the present company.

"Where did it happen?" the Dowager Countess asked. She swiped at her eyes.

"What happened?" He offered her his handkerchief.

"You know what I mean, Virgil—don't be difficult! That awful duel."

Oh. She'd been so obsessed with Hélène being named his wife; he'd assumed she hadn't noticed that part of the article.

He pointed from the bench to a distant corner across the park, which was greener than it had been a week earlier.

"The glade over there, past the vale of cedars. It's commonly used for such encounters. We were only to go to the first blood. Not to the death."

She nodded, still clinging to his arm. By then the Dowager Countess was completely engulfed in the unpleasant task of weeping. Being who she was, she made every effort to hide her sobs.

Fortunately, Sunny had a second handkerchief. He offered it.

"If anything had happened to you," she burst out, "I couldn't bear it, Virgil. I-I still can't bear it!"

And then Sunny understood. She wasn't just talking about him. She was talking about Robert. His father. Every sorrow that had ever weighed her.

"I'm here, Mother." His voice cracked too. "I'm safe."

"If you were to die—"

"But I didn't. I'm seated beside you. Alive." He patted her hand, which felt boney beneath his.

"Was it her influence that led to the duel?"

(By *her*, he understood she meant Angela.)

"My wife's name is Angela, Mother. The duel wasn't Angela's fault."

(He understood this was the real question his mother asked.)

"And you love this Angela?"

"With all my heart."

She blew her nose into his handkerchief. "Well, this is a mess. Think of the scandal, you marrying a Bartham! I'm not happy, Virgil."

"I know. You'll get over it."

After a very long moment and in a very small voice, she asked: "I don't have a choice, do I?"

On that bench in the Bois de Boulogne, Sunny couldn't contain his smile. "Not if you want to see your grandchildren."

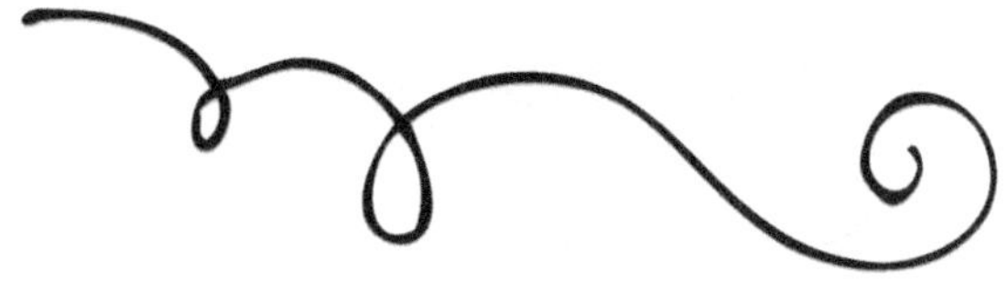

CHAPTER 33

Sunny and his mother lingered only a moment longer in the Bois de Boulogne. "I'm ready to leave," she said once she dried her tears. But, to his surprise, she refused to return to the chateau. Instead, she requested he send her trunk to the Hôtel Westminster on the Rue de la Paix.

"I think we've had enough conversation for one visit," she said. "I've also had enough of your cats. When you return to London, you may call on me once you're settled."

"With my wife?" he asked.

She let out a lofty sigh. "If it can't be avoided."

Once he found her a hansom for hire, his mother, the Dowager Countess of Sunderland, was gone.

Now alone, Sunny found himself fretful despite his rapprochement with his mother. Angela. He wished she was there so he could confide all that had occurred—she'd be astounded.

She'll write again soon, he told himself, hoping all was well with her parents. He'd go to her in Rome once she wrote back, he decided. They could even have a proper honeymoon there. Hell, he'd take her to the Alps, while he was at it.

His mood lighter, Sunny made his way back to the chateau. All about him, the Bois de Boulogne was filled with carriages and families. With his mother no longer accompanying him, there was no reason to avoid using the chateau's secret passage from the park; he'd fortunately brought the key. He'd sit in the greenhouse for a while, tend to the roses. Maybe he'd even invite the kittens in for a romp. Clover seemed especially mournful at Angela's absence; Sunny understood.

With the sun so high overhead, the door to the passage was hidden in shadows beneath a grotto on the other side of a duck pond. This time, as Sunny approached the door, he made out the silhouette of a slender woman in front of it.

I must be imagining this.

In all the years he'd known of the chateau and its passage, he'd never seen anyone pay mind to the door. From what he knew of Parisians, they probably shrugged at its existence, just as they did at secret entrances to catacombs and hidden gates to shopping arcades.

He squinted—how bright it was! It was indeed a young woman he'd seen. She appeared to be locking the door behind her.

The woman turned…and Sunny's heart felt as though it would leap from his chest.

For it was Angela, her silver-blonde hair tucked in plaits around her head.

Angela, dressed in a simple gown the color of roses, a Kashmir shawl wrapped about her shoulders.

Angela, grinning at the sunlight on her face as she scanned the Bois de Boulogne looking for someone.

For *him*.

Their eyes locked. He offered a nervous wave.

Her mouth opened. Surprise, that's what she felt. No, joy—for he knew she'd returned from Rome to find him at the chateau. To be with him.

Something had happened…but this time that something had been good.

He watched in silence—no, shock—as Angela raised the hem of her skirts so she could run. As she hurried in his direction, ducklings scattered in her wake, lilacs bloomed, and doves cooed, or so it seemed to his besotted heart.

And then, as she grew closer, she began to speak in such a manner that Sunny was astonished.

"I'm looking for my husband, the Earl of Sunderland," she shouted as she approached. "Do you know him? His manservant told me he was in the Bois de Boulogne."

Of course, she would tease him—such was her way. She'd always been so much lighter of spirit than he, so filled with joy. As for Sunny, he felt as though his relief at her return would crack the world open.

His steps gained in velocity. Well, if she could tease, he would too.

"How interesting," he called in return, unable to contain his grin. "I'm looking for my wife, the Countess of Sunderland. I last heard she was in Rome."

Now Angela was but a stone's throw away from him. He could sense her warmth, her vitality.

"She's returned from Rome, or so I've heard. A quick trip, but all is well. She received a *poste restante* letter from a certain Mademoiselle de Castel-d'Albret regarding her broken engagement."

Hélène had written Angela? She must have sent the letter as soon as he'd left her flat several days ago.

Sunny's smile widened. "Clever lady!" He should have thought to have written Angela *poste restante* in Rome.

Angela pouted. "But I still need to find my husband. He's ever so handsome and brave and valiant. I miss him so."

"I suspect your husband is closer than you realize. And he misses you too."

Four more steps and she'd be within arm's reach. He yearned to unpin her plaits, loosen her hair until it fell below her waist like the miracle that she was. Bring her back to the chateau and make love to her until they collapsed from satisfaction and exhaustion.

"As for my wife," he continued, "she's the most exquisite woman I've ever seen—"

One more step and he was before Angela. He grasped her hands in his.

"—and gives the best kisses in the world," he finished.

She smiled coyly. Shyly, even. "Does she? I heard the same about my husband."

He released her hands and wrapped her in his arms, never to let go.

"Hello, wife," he greeted. "Speaking of letters, I received yours."

"Hello, husband." A cloud of worry skittered across her face. "And what did you think of what I wrote?"

He tilted her chin in his direction, sensing the whole of their future life together. He imagined her dancing at the second wedding ceremony they'd hold, now that she was his true wife. Lying with him in his bed for decades to come in his country estate in Berkshire and beyond. The love they'd share, the family they'd create, even the kittens they'd raise.

He brushed his lips against hers, a taste of what was to come. He inhaled deeply. Her hair was scented with roses.

"I must admit I'm more intrigued by your kisses, countess. I need to make sure they're still the best in the world."

She smiled, her clear blue eyes crinkling at their corners. "I believe that calls for a demonstration, earl."

"Many, *many* demonstrations. Shall we begin?"

"Immediately," she agreed.

And so they did.

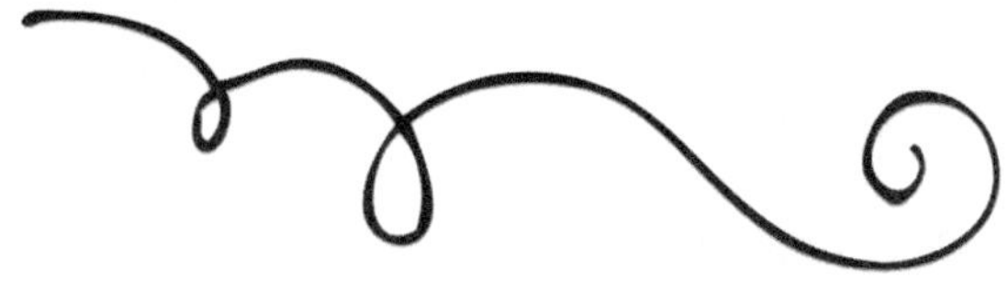

CHAPTER 34

COUNTESS OF SUNDERLAND REVEALED AT LAST TO SOCIETY

The Times, 21st May 1873: Virgil Sydenham, the Earl of Sunderland, officially introduced the new Countess of Sunderland last night in a private reception held in Rome. To the astonishment of many yet few, the earl's bride was revealed to be none other than Miss Angela Bartham, the noted beauty.

The bride's parents, who are currently in residence in the Eternal City, hosted the reception. The new Countess of Sunderland is the middle daughter of painter Neil Bartham, whose recent return from Jerusalem after a spate of ill health garnered much attention from the art world; her mother is the former Mrs. Clio Sutton née Hadley, known among some as the Muse of Scandal. It is presumed that their daughter's advantageous marriage will restore the Bartham family into society's graces.

Many will recall the earl and countess's nuptials were vehemently denied by both of their families when The Times first reported them in December 1872. In addition, it was rumored the earl wed a French debutante whilst abroad in Paris earlier this year.

When pressed for an explanation for the subterfuge over his marriage, the Earl of Sunderland responded, "I'm a most private person when it comes to my private life, as is my very private bride."

After an extended honeymoon in Paris, Rome, and the Alps, the couple plan to reside in London and Berkshire.

EPILOGUE
SIX MONTHS LATER

THE SECOND WEDDING of Virgil Sydenham, the Earl of Sunderland, was a far more joyous affair than the first. It took place soon after the couple's return to England on an exceptionally bright day in late November. The wedding was an intimate affair involving only their immediate family, held at a small but charming church near Sunny's Berkshire country estate. The ceremony was undertaken with a new marriage license, this one containing the bride's correct name for the sake of posterity: *Allegra Jane Bartham.*

Sunny used the occasion to replace his wife's signet ring with a lovely gold band. It was engraved inside with the dates of both their weddings.

Not that it mattered to Angela, Countess of Sunderland. She already felt as married as could be.

"Why a second wedding? You assured me we were married," she teased Sunny after the ceremony. "Grounds for annulment, not invalidation," she reminded.

Sunny said, after offering his bride a kiss, "Perhaps I've another reason for insisting on a second wedding."

"Because my father's here for this one?" Angela countered.

A month earlier, Neil and Clio Bartham returned to London from Rome and had been joyfully reunited with Musa and the twins. Her father was thrilled when Sunny announced the second wedding—he'd missed so much while away in Jerusalem.

"Not that, countess. Something else."

Angela scrunched up her face. "Because your mother didn't dare refer to me as 'the Bartham chit' this time?"

Sunny laughed. "Not that either, though I was pleased she was on her best behavior today."

The Dowager Countess had even offered a reluctant smile when the couple plighted their troth with a teary show of emotion. Afterward, she inquired about Angela's health, advising her to avoid dancing until she conceived a child for the sake of the earldom.

"Then what is it, earl? Why did you insist on a second wedding?"

"Patience, countess. You'll find out soon enough."

Angela's curiosity grew until she could barely stand it, especially since she had no chance to inquire further until after everyone departed for London in a flurry of hugs and kisses and happy tears and a last champagne toast. Then, the couple found themselves alone in their country estate for the first time since their wedding…though they weren't fully alone.

The kittens had accompanied them there from Paris. Now full grown, Clover, Dandelion, Ivy, Mari, and Hyssop had settled into their position with aplomb as guardians of the house. They'd gone into hiding during the wedding reception.

"Come with me, countess."

Sunny took Angela's hand as he led her from the ballroom to the reception room and then to the conservatory. His country home was statelier than the chateau, yet simpler, with walls the color of pale spring grass and cream. Angela loved it. How large it felt. How peaceful.

How empty.

"I've dismissed all the servants for the rest of the day," Sunny explained.

"We've only invisible ones, like old times?"

"No servants at all. Because I want you all to myself, Angela, Countess of Sunderland. Because I never got a wedding night with you the first time we married."

Oh. That was the reason for the second ceremony.

"And now I'm a bride again." Angela's stomach fluttered deliciously.

Sunny nodded, flushing. "And I'm your groom."

He draped his arms across her shoulders. Leaned his forehead against hers. She met his warm brown eyes.

"Hello, groom," she said.

"Hello, bride," he replied, his lips curving.

She returned his smile. "Tell me, groom, for a wedding night, am I expected to be innocent of the marital act?"

He raised an eyebrow. "Only if you want to be, bride."

"Hmmmm. It's more intriguing to have experience with one's spouse prior to the nuptials, don't you think? One can compare notes."

He laughed. "I'll leave that to your judgment. But first—" he pulled away "—I've something to show you. A wedding gift."

"I presume it involves consummating our marriage." Angela stroked his chest, feeling rather bold. "Is my gift down there?"

"That gift is for later, Angela, though if you keep touching me like that..." He drew a deep breath. "But this gift is for now."

A kiss on her chin. Another on her cheek. Then, a third on her forehead, all three kisses as gentle as rain and soft as flower petals.

Oh, she thought.

"I like these gifts, groom," she whispered, breathless. "Shall I give you gifts too?"

"If you like, bride."

She set a kiss on his cheek. A second on the tip of his nose. A third and final kiss at the base of his neck, where she could feel the warmth of his pulse.

"All lovely gifts," he said, taking her hand. "But, again, not the one I have in mind. Come."

To Angela's puzzlement, he led her out into the gardens where they'd spent so much time as children. It was still early enough in the day that it wasn't cold in the sunlight—it had been a mild November. Still, Sunny draped Angela's wool cloak over her bridal gown so she'd keep warm. The ivory gown was similar in style to a floor-length tutu, all net and lace and ribbons; Sunny had gasped when he spied her walking down the aisle wearing it.

As they strolled, the cats finally came out of hiding and followed the couple outside, Clover leading them in her dominant way. Soon they were beyond the garden hedge, past the grove of poplars that led toward the stream. Near where the *Rosa Angelus* roses would blossom in all their pink glory once spring returned. Beyond where sheep and cows grazed over green hills.

"Where are we going?" Angela asked, tugging at her husband's hand. Truth be told, she was wearing white satin slippers, which weren't meant for walking in the country.

"We're nearly there, Angela. I promise. Over here."

Sunny led her to the base of a thick oak tree, one that Angela knew to be the oldest and the tallest on the estate. He took off his greatcoat and settled it over the roots.

"Sit beside me," he said.

And then together, their backs against the oak trunk, Sunny pointed across toward the field facing it, one that remained lush even in the depths of autumn. It was then Angela noticed what appeared to be a small one-story house set in the center.

The house was painted a soft ivory hue. Pristine. New.

"There," Sunny said. "Your wedding gift."

"It's beautiful, whatever it is," she breathed, clutching his hand. "Is it some sort of greenhouse?"

"No. Guess again, countess."

"A shelter for the cats?"

Sunny laughed. "The gift is for you, not them."

Angela rose from the oak, careful not to get dirt on her gown. "I'll just have to go and take a look, won't I?"

Sunny followed after her. When they arrived, he handed her a thick brass key.

"For me, groom?"

"For you, bride."

The door to the small house opened easily, like it awaited Angela's arrival. Inside, she found a single large room, also painted in white. The room bore a spinet set in a corner. Beside it, a comfortable chaise and a chair. Along one wall, a ballet barre and a bookshelf for music scores. A fireplace with a small stove for warmth. Everything sparkled with light and beauty.

A place for me to dance in . . . but oh what a place!

Angela exhaled, feeling as though she was in a fairy tale. She blinked back tears as she threw her arms around Sunny. "I've never seen anything so beautiful in all my life."

"Happy second wedding, my love." He reached over to kiss her. "Now can we go back and consummate our marriage? I can no longer wait."

Angela laughed and pulled him against her. Toward the chaise. "Why not here?"

"Why not indeed."

Thank you, dear reader, for spending time with Angela and Sunny's love story. As an author, one of the happiest strokes of luck you can experience is when a character steps up to take over a story. This was definitely my experience with Sunny, whose appearance in *The Poetics of Passion* as Angela's sweet but ineffectual friend was initially intended as comic relief. However, while I wrote, Sunny proved to have other plans…and so did Angela. While I always knew Angela had a broken heart in her past—it's mentioned by Musa in *The Poetics of Passion*—I began wondering what it would take for the couple to fall madly and irrevocably in love.

And so here we are.

While *The Dance of Desire* is a Beauty and the Beast retelling with nods to the Jean Cocteau and Disney films, it was also inspired by *Ferdinand the Bull,* the classic children's picture book by Munro Leaf. If you have yet to encounter Ferdinand, he's a lover, not a fighter: all he wants to do is sit under a tree and sniff flowers. Fate intervenes when Ferdinand is stung by a bee one day, transforming the peaceful bull into Ferdinand the Fierce—much as Sunny transforms into a fighter as a result of Angela's letter of refusal.

Though I've visited Paris numerous times, I took liberties in my description of Sunny's chateau in *The Dance of Desire*. Since this is a fairy tale retelling, I hope the reader will understand—after all, fairy tales are about enchanted, liminal spaces.

The only residence on the Bois de Boulogne similar to Sunny's chateau is the Villa Windsor, the former home of the Duke of

Windsor and Wallis Simpson, which was built in 1929. To the best of my knowledge, the Villa Windsor does not have a secret passage with a greenhouse leading to the Bois de Boulogne (though how cool would it be if it did?). That bit of fancy was inspired by a secret passage in the palace of Versailles, which is rumored to have proven useful during the French Revolution. Nor does the *Rosa Angelus* rose exist; nor is the Bois de Boulogne as hilly as I described.

However, people regularly used the Bois de Boulogne in the nineteenth century for duels between men and, occasionally, women. Rapiers were a favorite weapon of choice for these affairs of honor, though pistols were used too. Paintings and prints abound of such encounters, which helped me envision Sunny's duel with Willie. What follows is a 1874 illustration by Godefroy Durand entitled *The Code of Honor—A Duel in the Bois de Boulogne, Near Paris.*

If you're curious about the Mozart adagio that spurs Sunny and Angela's truce, it's a truly sublime piece of music. The adagio is known formally as the first movement of the composer's Piano Sonata in E flat major, K. 282. A quick YouTube search will bring up multiple performances of it.

As for Angela's family history, Neil and Clio Bartham's love-at-first-sight elopement was inspired by the Pre-Raphaelite painter John Millais's marriage to Effie Ruskin, whose unhappy first marriage to famed art critic John Ruskin ended in scandal. The dissolution of the Ruskins' troubled marriage led to a high-profile annulment that left Effie permanently outcast from society, much like Clio Bartham.

Finally, though writing a book can be a solitary activity, I'm incredibly fortunate to be surrounded by supportive friends and family. I truly appreciate the community of reviewers, bookstagrammers, and readers who welcomed my debut romance *The Poetics of Passion* so kindly. On the author front, I'm especially grateful to Eliza Knight, Mimi Matthews, Harper St. George, Leanna Renee Hieber, Hope Tarr, and Molly Greeley for their friendship and support. Special thanks go out to Heather Webb, Karen Zuegner, and Crystal King, who read and offered helpful feedback and encouragement, as well as Jennifer Johnson and Greer Macallister. You're all the best!

So what's next? Unless another character steps forth, Lyra's Romeo and Juliet-inspired tale of forbidden love will be the focus of the third Muses of Scandal novel. To receive an alert when it's available, I hope you'll stay in touch with me via Instagram at @DelphineRossBooks and my author site at DelphineRoss.com— and thanks for reading!

Books *that make you think.*

Books *that make you feel.*

Books *that inspire.*

Thank you for reading *The Dance of Desire* by Delphine Ross. We truly hope you enjoyed it! As a small independent publisher, we rely on supportive readers such as yourself to get the word out. Here's three ways you can help.

1. REVIEW. Take a moment to leave a review on Goodreads, Bookbub, and retailers such as Amazon and Kobo.

2. REQUEST. Mention this book to your local library or favorite independent bookstore. Request they stock it. (Wholesale discounts are available via Ingram Books and Baker and Taylor.)

3. BOOK CLUB. Suggest this book for your book club. Reach out to us at ReadMuse.com to set up a virtual author visit.

Any other thoughts? Suggestions? We'd love to hear from you! Contact us at ReadMuse.com. Want to read more by Delphine Ross? Here's the prologue and first two chapters from *The Poetics of Passion*, the first book in the Muses of Scandal series.

With much gratitude,
MUSE PUBLICATIONS

DELPHINE ROSS
For Musa and Seb,
their secret identities
are about
to get real.
the Poetics of Passion
MUSES OF SCANDAL
A NOVEL
"A captivating blend of witty banter, historical details
and delightful characters ... that will enchant readers!"
—ELIZA KNIGHT, USA Today bestselling author

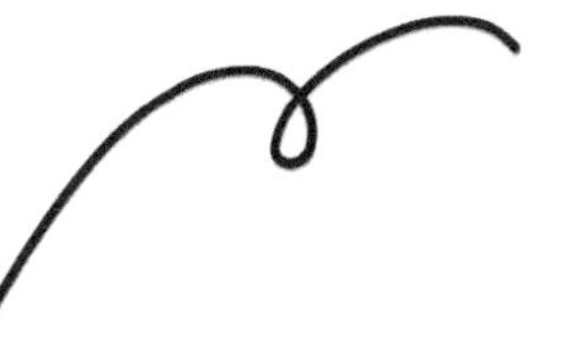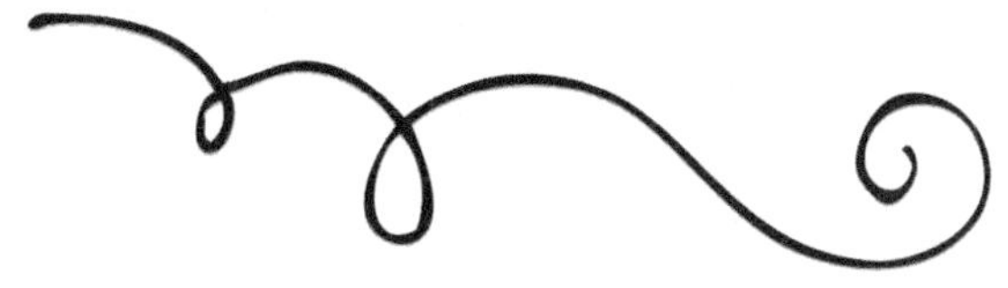

PROLOGUE
THE PAST

March 1845

THE FIRST TIME Musa Bartham's father saw the woman who'd become her mother, it was at a masked ball in Venice during Carnivale. The lady in question was the only one without a mask in a crowd of over a hundred. However, instead of standing out from a lack of sophistication, she glowed like a daffodil in a field of lavender. A falling star amid a cloudless night.

Later, Musa's father would tell his children this was the moment he knew he'd marry her.

He was not wrong. But it wouldn't be as simple as anticipated.

"Who is she?" he begged the ball's hostess, Lady Minerva Hadley. She was a widowed art collector with a palazzo on the Grand Canal in Venice.

"Neil Bartham? Is that you?" Lady Minerva retorted. "I must admit I hadn't expected your attendance! I thought you were too busy painting to mingle with society." She tapped his hand with her ivory fan. "You're interested in her?"

I'm not just interested, Neil thought. *I plan to wed her.* But this wasn't what one said, especially if one was an impoverished English artist in Venice.

While he considered the best way to reply to Lady Minerva's inquiry, he stole another look at the object of his marital ambitions.

The lady in question appeared only a year or two junior to his three and twenty. She wore no adornment save a slender choker of pearls and a cluster of pale gardenias pinned to her bodice. Necklace and flower were nearly the same shade as her silver-blonde hair, which hung in well-behaved curls to her waist. Her petite figure was set off in a simple ecru gown sewn of damask. A matching set of opera gloves covered her fingers, leaving Neil unable to tell whether she'd been claimed as someone's wife. This troubled him deeply.

But she's meant to be my *wife*, he thought madly and improbably.

And then her eyes met his. They widened as though she was struck by something wonderful yet terrifying. Her eyes were the same shade as cornflowers on an Alpine meadow. Not only were they beautiful, they bore kindness. An element of mercy. Even more so, he made out a spark of recognition in her eyes, as though they'd met before in another time and place.

This made no sense, but there it was.

"Well, Mr. Bartham?" Lady Minerva prodded. "Answer my question! Are you interested in her?"

"I-I'd like her to pose for me, my lady. Do you know her?"

Lady Minerva laughed. "Oh, I know her all right. She's my niece."

"What's your niece's name?"

Neil hadn't the self-control to play coy. By then he'd nicknamed Musa's future mother La Dame avec Merci, for she was as different from the La Dame sans Merci of Keat's poem as sugar from salt. As mad as it was, Neil sensed a thread tying him to his La Dame avec Merci—a thread that led all the way to his future, and his children's future, and beyond.

He saw his La Dame avec Merci seated beside him in his painting studio. He saw her in his future home, a mansion created by art and love. But, most of all, he saw four children tumbling about their feet, three girls and a boy, some bearing her light hair, others with his dark.

Before Lady Minerva could supply her niece's name, a rise of applause intervened. The guest of honor had arrived. Ethan Sutton, the powerful art critic who'd bankrolled Neil's travel from England to Venice and had insured his invitation to Lady Minerva's ball. Neil forced himself to turn from his *La Dame avec Merci* to acknowledge his benefactor. Besides, Neil hadn't seen Sutton in over six months, since the art critic's marriage to a woman whom Neil had yet to meet.

As for Neil's *La Dame avec Merci*, she approached Sutton. And then she was beside Sutton. Clutching Sutton's hand.

No. Neil was unable to think beyond that one panicked syllable.

"Here she is!" Sutton called to the crowd. "The former Miss Clio Hadley, now my bride!"

No, Neil thought again.

Neil awaited the thread he'd sensed to break, all those ripe scenes of artistic and domestic bliss scattering like beads from a broken necklace. The house, the children, the artistic renown. But, if anything, his desire was only renewed.

Even then, Neil knew this was not good. He didn't care.

"We're here on our honeymoon," Sutton continued. "But we're not without companions . . ." He pointed toward Neil, voice booming. "I see you, Bartham! Everyone, my protégé, Neil Bartham, the artist who will save British painting. Come, join us here!"

Somehow Neil set one foot in front of the other as he approached his benefactor. One step, another. And then he was before her, his *Dame avec Merci* who bore the unexpected name of Mrs. Clio Sutton.

The woman married to his benefactor.

The bride now on her honeymoon in Venice, the most romantic city in the world.

The muse who was meant to be *his* wife, not Sutton's.

"Good evening, Mr. Bartham," Clio said in a musical voice.

"The same to you, Mrs. Sutton," Neil replied.

And then Clio set her gloved hand in Neil's. The unexpected contact thrilled him beyond anything he'd ever experienced in his life.

Clio whispered, "Have we met before?"

"I was wondering the same, Mrs. Sutton," Neil whispered back. "I've never felt like this—"

He broke off, knowing he'd been madly forward. But, to his relief, a tremulous smile crowned her lips.

"I feel the exact same way, Mr. Bartham—I can't explain it." Then she pronounced the words that would seal their fates. "You must call on me tomorrow. I won't accept a refusal."

Ten minutes later, Clio and Neil were on an overly familiar first name basis.

Ten days later, they fled Venice together in the dead of night, winning Musa's future mother the snide nickname of the Muse of Scandal. The moniker was inspired by both circumstances and her namesake—Clio had been named after the Greek muse of history.

Ten months later, Clio and Neil returned to London. They wed after the Suttons' marriage was annulled for reasons Clio refused to reveal; her belly already swelled with child. The resulting scandal left the newlyweds exiled from polite society, but burnished Neil's artistic reputation to a fine sheen.

Ten years later, their four children, the first of whom was Musa, tumbled about their feet. Alas, as Musa and her siblings grew into adulthood, no one would receive them in society, leaving her sisters without marriage prospects, her brother shunned of opportunity. By the time Musa turned twenty, this realization led her father to undertake a desperate sacrifice—one which would have lasting repercussions for his family.

Neil gathered his paints and brushes. He kissed his beloved wife and children goodbye. Then he set off on a long and arduous pilgrimage for the Holy Land, where he planned to spend two years painting religious scenes of a treacle-hued sentimentality guaranteed to melt the heart of the frostiest London doyen. Through this act, Neil would rehabilitate the Bartham name into society's graces, thus restoring his children's futures and his wife's reputation.

He would never return.

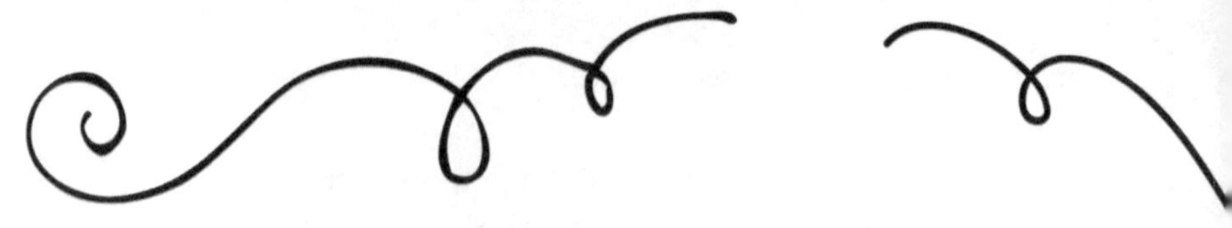

CHAPTER 1
THE PRESENT

In January of 1872, the inglorious Bartham family had been reduced from a West Kensington mansion of art to a shabby two-story townhouse in Brompton. This townhouse had been let only through the practical enterprises of Neil and Clio's eldest daughter, Musa. By then, Musa had reached the ripe age of twenty-six without an offer for her hand. This was in spite of her lustrous chestnut hair, willowy figure, and considerable intelligence—for the Barthams remained as outcast from society as they had prior to Neil's departure for the Holy Land.

For the best, Musa told herself. She didn't mind being a spinster. Unlike her tragically romantic parents, Musa bore a practical mind, the sort able to find solutions where others gave up. Thus, after a number of unsuccessful financial attempts, she'd taken upon herself to support her family through the means of poetry—and not just any poetry.

Poetry that dripped with florid emotion.

Poetry with rhyme schemes that brought flushes to cheeks and heat to groins.

Poetry that proved lucrative with gentlemen who yearned for forbidden encounters in nocturnal gardens scented with jasmine, and ladies who fantasized of kisses on chaise lounges hidden behind gilt-lacquered screens.

In other words, love poetry.

The irony that this love poetry was written by a young woman resolved never to wed was not lost on Musa, though her poems were shockingly passionate for one whose heart had never sped at the clandestine brush of a hand. But Musa had seen enough during the course of her life. She'd learned that grand passions, such as the one leading to her parents' marriage, led to grand scandals—and, if Musa were to have only one rule for her family, it would be no more scandals. To prevent further damage to their Bartham name, Musa's poetry books were written under the pen name of Felicity Vita.

Outside of her publisher, only Musa's sister Angela knew of Felicity's existence; their mother Clio remained too bereft to notice much beyond Neil's absence. She just assumed Musa found some way to monetize their father's art. Musa didn't dissuade her.

However, considerations of scandals were far from Musa's mind that winter morning. She thought only of providing for her family. Her father, for all his intentions, had left her mother with only enough income to survive for three years while he was off seeking respectability. Now, six years after his departure, they'd have been forced into the poorhouse had it not been for Musa's literary enterprises.

As Musa prepared to depart the Barthams' two-story town-house to provide for her family, she'd just finished imbibing a warming second cup of tea. (No sugar, only lemon.) It was Friday, which was Musa's usual day to run errands. That day, she'd visit her publisher near Fleet Street with fair copies of poems for her next book, which was several weeks overdue, and collect mail addressed to her *nom de plume*. All necessary tasks to keep the Barthams fed and housed…though she did take a disconcerting amount of pleasure in the mail. Especially one gentleman's correspondence. A gentleman she'd never meet in person, alas.

Henry Whitney was his name. It was a good name. A solid

name. The name of a man who wrote the best letters she'd ever read in her life. Her editor advised not to answer, but Musa hadn't been able to resist. Henry's last letter pressed to meet her, but she'd regretfully declined. It was impossible. Anyway, love was better in letters than in real life—of this Musa was certain.

However, that Friday morning would not be like others. As Musa approached the front door, satchel in one hand, umbrella in the other—she'd noticed a gray cloud suggesting rain rather than snow—the doorbell clattered.

"I'll answer it!" Musa called to their overtaxed maid of all work, the only staff they could afford.

By the time Musa reached the door, the bell pull had been deployed four more times, evidence of their visitor's impatience.

She thrust the door open. "Aunt Minerva?"

Musa let her mouth gape. Her elderly dowager of a great-aunt was not expected. Nor was she particularly welcomed. Not after all that happened.

Musa had only met Lady Minerva Hadley once. Seven years earlier, Minerva had confronted the Barthams at the funeral of an ancient cousin—an encounter that ended with the dowager shouting about how Neil ruined her niece Clio's life "because he was ruled by his stiff John Thomas instead of his brain." Whether Minerva had communicated since with Clio in the intervening years Musa did not know. But Musa had attempted such. After Neil's disappearance, she'd written Aunt Minerva five times apprising her of Clio's distress and their financial difficulties. Minerva never responded. This did not win Musa's favor.

And now here she was, at the Barthams' door.

Without a word of welcome Aunt Minerva pushed her way inside, her sharp eyes scanning the dank hallway, the water-stained wallpaper, which was barely hidden behind her father's oil paintings and other works of art. She offered a silent shudder, her aquiline nose wrinkling as though she'd smelled something foul. Musa recalled they had fish the night before; she'd grown accustomed to the stench. On top of this, a sour chord drifted from the parlor amid raised voices. Her fifteen-year-old brother, Theo, arguing with his twin sister Lyra over the piano, which hadn't been tuned in ages. The two youngest Barthams got along like oil and water.

"Your family's situation is worse than I've been informed," Aunt Minerva greeted. "And it's all your father's fault."

"Good morning, Aunt." Musa did her best to keep her voice free of shock. She recalled to bob a curtsey, hoping her aunt had reconsidered Musa's requests for help.

"You're the eldest girl then? Musa, if I recall. What a ridiculous name!"

Musa flinched. "I like my name. It means 'inspiration' in Italian—"

"I *do* speak Italian, you know. Perhaps you've forgotten I've a palazzo in Venice along with a townhouse in Mayfair. How tall are you, miss?"

"Tall enough, ma'am."

Musa was statuesque like her father. Lady Minerva's comment had intended to insult.

Moving past the slight, Musa said in her most ingratiating voice, "You look healthy, Aunt."

"Spare the flattery, miss. I didn't want to come here. You should know this and be grateful."

Well, excuse me. Musa clutched her poems against her chest, that second cup of tea churning in her stomach. She should have taken it with milk instead of lemon.

"Is Mama expecting you?" she replied, more alarmed than she cared to show. Clio rarely wrote to anyone these days. For the most part, all she did was lie in bed when she wasn't sleeping or rereading old love letters from Neil. Occasionally she'd venture downstairs or into the garden as though to remind herself the world still existed beyond her room.

"No, miss. Where is your sister Angela?"

"Why do you ask?" Angela was the beauty of the family, or so people said. She most resembled the ethereal Clio, who'd been a great beauty in her day. Angela danced with a grace equal to the great Taglioni of earlier in the century. Angela was kind. Sweet. Of all the Barthams, she'd taken their fall from society's grace the hardest, though she rarely complained. Musa had confessed to Angela about her poetry to reassure their family's financial woes were addressed.

"Aren't you saucy? If you must know, she's written me." Her brow arched. "A desperate letter too!"

"She hadn't told me." Why hadn't Angela confided in her? Why would Aunt Minerva respond to Angela but not Musa?

Aunt Minerva's tone rose. "Again, where is Angela?"

"I don't know," Musa lied, knowing perfectly well her sister was still in the dining room. When Musa last spied Angela, she was dolloping cream on her porridge with a voluptuous sigh; cream was a luxury for their household.

Musa's spine prickled with a dread she couldn't quantify. Her dread combined with the urge to protect Angela. Surely Angela made a mistake writing Minerva.

Then it was too late.

The disturbance of Aunt Minerva's arrival drew Angela into the hallway, looking as lovely as ever though she wasn't dressed for visitors. Her silvery-blonde tresses dangled in graceful curls to her waist, much like Clio's as a young woman. Angela's petite beauty was only enhanced in that she was wearing one of Clio's Japanese silk kimonos over her nightdress, which Neil had used as a painting prop in the early days of their marriage. Angela appeared a nymph of the woods, a fairy of old. Beauty itself as well as kindness.

Musa frowned as Angela thrust herself into Minerva's arms with a too familiar air.

"Oh, Aunt, thank you *so* much for coming!" Angela fawned in an overly sweet tone. "You'll help me find a husband then?"

"Husband?" Musa's stomach turned even queasier. "What's this?"

"Shush, Musa!" Angela whispered, eyes darting. "Don't spoil things for me."

Musa answered in a low firm voice, "You've no need for a husband, Angela. You know why."

Because no one worthy of you will associate with our family.

Musa believed Angela to be as resolved to spinsterhood as she was. Yes, there'd been that flirtation when Angela was eighteen with a dancer visiting from Paris. But that had been a slip of the heart. Nothing at all like their parents.

Aunt Minerva extracted herself from Angela's arms. She smoothed her purple day suit as though wiping off a child's muddy handprints. "You're Angela, I presume?"

Angela curtsied prettily, batting her thick eyelashes. "Yes, ma'am. I'm so delighted you're here!"

Minerva peered at Angela through her gold-rimmed lunettes. "How old are you, miss?"

"Twenty-three come April, ma'am."

"You're a beauty though a bit long in the tooth. No inappropriate suitors to gossip?"

Angela flushed. "Just as I wrote, ma'am. None at all."

"Angela, what's going on?" Musa pressed, growing even more alarmed.

"Hush!" Aunt Minerva snapped. To Angela: "No other scandals I should be aware of, miss? Perhaps something someone else in your family has done?" A glare in Musa's direction. "Or your sister?"

Angela met Musa's eyes for the briefest moment.

Musa again sensed dread rising from her stomach. Or curdled tea.

She thought of Felicity Vita, the scandal should anyone discover the truth. She'd been so careful to cover her tracks. Writing her manuscript fair copies with her left hand so no one would recognize her handwriting—it helped that Musa was ambidextrous. Destroying all her drafts—it helped they'd scant servants. But Musa had never considered her sister a vulnerability.

"No, Aunt. Nothing," Angela responded.

Musa pressed in what she hoped was a reasonable tone, "Angela, please tell me what you wrote Aunt Minerva."

"Something wise regarding her future. Unlike your parents, or you for that matter," Minerva said dryly. "Very well, Angela. I'll introduce you to society—from there it'll be up to you to win a husband. Though you're pretty enough, I must warn you'll have a difficult time thanks to your parents' foolishness. But first, I should speak to your mother. Where is she?"

"In her bedroom. Upstairs!"

Angela grabbed her great-aunt's hand and pulled her from the hallway. Musa followed, imagining what they would find in Clio's room. Clio half-asleep in her rumpled negligee, clutching the last love letters Neil sent before his disappearance. A trail of crumpled handkerchiefs next to her pillows. Bottles of medication and various herbal teas and potions intended to calm nerves and heal any imagined illnesses.

Friday morning or no, Musa's publisher—and Felicity Vita— would have to wait.

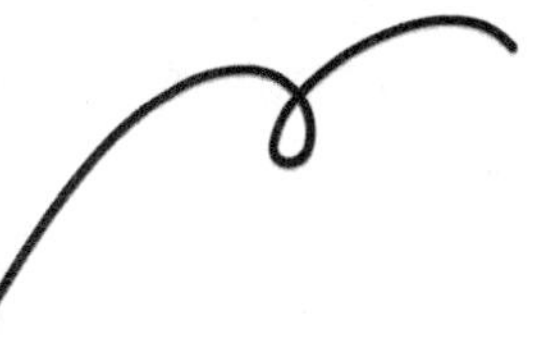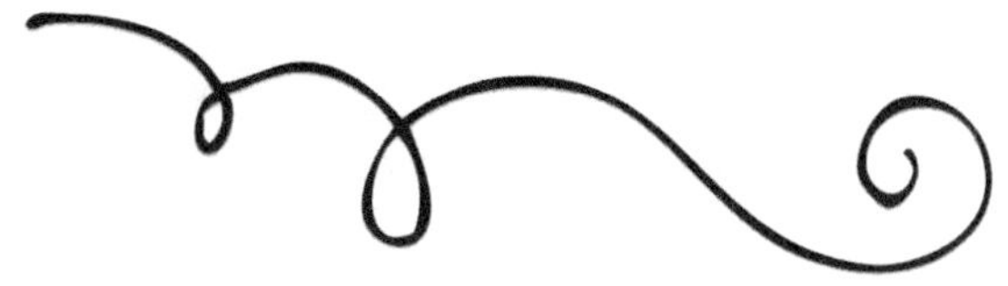

CHAPTER 2

On the other side of London, Sebastian Atkinson was embracing a dark-haired temptress, one with whom he'd exchanged plenty of letters. Though they'd never met in person, that night she'd miraculously arrived at his door. Now she laid beside him in his bed, which was more than he'd ever dared to dream. The temptress was dressed in yards of pink silk and expensive lace; fabric fine enough that her glorious body shimmered beneath it, for she wore no chemise or stays. The translucent fabric allowed Seb to recognize the nubs of her nipples, the dark valley between her thighs.

Seb's fingers trailed along the swell of her hips. The curve of her breasts.

He murmured against her neck, "You agreed to see me after all."

She laughed, but it wasn't a laugh of ridicule. No, it was a kind laugh. A laugh akin to a caress.

"I've been waiting for your invitation, Seb. Why did you take so long?"

Seb groaned. "Why indeed."

She leaned over his reclining form, her graceful fingers tracing the muscles of his arms. Her nipples teased his chest as her mouth traced the seashell curve of his ear, whispering sweet verses.

Poetry.

Poetry that awakened his deepest yearnings.

Poetry that evoked his most tender emotions, as if the author herself could see inside his very soul.

Poetry written by the temptress now pressing her lips against his neck—a temptress who bore the all-too-enticing name of Felicity Vita.

Felicity Vita was the love poet all of London buzzed about, for everyone yearned to uncover her identity. Some said she was a noblewoman in disguise. Others ventured she was someone far less genteel. Felicity's first book, *Verses of Love Lost and Love Found*, aroused quite the rumpus, though it was ever so tasteful in its descriptions of sensuality. From there, the poetess published a volume of poetry every six months like clockwork, her latest being *The Poetics of Passion*. However, though no one could figure out the secret behind her *nom de plume*, somehow he, Sebastian Atkinson, a twenty-eight-year-old gentleman artist with few guineas to his name, had somehow lured Felicity Vita into his bed.

Sebastian sighed with impatience as Felicity raised the hem of his nightshirt. He wished he'd gone to bed naked to expedite their intimacies, but the January chill was too sharp in his attic. Nor had he anticipated Felicity would show up at his door. Hadn't her last letter informed him they must never meet?

But this no longer mattered. Not anymore. Felicity was there. In his bed. Beside him.

Seb was swiftly undressed by Felicity's eager hands, his muscled torso a swirl of shadows beneath her lace-covered figure. He strained to make out her features in the darkened room.

"Please, show me your face," he begged. "I'll light a candle."

She laughed again, a honey-warm sound. "I can see well enough. Come here . . ."

Soon he was flat on his back. She reclined above him, her kisses growing bolder. He wove his fingers into her long dark tresses.

"Let me see you, Felicity. I'm begging."

Again, that low honeyed laugh. "Beg away."

Alas, no matter how close she approached, Seb still couldn't make out her features. It was as though she was there yet nowhere. Nothing yet everything. An amalgam of ideals, all too wonderful to exist. Like true love itself. Like a dream.

All of a sudden, everything began to shake and shudder like an earthquake about Seb.

"Are you alright?" Felicity asked in a strange, deep voice before she turned her attention to places south. She kissed and stroked him until he thought he could take no more.

Sebastian answered her with a long moan. Her caresses were so able and eager. Real. He felt on the edge of losing himself to the most exquisite pleasure . . .

More shaking in his bed. A splash of cold water.

❧

"Seb! Wake up! Are you alright?"

Seb's eyes blinked open. He was soaking wet, still in his bed. Any lingering arousal deflated.

Only a dream. But oh, what a dream!

It was morning, not night. He was still dressed from the day before. And he was alone in his room save for his best friend, Lucas Ward, who was shaking his shoulder with one hand, clutching a water jug in his other.

"You threw water at me," Seb gritted out.

"You were having a nightmare," Luke explained, setting the emptied water jug on a mantel. "You were moaning and shaking! You wouldn't wake up. I was alarmed."

"So am I."

Seb drew a deep breath, barely noticing his soaked clothes in the wake of his pounding head. A harsh gray glare streamed rudely into his room, which laid up a precarious stairway in an attic aerie overlooking the whole of Spitalfields. It was an expansive room, large enough for Seb's needs as an artist—one wall featured his oils, another his drawings and watercolors. There was a skylight, an array of windows. A sandbag hanging from one beam for exercise. Most importantly, the attic was cheap, which allowed him to save money so he could provide for his two sisters, who remained in their family home back in Kent. He'd been forced into daily labor upon the unexpected deaths of his parents a year and a half earlier.

Cheap room or not, right now the attic felt far too large and far too light-filled for his liking. Everything was spinning.

He groaned. A hangover, that's what he had. A monster hangover. Worse, he still felt mildly drunk. How could this be after hours of sleep?

Seb pulled himself against his pillow, which was thankfully drier than his bed. He gestured for a towel, which Luke handed him—Luke who'd brought him home in his protective way, though Seb questioned how they'd arrived there. He seemed to recall running out of funds…and yet somehow they'd gotten back to Spitalfields all the way from Kensington.

Had Luke stiffed the hansom? He probably did.

As Seb mopped his hair, he tried to puzzle through everything that had occurred the previous evening. He and Luke went to the pub near the printing house where they both worked, Luke as a journalist, Seb as a pressman. Seb was upset. (Well, he wouldn't think *why* he'd been upset—it was all too embarrassing in the context of his dream. Not until he'd gotten coffee into him, if his stomach allowed.) Luke was astute enough to notice Seb's distress. After all, they'd known each since they were boys in Kent. Luke even lived with Seb's family for a while, before making his way to London to seek his fortune as a writer. In an attempt to distract Seb from his emotions, Luke matched him glass for glass. Seb soon outpaced him, which led to them running out of money, which had probably encouraged Seb's all-too-intense dream.

Dreams of Felicity Vita, the poet.

Felicity Vita, his correspondent for the past year and a half.

Felicity, who sent intimate letters addressed to a postbox

bearing the name of Henry Whitney, a name Seb chose to protect his identity for reasons he couldn't quite explain.

Felicity, who'd written to him yesterday stating they could never meet in person, in response to a desperate letter Seb sent. *"Just meet me one time,"* he'd begged, *"though I hope it will lead to more than that."* He'd issued the invitation knowing he'd have to confess the truth that he was naught but an impoverished artist—but now this would never be.

The poet answered tersely in response:

> *Darling Henry,*
>
> *Let us enjoy the communion of our Souls through our Words, not our Bodies. True Love is an Ideal only spoiled by the intrusion of Life—this is a Truth I know from personal experience.*
>
> *I look forward to your next letter!*
> *Yours in literature and affection,*
> *Felicity*

Seb was devastated by her rejection, though he knew it was ridiculous. Who was he to presume so much of a famed poetess? To ask her to set her anonymity at risk? Anyway, they'd continue their correspondence. This would have to be enough.

It wasn't.

You can't love someone you never met, he lectured himself. *You've been swept away by your emotions. Again.*

"Sorry I threw water at you," Luke continued. "You were really—"

"Inebriated. I know."

Seb pulled on his boots in a quest to avoid the puddle of water beside his bed. He quickly changed into a dry shirt. It appeared fairly clean.

"You're too good to watch over me, Luke. About last night . . ."

"You weren't thinking straight," Luke finished, offering him a small glass of brandy for his hangover. "Don't worry about the hansom. He didn't mind us not paying."

Seb pulled a face at the brandy. "I don't believe that."

Luke offered a devil-may-care shrug, a gesture Seb recognized too well. "I told him you were deathly ill, and he'd be rewarded in heaven for his kindness."

"You never change. Next you'll tell me we did him a favor."

"Perhaps we did. What's better than the glow of a good deed?"

"The satisfaction of honesty." It was one thing to pull pranks, as they did while boys in Kent, quite another to skirt the law in London.

"Honesty . . ." Luke's blithe tone turned somber. "Very well then, I'll be honest with you."

Now it all came out, the conversation they'd avoided the previous evening. Not that Luke knew about Seb's correspondence with Felicity, which he kept locked away in his desk. Seb had simply confessed there was a woman who'd rejected him. Someone he thought he loved—Luke would have laughed at his moon-faced obsession with the anonymous love poet.

"Whoever you're enamored with," Luke said, wagging a finger, "it needs to stop. She's rejected you. Done. Move on."

Seb gagged down a sip of brandy before replying. "I know, I know. But the heart isn't so obedient."

"To be honest, I think you're still grieving your parents."

"Can't one grieve and also be infatuated?"

"I suppose you've a point. But here's something else to consider. You've barely painted in weeks." Luke pointed to Seb's latest painting, which was sketched in only sepia oil washes. "This looks like a pot of mud thrown at a canvas. What's it supposed to be?"

"Keats. La Dame sans Merci."

"Ah. Could have fooled me."

Seb gestured weakly. "I'm still in the early stages. Still figuring things out. Are you done criticizing me?"

"No," Luke replied. "You're distracted at work. Everyone's

noticed—you nearly incinerated a pile of newspapers, for god's sake! If nothing else, think of me. You're making me look bad since—"

"You recommended me for the job. And I do appreciate it, Luke, I really do."

"You can't continue like this, Seb. Whoever this woman may be, she must be trouble if you won't even confide to me who she is."

"I'm a gentleman," Seb protested, his face heating anew. "A gentleman never tells."

Luke scoffed. "Whenever you've taken a shine to someone in the past, I've always been the first person you told."

Another sip of brandy. "I've learned to be tactful."

"Tactful? You?" Luke laughed. "You're a waterfall of emotions. A seeping revelation of whatever hits your heart and soul. That makes you a great artist—yes, I do believe this—but also a terrible liar." He leaned in. "Tell the truth: are you involved with a married woman? Or a courtesan, though who knows how you'd pay for her? Is that why you're so secretive?"

Seb grimaced. "No! Nothing like that."

"Someone famous who refuses to be seen with you?"

This cut too close. "None of your business."

"Ooh feisty!"

"Anyway, it's over, Luke. Well, not exactly over—we're still friends. Just it won't progress further. She wrote as much to me. That's why I was so upset."

Though I desperately wish it wasn't so.

And here was the bitter kernel of Seb's obsession: writing to Felicity under the guise of Henry Whitney had allowed him to express truths he'd never dared admit even in the darkest hours of the night. Truths he didn't dare share with Luke or his two sisters.

Felicity was the only one who understood. Felicity was the only one who knew his true soul…though not enough to meet with him.

It was three weeks after his parents' unexpected deaths that Seb wrote Felicity Vita for the first time. It was a letter of appreciation, explaining how her poems offered comfort in the wake of his loss. He was shocked when she responded directly to his letter. *"I lost my father nearly five years ago,"* she'd answered in an elegant hand. *"I understand your sorrow—the loss weighs on one's Soul."* From there, their correspondence grew. In recent months, he found himself checking his postbox every day, rereading her letters over and over. All this had led him to issue his impetuous invitation to meet in person…and that dream.

Seb grew warm, recalling the dream's explicit quality. For all he knew, Felicity Vita was a fifty-year-old widow in Scotland with dozens of correspondents. She could even be a man.

Luckily, Luke didn't notice Seb's ruddy face. "Whatever's going on, let it go."

"I know I should. But I can't."

Luke led him toward the sandbag hanging from a corner beam. "Go! Punch it. Do whatever you can to get her out of your system."

"I've tried that many a time." Seb's muscles had become decidedly stronger in recent weeks.

"Try talking to her again. Convince her of your worth. You're talented, you've a manor house in Kent, damn it!"

"You mean a ramshackle house falling apart."

"It won't be once you make your fortune as an artist." Luke gestured at the canvas of *La Dame sans Merci*. "This could be good if you add other colors to it. You're not half-bad looking either."

"Am I?" At that moment, Seb didn't feel half-bad looking with his queasy, pounding head. There'd been a time when he'd felt very handsome indeed, when the world glowed with sunlight and promise. This seemed a lifetime ago. Since his parents' death, he'd been so focused on providing for his sisters that he couldn't recall the last time he had a haircut or a decent meal. He'd grown distinctly lanky and overgrown, like an untended garden that no one bothered to visit…especially since his obsession with Felicity Vita had overtaken his life.

Luke responded, "You can be quite charming when you're not mooning over someone who doesn't reciprocate your affections."

"Thank you, I think. Have you finished?"

"No. Whatever's going on with you and this woman, fix it. I can't bear to see you this way."

Fix it. This sounded easy enough. But how to fix something when you couldn't reach the object of your affection?

Seb's gaze drifted toward Felicity's books. They were stacked in a neat pile on his drawing board. Besides *The Poetics of Passion*, whose purple binding really drew the eye, there was *Verses of Love Lost and Love Found, The Triumph of Eros,* and several others with similarly themed titles. Felicity's books were works of art. Books to appeal to artistic sensibilities. They were printed on heavy paper stock with black and white illustrations, though not as fine as what Seb could offer as an artist.

An idea began to formulate in Seb's hungover brain. An idea that surprised him, one he'd never considered before. Even if Felicity refused to meet with him, there *was* something else he could do.

Seb grabbed his copy of *The Poetics of Passion* and his portfolio. He gathered his coat and bowler and turned toward the door.

Luke called, "You're not going out? It looks like rain."

"I am."

"You'll frighten people. Seriously. At least comb your hair if you won't shave."

"No time!"

"Tell me where you're going, so I can find you when the police pick you up for disorderly assembly."

Seb threw a smile from the threshold. "To find a way to speak to her. Lock the door behind you when you leave. Oh, and don't steal anything!"

In 1872 London, a scandalous love poetess and a passionate children's book illustrator are set at odds in this sparkling enemies-to-lovers historical romance.

Musa Bartham has a secret. To support her destitute family after her father's disappearance, she's been publishing steamy poetry under the pen name of Felicity Vita. As Felicity Vita, Musa's scandalous books have won legions of devoted fans—including an anonymous gentleman pen pal whose letters spark unruly desires she would never *ever* succumb to in her orderly daily life. But when Musa's cherished younger sister, Angela, is offered sponsorship by their aristocratic great-aunt for an advantageous marriage, Musa realizes her dangerous double life as Felicity must come to an end. Instead, she'll write books for children.

Sebastian Atkinson is a passionate artist reduced to working nights as a printer. Though Seb is infuriated by the prim yet alluring young woman who corners him into illustrating her insipid children's book, he can't turn Musa away: he suspects she may be Felicity Vita, the seductive poetess with whom he's been exchanging love letters for the past year. Egged on by his best friend, an ambitious journalist desperate for a break, Seb seeks to unmask Musa's secret identity. But the closer Seb comes to the truth, the more Musa entices him—and the more Musa finds Seb curiously attractive and even more curiously familiar. Could he have anything to do with her anonymous gentleman pen pal?

Unable to resist each other, the two shift from enemies to lovers just as their love letters are stolen, setting Angela's future at risk. As Seb and Musa frantically come together to contain the damage before it's too late, it's uncertain whose hearts and lives will be broken amid the most sensational scandal of all.

Available on all platforms and print.
Learn more at ReadMuse.com

ABOUT THE AUTHOR

Delphine Ross writes lush, witty, and angsty historical romances set during the nineteenth century. She is the author of the Muses of Scandal historical romance series. *The Poetics of Passion*, the debut novel in the series, was praised as "a beguiling Victorian romance" by *Historical Novel Review*. In her spare time, she loves traveling to places where she can imagine other lives in earlier times.

Under another name, Delphine writes critically acclaimed and bestselling fiction and nonfiction. She lives and works in Brooklyn. Learn more at DelphineRoss.com.

 instagram.com/delphinerossbooks

www.ingramcontent.com/pod-product-compliance
Lightning Source LLC
Chambersburg PA
CBHW021235310726
48971CB00006B/1832